A MOTHER'S WORST FEAR

"Mommy . . ."

The distant voice came through Laurie's baby monitor. It was a man's voice, teasing and singsong. *"Mommy . . ."*

"Oh, my God," Laurie whispered. "Vincent, call nine-one-one. Somebody's in my apartment. I think they're going to hurt Joey."

Dumbfounded, he stood in the doorway for a moment.

"Please!" she cried. "I'm counting on you, Vincent."

He quickly nodded and ducked back inside.

Laurie hurried to her apartment and threw open the door.

It was quiet. Her lungs burning, Laurie frantically glanced around the living room.

She ran up the stairs to Joey's room—where she'd checked on him less than five minutes ago.

But his crib was empty now . . .

Books by Kevin O'Brien

ONLY SON

THE NEXT TO DIE

MAKE THEM CRY

WATCH THEM DIE

LEFT FOR DEAD

THE LAST VICTIM

KILLING SPREE

ONE LAST SCREAM

FINAL BREATH

VICIOUS

DISTURBED

TERRIFIED

UNSPEAKABLE

TELL ME YOU'RE SORRY

NO ONE NEEDS TO KNOW

Published by Kensington Publishing Corporation

KEVIN O'BRIEN

NO ONE NEEDS TO KNOW

PINNACLE BOOKS
Kensington Publishing Corp.
www.kensingtonbooks.com

PINNACLE BOOKS are published by

Kensington Publishing Corp.
119 West 40th Street
New York, NY 10018

All Kensington titles, imprints, and distributed lines are available at special quantity discounts for bulk purchases for sales promotions, premiums, fund-raising, educational, or institutional use. Special book excerpts or customized printings can also be created to fit specific needs. For details, write or phone the office of the Kensington sales manager: Kensington Publishing Corp., 119 West 40th Street, New York, NY 10018, attn: Sales Department; phone 1-800-221-2647.

This book is a work of fiction. Names, characters, businesses, organizations, places, events, and incidents either are the product of the author's imagination or are used fictitiously. Any resemblance to actual persons, living or dead, events, or locales is entirely coincidental.

ISBN-13: 978-0-7860-3162-7
ISBN-10: 0-7860-3162-X

First printing: August 2015

10 9 8 7 6 5 4 3 2 1

Printed in the United States of America

First electronic edition: August 2015

ISBN-13: 978-0-7860-3163-4
ISBN-10: 0-7860-3163-8

*This book is for Tim Curtis, Denny Kinsella,
Mike Leonard, Judy O'Donnell O'Brien and
Tom O'Brien . . .
With love from your brother-in-law.*

You guys are the greatest!

ACKNOWLEDGMENTS

Thanks to my marvelous editor and friend, John Scognamiglio, who has been there for me for fifteen novels—so far! John, you're amazing. The same goes for everyone at Kensington Publishing Corp. What a terrific group. Without you, I'm nothing!

Thank you to Meg Ruley, Christina Hogrebe, and the gang at Jane Rotrosen Agency. It's because of you that I'm an International Man of Mystery.

Another great big thank you goes to my Writers Group: John Flick, Cate Goethals, Soyon Im, David Massengill, and Garth Stein. You guys are the best.

Speaking of Writers, I'm grateful for the support of my Seattle 7 Writer friends, especially my fellow board members: Garth (again), Jennie Shortridge, Kit Bakke, Erica Bauermeister, Dave Boling, Carol Cassella, Randy Sue Coburn, Laurie Frankel, Stephanie Kallos, and Tara Austen Weaver. Check us out at www.seattle7writers.org.

Thanks also to the terrific people at Levy Home Entertainment.

A special shout-out and thank-you to Doug Mendini.

I'd also like to thank the following friends and groups who have been incredibly supportive: Nancy Abbe, Dan Annear and Chuck Rank, Pam Binder and the gang at

PNWA, Marlys Bourm, Amanda Brooks, Terry and Judine Brooks, George Camper and Shane White, Barbara and John Cegielski, Barbara and Jim Church, Pennie Clark Ianniciello, Anna Cottle and Mary Alice Kier, Tommy Dreiling, Paul Dwoskin, my friends at Elliott Bay Book Company, Tom Goodwin, the wonderful people at Hudson News, Cathy Johnson, Elizabeth Kinsella, David Korabik, Stafford Lombard, Roberta Miner, Dan Monda and Kyle Bryan, Jim Munchel, the fantastic people at The News Group, Meghan O'Neill, my pals at Open Road Media, Midge Ortiz, Eva Marie Saint, John Saul, and Mike Sack, the gang at Seattle Mystery Bookshop, John Simmons, Roseann Stella, Dan, Doug and Ann Stutesman, George and Sheila Stydahar, Marc Von Borstel, Michael Wells, and Ruth Young.

Finally, thank you to my family. I love you guys!

CHAPTER ONE

Laurie Trotter had a bad feeling about the man who stepped inside the restaurant just ten minutes before closing. There were no other customers in the place. The last one had left about five minutes ago.

The Superstar Diner off Interstate 90 was isolated—a Texaco station on the other side of the highway was its closest neighbor. Laurie hated working this "bare-bones staff" late-night shift. Somewhere along the line, the owner, Paul, had done a survey and determined their slowest evening for business was in the middle of the week, especially in the summer, when most of the students at Central Washington University had gone home. So from nine until closing on Wednesday nights, the menu was limited to grill food.

A trained chef, Laurie reluctantly emerged from her sanctuary in the kitchen to double as a waitress and short-order grill cook on those nights. The only other person working the shift was the dishwasher, Duncan, a sweet, nerdy eighteen-year-old with a puny build and a nervous manner. He always seemed overwhelmed, rushing around, bussing tables and washing dishes as if it were his first day on the job. Whenever he became flustered—which was often—he got tremors, which made him shake from the neck up like a bobble-head figure. If some creep were to wander into the diner and make trouble, poor Duncan could hardly come to Laurie's rescue.

In fact, it was sort of the other way around. A while back, a trio of jerks from Duncan's high school had come in. They'd sat down at the counter, where they could see him through the pass-through window while he'd toiled away in the kitchen. They'd started teasing him.

"Hey, retard, how many plates did you break today?"

"Shit, look at him shaking . . ."

"When I grow up, Duncan, I want to have a real cool job like the one you have!"

Laurie had spotted Duncan, bent over the sink, trying to ignore them. All the while, his head trembled on his skinny neck.

Instead of handing menus to Duncan's tormentors, she'd just glared at them. "If you guys ever want to eat in here again, you'll shut the hell up right now," she'd growled. "I'm serious, knock it off."

And they'd clammed up.

Laurie had that kind of pull at the Superstar Diner. In the two years she'd been employed there, business had almost doubled. Thanks to her daily specials and the desserts she added to their menu, the once-foundering truck stop had become a popular dinner spot in Ellensburg—like one of those places profiled on *Diners,*

Drive-Ins and Dives. Plus, Laurie was well respected in town. A graduate of Central Washington U, she'd been married—too briefly—to the star player on their football team before he'd joined the army and been sent overseas. At least Brian Trotter had gotten to see his infant son, Joey, before dying a hero five months ago. He was awarded the Distinguished Service Cross and a Silver Star posthumously. They had a big ceremony at City Hall, and the event made the front page of the *Daily Record.* As Brian's widow and the mother of his child, twenty-six-year-old Laurie was revered around town. Sometimes that wasn't easy. The perfect widow wasn't exactly something she'd aspired to be.

The local high school boys were especially in awe of her—and it wasn't just due to her dead husband's heroics on the football and battlefields. Laurie was cute, with auburn hair and a buxom figure. Laurie thought she was a bit too buxom. She still hadn't completely shed the extra baby weight, and working in a kitchen didn't help.

At the moment, she would have welcomed a familiar face or two. These last few lonely minutes before closing were sometimes a bit unnerving. There was always the chance of a stranger wandering in there, a stranger who might want to cause trouble or rob the place.

Laurie wasn't usually this paranoid. But six nights ago, only thirty miles away at Paddy's Pantry off Highway 82 near Yakima, a waitress and a cook had been viciously beaten by a pair of armed robbers. It had occurred just minutes before closing.

The gunmen had emptied out the register, stealing

close to seven hundred dollars. They'd also made the waitress, cook, and a busboy surrender their wallets. Laurie had followed the story closely. The waitress and cook resisted. She ended up with a black eye and a split lip; the cook spent three days in the hospital having his broken jaw wired. Their attackers were still at large. Paddy's Pantry had surveillance cameras. Blurry shots of the perpetrators were printed in the newspaper, and distributed to several restaurants in the area. The photos were plastered in the break room at the Superstar Diner. Laurie thought it was pretty ridiculous that they were expected to recognize the assailants from those fuzzy snapshots. Both men had medium builds and dark hair; one looked pale, and the other might have been Latino—that was all she had to go on. The descriptions from the waitress, cook, and busboy could have fit half the men who had walked into the Superstar Diner tonight.

"My Sharona" was churning over the jukebox, Laurie's selection. That *thump, thump, thump* rhythm always helped revive her at the end of a long day on her feet. "Walking on Sunshine" was another song selection that reenergized her near closing. Both tunes were probably brand new when Paul had last changed the jukebox selections.

Duncan had already brought in the sandwich board sign from the sidewalk by the entrance. He was mopping the kitchen floor—always his last chore for the night.

As she wiped down the counter with Windex and a sponge, Laurie prayed no last-minute customers would show up. In just a few minutes, she could lock the door and hang up the CLOSED sign. She was hoping to get out of there by 11:15.

She was about to pull the keys from the pocket of her waitress uniform when the man strutted through the doorway.

Laurie hadn't noticed a car pull into the parking lot. She couldn't help wondering if the guy had switched off his headlights as he'd approached the diner. But why would he do that? Was it because he didn't want anyone identifying his car later?

Laurie felt dread in the pit of her stomach. She put down the sponge, and nervously wiped her hands on her apron. She tried not to stare at the man: *dark hair, pale complexion, medium build.* She guessed he was about thirty. He looked unwashed with his five o'clock shadow and greasy, unkempt black hair. Still, he was sort of sexy in a strange, dangerous kind of way. Maybe it was the unabashed, flirtatious grin on his face as his dark eyes met hers. He seemed so smug. Any other time, she might have been amused, maybe even slightly intrigued despite herself—but not now.

Please, she thought, *just order a Coke to go, take it, and get out of here.* Hell, she wouldn't even charge him for it if that was all he wanted.

The camouflage-pattern army fatigue jacket he wore seemed too big for his frame. With a grunt, he plopped down on one of the middle stools. Then he began to slap his hands on the countertop, keeping time with "My Sharona."

Laurie worked up a smile and handed him the grill

menu—which, thankfully, got him to stop pounding on the counter. "We're about ready to close," she said over the music. "But I can still fix you something to go."

He studied the menu and frowned. "What the hell is the Rita Moreno Burger?"

Laurie took a deep breath. "It's a ground chicken burger with hints of chili, lime, and cilantro, topped with guacamole, and served with beans and plantain fries." The description was plainly there on the menu. Still, she refrained from asking, *Can't you read?*

"Doesn't sound very Italian," he muttered.

"It's Puerto Rican," Laurie explained. "Rita Moreno is from Puerto Rico."

"Moreno sounds Italian to me," he grumbled.

Laurie just shrugged.

Paul, the owner, was a big movie fan. His collection of framed vintage movie posters and autographed film-star portraits decorated the walls of the Superstar Diner. Every item on the menu was named after a movie star—from the Crepes Suzanne Pleshette to the Lee J. Cobb Salad to the Spencer Tracy Steak. Laurie figured this clever concept was lost on most of the truckers who wandered in for a fast meal.

His eyes on the menu, the stranger let out a long sigh. "Okay, give me three of those, two Myrna Loy Soy Burgers, three of the Gary Cooper Classics, one with cheese, and two Jon Hamm and Egg Sandwiches." He slapped the menu down on the counter and smirked at her. "To go."

Oh, crap, Laurie thought, scribbling it all down. She'd be lucky to get out of there by 11:40 now.

"Regular french fries with each order, okay?" he

grunted. "None of that plantain shit." He reached inside his fatigue jacket, pulled out a pack of cigarettes, and lit one up.

Laurie shook her head at him. "I'm sorry, but you can't smoke in here. It's against the law."

He drew in, and then deliberately blew smoke rings in her direction. "Know what else is against the law?" he asked. "Carrying a concealed weapon."

Laurie froze and stared at him. Was he hiding a gun inside that baggy fatigue jacket? For a second, she couldn't breathe.

"My Sharona" finally ended. She could hear Duncan in the kitchen, wringing out the mop. He had no idea what was going on. The sound of the kitchen door slamming made her flinch, and she realized he'd just stepped outside to empty the mop bucket.

Now she and this man were alone.

He took another long drag from his cigarette, and then he cracked a smile. "Hey, relax," he whispered. "I'm just having a little fun with you, Laurie, that's all."

For a second, it baffled her that he knew her name. Then she remembered the name tag on her waitress uniform. She wore the uniform only on Wednesday nights.

With a shaky hand, Laurie grabbed a saucer and set it on the counter in front of him. It wobbled and clanked against the linoleum. "No smoking," she said, hating the little tremor in her voice. "Put out your cigarette, please."

He drew in one last puff, stubbed out the cigarette, and then exhaled a cloud of smoke in her face.

Laurie glared at him. Her stomach was in knots. "I'm sorry, but with a big order like this so late at night, you'll have to pay in advance. I'll total it up . . ." She started toward the cash register at the end of the counter. She remembered, in case she needed it, the button was there under the counter by the register—a silent alarm to the police department.

Suddenly, he grabbed her arm. "Listen, why don't you skip that for now and start cooking up the shit you're passing off as food, huh?" he said. "The sooner you get my order on the grill, the sooner you can wrap it up here and go home to your baby boy. Am I right, Laurie, or am I right?"

She automatically wrenched her arm away from his grasp. But she couldn't move. Staring at him, she felt as if her feet were cemented to the floor. She couldn't figure out how he knew about Joey.

He grinned. He could tell she was scared. That was the thing about him—it was as if he knew her every thought.

"Who are you?" she whispered.

Laurie barely got the question out when she heard the kitchen screen door slam again. It gave her another start. She turned to see if Duncan was coming back inside. But she couldn't spot him through the window. For a moment, she imagined someone following him into the kitchen—with a gun at his bobbing head.

Laurie stole a glance at the silent alarm, just a few feet away. She had to go for it—even if it meant a split lip and a black eye.

"Is someone smoking out there?" Duncan called.

She swiveled around, and was grateful to see him—alone—peering at her through the pass-through window.

"Go back to your mopping, Einstein," the stranger snarled. "Laurie and I are having a private conversation. Go on . . ."

Duncan blinked at him, and his head started to shake.

"Loser," the man grumbled.

Behind the man, out the plate-glass window, Laurie noticed a pair of headlights coming up the road from the Interstate's off-ramp.

"Laurie, are you okay?" Duncan asked.

She watched the vehicle turn into the lot. To her utter relief, she saw it was a police car. "Everything's fine, Duncan," she said evenly. "The gentleman's just leaving . . ."

The man fiddled with a salt shaker. He looked so smug. He didn't seem to catch on that a patrolman was just outside the restaurant.

Duncan retreated from the pass-through window. A moment later, Laurie heard the bucket clanking as he put it away.

"I have no idea how you know me," Laurie said to the stranger. Her heart was racing. "But you're acting like a total creep. Now it's past closing time, and I don't have to put up with you. Do you understand me? You need to leave—*now*."

In response, he unscrewed the top of the salt shaker, and slowly poured out the salt. A little white mound formed on the counter.

Laurie nodded toward the window in back of him. "You're going to have a tough time explaining that little trick to the state trooper out there."

The man glanced over his shoulder, and then turned toward her again, stone-faced. "If he's a friend of yours, he might be interested to hear how much you whored around while your hero-husband got shot at in Afghanistan. I could give him an earful, sweetie. You have everybody in this town thinking you're somebody special, the sweet war widow . . ." He stood up. "But you're just a fraud."

Dumbfounded, she stood there with her mouth open. It wasn't true. He didn't know what he was talking about. She wanted to say as much, she wanted to scream it at him. But a grain of truth in his tirade kept her mute.

He sauntered toward the exit, slipping out just as the state patrolman opened the door to come inside. "Thanks, pal," he muttered to the cop.

The husky, baby-faced patrolman scowled at him. Then he seemed to shrug it off. "Is it too late for a cup of caffeinated to go?" he asked, lumbering toward the counter.

Laurie listened to an engine start up outside. Through the window she watched an old, beat-up silver minivan pull out of the lot. This time his headlights were on. She thought she saw someone with him in the front passenger seat.

She had a pretty good idea who it was.

"Is it too late to get a cup of coffee to go?" the patrolman asked again.

Rattled, Laurie gaped at him, and quickly nodded, "Sure thing, coming right up." She headed for the coffee station. She hadn't switched it off yet. "It's on the house," she said, reaching for a Styrofoam cup. Her hand was shaking a little. "You want a large?"

"Sure, thanks," the cop replied. He squinted at the white mound of salt on the counter—and the cigarette stubbed out on the saucer. "What's this?"

"Oh, that's nothing," Laurie said, pouring coffee into the large container. She set the container and a lid in front of him, and started to clean up the stranger's mess. "Did you need cream or sugar with that?"

"Black's fine," the policeman said.

Laurie wanted to tell the cop what had just happened, but she couldn't. Right now, she couldn't tell anyone.

She stole another look out the side window—at the access road. The minivan's front beams and taillights disappeared in the darkness.

But she didn't feel any relief. The dread was still rooted in the pit of her stomach.

She knew it wasn't over. The silver minivan would be back.

Tonight was just the beginning.

CHAPTER TWO

Wednesday, 11:12 P.M.

The code to set the alarm was *72. The keypad was on the kitchen wall by a pair of saloon doors to the dining area. Once she set the alarm, Laurie had sixty seconds to leave through the front exit and lock it—or the damn thing would go off. As usual, Duncan waited for her outside, because the whole business of having to get out of there within a minute flustered him. Tonight he had the state patrolman keeping him company. After what had happened at Paddy's Pantry six nights ago, the cop said he'd stay until she'd closed up—just to be safe.

Laurie knew her last customer of the night had nothing to do with the armed robbery at Paddy's Pantry. He'd had no intention of robbing the diner tonight.

No, he'd come there for her.

But she couldn't admit that to the cop—or to Duncan. For them, she tried her damnedest to act as if nothing was wrong. Yet all the while she felt as if her whole world was about to crumble. She couldn't breathe right.

She just wanted to get home and make sure Joey was safe.

At closing, they always left on the big lighted Coke clock and the red neon sign in the window spelling out BREAKFAST-LUNCH-DINNER. The dim, scarlet-hued light was enough for Laurie to navigate her way through the shadowy restaurant.

She slipped out the front door and locked it with thirty seconds to spare. A cool night breeze hit her, and she clutched together the front of the black cardigan over her waitress uniform.

Duncan said he'd see her tomorrow, and then he mounted his moped, which always sounded like a defective lawn mower whenever he started it up. Waving good-bye to her and the cop, he took off. The sound of the sputtering engine grew fainter as Duncan headed up the access road toward town.

Laurie turned and smiled at the state patrolman. He had no idea how he'd rescued her tonight, even if it was just temporarily. "Well, thank you for sticking around," she said. "It was a comfort—"

A static-laced announcement came over a mic strapped to the cop's shoulder, interrupting her. The patrolman pressed a button on the device and spoke into it. "This is car seventeen responding . . ." There was more gibberish from the mic, which apparently he understood. "I'm at the Ellensburg exit by I-90 right now. I'm on my way. Over . . ." He turned to Laurie, his eyebrows raised. "Are you okay on your own from here?"

Nodding at him, she reached into her purse for the car keys. She backed toward her Toyota Camry on the other side of the small lot. "Oh, yes, I'm headed straight home . . ." She turned and pressed the device on her key ring. The car lights blinked.

She glanced back at the cop, who was already ducking inside his patrol car. He started to talk into his mic again, and then shut the door.

She was about to call, "Thanks again," but he wouldn't have heard her.

With a sigh, Laurie climbed into her car. She put the key in the ignition, and then remembered something she'd left behind in the diner.

The prowler's headlights and rooftop red strobes went on as the cop pulled out of the lot.

Biting her lip, Laurie watched him drive away.

She'd promised Paul that when she got home tonight, she would bake four orange cakes for tomorrow. So on the way to work, she had stopped by the grocery store and bought all the ingredients, which she'd stashed in the diner's refrigerator. Her orange cake was a hit at the Superstar Diner, and would go on the special dessert menu Thursday night. She would be baking one more cake—to send to Cheryl Wheeler, the owner of Grill Girl, a popular Seattle food truck recently profiled on the Food Network. Paul didn't know it, but for the last two months Laurie had been sending her desserts to various Seattle and Portland restaurateurs in hopes of getting hired—and getting out of Ellensburg.

She nervously tapped her fingers on the steering wheel. One of the last things she wanted to do right now was go back inside the diner, deactivate the alarm, and retrieve a bunch of groceries. She'd have to go through the whole lock-up procedure all over again, alone this time. And she couldn't be certain if her last customer of the night hadn't stuck around to see if the cop would leave before her.

Did she dare push her luck?

Laurie told herself she'd be back inside the car within two minutes. That was certainly a lot less time and hassle than making a special trip here tomorrow morning. Just getting Joey dressed and strapped in his car seat always added an extra ten minutes to every trip—each way.

"Damn it," she hissed, fishing her cell phone from her purse. She slipped it into the pocket of her waitress uniform, and then climbed out of the car. She warily glanced toward the access road. She didn't see any cars. There was nothing, no sign of the silver minivan.

As she unlocked the restaurant door, the alarm went off. She rushed inside, shut the door and bolted it behind her. Leaving the key in the lock, she hurried into the kitchen. Laurie tried not to let the alarm's incessant beeping unnerve her. She knew the disable code by heart: 8291940. The saloon doors were still swinging back and forth as she punched in the numbers on the lighted keypad. All at once, silence. It was a relief. But her heart was still racing.

In the darkness, Laurie made her way to the big refrigerator, and opened it. "Let there be light," she whispered. Even for a normal evening, it would have been a bit scary poking around here in the dark.

She imagined stepping out of the kitchen—only to see her last customer standing on the other side of the plate glass window, staring in at her.

Laurie grabbed two large to-go bags, doubled them

up, and quickly loaded the butter, milk, eggs, and orange juice inside. She closed the refrigerator door, and the kitchen was dark again.

The bag felt heavy and awkward as she lugged it toward the saloon doors. She set the activate code again, and then made a beeline for the entrance. She didn't spot anyone out there, thank God. She unlocked the door, swung it open, and hurried outside. The bagful of groceries got in the way as she tried to lock up, and she couldn't keep her hands from shaking. But she finally got the door locked.

Glancing toward the access road again, Laurie didn't notice any headlights. She let out a sigh of relief, but then it caught in her throat.

There in the moonlight, she saw a vehicle slowly moving up the road—toward the restaurant, toward her. The headlights were off.

She wasn't certain, because of the distance and the night, but it looked like a minivan.

Bolting toward the Camry, she dug the key from the pocket of her waitress uniform. She clicked the unlock button on the key ring device, and the Camry's lights flickered. Pulling open the car door, she jumped inside and tossed the bag on the passenger side floor. She heard something crack inside the bag, but was too frazzled to care right now. Fumbling with the key, she struggled to get it in the ignition. "C'mon, c'mon, c'mon," she breathed.

Even with the window up, Laurie could hear the minivan's engine now—and stray pieces of gravel crunching under its tires.

At last, she got the key in the ignition and started up the car. She backed out of the parking space, and then shifted gears. She was about to put her foot down on the accelerator when all at once, something blinded her. She hit the brake.

The minivan's driver had switched on his brights. The van stopped at the narrowest part of the drive, where a curbed sidewalk jutted out at the edge of the parking lot. It was her only way out, and they had it blocked.

Squinting in the headlight beams, she could just barely make out the two silhouetted figures inside the front of the minivan. Someone climbed out on the passenger side, but she couldn't quite see him. She heard the vehicle's door shut.

Laurie immediately reached for the armrest, and with a click, locked the car doors.

The tall, lean man came into view, weaving toward her. He looked as if he were drunk. He banged his fist on the hood of her car. "Roll down your window!" he yelled, his voice only slightly muffled by the glass. "C'mon, Laurie, roll it down, before I break it!"

Reluctantly, she reached for the armrest switch. The window hummed as she lowered it a mere couple of inches. He glared at her through the narrow opening. Laurie stared back at him. "That was your brother, Ryder, in the restaurant earlier, wasn't it?" she said. "I should have seen the family resemblance. What do you want, Tad?"

He drummed his fingers on the roof of the car—just above her head. His face came even closer to the glass.

For Laurie, seeing him again for the first time in four months was a shock. He looked terrible—like someone who was strung out on drugs or living on the streets. He used to have a sweet, goofy cuteness that made him endearing. But it was gone now.

He hadn't answered her question. He just shook his head at her.

"What do you want?" Laurie asked again. Her foot was still on the brake.

He just glared at her, and kept drumming his fingers on the car roof.

"I can't believe this," Laurie said. "You used to tell me that your brother was bad news. You didn't want anything to do with him. That therapist you were seeing called him a *sociopath*. Remember? So why did you send him into the diner to harass me? Or was that *his* idea? Are you two buddies now?"

"I just want to see my kid," he replied—at last.

"He's not your child," Laurie said steadily. "You know that, Tad. I gave you proof—and it cost me dearly. It almost ended my marriage."

"Well, your marriage did end," Tad said. "The guy died. And I'm alive. Goddamn it, Laurie, you care about me! Quit trying to be the great, suffering, noble war widow. That routine might fool some people, but I know you—"

"Stop it," she whispered. Her eyes were starting to hurt from the headlights' blinding glare. "Just leave me alone."

"I still have a right to see my own kid," he argued.

"Good God, how many times do I have to tell you? Tad, I showed you the test results—"

"Ryder says you probably paid off some doctor to fake those documents. And I wouldn't be surprised if you did, you lying bitch."

"'Lying bitch?' I think that's your brother talking. That's not you. Why are you even listening to him?" She studied his ravaged face. If she weren't so frightened, her heart would have been breaking for him. "What happened to you? You used to be sweet."

"You can't just *dump* people—"

"That was two years ago, Tad. Two years . . ."

"I was in love. We had something together. You can't just pretend it didn't happen. If I can't have you . . ." He trailed off, and then suddenly banged on the hood.

Startled, Laurie reeled back.

"Get out of there!" he shouted. "Get out of that goddamn car right now!"

Laurie gaped at him, and then she realized her foot had been on the brake all this time. She turned and switched on her high beams. Tightening her grip on the wheel, she pushed down on the accelerator. The tires let out a loud screech as she sped toward the narrow section of road between the minivan and the edge of the sidewalk.

Tad jumped back from the car, and fell down on the pavement.

Laurie saw him only out of the corner of her eye as she plowed forward. For a second, the minivan's headlights blinded her. Then she felt a jolt as the front passenger-side tire hit the curb and the car bounced up onto the sidewalk. She thought the Camry might tip over and crash into the other vehicle. The car's underside scraped against the concrete, and she winced at the grating sound. She got another jolt when the back tire slammed into the curb. One side of the Camry careened along the walkway. She kept her foot on the accelerator, and didn't let up.

Clearing the minivan, Laurie swerved back onto the driveway. She was almost certain she'd damaged the underside of the Camry, but she didn't stop. She checked her rearview mirror to make sure Tad and his brother weren't following her.

She didn't see anything back there. Ryder must have turned off the minivan's headlights. She turned down Canyon Road, and headed toward the center of town. There were other cars on the road, and that made her feel better. If the Camry were damaged and broke down on her, at least other drivers were around. She wouldn't be totally helpless.

She tried to tell herself that everything was okay. But her heart was still racing.

Laurie pressed the switch on her armrest, and her window descended. The cool breeze through the open window was refreshing. She thought about calling the police. But what would she tell them? *I'm worried, because the guy I slept with a few times while my husband was fighting in Afghanistan is now harassing me—him and his sociopath brother.*

She kept thinking that she deserved this. Everyone who knew her—or knew of her—would think the same thing.

No, she couldn't call the police.

Right now, she just wanted to get home. She glanced in the rearview mirror again. She didn't see the minivan anywhere back there. They weren't following her. Then again, they didn't have to.

They knew where she lived.

* * *

Her home was on Wilmington Court, a cul-de-sac about half a mile from the university. As she turned down the block, Laurie kept a lookout for the minivan. Tad and his brother couldn't have made it there before her. She'd gone over the speed limit most of the drive home. Still, she kept her eyes peeled.

Laurie pulled up in front of her duplex, a charmless, beige stucco—one of four that made up the Bancroft Townhome Apartments. Her apartment was on the first floor. The inside of the unit was just as drab as the exterior. With the imitation parquet floors and the cheap-looking wood doors, cabinets, and accents, Laurie figured the place must have been built in a hurry sometime in the mid-eighties and never been updated.

She'd always hated it.

After Brian had joined the army and been shipped to a base in Heidelberg, Laurie vacated their old apartment, put everything into storage, and traveled to Paris. She'd studied with master chefs at the École Ritz Escoffier and lived in a tiny, ridiculously expensive studio—with a view of the Eiffel Tower if she stood on a chair and stuck her head out the window. She was blowing her entire savings from years of waitressing, but she'd never been so happy. She and Brian would get together practically every weekend. Cramming in as much as they could during those forty-eight-hour increments, they'd explored cheap places to stay all over Europe.

Then he'd gotten his orders to go to Afghanistan. They'd given him a two-week furlough, and Brian had decided they should take that time to return to Ellensburg and establish a home base. Laurie had resisted.

But he'd made it clear to her. They were running out of money. If she stayed on in Paris, they'd be broke within a month. He wanted her stateside or at least at one of the resident facilities on the base in Heidelberg, someplace where he knew she was safe. He'd have enough to worry about while in Afghanistan. He didn't want to be worried about her, too. Five weeks away from earning her diploma from the cooking school, Laurie had to quit.

Brian had chosen the dumpy two-bedroom at Bancroft Townhomes because it was within their budget, and the extra room would come in handy in case her mother ever wanted to visit. Brian had no family, and he'd gotten close to her mom. That was the way it was. Everyone liked Brian. But Laurie couldn't help resenting him a little. Even though she'd fixed up the apartment the best she could, she was miserable there. But she didn't dare complain. After all, Brian had it far worse than she did.

Still, she'd gone from a culinary class at the Ritz Hotel in Paris to the Superstar Diner in Ellensburg. Instead of looking out her window at the City of Lights, she had a view of another lousy, rundown apartment complex on Wilmington Court.

Laurie turned off the ignition, and stared at the duplex.

Through the living room picture window, she could see her neighbor and Joey's babysitter, Krista, curled up on the sofa, working on her laptop. Laurie often sat in that very same spot while watching TV, reading, or playing with Joey. But it wasn't until now, looking in from the outside, that she realized how truly vulnerable and exposed they were.

The light from the computer illuminated Krista's face as she focused on her studies. She was cute, with short-cropped strawberry blond hair, freckles, and a curvy figure. Krista and her husband, Nathan, were working on their master's degrees. They lived in the next apartment complex down—at the end of the cul-de-sac. Krista often said how much she admired Laurie for working full-time and raising a baby on her own. But Laurie knew she couldn't have managed without Krista's help. Nathan had a job as a campus security guard from five until midnight. That left Krista free to babysit Joey three nights a week while Laurie had the closing shift at the Superstar Diner. Joey was in Happy Train Daycare the other two days Laurie worked.

Laurie hoisted up the bag from the passenger floor. It was leaking. At least a couple of the eggs must have broken, maybe the whole carton. "Fine, terrific, one more thing," she muttered, climbing out of the car. The Camry let out a beep as she locked it with the remote device. Then she headed toward her front door.

From inside came a bark. It was Krista and Nathan's black Lab, Frannie. The door flung open before Laurie got the key in. "Shhhhh, Frannie," Krista whispered. "You'll wake Joey." She looked at Laurie, and then at the bag. "You're dripping."

Laurie nodded glumly, and stepped inside. "Broken eggs. It's been a rough night." She carried the messy bag around the corner into the kitchen. With the faux-wood cabinets and chipped, yellow Formica countertops, it was an ugly work space, but at least the oven was reliable—for an electric.

Frannie licked up the trail of raw egg that was leaking. "Is it okay for her to eat that?" Laurie asked, setting the bag down on the counter.

"Oh, yeah, gives her a shiny coat." Krista petted the Labrador. "Doesn't it, girl? You're the best combination mop and vacuum cleaner in the world. Yes, you are." She looked at Laurie, and suddenly seemed serious. "You said it was a rough night. Are you okay?"

Laurie unloaded the milk and orange juice. She nodded a few more times than necessary. "Oh, yeah, I'm fine now."

Krista sighed. "Well, we had a—situation here."

With one hand in the bag, Laurie stopped and gaped at her. "What? Is Joey okay? When I called two hours ago, you said—"

"He's fine, went to sleep without a fuss. This is something else—"

"What?" Laurie asked anxiously. She was thinking about Tad and his brother, Ryder. Had they phoned here—or come by before heading to the diner?

"Those lemon bars you made," Krista whispered. "I ate four of them. They're like crack. I couldn't stop. If I end up looking like a beached whale, it's your fault."

Laurie sighed, and then worked up a smile. "You scared me for a minute there . . ." She continued unloading the bag. "I made those for you. Take some home to Nate. In fact, speaking of your sweet, understanding husband—"

"Who called twice tonight, by the way," Krista interrupted. "They're training a new guy for the midnight to morning shift, so they let Nate out early. He's heading home now, and ready to chase me around the bedroom—so he claims. I should scram."

Laurie and Frannie followed her back into the living room. Krista closed up her computer laptop and started collecting her books and spiral notepad. Frannie nuzzled up beside Laurie, and she scratched the dog behind her ear.

"You started to say something about my 'sweet, understanding husband,'" Krista said.

Laurie had wanted to ask if her sweet, understanding husband would mind if she and the dog spent the night here. But she couldn't bring herself to ask now. She shrugged awkwardly. "It was nothing. Let—let me pack up some lemon bars for him . . ."

She retreated to the kitchen and put some of the dessert bars into a Tupperware container. She really didn't want be alone right now. She was wondering if Krista would mind leaving Frannie here for the night. But the dog always went into a barking fit whenever Krista left her, and Laurie couldn't risk waking Joey. She didn't have a gun in the house. The next best thing was Brian's old aluminum baseball bat. She'd had a few nervous nights when she'd slept with the bat at her bedside. It looked like tonight was going to be one of them.

Laurie walked Krista and Frannie to the door and stepped outside with them. Frannie darted over to some bushes to pee. From the front stoop, Laurie gazed up and down the street once again.

"What's wrong?" her friend asked, hugging her books and the Tupperware container to her chest. "You seem tense. Is everything okay?"

"My last customer at the restaurant was kind of creepy, that's all."

"Why didn't you say something? What happened?"

"Nothing," Laurie said. She couldn't tell Krista the whole story. Hell, Krista looked up to her. "Nothing happened. He just—it's silly. It's really not worth going into. I'm fine."

Krista stroked her arm. "Well, lock up, and don't hesitate to call if you get scared. I mean that. And have a glass of wine to take the edge off. What the hell? Have two."

Laurie nodded. "This may be the night for it." She clutched together the front of her cardigan. "Would you do me a favor? Could you blink the outside lights once you're inside to let me know you're safe?"

They'd gone through this routine three months back, when someone had been assaulting women on the college campus. The assaults stopped, but they never did find the guy. They'd kept up the blinking lights ritual for three weeks—until Krista had deemed it no longer necessary.

But she agreed to it tonight. She and Frannie headed down toward the end of the cul-de-sac. Biting her lip, Laurie watched from the front stoop as they disappeared behind some bushes near the front of their townhouse apartment. It was quiet on the cul-de-sac, but Laurie didn't hear Krista's door open or shut. She nervously rubbed her arms and waited. At last, she saw the outside front lights blink three times.

Laurie ducked inside, closed the door and double-locked it.

She drew the front window curtains, and then turned on the TV for some soft background noise—and a little bit of company. A *Frasier* rerun was on. She headed toward Joey's room to check in on him. But something near one end of the sofa caught her eye. It was one of Krista's textbooks, half-hidden by a throw pillow.

Laurie figured Krista wouldn't need it anymore tonight. She set the book on the coffee table, and made a mental note to call her about it in the morning—if Krista didn't call her first. She peeked into Joey's bedroom. It was the nicest room in the place: new blue carpet, all new furniture from Ikea, including a rocking chair, and a night-light that created a starry pattern on the ceiling. Joey was asleep under a yellow blanket with cartoon elephants on it.

The home-line phone rang, breaking the silence. Laurie quickly headed toward the kitchen to grab it before the ringing woke Joey. She figured Krista must have needed her book after all. She snatched up the receiver. "Yes, you left your book here," she said. "I didn't think you'd want it tonight."

There was no sound on the other end.

Laurie hesitated. "Hello? Krista?"

She heard a sigh. "I no your loan now," he whispered.

Laurie didn't understand. There was a click on the other end, and then the line went dead.

Her hand still clutching the receiver, she looked at the caller ID box: NUMBER BLOCKED.

What had he said? Was it Tad? Then she realized.

"I know you're alone now."

For a moment, Laurie couldn't move. She wanted to phone the police. But what would she tell them? And if she called Krista, she'd have to explain to her about Tad—and his brother.

She quickly checked to make sure the windows were locked. She kept telling herself that Tad was just screwing with her head, trying to get her attention. She knew him. She'd dealt with him before. He would never hurt her or Joey.

But then, she didn't know his brother.

Laurie didn't bother going to bed that night. She knew she'd never fall asleep. A glass of Merlot didn't help. She nodded off only briefly, forty-five minutes at the most.

She spent the entire night in the rocking chair in Joey's room—with her dead husband's aluminum baseball bat across her lap.

CHAPTER THREE

"**O**kay, so what's the situation here?" Maureen asked, stepping inside the food truck.

It was like walking into a sweatbox. Despite the vents blowing at full speed, the trailer was twenty degrees hotter than the mid-60s temperature outside. The savory aroma of caramelized onions and meat on the grill always smelled so good at first. But by the end of her four-hour shift, the stench would saturate Maureen's clothes, and she'd be sick of it.

"God, you're a lifesaver," said her boss, Cheryl, turning from the grill to smile at her. She held a spatula in one hand and a salt shaker in the other. "Thanks for doing this. The 'situation here' is we're out of the Philadelphia cheesesteak, and some customers are mighty pissed off about it . . ."

"Well, they'll live," Maureen said, stowing her purse under the cash register. "I'll put a sign by the order window—*If you want a cheesesteak sandwich, you're shit out of luck. Go to Philadelphia.*"

On the grill, six buns were toasting. Maureen could tell at a glance what else was cooking: a teriyaki chicken and Swiss, two cheeseburgers, two pulled pork, and a turkey cranberry.

This was supposed to be her day off. Fridays during the summer, a lot of office people worked a half day and skipped having lunch downtown. So Cheryl had decreed that one of them would get every second Friday off, while the other worked alone. It was hectic, but manageable. The rest of the week, the workload would have been impossible for anyone to handle by themselves. It wasn't just about cooking the food, which was tough enough. They had to take orders, collect money, and get that food to the right customers.

Though she'd only had the job for three months, Maureen had learned fast. She and Cheryl had work chemistry. They usually fell into a perfect rhythm together whenever they had a mad rush.

Except for the cheesesteak crisis, Cheryl seemed to have things under control. Maureen had checked the crowd outside on Fourth Avenue, by the downtown library. Five people waited in line at the window of the pale green truck. They didn't look too restless.

On the side of the vehicle was their logo—a fifties-inspired cartoon of a plump, middle-aged waitress holding up a tray of food with one hand. Alongside this illustration, it said in big letters:

GRILL GIRL
Your Lunch Break Starts Here!
Sliders, Sandwiches, and Burgers to Die For!

Maureen often wondered if their customers thought the cartoon waitress was her—or possibly Cheryl, who owned Grill Girl. They were both full-figured blondes. Pushing sixty, Maureen was flattered whenever patrons mistook her for her boss. Cheryl looked like her much younger sister, but their age difference was only three years. Cheryl had a slightly careworn, still pretty face. She was sexy in an earth mother sort of way.

Maureen was having her over to dinner tonight. In fact, she'd been in the checkout line at Safeway with a cart full of provisions for the lasagna dinner when she'd gotten Cheryl's distress call. Her boss had an "emergency meeting" with a potential client for some big catering gig. The people wanted to meet at 1:30, and Cheryl needed Maureen to finish up the last hour with the lunch crowd.

"By the way, you owe me thirteen bucks for cab fare," Maureen announced, rolling up the sleeves of her lightweight pink pullover. "I'll start bagging while you finish up this batch. Then you can get the heck out of here . . ." She started examining the orders on the chef's clipboard. Maureen got the side portions of garlic green beans and mixed balsamic veggies out of the refrigerator and into the microwave. Then she started stacking up the refrigerated six-ounce containers of Cheryl's homemade coleslaw and potato salad.

"So this catering job thing, who's the big, important client you're meeting?" she asked.

"I don't want to jinx it by saying," Cheryl answered, hovering over the grill.

"It's not Gil Garrett and Shawna Farrell, is it?"

She noticed her boss pause for a moment.

Gil and Shawna were on the top of Cheryl's wish list for special catering gigs, a list that included notables like Bill and Melinda Gates, Paul Allen, and Jeff Bezos, and for reasons Maureen didn't fathom, a perfectly nice but nothing-special rest home called Evergreen Manor.

Gil and Shawna were almost an obsession with Cheryl. They lived in one of those Medina mansion-fortresses on the lake with all the other multimillion-aires. Gil was a retired major film producer, and his wife, Shawna, had won an Oscar about forty or so years ago. Now she had a line of yoga and exercise at-tire for women. They had one of her stores in Bellevue Square and another at Pacific Place, downtown. Mau-reen imagined only the most hoity-toity malls had Shawna Chic stores. Shawna Farrell wouldn't deign to sell her wares next to an Applebee's. And there was no way in hell a health nut like Shawna was going to hire Grill Girl to cater her next soiree.

It was obvious that Cheryl figured differently. And maybe she was right. With a profile on the Food Net-work, and write-ups in the *Seattle Times* and *Seattle Met* magazine, it wasn't totally out of left field that Grill Girl might land a catering job with Mr. and Mrs. Gil Garrett. Cheryl had certainly tried hard enough to make it happen. She'd sent flyers and coupons to Gil's house, and had even gone to Shawna Chic in Pacific

Place and left sample containers of her best, low-cal lunches for the sales staff. She'd also gushed about Gil and Shawna in the *Seattle Met* piece, making no bones about the fact that she wanted to cater an event for them.

Maureen stopped to stare at her boss, and wondered if all of Cheryl's campaigning had paid off at last. "Well, did we finally land a catering job for the Garretts?" she asked again.

Cheryl gave an evasive shrug. "Let's just say this potential gig is very 'movie-related.'" With her spatula, she set two more sandwiches on foil wrappers laid out on the counter. "I'll give you the whole scoop at dinner tonight, I promise. We're still on, aren't we?"

"You bet," Maureen said, wrapping the hot sandwiches. "Six-thirty, my place."

Maureen had a scoop for her, too—a revelation actually. It was why she was having this dinner. Whatever Cheryl might disclose about this potential catering gig, the news would pale in comparison to what Maureen had to tell her.

Before she left for her big meeting, Cheryl took off her apron and gave it to Maureen to put on. Cheryl's name tag was still pinned to it.

For the next hour, while Maureen worked alone, several customers—even a few semi-regulars—mistook her for Cheryl. She probably could have taken off the name tag and made things less confusing. But Maureen left it on.

It was strange how some people could come to a place again and again, and never really notice the person serving them. That was especially true of the texters and cell phone talkers. Flattering as it was to be mistaken for Cheryl, at times it was kind of irritating. It was as if she and Cheryl were just a couple of faceless blobs inside a truck filling food orders.

Maureen tried not to take it too personally.

By 1:45, lunch hour was over for most office workers. The mad rush had dwindled to a steady trickle.

No one was waiting behind the pale, thin-faced woman who had just ordered the salmon burger with arugula and aioli, and a side of green beans. "Are you Cheryl?" she asked, sizing up Maureen from behind a pair of sunglasses. "You look a little different from your picture in that magazine—and that time you were on TV."

"Yeah, I'm Cheryl," Maureen lied. She was tired of correcting people. She fetched a salmon patty out of the fridge and set it on the grill. The patty let out a sizzle. "It's amazing what some Photoshopping can do. And that's a big misconception about how heavy you look on TV. The camera actually *subtracts* ten pounds . . ."

The woman didn't seem to catch on that Maureen was kidding. Her face was expressionless—without even a hint of a smile. Maureen had noticed earlier the skin-tight, black long-sleeve T-shirt and black jeans. Sticking her head through the order window, the woman seemed to study the interior of the food truck.

Maureen handed her the bag of food. "Thanks a lot. Hope to see you back real soon."

"Nice little establishment you have here, Cheryl," the woman replied, with a tiny smile—at last. "I'll be sure to tell my friends."

"You do that, honey."

With no other customers waiting, Maureen stood by the order window and watched the woman walk away. She was barely thirty feet from the truck when— without breaking her stride—she tossed her unopened bag of food into a garbage can.

"What the hell?" Maureen muttered. She couldn't believe the waste of perfectly good food—and of her time. The stupid woman hadn't even tasted any of it. Maureen wanted to chase down the horse-faced bitch and give her a piece of her mind.

But then a thirty-something brunette with a cell phone to her ear came to the window. "Hi, Cheryl," she said, barely looking at her. "I need a teriyaki and Swiss with potato salad, and a Diet Coke."

Maureen scribbled down the order. "I'm not Cheryl," she growled. "I just have on her apron. I'm Maureen . . ."

She didn't wait to see if the woman understood or was even listening. Maureen turned away and started to prepare the order.

The customer who had just thrown away her untouched sandwich hadn't been lying when she'd promised Maureen she'd tell her friends about Grill Girl.

One block away from the food truck, she stood on the corner of Fourth and Spring Street. She was on her cell phone with a cohort. "So that's the layout," she was saying. "Our friend is in there by herself. It's kind of slow at the moment. So get over here and take care of things. I'm talking about within the next five minutes. Got that?"

"We're on it," replied the man on the other end of the line.

Maureen figured the two men would be her last customers of the day.

They looked like they were in their late twenties. One of them was on crutches. They dressed a little too casual to be office workers, even for casual Fridays. But they were friendly enough. In fact, the one on crutches was a real charmer with his shaggy brown hair and cute smile. She didn't recognize either one of them. But they acted like friendly regulars with a "Hi, how are you today?" and slipping in a *please* and *thank you* when it was warranted. The one on crutches even winked at her, and tipped her five dollars.

With their burgers almost ready, Maureen decided to throw some teriyaki chicken on the grill for herself. She hadn't had any lunch and needed to keep body and soul together until tonight's lasagna dinner.

Maureen bagged their food and brought their orders to the window.

But no one was there.

She noticed the brown-haired one, not far away at all, in front of the library, on one of the benches where a lot of people sat eating their lunches. He had his crutches leaning against the wall.

"Hey!" Maureen called. She wondered where his friend was.

He saw her, and his face lit up with a smile. He waved.

"Your food's ready!" she called.

He nodded emphatically, and then reached for his crutches. But they fell to the pavement. He looked so helpless and awkward as he tried to reach for them again. No one around seemed to notice. He waved at her again. "Just give me a minute! I'll be right there!"

"No, no, stay put!" Maureen yelled. "I'll bring it to you!"

On her way to the food truck door, she glanced at her teriyaki chicken on the grill. It was still a bit raw-looking, nowhere near ready. She left the food truck door ajar as she stepped outside and down to the street. Winding around to the front of the truck, she saw that he'd somehow managed to retrieve his crutches, but he was still sitting down. She also noticed for the first time that he wasn't actually wearing a cast, none visible anyway. Maureen figured it must have been hidden under his trouser leg.

"Thank you so much!" he called as she came closer. He grinned at her as if this little gesture was just about the nicest thing anyone could have done for him. "I didn't mean to put you to all this trouble . . ."

A bit breathless from running, Maureen handed him the bag. "No problem. What happened to your buddy?"

The young man shrugged. "Oh, he saw some girl he thought he knew, and ran off. The way he is, I'll be lucky to see him again today." He glanced into the bag. "Which one's mine?"

"Either one," she laughed. "You guys ordered the exact same thing." She glanced back at the truck. No one was waiting by the order window.

"Must be really interesting working in a food truck," he said. "Have you been at this location a long time?"

"A couple of weeks," she said, turning to smile at him again. "We keep changing around where we are." She wiped her hands on the front of her apron and sighed. "Well, I should get back there . . ."

"I don't see any customers," he said. "Why don't you sit and talk for a moment?"

"Oh, I wish I could. But I can't desert my post—"

"Huh, speaking of *dessert*," he said, "I saw the sign you have by the window with the desserts listed. I was tempted to get a piece of the key lime pie. Did you make it yourself?"

"No, my partner did," Maureen said. She started to back away. "Listen, I'd love to chat. But I left something on the grill in there. It's probably burned to a crisp by now. If you're still around after I close up the truck, I'll bring you a piece of the key lime pie. Okay?"

"That's a deal," he said. "Thanks, Cheryl!"

Maureen didn't have time to correct him. She just waved and hurried back toward the truck. Around the back, she found the door still ajar. Climbing up the metal grated steps to the door, she expected to be assaulted by the smell of burned teriyaki chicken. But once inside, she only got the familiar aroma of meat and onions cooking. Maureen shut the door behind her, and checked the grill. By some kind of miracle, the chicken wasn't burned at all. In fact, it still needed another minute or two to cook. She picked up the spatula, and turned over the chicken breast.

Then she glanced out the order window to check if any customers were waiting. No one was there. She looked for her brown-haired friend among the people on the benches outside the library. It took a moment, but

Maureen finally spotted him—along with his buddy—walking away. He wasn't on his crutches. He was carrying them. He wasn't even limping. His friend was holding the bag of food. The brown-haired one glanced back toward her for a moment. Then they picked up the pace and turned the corner.

It didn't make any sense.

Another thing that didn't make sense was the silence.

The vents weren't on. And why wasn't the food hissing on the grill? The chicken just sat there, not quite completely cooked, no juices bubbling or sizzling. Had the pilot light gone out?

She peeked under the grill and didn't see a flame. At the same time, Maureen detected—past the smell of grilled meat—a slight gassy odor.

She heard something crackle. But it wasn't coming from the grill. It was the microwave. She glanced up and saw the digital clock counting down the remaining minutes and seconds. Whatever was in the oven gave another sputter. She hadn't turned on the microwave—at least not for the last few orders. She hadn't nuked anything since the garlic green beans for that creepy, horse-faced woman.

Maureen had stepped out of the food truck for only a couple of minutes. But it was obvious to her now that someone had snuck in. They'd tinkered with the gas line, and blew out the flame under the grill. They'd also put something in the microwave oven. She heard it sputter again. She saw the minutes and seconds descend on the microwave's digital clock: 1:06, 1:05, 1:04 . . .

Through the window in the oven door, she saw the sparks.

Someone had wadded up a ball of aluminum foil and put it in there.

1:01, 1:00, 0:59, 0:58 . . .

Maureen froze.

Inside the microwave, she noticed another spark. Then there was a bright flash.

It was the last thing she saw.

The blast ripped through the food truck. Witnesses said it was a small miracle the explosion didn't start off a chain reaction with the food trucks parked on either side of the Grill Girl. Bus and car windows shattered—along with a few windows on the library's ground floor. Thick black smoke billowed up between the buildings on Fourth Avenue while car alarms blared.

"I thought it was some kind of terrorist attack," one passerby later told KING 5 News.

Twenty-two people were injured—mostly from flying glass and debris. Eighteen of them were treated at Harborview Medical Center and released that afternoon. Three remained hospitalized in stable condition, and a fourth—a nineteen-year-old woman—was in the ICU with burns from the explosion. She'd just been approaching the Grill Girl's order window when the truck blew up.

There was only one fatality: sixty-year-old Maureen Forester, described in news reports as "a cook at Grill Girl."

She was more than that to Cheryl Wheeler. She was just about Cheryl's only friend, even though they really hadn't known each other long. What the newspapers and TV didn't say was that Maureen wasn't even supposed to be working that day.

She was dead, because she'd decided to help out her friend.

Cheryl knew she'd never forget that.

She already knew what it was like to be haunted by an incident for years and years.

It was Monday afternoon, and she stood in line at the post office on Union and Twenty-third. She had a pale green slip in her hand. Cheryl was still in shock over everything that had happened. All weekend, the police and fire department investigators, lawyers, and insurance people kept her occupied—when she just wanted to be left alone to grieve. They said a faulty gas line might have caused the explosion. Cheryl pointed out that the food truck had passed a safety inspection just three weeks ago. It was her polite way of telling them they didn't know what the hell they were talking about.

Maureen had been a widow with no known family. It was up to Cheryl to arrange the burial. She wasn't quite sure how to go about it. She'd been on the phone all morning with the King County coroner's office, St. Joseph's Catholic Church, and Bonney-Watson Funeral Home.

All the busywork kept her emotions in check—up to a point.

But now, in the post office, it suddenly hit her that

she'd lost her friend and the livelihood for which she'd worked so hard for so many years. She felt a pang in her gut. Her throat tightened. The sadness swelled up inside her, and she let out a gasp.

Of all places to start tearing up, it had to be here. She covered her mouth and faked a coughing spell to disguise her sobs. In front of her in line, a man with packages gave her a strange look. Had he recognized her from the local TV news over the weekend? Or could he see that she was crying? Cheryl turned away, and took a couple of deep breaths. She wiped the tears from her face.

There was always a line at this stupid post office. Unfortunately, it was where she had the P.O. box for Grill Girl. And every so often, like today, she found a slip of paper in there for a package to pick up. It was probably something she'd ordered ages ago for the food truck, now up in smoke.

Now third in line, Cheryl dug a Kleenex out of her purse and blew her nose.

She never got to tell Maureen about the potential client she'd met on Friday. The catering job wasn't for the elusive Gil Garrett and Shawna Farrell. No, while her poor friend had been working in her place, Cheryl had signed a contract with Atlantis Film Group to cater a six-week movie shoot here in Seattle. It was a major motion picture, too—very high profile. The starting date was less than a month away.

The fact that she still cared about the job made Cheryl feel horrible. What kind of person was she? She hadn't even buried her friend yet, and she was wondering how to pull off this catering gig without her truck and her coworker.

The stout, forty-something Asian woman behind the counter took her slip and her ID, and then returned with a package that was slightly bigger than a shoebox. From the uncomfortable, somber look on the woman's face, Cheryl could tell she recognized the name—and the now-defunct business on the package address label. The woman gave her back her driver's license, and the slip. "Sign here, please," she said.

With the pen on a chain, Cheryl signed the slip. When she looked up again, the woman sadly shook her head. "I heard about what happened," she whispered. "And I'm awfully sorry."

Cheryl nodded. "Thank you," she replied, but the words caught in her throat. She grabbed the package and got out of there before she started crying again.

In the parking lot, she stopped to wipe her eyes once more. It seemed almost pointless keeping her face dry—what with the dull, steady drizzle. She glanced at the return address on the package. Rain dotted the brown paper wrapping. The sender didn't include a name, just an address in Ellensburg, Washington. Cheryl didn't know anyone in Ellensburg. The package was fairly light, and marked PERISHABLE.

That was how Cheryl felt. Suddenly, she was very perishable.

The explosion on Friday that had killed Maureen hadn't been the result of a leaky gas line. She was almost certain of that. It was no accident. Cheryl had good reason to believe she was the one who was supposed to have died in the blast. But she couldn't admit that to the investigators—not without getting herself into deeper trouble.

Standing in the parking lot with the rain matting down her ash-blond hair, she couldn't help wondering about this mystery package in her hands. Was it a bomb of some kind?

Perishable.

People didn't send bombs in the mail. They sent anthrax.

It was probably just food of some sort. But who would be sending her food?

She started toward her red 2005 Saturn. Since Friday afternoon, every time she climbed inside the car and started the engine, she held her breath. It was probably pretty simple to wire a car for detonation. If they hadn't succeeded in blowing her to bits the first time, they would certainly try again.

Or perhaps they planned to kill her some other way now—something that would look like an accident or suicide.

Last month, she'd bought a gun and had a security system installed in her apartment. She felt more vulnerable outside, away from home. Doing something to her car seemed the obvious choice for whoever wanted her dead.

Setting the mystery package on the roof of the Saturn, Cheryl dug out her car keys. She imagined the bomb going off when she opened the door. The big storefront window to the post office would probably shatter from the explosion. On the street corner, she noticed a woman with an umbrella, holding a toddler by the hand. Cheryl waited until they crossed the street—away from the parking lot. Then she took a deep breath, unlocked the car door and opened it. No white flash, no thunderous boom, nothing. She was still standing—and in one piece.

Cheryl grabbed the package, and slid inside behind the wheel. Dropping her purse on the floor, she set the parcel on the passenger seat. She checked under her dashboard, and didn't see anything strange there. In the movies, it was almost always when the person turned the key in the ignition that the bomb went off. At least that was the way it was with Robert De Niro in *Casino,* and Sam Shepard in *The Pelican Brief.* Cheryl decided just to get it over with, and she slipped the key into the ignition and gave it a turn.

The car started.

She uttered a pathetic, little laugh. While the engine purred, rain tapped lightly on the car roof. Cheryl took a pocket knife from her purse, and cut open the parcel. Inside, she found a Tupperware cake container—with an envelope taped to the top. She pried off the lid, and got a whiff of something citrusy and sweet. It was a golden brown Bundt cake—saturated with orange or lemon juice or both—and drizzled with a sugary glaze. One look and one sniff, and Cheryl could tell whoever had made this knew how to make desserts.

She pried the envelope off the Tupperware lid, opened it, and pulled out a postcard. It was a photo of one of those restaurants that went up about thirty years ago, trying to emulate a fifties diner. Emblazoned across the top of the card, it said:

SUPERSTAR DINER

Just Off I-90!

ELLENSBURG, WASHINGTON

On the back of the card was a note:

Dear Cheryl,
Please help me get out of this place! Actually,
I enjoy working here as a chef, but I'd love to
be in Seattle, cooking for you at Grill Girl. Here
is a sample of one of my desserts. But I'm
very creative with sandwiches, too. If you're
interested, don't hesitate to get in touch.

Bon appétit!
Laurie Trotter

PS: I read in Seattle Met mag that you'd love to
cater a party for Gil Garrett. He's my godfather
& an old family friend!

Cheryl broke off a piece of the cake, still moist—
with just the right firmness along the glazed exterior.
She took a bite, and closed her eyes.

It was incredible.

CHAPTER FOUR

"Just wait. She'll try to make out like it was our fault the wrong bitch got blown up. I'll bet she wants us to whack this Cheryl Wheeler for free—or on the cheap. I say, no way. It was her mistake, and she should pay us full price to correct it."

In the car's passenger seat, Keefe Grissom wondered if his work partner, Jay Trout, was even listening to him. Trout sat at the wheel, watching porn clips on his mobile device. "You like that?" the porn actor was asking, between grunts. The girl was panting and groaning in ecstasy.

The silver Audi was parked by the loading dock of an abandoned warehouse. They'd been sitting in the car with the engine off for about ten minutes. Graffiti covered the big door, crabgrass sprouted through the cracks in the driveway, and on the dock sat an old shopping cart full of rags and garbage some derelict must have left behind.

Whenever they met with this client, she'd always set the meeting in some bizarre, godforsaken spot. Shit like that came with the job. They rarely knew the names of their contacts. They nicknamed this one Zelda. She didn't know that, of course. She was a funny-looking bitch, with her wiry build, long face, and pale complexion. She always wore black—maybe to match her short-cropped, coal-colored hair. And she never smiled. But she'd paid them well for their last couple of jobs, so Grissom wasn't going to complain.

However, this last job was her screwup. They'd acted on her instructions to the letter. While his partner had lured the woman out of the food truck, Grissom had gone to work quickly and efficiently. He'd even come up with a piece of improvisational genius: nuking some aluminum foil in the microwave to set off the gas explosion. And not that he gave a crap one way or another, but the collateral damage had been pretty minimal. They'd done a damn fine, neat job—on the wrong woman.

"Harder, do it harder!" screamed the porn actress on the video Trout was watching.

With a sigh, Grissom leaned back in the passenger seat. "What the hell is the point watching a movie on a screen that size? Her tits are about as big as a couple of pinheads. I mean, can you see anything at all?"

"I can zoom in," his friend said, eyes riveted to his mobile device.

Suddenly, as if out of nowhere, Zelda appeared at the driver's window, staring in at them. Grissom saw her first and flinched. "Shit!"

The woman had a way of sneaking up on them. They

never heard her, never saw her coming. But all at once she was there.

Trout glimpsed her on the other side of the glass, and he dropped his device. Fumbling to retrieve the phone, he finally snatched it up and switched it off. He restarted the engine so that he could lower his window. "Jesus, you scared the shit out of me," he said to the woman.

Stone-faced, Zelda put her arm up on the edge of the door. Grissom noticed she wore some kind of weird, studded black leather cuff that went almost all the way to her elbow. "We have a problem," she said in a quiet voice. "As you must know by now, the wrong woman was killed. Cheryl Wheeler is still alive, and my client isn't too happy about it—"

"Well, that's not really our fault," Grissom said. "I mean, c'mon, you—"

"Now Cheryl's in the spotlight," the woman said, talking over him. "And we can't touch her for at least another couple of weeks, not without the police catching on. That's really unfortunate. You two did excellent work on the Hawaii job—as well as the L.A. assignment. But this mistake on Friday, it's disappointing . . ."

"Hey, you gave us the go-ahead," Grissom said. "It's not like we went in there on our own . . ."

Zelda stared at him. Her mouth seemed to tighten.

Grissom shut up. He didn't want to push his luck with her.

But his friend didn't seem to care. "We carried out your orders," Trout said, one hand on the steering wheel. "If the wrong woman is dead, that's your fault, not ours. Now, we don't mind correcting this screwup, but it'll be at our regular fee. Don't think you can get a freebie by shifting the blame on us."

Zelda took a small step back from the window. She tugged at the leather cuff on her arm.

Grissom squirmed in the passenger seat. "Listen, what Trout's trying to say is—"

"Oh, for Christ's sake . . ." Trout interrupted, turning toward him. "A minute ago you were going on about how if she tried to pin the blame—"

He didn't get another word out—just a deep gasp.

The woman had reached inside the car. It had happened so fast. Grissom had thought she was swatting a fly off his friend's shoulder.

Now he realized what was happening. Trout started to twitch as if he were having convulsions. Then his body suddenly went limp and slumped toward him.

The woman was wiping the blood off something that looked like a meat thermometer. She must have pulled it out of a pocket in that leather cuff on her arm. She slipped it back inside the cuff.

All the while, blood gushed from a hole on the side of Trout's neck, just under his ear.

Grissom glanced over at the woman in the window once again. Her face was expressionless. She pointed a gun at him.

"Oh, Christ, no," he cried. "Wait—"

Two shots rang out, one right after another.

The first bullet went through his hand, a defense wound.

The second one went through his eye.

* * *

Without passion, she stared at the two dead young men in the front seat of the Audi. Blood dripped down the passenger window—and the windshield.

Her paid assassins had been more like gifted amateurs than professionals. They'd been subcontracted by her—and they'd been reliable up until this last job. She didn't blame them for killing the wrong woman. That wasn't why the two men were dead now.

She kept tabs on all the police and fire department bulletins. There had been one this morning—from a witness to the food truck explosion on Friday afternoon. The waitress had seen Maureen Forester's last customers: two men in their twenties, one on crutches. A vague, but accurate enough description of the two young men had gone out on an APB. The police regarded them as "persons of interest" in the incident.

Now the woman needed to make sure the police never found them. Climbing inside the blood-splattered car, she collected their wallets and their phones. She wasn't too concerned about staining her clothes. It was one reason she always wore black while on the job. The blood didn't show.

Once she was outside again, she tossed the wallets and phones into a small plastic bag. Then she pulled out her own phone and made a call. A man answered: "Yeah?"

"I need you to come clean this up and make it disappear for me," she said.

"Will do," said the man on the other end of the line. Then he clicked off.

Like her, he was a professional. He'd get the job done.

The woman clicked off. She stared at the two corpses inside the crimson-stained car, two talented, young amateur killers. No one would ever find them or connect them to her client.

That was a problem easily fixed.

But Cheryl Wheeler was still alive.

The woman told herself she was working with another professional now. No subcontractors this time. She'd just have to be patient and wait it out a couple of weeks.

Then Cheryl Wheeler would be another problem easily fixed.

CHAPTER FIVE

The third Molly Ringwald Heavenly Chocolate cake still had twelve more minutes in the oven until it was ready. Two were already baked, frosted, and in their Tupperware containers. Laurie had promised her boss, Paul, the cakes tomorrow if he put one of the other cooks on tonight's solo closing shift.

She just didn't want to be there today, not after last night. Joey had had a fever—and a bad cough. Listening to him hacking away was heartbreaking. Laurie had spent a good chunk of the evening in the bathroom, rocking him while the hot water in the shower had gone full blast. The steam had helped clear out his little lungs. But he hadn't fallen asleep until three-thirty in the morning.

Joey's temperature was near normal today, thank God. Now he was asleep in his room. Some Jennifer Aniston movie provided harmless distraction during the lulls in baking. Laurie also kept busy with an ongoing project—emptying out her big antique desk in the living room. In preparation for moving, she'd been cleaning out all the drawers, cabinets, and closets this week. It was amazing how much crap she'd accumulated in three years. She'd filled five big plastic trash bags with junk.

Yesterday, she'd given Paul her two weeks' notice, asking him to keep quiet about it. She didn't want it getting around that she was leaving. She'd even stuffed those trash bags in two different dumpsters, so nobody would catch on that her unit was being vacated.

In two weeks, it would be as if she and Joey had disappeared.

She'd wanted to move for a while. But Tad McBride and his brother, Ryder, had helped set things in motion. They were also the reason the move had to be sudden—and secret.

Laurie had hoped to have a job waiting for her when she relocated. Working at Cheryl Wheeler's Grill Girl food truck in Seattle would have been ideal. Between the dessert she'd sent to Cheryl and dropping her famous godfather's name, Laurie had figured she'd be a shoo-in for at least a follow-up call or e-mail.

Of course, she didn't want to admit to Cheryl that "Uncle Gil" Garrett had met her only once—when she was eleven months old. But he really was her godfather. She had a photo of Gil holding her—and a silver spoon with her name engraved on it that he'd sent. Actually, Laurie figured someone on his staff had probably sent the baby spoon to her mother for him. Gil and her grandmother had been high school sweethearts in Boulder, Colorado, back in the early fifties. They'd stayed in touch—even after he'd become a famous Hollywood producer. Gil had agreed to be Laurie's godfather as a favor to her grandmother. He barely knew Laurie's mom.

And he barely knew her. But last Christmas, on a lark, she'd sent him and his wife, Shawna Farrell, a batch of her Holiday Spritz cookies. She'd included a Christmas card, telling him that she was Emily Hatch's granddaughter and his godchild. She'd mentioned that her husband was stationed in Afghanistan, and that her mother had died earlier in the year.

In reply, she'd gotten an expensive-looking Christmas card, perfectly square, the kind that required extra postage. GIL AND SHAWNA GARRETT was preprinted under the greeting inside. A note was scribbled below their names:

Thanks for the delicious treats! Happy holidays!

Laurie wasn't sure if Gil, Shawna, or some secretary handling their fan mail had written the personal note. But at least someone from Gil Garrett's camp had acknowledged her existence.

So why not drop Gil's name if it might help her land a job she wanted?

Too bad her timing totally sucked. The day after she'd sent that package to Cheryl Wheeler, the Grill Girl—and Cheryl's poor coworker—had been blown to smithereens in a freak explosion. Laurie couldn't help thinking that it might have been her.

Still, she planned to move to Seattle anyway. She had money saved, and also received a nice check every month from Brian's military insurance policy. She and

Joey wouldn't starve. Once she found a good daycare place for him, she could go out job hunting.

There was nothing for her in Ellensburg anymore, no reason to stay. Most of her and Brian's college friends had already moved away. The ones who remained seemed uncomfortable around her now that she was a widow. Her only real friends were Krista and Nathan—and the people at the diner.

Yet here she was, sifting through dozens of sympathy cards from the desk's bottom drawer. Where were these people now?

She couldn't lug all this stuff to Seattle. She had to be ruthless. She would only save the cards that said something personal about Brian. But she couldn't actually read the notes, because she didn't want to start crying. There was no time. She still had a cake in the oven, and she wanted to empty out this desk before she went to bed.

While she narrowed down the cards to a select few, Laurie kept glancing out the living room's picture window. She couldn't help feeling on edge. The graduate student who occupied the unit above hers was out of town. He wasn't the chummiest guy around, but having someone up there at least gave her a sense of security.

But not tonight. She and Joey were all alone.

It had been around this time last week that Tad and Ryder had pulled their surprise visit to the diner. Laurie imagined them returning there tonight, only to find her coworker behind the counter. They'd probably come here next. Every time she looked out the window, she half-expected to see the beat-up minivan in front of the town house.

She'd spotted the minivan in her cul-de-sac twice this past week. She was certain it was Tad and Ryder's van, too. Last Friday night, it had cruised up and down the block several times, always slowing to a stop in front of her duplex. Joey had been in his playpen at the time. She'd scooped him up, carried him into his room, and put him in bed. He screamed and cried in protest. But she just couldn't have those creeps looking at him, sizing him up. She was about to call the police when they finally drove away. On Monday night after she'd put Joey to bed, the minivan came back. It switched off its headlights and parked across the street. Laurie could barely make out two silhouettes in the front seat. She thought about shutting the curtains so they couldn't see her, but then she wouldn't have been able to see them. After ten excruciating minutes, she couldn't take it anymore, and finally phoned 911. The vehicle took off before the squad car arrived.

Laurie told the police that someone in an old, silver minivan was stalking her. She knew if either one of the McBride brothers were arrested, they'd probably go public with all the sordid details of her brief affair with Tad. Laurie told herself she was moving; she shouldn't really care if people knew. But she did. The people who adored Brian didn't need to know about his wife's stupid infidelity. So when the police asked her if she knew the minivan's owner, she lied. "Some customer from the restaurant, I suppose," she told them. She hoped they'd beef up patrols of the cul-de-sac, and maybe that would discourage Tad and his brother.

She told the police, too, about the dozen or so strange calls to the house at odd hours—all from a blocked number. They weren't hang-ups either. The person on the other end would wait for her to answer, and then stay on the line, saying nothing. Laurie always hung up first. She kept remembering the one time he'd said something: *"I know you're alone now."*

She hated having Joey out of her sight. She told the staff at Happy Train Daycare that she had a stalker situation, and that she was worried the person might come after Joey. So they were on their guard. She gave the same story to Krista and Nathan. Krista had a great solution. She simply invited her study group over to Laurie's those nights she babysat. Laurie fixed them treats, which were a big hit. Still, she couldn't breathe right until she was home and saw her baby boy was safe.

Laurie had asked her boss and the wait staff to let her know if they happened to spot the banged-up, silver minivan in the Superstar Diner's lot. She'd chalked up several false alarms last week. But on two occasions, the silver minivan parked in the lot for several minutes, but no one ever got out—until yesterday.

One of the waitresses had given her the heads-up that the vehicle was in their lot. Laurie had already come close to burning a few meals this week because she'd let these alerts distract her. So she tried to stay focused on her work. They were in the middle of a rush, and she had seven sandwiches on the grill, and two dishes in the oven.

"Hey, someone got out of that silver van I told you about," Laurie's waitress friend said, passing her with a tray of dirty plates. "She just walked in. *Freak,* party of one . . ."

Laurie stepped away from the grill and glanced out the pass-through window. She saw a lanky young woman with brown dreadlocks. She wore a black tank top and camouflage pants. Her face was studded with piercings, and tattoos covered her skinny arms. There was some strange star-pattern tattoo on the side of her neck. She looked like she hadn't had a bath in days. With a bizarre grin on her face, she stood by the door, talking to Duncan. She handed something to him, then turned and sashayed out the door.

Laurie figured it was another false alarm, and went back to work. But a few moments later, Duncan came into the kitchen. "Behind!" he announced, clearing his throat. One of the other cooks had once given him a hard time for getting into their work space, and poor Duncan had never forgotten it. "Um, Laurie, I've got something for you . . ."

She turned around to see him holding a small sailor boy doll in his hand. It was so dirty and tattered it must have been plucked out of the garbage. A few clumps of its yellow-blond hair were missing. The realistic detail on the doll's face and its slightly demonic grin made it look more creepy than cute.

"A customer wanted you to have this," Duncan explained. "She said it was for Joey—from his dad and his uncle . . ."

Laurie ran toward the kitchen's saloon doors and gaped at the parking lot outside. She caught a glimpse of the silver minivan driving away.

"I told her I didn't know what she was talking about," Laurie heard Duncan go on, "because Brian passed on and he didn't have any family. But the woman said *you'd* know what she was talking about."

Laurie thought she smelled something burning on the grill, and she rushed back to the stove.

"Don't you want the doll?" Duncan asked.

"Throw it out," she snapped, taking the food off the stove. "Please, just—just get rid of it. And you better wash your hands. That thing looks filthy."

She'd forgotten that Ryder had six friends who lived with him on the McBrides' small farm outside Cle Elum. According to Tad, these people were like his disciples. "They're all screwups—runaways, addicts, homeless," Tad had told her. "Ryder is like their guru. I don't know how he does it. He seems to know what they want, what they're afraid of, what makes them tick. Of course, it helps that he gets them drugs—and his guy pals have their pick of any of the girls. Whatever Ryder wants them to do, they do. He calls the shots. They worship him."

Tad had shared this tidbit with her almost two years ago.

Now Tad and Ryder seemed like a regular team, united in their effort to torment her. She had no idea what had happened to form this unholy bond—and why they'd decided to go after her now. Her pathetic little episode with Tad had lasted a mere two weeks— nearly two years ago. How could he still be angry with her?

She wondered about Ryder's tribe of followers. Obviously, it wasn't just Tad and his brother going after her.

Laurie was looking out her living room window

when the cake-timer chimed. Getting to her feet, she hurried into the kitchen, then grabbed her oven mitts. She felt a blast of heat as she opened the oven door, and reached in for the cake tins.

As she was pulling out the second cake, the telephone rang. She almost dropped the tin.

Biting her lip, she set down the cake and glanced at the stove clock. It was after ten. She didn't have to wonder who it was. She reached for the phone, and checked the caller ID: a blocked number. Laurie picked up the receiver, and didn't say anything. She figured two could play this silent game.

On the other end, she thought she heard traffic in the background. Were they on their way over?

Jennifer Aniston was yelling at someone on the TV. Laurie wondered if they could hear it on the other end of the line. She held on for another few moments until she couldn't take this standoff any longer.

"Leave me the hell alone," she finally said into the phone. She hated the quiver in her voice. "I've told the police about you. Do you understand me? They know. They're just waiting for you to make one more stupid move . . ."

She heard a man chuckle.

For a second, Laurie panicked.

The sound wasn't coming from the phone. It was from inside the house.

She froze. She couldn't even breathe. She glanced over at Joey's bedroom door.

She heard it again, and realized the low, guttural snicker was coming from the TV.

Laurie took a deep breath. "Listen to me," she said

into the phone. "If any one of you comes near me and my baby, I swear to God you'll regret it."

She clicked off the line.

Her heart was still racing as she made her way into Joey's room. The mobile of zoo animals swayed gently over his crib. If anyone else had just been in there or near the crib, the motion-sensitive mobile would have been swirling a lot more.

She watched Joey breathe, no cough, no raspy sounds. Then she reached down and tucked his blanket under his chin. He stirred a bit, kicked his little feet, and went back to sleep.

With his brown curly hair and cherub face, he looked just like Brian did in his baby pictures. If Tad saw him, maybe he'd finally acknowledge that Joey wasn't his. But that wasn't going to happen. She meant what she'd said.

She wasn't letting him get anywhere near Joey.

Cle Elum, Washington

"I don't know about this." Tad sighed. "I mean, she said she told the police about us."

"She's lying," his brother replied.

Ryder sat at the table in the grimy kitchen of the McBrides' farmhouse. The old Harvest Gold fridge and the avocado-colored electric range were relics from the seventies. The kitchen smelled of rancid cat food—thanks mostly to the four felines that seemed to own the place. The glass-topped wrought iron table was meant for a patio, but worked fine in this kitchen. It was especially good for snorting cocaine. Ryder was tapping a credit card against the glass as he made two lines of the white powder for his brother. "She's a lying bitch," he went on, over the tap-tap-tapping. "She lied when she said she cared about you. She's been lying to you for the last year and a half about *your* baby. And now she's lying to you about the cops. Believe me, she's milking her war widow routine for all it's worth. She's not going to admit to the cops or anybody else that she was banging you while her husband got shot at in Afghanistan or wherever the hell he eventually bought it."

"I guess you're right," Tad muttered.

He stood by the sink, which was stacked with dirty, mismatched plates and glasses. He was shirtless. One of Ryder's girls, Dawn, was behind him. He heard her rip off another piece of duct tape. Then she slapped and pressed it firmly on the right side of his lower back. The tape held a leather sheath to his skin. And inside that sheath was a hunting knife with a sharp, serrated edge.

"Of course I'm right," Ryder said. "But you don't sound too sure. Hell, if you want to chicken out, that's fine by me. We don't have to do this tonight. It's not my kid. I don't care. This was your idea, bro."

"I know it was," Tad said, staring at his reflection in the darkened window above the sink.

"You were too good for her. She treated you like shit, man. I know it was two years ago, but let's face it, you're still pretty raw about it. If your baby wasn't involved, I'd just say fucking forget about her. She's not worth it. But then she's got your kid, your son . . ."

Tad nodded. He felt his heart racing. "Damn it, I

have a right to take what's mine. We're doing this tonight . . ."

Dawn tugged at the knife sheath. It pinched and pulled at the skin on his back. "That's on good and tight," she said.

"Come over here and get a little Dutch courage," Ryder said to his brother.

Taking the straw from Ryder, Tad bent over and quickly snorted up one line, then the other. Shuddering gratefully, he rubbed his nose. "More," he murmured.

Ryder shook his head. "You know how too much coke makes you sweat. Might loosen the tape, and you'll want to have that knife tonight."

Tad picked at the remnants of white powder on the glass tabletop, and then licked his fingers. "I'm just going there to get my son. What do I need the knife for anyway?"

Ryder gave him a tiny little smile. "For when that cheating whore gives you an argument," he said.

CHAPTER SIX

Thursday, June 5
Ellensburg

Joey let out a little cry.

Laurie blindly felt around for the nightstand lamp and switched it on. She squinted at the clock at her bedside: 2:51 A.M.

After that phone call at ten, there hadn't been another. Maybe her threat had made some impact. At least that was what Laurie had told herself while frosting the third cake. She'd finished emptying out her desk, and started nodding off during the Jennifer Aniston movie. She'd woken up in time for the gag reel along with the end credits, which looked like the best part of the movie. She'd peeled herself off the sofa and crawled into bed shortly after midnight—with Brian's baseball bat by her side.

Now propped up on one elbow, Laurie pushed her hair away from her face and stared at the baby monitor on her nightstand. *Please, don't start coughing.* It wasn't unusual for Joey to let out a little cry in his sleep now and then. Most nights, she'd just ignore it. But now, each little noise from his room was cause for alarm. And she wasn't just worried about his cough either.

She listened and waited. She didn't want to go in there if he was about to nod off again. She would give him sixty more seconds—and if there wasn't another peep out of him, she'd switch off the light and go back to sleep.

On the nightstand was a small photo of her and her mom. Laurie had found it earlier tonight in an envelope in the desk's bottom drawer. She'd propped the snapshot against the baby monitor on her nightstand. It was one of those photo-booth snapshots. She had no idea what had happened to the other three pictures from the strip. Maybe they weren't very good shots of her mother, so she'd gotten rid of them. Then again, Teri Serrano hardly ever took a bad picture in her younger days. In this photo, she was movie-star gorgeous—with exotic eyes and shimmery, shoulder-length black hair. In the photograph, she was laughing. Crammed inside the booth with her was Laurie's skinny, serious, eleven-year-old self.

"You're no fun at all," her mother was forever telling her.

Her mom didn't leave her much choice. One of them had to take on some responsibility. From an early age, Laurie got up, dressed, fed herself, and then went off to school—all while her mother slept. Laurie did the housework and prepared the meals. Teri was a lousy cook. She would have lived on Chardonnay, cupcakes, Bugles, and microwave burritos—if her young daughter hadn't intervened.

Life with Teri was anything but dull. Her mom was always moving them—usually to get away from either a lousy boyfriend or trouble at work. Laurie would just get used to a place, and her mother would suddenly up and move them again. She often chose their next destination by opening a Rand McNally map of the U.S., closing her eyes, and going wherever her finger landed. Then Laurie would help her mother load up the old Ford Celebrity, and they'd head to the next city.

She didn't make any close friends. There didn't seem much point in trying. So cooking became her companion. In the kitchen, Laurie had control. She could be creative, and it was the one thing she did that her mother appreciated. Teri never noticed that Laurie had done the laundry or cleaned the apartment, but she really enjoyed a good meal. Whenever one of her boyfriends treated her to dinner at a classy restaurant, Teri would charm her way into the kitchen and get the recipe from the chef. Then she'd give it to Laurie to duplicate.

Laurie could still see her sitting in front of the TV with the dinner plate on her lap. "Oh, sweetie, this is even better than what I had in that hoity-toity restaurant," her mother would say, gobbling up Laurie's rendition of the latest borrowed recipe.

Every new place they moved into, Laurie checked the kitchen first, and then she took a look at her bedroom—if she got one. Often she shared a bedroom with her mom, which became awkward whenever Teri had a man over. Many a night, Laurie cooked an elaborate dinner for her mom and the latest boyfriend—and then at bedtime, she was relegated to the sofa in the living room.

Her dad wasn't in the picture at all. He'd played the bass guitar in a band called Sump Pump. Apparently, they'd been a real hit in Jacksonville, Florida, in the mid-eighties. That was where he and Teri had gotten married. When the band split up, he split, too—for good. He just took off one morning. Laurie had been thirteen months old. She and her mother didn't hear from him again. But Teri never filed for divorce.

"Sweetie, the things you should know about your father are this," her mother told her. "He was a very talented musician, sexy, a lot of fun—and, well, you know how some people have a severe reaction to nuts, like an allergy? They eat one nut and suddenly their throat closes up and they go into a coma or something. Well, that was Art Serrano with responsibility. He just couldn't handle it—not even a little bit."

Laurie wanted to tell her mother that it took one to know one.

Early on, she'd made up her mind that she wouldn't be anything like Teri. She would be a terrific mother to her children.

Yet here she was, planning a sudden, furtive move to another city to get away from a pissed-off former lover. And here she was, switching off the light and ducking back under the covers—when her child had just cried out in the middle of the night.

He's fine, everything's fine, Laurie told herself. She'd waited three whole minutes without another sound from him. If Joey was still awake, she'd have heard him on the monitor. And if by chance anyone had climbed in through his bedroom window, she'd have heard that, too. Besides, no one could break in that way. A few days ago, she'd sawed off part of a broom handle and vertically wedged it into the window frame for extra security.

Laurie assured herself once again that Joey was okay, she should go back to sleep. But she lay there in the dark, staring up at the popcorn ceiling.

It was just her and Joey, no grandparents, no relatives, no one else. It had been the same setup with her and her mother. They only had each other. Laurie wondered if Joey would spend most of his childhood and teen years resenting her the way she'd resented Teri. Yet she and her mom had been a team, nearly inseparable.

When she'd headed off to Central Washington University, Laurie had been horribly homesick—even though she'd never really had a steady, stable home. She'd worried about Teri on her own. Her mom wasn't as pretty as she used to be. She no longer had guys doing things for her—or a daughter to look after her. Teri lived only two hours away in Spokane. But Laurie was busy with school and waitressed most weekends, so weeks passed between visits home. Each time she made that bus trip to Spokane, she noticed her mother getting heavier and more sedentary—old before her time. Her beautiful black hair had lost its luster, and was ceding to gray; so she'd cut it short.

When Laurie and Brian were engaged and the wedding date drew near, her mother had a meltdown trying to find a decent dress to wear to the ceremony. "I can't fit into anything," she lamented. "I'm so big. God, what's happened to me?"

Laurie tried to convince her that she was still beautiful. But Teri didn't want to believe it. She didn't want Laurie to take her shopping at Lane Bryant. She didn't want to hear about all the gorgeous, self-confident TV and movie personalities who were full-figured, plus-size women. Three days before her wedding, Laurie received a letter from her mother—with a check for a hundred dollars, which she could hardly afford. There was also an apology note:

> *Dear Laurie & Brian,*
> *Please forgive me for not coming to your*
> *wedding. I just can't let people see me looking*
> *this way. Give my best to everyone there. I'm*
> *so proud of you, Laurie & so happy you're*
> *marrying such a wonderful man. Be happy,*
> *you two.*
>
> *XXXX—Me*

The worse Teri felt about her weight, the more she stayed at home—and ate to compensate for her misery and loneliness. She just didn't know how to take care of herself.

Not long after Laurie had returned from Europe and Brian had been sent to Afghanistan, Teri fell and badly sprained her ankle in the Safeway parking lot. Laurie drove to Spokane to take her to Ellensburg, where she could look after her for a while. They would make use of that second bedroom after all. During the drive home, her mom suddenly started sobbing. "When I fell, I felt like such an idiot. And, oh, sweetie, it hurt so much when I hit the pavement. But worse was my grocery bag ripping open. My stash fell out—the candy bars and donuts, everything I shouldn't be eating. And I saw these people in the parking lot laughing at me—me, the fat lady falling on her ass with all her junk food around her."

Staring at the road ahead, Laurie took one hand off the wheel, reached over, and squeezed her mother's arm. "Fuck them, Mom," she said. "Pardon my French, but fuck them."

Her mother didn't stay in the guest room long. After a couple of days, she complained of stiffness in her joints and trouble getting her breath. On her day off from the diner, Laurie took Teri to Kittitas Valley Hospital. Her mom rolled her eyes while the examining doctor mentioned that she needed to lose some weight and exercise more. He wanted to set her up for an X-ray and an EKG that afternoon. Both procedures were done in a different building. It was only a block away, but Laurie knew her mother couldn't walk it. She had her wait in the lobby of the main building while she brought the car around. By the time Laurie helped her into the passenger seat her mother was huffing and wheezing.

"Mom, are you okay?" she asked, bent over by the passenger door.

Teri nodded impatiently. "Let's go . . ."

Closing the door, Laurie hurried around to the driver's side. She started up the car and then glanced at her mom, who had a hand over her heart. She looked chalky.

"I'm lowering your window," Laurie said, flicking

the master switch on the armrest. "Are you sure you're okay?"

Her mother nodded again. Laurie pulled out of the main lot and started down the block. That was when her mother gasped. "Oh, sweetie . . . I can't—I can't breathe . . ." She was tugging at the collar of her sweatshirt.

Laurie saw the emergency room entrance up ahead, and pushed down on the accelerator. The tires let out a screech as she turned into the driveway. "Hold on," she said, clutching the steering wheel. "Hold on, Mom . . ."

By the time Laurie pulled up to the entrance, her mother had passed out. It took three orderlies to pry her out of the car and onto a gurney. One of them put a respirator mask over Teri's mouth and nose. Then they wheeled her down the corridor. Laurie followed them—until a tall, stern-looking nurse stepped into her path. "This is far as you can go. I'm sorry . . ."

She watched them push her mother on the gurney through a set of double doors.

Another nurse with a clipboard sat her down in the waiting area, and started grilling her about her mother's medical background, and when she'd last eaten. The nurse was just getting to questions about insurance when a doctor came through the double doors. He was a pale, handsome, thirtyish man in scrubs. He whispered something to the nurse, who showed him the form she'd been filling out.

Laurie stood up. The doctor turned to her. "Laurie?"

She nodded.

"I'm Dr. Lahart. I'm really sorry. We did everything we could . . ."

Wide-eyed, Laurie stared at him. She kept expecting him to say that her mother would need surgery, or that they had to keep her in the hospital overnight. Instead, Dr. Lahart sadly shook his head. "We lost her."

They told her later that a blood clot must have formed after Teri's ankle injury in the Safeway parking lot. And that blockage was what caused the respiratory problems, which led to her death.

Brian got a five-day furlough to attend the funeral. They drove to Spokane and cleaned out her mother's apartment. Laurie found a manila envelope full of restaurant recipes her mother had scribbled down for her. When she was growing up Laurie had figured Teri had done that just so she could enjoy a restaurant-quality dinner at home—courtesy of her daughter. And of course, she'd probably enjoyed flirting with those chefs, working her charms on them to get their culinary secrets.

But it wasn't until Laurie found the manila envelope in Teri's sad little apartment that she realized her mom had collected those recipes all these years for her—to encourage her to become a good cook.

Teri hadn't any insurance. There were medical bills and funeral costs. Brian had been worried about them going broke if she'd stayed in Europe another five weeks. And now here they were, broke anyway.

After Brian left again for Afghanistan, Laurie took on waitressing shifts at the Superstar Diner. She sometimes worked sixteen-hour days—cooking for eight hours, and then washing up and changing into a uniform to wait tables.

She could hardly afford it, but Laurie hired a private

investigator in Seattle to track down the whereabouts of Arthur Serrano. Suddenly, it seemed more important than ever to find her father. If nothing else, Laurie figured he should be told that Teri was dead.

It didn't take long for the investigator to find her dad.

"Art Serrano passed away seven years ago, Hodgkin's lymphoma," the man told her over the phone.

He'd never remarried. He'd been with several different bands in several different cities—until he got sick. He'd left what little he had to a woman he'd been living with in Raleigh, North Carolina, at the time of his death.

The investigator asked Laurie if she wanted the woman's name and contact information. She told him no thanks.

She had never been so miserable and lonely as she was in those months following her mother's death. A part of her still resented Brian for making her return to Ellensburg. She'd rather have been miserable in Europe. But then, of course, her mother still would have tripped in that Safeway parking lot, and within the week she would have died alone in her apartment. Living in Ellensburg had at least allowed Laurie to be with her mom at the end. Besides, she really couldn't be too angry at Brian—not when she thought about where he was, not when she considered the very real possibility that he might not come back.

Tad McBride first started showing up at the Superstar Diner in late September. Something about the season change—with a chill in the air and it getting dark earlier—made Laurie even more melancholy. She was strangely drawn to the cute, dark-haired twenty-something man. Maybe it was because he seemed even lonelier than she was. Or maybe it was because the first time she waited on him, he looked up at her. "Thank you for the smile," he said. "I really needed that today."

He came in every few nights, and always sat alone by the window. He spent most of his time writing—not on a laptop, but in an old-fashioned spiral notebook. He was one of those breakfast-for-dinner guys. He usually ordered the Kevin Bacon waffle with the Samantha Eggar scramble on the side.

Soon they were on a first-name basis. She found out that Tad's constant scribbling in that notebook was a novel in progress. He told her it was his attempt at another *Catcher in the Rye*. He admitted he'd had a "sort of nervous breakdown" a year before, and was still seeing a therapist. He lived in a studio apartment near the CWU campus, and worked as a custodian there. It was his "fallback job" until his novel sold. His parents were dead, and he had an older brother who lived on the family farm near Cle Elum—only Tad didn't want anything to do with him. "He's bad news," Tad said. "My shrink helped me realize that Ryder's pretty manipulative—and, well, let's just say I'm better off keeping my distance."

He asked her out. Laurie told him she was flattered, but she didn't think her husband would like her going on a date with another guy. Tad never asked her out again. But he often stayed until closing, claiming he wanted to make sure that no one bothered her and that she got to her car okay. It felt nice to have someone concerned about her.

Those nights he stayed until closing, they sometimes stood and talked in the parking lot for fifteen or twenty minutes. Though she was dead on her feet, it was always the best part of Laurie's day. She told him things she wouldn't dream of telling anyone else— about how miserable she was. She admitted to him that sometimes she felt as if Brian didn't understand her, and maybe she would have been better off not marrying him—or at least waiting until he'd finished up his tour of duty.

The nights Tad didn't show up at the restaurant always seemed so empty. But those occasions also gave her a little reality jolt. Though her marriage wasn't perfect, her husband was a pretty wonderful guy, who put his life in danger every day for his country. And here she was, getting a crush on a lonely, screwed-up janitor. She had to keep things with Tad in check.

When Brian said he might be home for Thanksgiving or Christmas, it helped her put things even more into perspective, and strengthened her resolve. Plus at long last, she had something to look forward to.

But then, in early November, Brian texted her that a holiday furlough wasn't going to happen. Laurie was crushed.

On a cold, bleak night two weeks before Thanksgiving, she closed up the diner and discovered her car wouldn't start. Tad was there—once again. He drove her home in his old VW Bug. But when he pulled in front of the duplex, Laurie gazed out the car window at that dark, empty first-floor unit, and she started to cry.

Tad put his arm around her and kissed her. Though she knew it was wrong and stupid and reckless, she kissed him back.

They made love in the guest room. A part of her just wanted to be crushed to death beneath him. They were clumsy and awkward together, especially when he hunted through his wallet for a condom he'd tucked in there months ago. He was shy about putting it on in front of her. Laurie hadn't been with anyone else since meeting Brian, and try as she did, she couldn't quite get comfortable with this other body. When Tad was finished and still on top of her, he started to weep. This time, he was the one crying. He seemed so grateful, so moved. All Laurie could do was hold him.

As the days passed, when Tad wasn't at the restaurant at closing, he was usually waiting for her outside when she got home. They had sex only two more times after that first night. Laurie simply couldn't relax with him—and in a way, she didn't want to. There was just too much at stake. She made it clear to Tad that all evidence to the contrary she still loved her husband and didn't want to give him up. Yet as guilt-stricken as she was over her infidelity, she didn't want to give up Tad either. He made her feel needed.

Tad was good at keeping things clandestine. No one at the diner seemed to have a clue. He acknowledged that this thing between the two of them was just temporary. He told her that Brian seemed like a terrific guy, and he didn't want to hurt their marriage. When the time came, he'd go quietly. But would she mind if he dedicated his novel to her?

Both of them had nowhere to go for Thanksgiving, and the diner was closed for the holiday. So Laurie promised to have him over for an elaborate dinner—turkey, stuffing, all the trimmings. She used to do the same thing for her mom. Tad said he hadn't had a home-cooked Thanksgiving dinner since his own mother had died six years before.

That Tuesday afternoon before Thanksgiving, Laurie worked only one shift—in the kitchen. When she got the order for the Kevin Bacon waffle with the Samantha Eggar scramble on the side, she knew Tad was there for a late lunch or early dinner. She gave him a furtive smile at the pass-through window. About fifteen minutes later, one of the waitresses came into the kitchen. "Laurie, we have a customer who isn't happy with his spaghetti and meatballs," she announced. "He says he wants to talk to the chef."

She'd never had any complaints about the Sophia Loren spaghetti and meatballs. It was one of their most popular items—from a recipe her mom had procured for her. With three orders going on the grill, Laurie nodded distractedly. "I'll have these plated in a minute. Meantime, could you please tell the customer to shove the meatballs up his ass?"

The waitress cracked a smile. "Tell him yourself. I'll let him know you'll be out to see him soon. He's at table two. Better not keep him waiting too long."

Laurie got the grill cleared and the orders plated. As she set the food under the heat lamp in the window, she glanced at Tad again. He was just finishing his break-fast-for-dinner, and didn't see her. Laurie tried to get a peek at Mr. Complainer, but it was impossible to see table two from the pass-through window.

Wiping her forehead with her arm, she took a deep breath and headed out the saloon doors to the restaurant area. She started toward table two. The man was sitting alone with a near-full plate of food in front of him.

He wore an army uniform.

Laurie stopped in her tracks. "Brian!" she screamed.

He sprung to his feet, nearly tipping over his chair. Elated, Laurie ran into his open arms, and kissed him all over his face. She hadn't realized just how desperately she'd missed him until now. She started crying.

The waitresses broke into applause. Everyone else in the restaurant joined in the ovation, clapping and cheering. With one arm still on her shoulder, Brian broke apart from her and waved to the customers. But he still had one arm around her shoulder. Laurie clung to him. She looked at all the happy faces in the diner— all but one.

Sitting alone at his window table, Tad didn't applaud. And he didn't smile.

Laurie saw the hurt in his eyes.

All she could do about it at that moment was hope he didn't stay too hurt or angry.

Once they were home from the restaurant, Brian took her into the bedroom. Her work clothes and his army uniform were off in a matter of seconds. He didn't even give her time to wonder if she seemed different to him. Brian was the exactly the same: a big, sweet, sexy teddy bear. But she wasn't the same. For the first time in their marriage, she couldn't get completely comfortable with him. She didn't have to wonder why.

Afterward, Laurie held her breath every time he stepped into the guest room. Though she knew Tad hadn't left anything behind in there, she couldn't help thinking Brian would somehow sense what had happened in that room. It was ridiculous. But then *she* was ridiculous to have cheated on him.

She was terrified he'd discover her infidelity. While she cooked dinner, Brian innocently asked why she'd bought so much food for Thanksgiving when she hadn't known he was coming. Laurie lied and told him she'd planned to bring Thanksgiving dinner over to a regular customer, an elderly man who lived alone.

"Well, what the hell? Let's invite the old guy over here," Brian said, sticking his finger in the pot to sample her beef stew on the stove. "He'll probably get a real kick out of spending the holiday with us. Plus most old farts love us military dudes."

"Oh, I don't want to share you with anyone else," Laurie said, working up a smile. "He'll understand. I'll bring him some leftovers on Friday. I'll call and let him know."

After dinner that night, while Brian dozed in front of the TV, Laurie snuck out the kitchen door and phoned Tad. "I'm sorry about today," she whispered, shivering in the cold.

"Don't say you're sorry," he replied, "not when you looked so happy. I suppose I should be glad for you. But I'm not. So, our Thanksgiving is officially canceled. Is that why you're calling?"

"Yes." She sighed. "I'm afraid we—well, we're officially canceled, too. We both knew this was coming—only not this early."

"You'll change your mind as soon as he ships out again."

"No, I won't. I don't want to do that to him—and I don't want to do it to you."

"You can't just break up with me on the phone like this," he insisted. "I deserve better. I want to see you in person—"

"Tad, I don't think that's a good idea—"

"I thought you cared about me."

"I do," she said.

"If you don't see me again, I swear to God, I'm going to raise such a stink . . ."

"All right, all right," she sighed. "I'll see you on Friday, okay?"

Laurie wondered what the hell had happened to the sweet, sensitive guy who didn't want to hurt her marriage, the one who had vowed to "go quietly."

With three Tupperware containers full of food, she drove over to Tad's small, dingy studio apartment on Friday afternoon. Tad opened the door and frowned at her. "C'mon in," he grumbled.

Laurie stood in the dim corridor. The beige carpet was stained and tattered. She shook her head. "No, I can't come in. That wasn't part of the bargain. You wanted to see me, and here I am." She handed him the food containers. "Also, I wanted to make good my promise to cook you a Thanksgiving dinner. It's a day late and a dollar short, but it's still pretty good if I say so myself."

"Leftovers," he muttered, scowling at the containers in his hands. "So, that's it then?"

She shrugged awkwardly. "That, and I'm sorry it's turned out this way. I hate to see you hurt. You're a good guy, Tad. It's like you said on the phone the other day. You deserve better. If it's any consolation, I'm going to miss you."

He shoved the Tupperware containers back in her hands. "Why don't you say what this is really about?" he muttered. "I'm in the way now, and you want to get rid of me. You're just being nice about it so you can think of yourself as a decent person."

Her mouth open, Laurie stared at him. In many ways, his assessment of her was spot-on.

He stood in the doorway with his shoulders slumped. His eyes started to fill with tears. "What am I supposed to do now?" he whispered.

"Tad, please . . ." She wanted to reach out to him, but couldn't.

He shook his head at her. "You fucking bitch," he whispered. Then he stepped back and shut the door in her face.

Laurie clutched the food containers to her chest. "I'm—I'm really sorry," she murmured to the closed door. She turned and retreated down the hallway.

The people at the diner had been incredibly nice. They all pitched in and took turns working her shifts so she could spend the holiday weekend with Brian. After he shipped out and she came back to work, Laurie often found herself checking the table by the window for Tad. Maybe it was because of Christmas approaching, the red and green lights in the diner's window, the tacky fake poinsettia plants on the tables, "Goodwill to Men," and all that. But she did indeed miss him—only the Tad she missed was from weeks back when he'd just starting coming into the diner, before she'd mucked it up by having sex with him. She had no desire to pick up where they'd left off.

He never set foot inside the diner again. But once in a while his old VW Bug would pull into the lot and park. He'd just sit at the wheel and stare at her while she waited tables. It was unnerving.

Two weeks before Christmas, Laurie went back to working just one shift—in the kitchen. The waitress duties on top of cooking had become too exhausting. One advantage to being in the kitchen was she didn't see Tad out in the parking lot. But he still made his presence known. One morning, when Paul was opening the place, he discovered that during the night someone had scratched the word WHORE on the front window—only the culprit had misspelled it, H-O-R-E. Laurie didn't say anything, but she was pretty certain it was meant for her.

That afternoon, Paul had a windshield repair place buff the scratch marks from the big window.

Laurie wished she could erase her own mistake just as easily. She tried to wax optimistic. Maybe with that misspelled slur on the restaurant window, Tad had finally gotten it off his chest. Maybe he was finished with her. Though things with him had ended badly, Laurie told herself it could have been a lot worse. Although she would be all alone at Christmas—her first without her mom—Laurie decided her credo for the yuletide was "Count your blessings."

But that Christmas week, she felt more and more tired each day. She would get nauseous at work smelling certain foods, even foods she ordinarily liked. And her breasts felt tender and swollen—the way they did before she got her period. But she hadn't gotten her period.

Laurie realized she might not be so alone after all.

It was almost as if Tad had masterminded the whole thing with the timing of his Christmas card—a cheap variation of a Currier and Ives scene from a set of cards he'd obviously gotten in the mail for free from the Veterans' Association. Inside was a Trojan brand lubricated condom still in its wrapper. There was also a note:

> *This is like all the others I used*
> *when I was with you.*
> *I'm still inside you & always will be.*

"No," Laurie murmured. Her hand shook as she examined the wrapper, which had been opened. "God, please, no . . ."

The card fluttered to the floor as she rushed to the kitchen sink with the condom in her hand. She put it under the faucet, and the thing started leaking through the dozen or so pinholes before she even had it halfway full.

"Goddamn him!" she screamed.

Tad was not finished with her.

And now, his sociopathic brother had teamed up with him to make her life even more miserable.

"You really know how to screw things up," Laurie muttered to herself, lying in bed, hugging Brian's pillow. What an idiot she'd been to let Tad into her life, and eventually her home. Hell, he'd even been in Joey's room—back when it was just the second bedroom. She'd ignored all the signs. Yet Tad couldn't have made it any clearer to her at the start. He'd had mental health issues, which obviously ran in the family. And commendable as it seemed that he was writing his own *Catcher in the Rye*-type of novel, that brilliant book was also a source of inspiration for some deeply disturbed individuals—including John Lennon's killer, the creep who stalked and murdered actress Rebecca Schaeffer, and the guy who tried to assassinate Reagan.

What in God's name had she been thinking?

Laurie threw off the bedcovers. She sat up and frowned at the nightstand clock: 3:44. She didn't need to turn on the light. Her eyes had long ago adjusted to the darkness. She got to her feet. All she had on were a pair of panties and one of Brian's U.S. Army T-shirts, which was huge on her. She just wanted to check on Joey. But she was still feeling a bit edgy and paranoid, so she grabbed the aluminum baseball bat.

She didn't switch on any lights. She didn't want to disturb him.

The door creaked as she tiptoed into his room. She gazed at Joey in his crib, lying on his side with the blanket up to his chest. He had his tiny fist tucked under his chin. His breathing sounded healthy, no signs of any lingering congestion. She touched his forehead—a tad warm, but nothing to be alarmed about. The zoo-animal mobile above him moved ever so slightly. Laurie looked over toward the window—with the broom handle fixed in place.

She heard a rustling sound outside, but figured it

was just the wind. If the McBride brothers really wanted to get at her and Joey, they would have tried at midnight or one in the morning, not now. In another hour, it would be light out.

Laurie heard it again, the same rustling sound. Then there was a soft tinny clank—like a screen door closing. It seemed to come from the kitchen. "Your refrigerator is possessed," Krista had told her recently. "It makes all sorts of weird noises." That was probably what she heard. The squeaking and clicking sounded mechanical.

Laurie tiptoed out of the nursery and down the short hallway to the living room. She had the aluminum bat resting on her shoulder.

She saw something move in the darkened living room, and gasped. Then she realized it was her reflection in the glass door of the tacky trophy case where Brian displayed his football awards as sort of a joke. A hand over her heart, Laurie stared at the largest faux-gold cup in the case, one he had made for her—before Tad had come along. The trophy was alone on the middle shelf, and on the pedestal plaque it said:

WORLD'S GREATEST WIFE

TO LAURIE TROTTER

Master Chef, Curvaceous Cutie, Bedcover Hog, And the Love of My Life

"Oh, What a Woman!"

She ached inside, and tears welled up in her eyes. Laurie felt she didn't deserve that award at all. What she wouldn't give to have him sleeping in their bed right now.

Wiping her eyes, Laurie took a deep breath and headed into the kitchen. At the threshold, something crunched under her bare foot. It was a stray Honey Nut Cheerio. Joey gobbled them up by the fistful as a snack—and lately he was also learning to throw things. So she had cereal in every nook and cranny in the kitchen. She wiped the cereal crumbs from the bottom of her foot onto the floor, and made a mental note to attack the place with the Dirt Devil in the morning. She flicked on the light switch on the kitchen wall.

The sudden bright overhead almost blinded her for a moment. She blinked a few times and focused on the kitchen door. The chain lock was still in place. Through the window in the door, she didn't see anyone outside— just a dim reflection of the kitchen.

She noticed the refrigerator sounds had stopped.

Laurie figured there was still a chance to nod off if she went back to bed right now.

She took one last look at the door, and then at the window by the breakfast table. It was closed, but something wasn't quite right. The glass was too clear. It took her a few seconds to realize that the outside screen was missing.

Laurie warily stepped closer to the window, and spotted the screen outside, leaning against a recycling bin. There should have been two recycling bins, but she only saw one. Taking another step toward the window, she spotted the second bin, turned upside down— against the side of the house. Someone had used it as a makeshift stepladder to the window. The same some-one had pried off the screen.

"Oh, dear God," she murmured. Her first thought was to call the police. She turned to reach for the phone on the wall. But she froze. Out of the corner of her eye, she glimpsed someone on the other side of the kitchen door. She saw only his tall silhouette.

Within in a second, he was gone.

The phone rang, and she let out a startled cry.

Laurie hesitated, and then she snatched up the re-ceiver. She listened. Someone breathed heavily on the other end.

"I have a gun!" she screamed into the phone. "God-damn it, leave me alone!"

The person on the other end didn't say anything.

From the nursery, she heard Joey crying. The phone ringing and her yelling must have woken him.

"Liar," whispered the person on the other end. Lau-rie didn't recognize the raspy voice. She couldn't tell if it was male or female. "You don't have a gun. All you have is a baseball bat."

She heard someone chuckling—someone else. The other voice came from right outside the kitchen win-dow.

Two of them were out there.

Laurie pushed down the receiver cradle to break the connection. With her hand trembling, she tried to call 911, but it didn't go through. She couldn't even get a dial tone. They still hadn't hung up on their end.

Joey was wailing now.

Someone started pounding on the kitchen door.

Panic-stricken, Laurie turned and spotted Tad banging on the window in the door. She thought he might break the glass. He was shirtless. "Goddamn it, Laurie, let me in!" he shouted.

He didn't even seem to care that the neighbors might hear him. A dog started yelping in one of the nearby duplexes. "C'mon, open up!" Tad demanded, pounding on the door more violently. "I'm tired of this shit! At least let me in so I can get my stuff . . ."

She didn't know what he was talking about. Was he on drugs or something?

Past Tad's tirade and Joey's cries, she thought she heard a squeaking noise—a window opening in another part of the house. She immediately thought of Joey's room. Had they somehow gotten in—past the broom handle in the window?

Laurie rushed through the living room, and then down the short hallway to the nursery. She had the aluminum bat raised for whoever was trying to get at her little boy. Charging into the darkened room, she stopped dead. It didn't look like anyone was in there—except Joey. Sitting up in his crib, he had his blanket scrunched around his feet. He wouldn't stop crying. The window was still closed, the broom handle still in place. Outside, she could see a neighbor's light go on. Was it too much to hope that they might call the police? Tad was still yelling and pounding on the kitchen door.

Laurie patted Joey on the back. But her hand still shook, and he must have sensed her anxiety, because he screamed even louder. She longed to pick him up, but then she couldn't have swung the bat—at least, not so it would do any good. A part of her just wanted to stand here in the nursery guarding her baby until the police came—if a neighbor had indeed called them.

There was a loud clatter in her bedroom next door. It sounded like someone had tipped over a piece of furniture.

At the same time, Tad's banging on the door and his shouting abruptly ceased.

Had he given up? She wasn't sure. All she knew was that someone else was inside the house now—in her bedroom.

Hovering near Joey's crib, Laurie clutched the bat even tighter.

A shadow swept across the nursery's wall. Laurie spun around in time to see a figure darting past Joey's window.

She wondered how many people were out there— and how many were inside the house. "Leave us alone!" she screamed, her voice cracking.

Past Joey's cries, she heard the chain rattling on the front door.

Laurie moved toward the small hallway. She peeked around the corner in time to glimpse someone running out of the house. The intruder wore dark clothes and a ski mask. From the slight build, it could have been a woman. Whoever was working with Tad, they left the front door ajar. Laurie didn't see anyone outside.

Baffled, she glanced back into her bedroom. The window was open, and the curtains billowed slightly. A lamp on a dresser near the window had been knocked over. It lay on the floor, unbroken, the shade askew. Be-

side the fallen lamp was a trail of clothes on the floor—
a man's sneakers, trousers, a shirt and underpants.

"I came for my son."

Laurie swiveled around to see Tad standing in the
front doorway. He was completely naked. His body
looked ravaged, sickly thin, with a row of scars on one
arm that looked like the result of self-mutilation. His
feet were filthy from walking outside in the mud. He
had his hands out in front of him—as if prepared to
fend off an attack.

"Good God, what are you . . ." She trailed off. The
bat poised, Laurie just stood there, paralyzed. She
couldn't understand what was happening. Was Tad's
partner still around?

He took a step toward her. "You can't just invite me
into your bed, and throw me out. At least let me get
dressed first . . ."

Laurie shook her head at him. She realized why the
other intruder had left a trail of clothes in her bedroom.
In some weird, screwed-up way, it was a clever ruse. If
the police came, he had a story for why he was there—
and why he'd created a disturbance. And Tad would
certainly tell the cops that he'd slept with her before
tonight. Was she going to deny it?

"Now, no one's getting hurt," he said. "You can see I
don't have anything on me. So, how about putting
down the baseball bat, okay?"

Laurie kept the bat raised. She didn't budge.

All the while, Joey kept screaming.

Tad cracked a tiny smile. "Quite a set of lungs on
my boy," he said, moving toward her.

"Don't," she said, brandishing the bat. "I mean it.

You turn around and get out of here—now! I'll throw your clothes out the door after you go." She kept thinking the other one was still lurking around the house, just waiting to get at Joey.

"I'm going to see my kid, goddamn it," he growled, coming toward her. He made a strange gesture, reaching back like he was going to scratch his tailbone.

"How many times do I have to tell you? He isn't yours, Tad. Don't you get it?" Laurie stepped back and bumped into the wall.

He kept getting closer and closer.

"I'm not letting you near him . . ."

"Get out of my way, you unfeeling bitch."

Laurie thought he was going to grab her. She slammed the aluminum bat down on his arm. She heard a crack. Something shiny flew out of his grasp. A jagged-edged knife landed on the carpeted floor.

Tad howled with pain, and he recoiled. Cursing at her under his breath, he rubbed his arm. It looked like he was backing away. But then he suddenly lunged at her again.

Laurie swung the bat once more, connecting with the side of his head—just below the ear. He let out a groan and fell against the trophy case, shattering the glass. The tall case tipped over and crashed to the floor. Tad staggered back, almost tripping over the trophy case. Laurie glanced down at all the glass on the floor—around Tad's bare feet. Then she saw the blood running down his right leg and onto the carpet.

Horrified, she gazed at the crimson stream running down his pale chest and torso. It gushed from a large shard of glass wedged in his neck.

Tad was still standing, gaping at her as if he didn't know what had happened. It looked like he was trying to say something. He brought a hand up to his throat, and collapsed to the littered floor. Broken glass crunched under his weight.

Laurie stood there with the bat clutched in her fist, watching him die. She was afraid to move, afraid his friend was still around.

Blood bubbled from the gash in his throat as he took his last few gasps. But Laurie couldn't hear him.

She could only hear her son's cries.

CHAPTER SEVEN

Thursday, June 5, 9:55 P.M.
Ellensburg

"No, you can't confiscate them as 'evidence,'"
Detective Donald Eberhard said into the phone.
He sat at his desk in his small office. Behind him was a
bulletin board crammed with "wanted" fliers, restaurant carryout menus (including the Superstar Diner's),
business cards, and newspaper clippings. His desk was
just as messy with piles of paper everywhere. A com-
pact digital recorder sat on top of one stack of papers.
At the desk corner closest to Laurie was a bobblehead
figure of Linus from *Peanuts*.

During most of their talk, Eberhard nibbled at the
tip of a cinnamon stick. He'd explained that he'd just
given up smoking, and gnawing at cloves and cinnamon sticks helped get him through withdrawal.

Laurie sat across from him, her back to the window,
which looked into the general office area. There were
about ten desks with computers that desperately needed
to be updated. Laurie figured most of the cops there

had known Brian—or knew of him. They'd spent the morning fawning over Joey, who got passed from desk to desk—until Krista, bless her heart, had come to pick him up about an hour ago.

The notion that she might have to spend time in jail gnawed at her. She'd never been away from Joey for a night, not since coming home from the hospital with him.

Laurie tried to convince herself that everything would be all right. Considering she was a manslaughter suspect, they were certainly treating her well. Of course, being the widow of a local football star and a war hero helped. Plus most of the cops were regulars at the diner. They'd clearly seen she'd been traumatized by what had happened. At the apartment, they'd let her wash her face and change into a black V-neck top and jeans. Once they'd arrived at the station, they'd photographed her, and gotten her coffee and a Croissan'wich from Burger King. But her stomach was on edge, and she'd only been able to eat a few bites.

Eberhard covered the mouthpiece of the phone and peered across the desk at her, one eyebrow raised. "The guys at your place want to know if they can have some of that chocolate cake you left on the kitchen counter."

She shrugged. "Actually, the cakes are for the restaurant. I was going to take them to work this afternoon."

"Nope, they're not *evidence,* Mike," the detective said into his phone. "I need one of you guys to run the cakes over to the Superstar Diner, and let them know Ms. Trotter probably won't be coming in today. And don't sample the evidence on the way. Got that? Now, anything else?" He paused.

Laurie watched for any change in his expression. The detective was a handsome man in his mid-thirties. He had a slight five o'clock shadow, which suited him well, and dark brown hair that probably had too much hair product in it. At least it looked kind of stiff. His navy blue shirt was slightly rumpled and his black tie was loosened around the collar.

She couldn't help wondering if the cop at her place was telling Eberhard about some new discovery. So far, everything they'd found backed up her story about the bizarre, predawn home invasion and the dead naked man on her living room floor. Taped to his lower back was a holder for the hunting knife found on the floor near his body. The screens had been removed from one window in the kitchen and from another in her bedroom. The police on the scene uncovered two sets of footprints around the outside of the house—one matched Tad McBride's bare, dirty feet. The other set of footprints appeared to belong to a woman. Most of those prints were on the ground outside Laurie's bedroom window, and some on the bedroom carpet. Compared to the shoes found in Laurie's closet, there didn't seem to be a match. Finally, there were the neighbors who had heard the screams and commotion. One neighbor in particular was pretty certain she'd seen someone dressed in dark clothes running across the lawn in front of Laurie's duplex around 3:30 A.M.

Perhaps making her story even more believable was her report to the police earlier in the week that someone in a silver minivan had been stalking her. The detective told her that Tad's brother in Cle Elum owned a 2004 silver Town & Country minivan. The local police had already had several brushes with Ryder McBride. "Him and his gang on that farm off Highway 97 have been a major thorn in my side," Don Eberhard had said earlier, switching off the tape recorder on his desk for a moment. "McBride's been arrested several times—and each time he's walked. We couldn't make any of the charges stick. The scumbag is as slippery as a greased flagpole."

Laurie figured whatever Ryder had to say, it would be the scumbag's word against that of the war widow. Still, that didn't boost her confidence. So far, all she'd told Eberhard about Tad McBride was that he'd been a regular customer at the diner for a while—in the fall of the year before last.

They'd been interviewing her for nearly five hours now. But the detective still hadn't asked the ten-thousand-dollar question, the one she dreaded: *Exactly how well did you know the deceased?*

"Yeah, that's fine, go for it," he said into the phone. "Over and out." He hung up, and then reached over for the recorder again. "Sorry about that."

Laurie straightened in the hard-backed chair. "Thank you for having them deliver the cakes," she said. "But I—well, I couldn't help overhearing that part about me not coming to work today. Does that mean you'll be keeping me here?"

"Oh, no, don't worry—"

"I mean, my shift doesn't start until four. And there's Joey—"

He gave a wave of dismissal. "We should have this wrapped up before lunchtime. No, I just figured you were in no shape to be cooking John Wayne burgers

today. In fact, it's going to be a little while before
things get back to normal for you and Joey. You won't
be able to stay at your place for at least another couple
of days. It's a crime scene now. I'll make sure you get anything out of there you might need, within reason. I recom-
mend the Hampton Inn—if you can't find a friend to stay
with for the duration."

All Laurie could think was that she didn't have to go
to jail or be separated from Joey—at least not yet.
Nodding, she let out a sigh of relief. "Thank you."

Eberhard adjusted something on the tape recorder.
"So, before Tad started stalking you, he'd been a customer at the diner eighteen or nineteen months ago. To
your knowledge, was he ever inside your apartment before the incident early this morning?"

She hesitated. "Yes. I—I had car trouble one night—
back in November, the year before last—and he drove
me home. I invited him inside . . ."

Eberhard nibbled on his cinnamon stick and frowned
at her. "What for?" he asked. "A glass of water? Cup of
coffee?" He paused. "A game of Parcheesi?"

Laurie gripped the chair's armrests. She figured
Ryder was going to tell them the whole story anyway—or at least, his version of it. If she didn't tell the
truth now, it could end up biting her in the ass later on.
She took a deep breath. "He spent the night."

Eberhard's mouth twisted to one side. "Did he crash
on the living room couch or . . . ?"

"We slept together—in the guest room bed."

"Was this a one-shot deal or a long-term thing?"

Laurie sighed. "I really don't see what this has to do
with—"

"I'm trying to determine how well he knew the inside of the apartment, Laurie."

She nodded. "I'm sorry, of course. He was in the apartment on several occasions, maybe eight—or nine. We . . ." Laurie trailed off. The cop didn't need to know that she and Tad had had sex only three times. "I—I stopped seeing him when Brian came home for a surprise visit during Thanksgiving week."

"Some surprise," the detective murmured. Then he cleared his throat. "And you didn't see McBride again?

"Not intentionally," Laurie replied. She explained about his vigils outside the diner, and the graffiti on the restaurant's front window. "I was working full-time in the kitchen by Christmas, and if he came to the diner after that, I didn't see him," she said.

Laurie remembered that once in a while she'd get an order for the Kevin Bacon waffle and the Samantha Eggar scramble, and her stomach would automatically clench. But then she'd peek out the pass-through window, and realize it wasn't him.

"I didn't see or hear from him again until I was about six months pregnant," she told the detective. She nervously fingered the Burger King bag on the table at her side. She figured she had to tell Eberhard about the paternity issue. After all, it was the main reason Tad wouldn't leave her alone.

"I didn't realize he'd been watching me," she explained. "But I guess he had been, because he called me one night after work. He said, 'That's my baby you're carrying, isn't it?' I told him that he was mistaken. But the truth is once I found out I was pregnant, I wasn't really sure if it might not be his. I thought we'd been using protection, but—well, it's a long story. Anyway, the time I was with him and when Brian had returned home—it was just too close to call. I told my doctor my predicament, and he advised me just to focus on taking care of myself and my baby. We could work out the paternity issue with a simple test once the baby was born."

"Did you consider having—" Eberhard stopped himself. He sat back in his chair and quickly waved away the question. "Sorry. It doesn't have anything to do with the investigation. Go on . . ."

Laurie figured she'd answer his question anyway. "I wasn't going to terminate the pregnancy just to keep covering up what happened." She shrugged. "Then there'd have been one more awful thing I'd have to hide from my husband."

"While you were pregnant, did McBride call you again—or harass you in any way?"

She nodded. "There were a few more calls—basically the same thing over and over. He asked me when I was due, and he threatened to tell Brian. He was convinced the baby was his."

Her throat went dry, and Laurie took a sip of the bottled water they'd gotten for her. "In my eighth month, someone left a used high chair in front of the restaurant one morning. My coworkers figured it was some nice customer who had spotted me in the kitchen and thought they were doing me a favor. But I have a feeling it was Tad. Anyway, I didn't keep the high chair. I didn't even take it home. I dropped it off at Goodwill."

"Did you ever spot him outside your house during this time?"

"It was hard to be certain," Laurie replied. "I never saw him sneak up to the duplex or anything like that. But several times, I wondered if it was him driving by. Tad had an old, red VW Bug. And—well, you know, this is a college town . . ."

"Crawling with VW Bugs," Eberhard said, nodding.

"Every time I saw one come down the block, I couldn't be sure."

Laurie let out a sad little laugh. In a strange way, she was glad to tell someone—at long last. Yet she was trembling inside, and she perspired so much that her sweater stuck to her skin.

It was sort of how she'd felt when she'd told Brian the truth. She'd decided to wait until his next furlough home. It wasn't exactly something she could tell him over the phone or in an e-mail. Just deciding to come clean with Brian had given her an edge over Tad and his threats.

Joey was born on September first. Brian finally saw his baby son on Halloween. By that time, Tad was calling with more frequency, demanding to see his child. By then, she was almost certain Joey was Brian's son. Still, that wasn't enough. She'd need Brian to take a paternity test to get Tad off her back. Though she hated breaking Brian's heart and risking their marriage, she had to tell him. Besides, she owed him the truth.

She told him in the kitchen while they were washing the dinner dishes together. They'd already put Joey to bed. It was Brian's fourth night home. Laurie had considered it a minor miracle that Tad hadn't called to harass her during Brian's stay. Or had he been watching

the house? Brian had another three days left before he
shipped back.

Laurie tried to brace him for what she had to say. "I
have something to tell you that's going to be really difficult, Brian." She took the pot and the dishtowel out of
his hands and pulled him over to the breakfast table.
Brian had a sort of mystified half smile on his face—as
if he thought this might be a joke.

"First off, you should know, this—*thing,* it was like
a blip. And I'm so sorry. It was over with by the time
you came home last year. But I need for you to know
about it." She sat him down in one of the chairs, and
watched the smile run away from his face. "I don't expect you to forgive me," she continued, tears in her
eyes. "What I did was utterly stupid. It wouldn't have
happened if I hadn't been so lonely . . ."

"Oh, Jesus," was all he said. She'd seen that same
look of hurt in Tad's eyes on the Friday after Thanksgiving when she'd tried to apologize to him.

She told Brian everything—including the perforated
condoms and Tad's recent harassment. Brian just kept
shaking his head. Then he finally got to his feet and
slammed his fist into the kitchen wall. Laurie flinched
at the loud crack. There was a small explosion of plas-
ter particles and dust.

Then Brian stormed out the front door.

An hour later, the phone rang, and she'd snatched it
up. "Brian?"

"I'm coming over there. It's time I saw my son!"

"Oh, God, Tad," she said, rubbing her forehead.
"Would you leave me the hell alone? Brian's here and the

baby's asleep. What is wrong with you? Does your therapist know you're doing this? Are you still seeing him?"

He hung up.

An hour later, Laurie heard someone at the front door. She ran from the kitchen to the living room in time to see Brian step inside with a bag from Lowe's. She figured he must have driven to the nearest Lowe's—in Yakima. His head down, he brushed past her into the kitchen. He wouldn't look at her.

Her arms folded, Laurie stood behind him and watched as he set an old newspaper on the floor beneath the fissure on the wall that he'd created with his fist. From the Lowe's bag, he pulled out a five-pint container of Patch 'n' Paint, and a spackling knife. He started to work, repairing the crack in the kitchen wall.

Laurie was afraid if she said one word he'd erupt again.

"So, what do I have to do to prove I'm Joey's dad, take a blood test or something?" he asked, finally breaking the silence. His back was to her.

"The doctor said they just have to take a swab from the inside of your cheek," she replied, her voice quivering. "They do the same thing with Joey. It doesn't hurt at all."

"Believe me, it's going to hurt," he muttered, focused on his work.

She'd remained in the kitchen the whole time, saying nothing and staying out of Brian's way.

He was cleaning up the area when there was a sudden pounding on the front door. It woke up Joey, and he started crying.

"Oh, no," Laurie gasped. "That's Tad. He called earlier, threatening to come over. I didn't believe him. I . . ."

Brain dropped the crunched-up newspaper and stomped past her.

"Honey, don't, please—"

He flung open the door. From the kitchen entry, Laurie couldn't see Tad. Brian stood between them, his hands at his side, clenched into fists.

"I want to see Laurie," she heard Tad say—past the baby's cries. "I have a right to—"

"You don't have any rights here," Brian cut him off. "If you bother my wife or my child again, I'll kill you. Did you hear me? And yeah, I said *my* child. He looks just like me." He paused. "And I know what you're thinking, bub. You'll just wait until I ship out again, right? Well, I have friends in this town. If they see you hanging around here or the diner, you'll wish to God you were never born. Now, get the hell off my front stoop before I tear you limb from limb." He paused again. "GET OUT OF HERE!" he bellowed.

Laurie could hear Tad's retreating footsteps on the front walk. Then there was a faint, cowardly call: "Fucker!"

Brian closed the door. He shook his head. "Jesus, what were you thinking?" he muttered, on his way back into the kitchen. "I thought the guy would look like Brad Pitt or something. I mean, if you're going to cheat on me, at least pick somebody who's good-looking. Trade up. You could have done a hell of a lot better than that weasel." He started cleaning up the mess again.

Joey began to quiet down on his own.

Laurie nervously rubbed her arms as she watched him. "Brian, what if—" she hesitated, "what if the tests show Joey isn't yours?"

"We'll drive off that bridge when we come to it," he grumbled, his head down. "Now, could you do me a big favor and stop talking to me? You really need to leave me alone, because right now, I can't even look at you . . ."

That night, Brian slept on the living room sofa. There wasn't another peep from Joey. Laurie didn't hear any crying from the nursery.

But she heard the muffled sobs in the living room.

The paternity test showed that Brian was Joey's father. Laurie mailed a copy of the results to Tad. She didn't attach a note to it. She didn't want to encourage any kind of further communication.

"I guess Brian must have put the fear of God in him," she told Detective Eberhard. Laurie hadn't realized that she'd had one foot so tightly wrapped around the chair leg that it now started to hurt. She rubbed her ankle, and straightened up in the chair. "Or maybe it was me sending him the test results. Either way, I didn't see or hear from Tad for a long while after that."

Slouched behind his desk, Eberhard nibbled on one end of his cinnamon stick. "So, when did he start up again?"

"A few days after Brian's funeral, he came by the diner around closing time. Tad made it pretty clear he wanted to pick up where we'd left off now that I was single. I told him it wasn't ever going to happen, and he needed to leave me and my baby alone. He didn't like that answer, so I reminded him of what Brian had said. I told him Brian still had several loyal friends in town who would be looking out for me and the baby."

"Did that nip things in the bud?"

Laurie nodded. "For about four months," she said. "Then last week, he and his brother came by the diner to harass me when I was ready to close the place. I'm guessing some time during the last few weeks he got chummy with Ryder again. Tad was always kind of a lost soul, and his brother—well, I think Ryder enjoys manipulating people. I think he encouraged Tad to go after me again. If Tad still had some issues about me, I'm sure his brother fanned the flames. God knows why, maybe for his own amusement. But this last week has been pretty scary."

Eberhard put down his cinnamon stick and leaned forward. "So, last week, when you reported to the police that someone in a silver minivan was stalking you, we weren't getting the whole story. You knew the perpetrators were Ryder and Tad McBride."

"Yes, I knew," she murmured, looking down at the floor. "I'm sorry. When you're the widow of the town hero, you have reputations to protect. I didn't want them going public with my stupid, little mistake. I didn't want it for Joey—or Brian. I didn't want it for myself. I figured if there was a police presence on my block and outside the diner, it might be enough to discourage Tad and his brother." Laurie sighed, "And maybe then I could keep the whole sad, sordid business with Tad from leaking out."

She looked across the desk at Eberhard and saw the

pity in his eyes. "I guess it doesn't really matter anymore at this point," she said. "Everyone will know now, won't they?"

He nodded glumly, then reached over and shut off the recorder. "We'll try to keep it on the down low," he said. "But I'm afraid they set up that home invasion so that people would jump to all sorts of conclusions. And I doubt we'll be able to prevent Tad's brother from sounding off about it." He sighed. "While you were handing off Joey to your friend earlier, I got a call from one of our guys down in the morgue at Kittitas Valley. They brought Ryder in to ID Tad, and apparently he went pretty crazy. He started tearing the place apart. They had to restrain him . . ."

Wide-eyed, Laurie stared at the detective. "Aren't they going to charge him with anything? I mean, he must have had a hand in this."

Eberhard frowned. "From two-thirty until five this morning, he was at an all-night truck stop in Yakima with one of his cronies. They have plenty of witnesses. Pretty convenient, huh? Still, I wouldn't be surprised if one of the girls at his farm doesn't have the same shoe size as the second intruder. We'll look into it, Laurie. It may take a while, but we'll keep at it. That slippery bastard hasn't wriggled out of this one yet."

"'It may take a while?'" she repeated, crestfallen. "I was really hoping to leave Ellensburg—as soon as next week, in fact."

"Where are you headed to?" the detective asked.

"Seattle. I was going to move there."

"Do you have a job waiting?"

Laurie sighed. "I had something in mind, but I don't think it's going to pan out now. Still, job or no job, I want to make this move."

"I think it's an excellent idea," Eberhard said, chewing on his cinnamon stick. "As long as you don't leave the state, and I know how to reach you, I see no reason why you can't relocate."

"It sounds like you're encouraging me to go."

The detective nodded soberly. "I am. I think it's only fair to tell you that while he was going a little crazy down in the morgue, Ryder McBride said some things about finishing up what his brother had started with you." Frowning, Eberhard tossed the cinnamon stick in the trash. "We can do only so much to protect you. As I said, he's pretty damn slippery. Of the two McBride boys, Tad was nothing compared to his depraved brother. So, you take your little boy and make that move to Seattle, Mrs. Trotter, as quickly and quietly as you can."

CHAPTER EIGHT

"Sounds like a colossal snooze," Kent MacArthur said. "Why the hell would I want to look inside some dead lady's apartment?"

"Because she's the one who got blown up in that food truck, remember?" replied his friend, Derek. "Her apartment's like—four blocks from here. Danny Flick and John Reich went by there last week, and said there was even a police sign and yellow tape on the door. Don't you want to check it out, see if we can peek inside the windows?"

"You guys can go if you want," Kent said. "I'd rather head home and see what's on Skinamax."

"I think it sounds kind of cool," Gwen Carney piped up. "I'll go with you, Derek." She turned to Kent. "Are you sure you don't want to go?"

She was going to ask Kent only once—for fear he might change his mind if she asked a second time. She'd been itching to get rid of him all night. Gwen had a crush on Derek, despite noticing last week during a casual, shirts-versus-skins basketball game that he had a bad case of bacne. Ordinarily that would have been a deal breaker for Gwen, but Derek had soulful blue eyes and tousled brown hair. Plus he was one of the few sophomores at Garfield High School who noticed she was alive.

She hadn't planned on having Kent along this evening. She'd had to babysit for one of her regulars, the Gottliebs, who lived practically next door to Derek. Mrs. Gottlieb had said they'd be back by eleven, so Gwen had asked Derek ahead of time if he wanted to get together after. He'd said his parents were gone and maybe his older brother could score them some booze, which sounded awesome to her.

But surprise, surprise, he'd decided to invite Kent over. And their booze-fest consisted of one six-pack of Mike's Hard Lemonade, which they split among the three of them. And Kent, the pig, downed three bottles. Gwen had barely gotten a buzz off the one bottle she'd drunk. Afterward, they'd headed to the Olympia Pizza and Spaghetti House and split a large pizza. Kent guzzled down half her Diet Pepsi, and then the jerk had the nerve to complain about how he really didn't like Diet. Thank God they had free refills.

Now they stood in front of the restaurant on Fifteenth Avenue. Though midnight, the evening was still relatively young—and looking more promising with Kent finally going home. The notion of sneaking around some apartment building looking into a dead woman's windows didn't exactly thrill her. But if it meant being alone with Derek, then Gwen was all for it.

"Why don't you want to check out this place with us?" Derek pressed his friend. "Are you too chicken?"

"No, it just sounds boring," Kent replied, starting to back away from them. "But you guys knock yourselves out. Call you tomorrow, doofus."

Gwen watched Kent turn around and head toward his house near Volunteer Park. She got ready to take hold of Derek's hand. "So which way is it?" she asked.

He shoved his hands in the pockets of his jeans. "This way," he said, moving in the opposite direction of his friend. "It's on Howell, about three blocks from John Reich's house."

Gwen hurried to catch up with him. "Hey, slow down . . ."

"We better get off the main drag here, before a cop stops us for being out so late," he explained. They turned down at the next cross street, leaving behind the lights of passing cars and the twenty-four-hour Quality Food Center. It was suddenly quiet and dark in the residential area off Fifteenth. Clouds covered the moon, and a soft, chilly breeze stirred the leaves on the trees.

"I should have brought along a sweater," Gwen said. "It's getting cold."

Derek didn't seem to get the hint that she wanted him to put his arm around her. She'd worn her favorite, sexy yellow top and washed her long blond hair tonight. But her efforts seemed wasted on him. As they strolled down the sidewalk, there was room for practically another person between the two of them. Gwen narrowed the gap. She thought about slipping her arm around his, but she was afraid he'd pull away. "So, do you know this place we're going to?" she asked.

"Like I said, it's on Howell. It's called La Hacienda. John and Danny said it's like a Spanish-style place with a courtyard. The lady who got blown up was named Foster or Forester or something like that." He stopped abruptly. "Shit, it just occurred to me. If the lights aren't on inside the apartment, we won't be able to see anything from outside."

"Well, I've got a flashlight mode on my phone," Gwen said. "Don't you?"

He grinned at her, and then slapped her on the back. "You're a genius!"

They started walking again, and he put his hands in his pockets once more. Gwen figured she'd have to act pretty scared at this La Hacienda place if she wanted Derek to put his arm around her. Until they got there, a stupid, chummy-chummy slap on the back seemed about as far as he'd go with her.

It was almost too dark to read the street signs. While they'd been walking along the side street, not a single car had passed them. Most of the houses they passed had all the lights off. By the time they reached Howell Street, Gwen realized they were at least a mile from her house. That wasn't too far a hike, but at this hour she didn't want to walk it alone. Certainly, Derek would walk her home after this, wouldn't he?

"I think that's it over there," he said, touching her arm.

On the next street corner, Gwen saw a two-story structure with a Spanish tile roof. But it looked like the back of a house.

He grabbed her hand, and they hurried down the block. Gwen was ecstatic. He pulled her along the sidewalk and then across the street. She saw the place with the Spanish tile roof was actually an apartment complex. They stopped in front of a tall wrought iron gate, and a post with a carriage house lamp on top of it. On the front of the post were multicolored tiles that said LA HACIENDA, and the street number. Around the corner on the same post was a call box. Counting from the bottom up, Gwen noticed there were eight apartments. Someone named C. Wheeler was in number 8.

"There it is," Derek said. "They haven't taken her name off yet. M. Forester, three."

"Yeah, well, how are we getting past this gate?" Gwen whispered. "It's not like she'll buzz us in."

The property was surrounded by shrubs and a tall fence. Beyond it was a charming, though slightly shabby courtyard with a patchy lawn, a walkway, some trees, and a fountain, which wasn't running. It was deathly quiet. Except for a couple of dim lights in two windows, it looked like everyone in La Hacienda must have been asleep—or away.

The beige stucco complex was U-shaped, with two-story apartments all connected—each having its own outside entrance. Only three units had their outside lights on.

Derek let go of her hand to push at the gate. To Gwen's amazement, it squeaked open. "Someone must not have shut it all the way," he whispered.

Gwen couldn't help thinking something was wrong. It was almost too easy getting inside. They crept into the courtyard. She was careful not to shut the gate all the way behind them—in case they had to make a quick getaway.

Now that they were here, it was kind of exciting and scary. Derek was holding her hand again as they crept toward the corner unit. Gwen saw the number on the door: 8. It was C. Wheeler's apartment.

"Number three must be on the other side," she said under her breath.

They hurried across the courtyard. Derek accidentally kicked a small rock that ricocheted off the side of the fountain with a loud crack. "Get down," he hissed. They ducked behind the fountain and waited. They didn't hear anything. No lights came on inside any of the apartments.

After another minute, he finally nodded at her and they continued across the courtyard. They found apartment 3. The outside light was off. But someone must have left a lamp on somewhere inside, because past the open slats of the window's mini-blinds, Gwen could just make out the shape of furniture. There were pictures on the walls, but Gwen could see only the random black squares in the murky darkness.

Maneuvering between some bushes, they moved closer to what must have been M. Forester's living room window. The bushes' branches scraped against their bodies and at the glass. Gwen wondered if anyone heard it. The expression *Enough noise to wake the dead* came to mind, and she shuddered.

It didn't seem all that exciting anymore—just creepy. "Listen, I think we should go," she whispered.

"Just a sec," Derek murmured, pulling out his phone. He held it up to the window, and pressed the flashlight function. The living room was bathed in an eerie bluish light—with shadows sweeping across the walls as Derek moved his phone. For some stupid reason, Gwen had thought the dead woman's place would look like a Victorian haunted house inside—with big Tiffany lamps, overstuffed old furniture, and doilies on antique tables. Instead, it looked like a normal living room with the type of furniture she saw in Macy's. One of those mysterious, dark pictures on the wall was actually a framed print of the Eiffel Tower, which Gwen could have hung in her own bedroom.

She thought of the woman who had lived here up until twelve days ago, and how she'd been blown to pieces in that food truck. She'd been sixty years old, not that much older than Gwen's mom.

"Derek, I really want to get out of here," she whispered.

"Hold on, I just want—"

He fell silent at the sound of the wrought iron gate squeaking open.

They both turned to look toward the courtyard. It sounded like one of La Hacienda's residents must be coming in late. Gwen and Derek waited to see who it was, and which apartment was home to the night owl. They cowered in the bushes by the dead woman's unit, and tried not to make a sound. Gwen still couldn't see anyone, but she heard pebbles crunching underfoot.

Then it dawned on her that whoever else was here must not have wanted to be seen either.

She caught a glimpse of something moving in the shadows over by number 8, C. Wheeler's unit. It happened so quickly that she wasn't sure who or what it was.

She wondered if Kent had followed them here. Maybe the two guys were pulling some kind of gag on her.

Well, it wasn't funny. It wasn't a bit funny.

"Did you see that?" Derek whispered, nudging her. He nodded toward the apartment across the way.

"I saw," she whimpered. Gwen noticed him trembling. It wasn't an act. If this was some kind of joke, Derek didn't know about it.

She heard a twig snap. It sounded close.

"I think we should just make a run for it—head for the gate," she said under her breath. "If we stick around here, we—"

Derek shushed her. "Someone's trying to break into the unit across the way." He slowly raised his phone.

At first, Gwen thought he was going to call 911. But instead, he shined his flashlight across the courtyard toward apartment 8. Gwen couldn't believe how stupid he was—giving away their location like that.

A man in black with a dark ski mask over his face stood in the doorway, caught in the spotlight. He had something in his hand. It looked like he was trying to trip the door lock. He swiveled around. Even with that mask covering his face, Gwen could tell where his eyes were. He was looking directly at them.

He took off, ducking behind one of the trees.

Derek directed the flashlight at the tree trunk. The unsteady bright spot revealed his nervousness. The man didn't seem to be there anymore. It was as if he'd vanished. Derek tilted the phone, and the flashlight's jittery beam swept across the bushes outside C. Wheeler's apartment.

"Where is he?" Gwen whispered. They'd lost track of him. But thanks to Derek's flashlight, the man knew exactly where they were. "Turn that damn thing off," she hissed.

He finally switched off the flashlight. "I think we're closer to the gate than he is," Derek whispered. "Let's make a run for it. Then we can call the cops . . ."

Crouched down between the bushes and the side of the building, they scurried toward the gate. Gwen felt a branch scratch her face—just missing her eye. She let out a little yelp of pain, but didn't stop. She couldn't tell if she was bleeding or not. Right now, she didn't care.

They paused at the corner of the building. From there, they could see the wrought iron gate. Whoever had broken in must have closed it.

"I don't see any sign of him," Derek said. "Do you suppose we scared him off?"

"I don't want to stick around to find out," Gwen said, trying to catch her breath.

He turned to give her a reassuring smile, but then his eyes narrowed. "You're bleeding . . ."

She touched her cheek, and felt it sting. She looked at the blood on her fingertips, and swallowed hard. "Let's just get out of here," she whispered.

"We'll make a run for it, okay?"

Gwen nodded.

He grabbed her hand and they sprinted toward the gate, their footsteps echoing in the courtyard. Gwen prayed the gate wasn't locked. She kept thinking that at any moment now, someone would lunge at her from behind.

They finally reached the gate, and Derek tugged at

it. The latch was down. Gwen quickly reached up and lifted it. She heard footsteps in the courtyard—coming at them.

Derek flung open the gate and they hurried out toward the street.

But suddenly someone stepped out from behind a spruce tree on the parkway—right in their path. Gwen and Derek stopped dead. She gasped.

It was a thin woman, dressed in black pants and a tight black top. Her black hair was slicked back, and she had ghostly pale skin. "Hold it," she murmured, with her hand out—almost like a cop directing traffic. "Seattle Police, Special Investigations Unit. What were you two doing in there?"

Though the woman was dressed like the man in the ski mask, Gwen knew they weren't one and the same. From the build and height, the other was almost certainly a man. Gwen didn't know what to say. She just shook her head.

She felt Derek squeeze her hand. He squinted at the woman. "How do we know you're a cop?" he countered—with a hint of defiance. "Where's your badge?"

"Here," she said, reaching inside a long black leather cuff around her left arm.

Before Gwen could even step back, the woman grabbed Derek by his hair, and then plunged what looked like a big knitting needle into his ear. His body seemed to tense up, and a strange choking sound came out of him. Then Derek collapsed on the grass—near Gwen's feet.

She started to scream. But all at once, the woman hit

Gwen across the face with the back of her hand. She tumbled into the spruce tree. Dazed, she fell to the grass. The blow left her practically blind. All she could see were spots. She couldn't move. Past the ringing in her ears, she could hear footsteps approaching.

"We'll have to abort," the woman was saying to her friend. "Goddamn it, I knew it was too soon to go after her again. It's still too hot here. Now we'll have to dispose of these two. The boy's dead."

"Stupid kids," her friend muttered. He kicked at something. It must have been Derek's body.

Gwen blinked several times and tried to focus. Her head throbbed horribly. But she could see shapes now—and the woman bent over her. "Does anyone know?" she whispered. "Did you tell anyone you were coming here?"

Gwen figured the woman wanted her to say no. That was the answer she was supposed to give, wasn't it?

The blow to her head had screwed up her thinking.

"No one knows we're here," she murmured.

"Good," the woman said. "That's a girl . . ."

Then Gwen felt something sharp tickling her ear. And in an instant, she knew she'd given the wrong answer.

CHAPTER NINE

Tuesday, June 10, 2:10 P.M.
Ellensburg

"C'mon, please, I'm begging you," she said, tugging at the thick straps on her shoulders. "Give Mommy a break . . ."

Joey usually loved sitting in his backpack—complete with the little blue awning over his head to protect him from the sun and rain. For Laurie, with all the bars, clips, and straps, it felt like someone had pitched a tent on her back—with a wiggling, bawling twenty-pound occupant. She still hadn't mastered how to move Joey from the car seat to the backpack without it taking at least ten minutes of contorting, pleading, and praying.

At last, she had him secured in the backpack seat, but he was still fussing a bit. He wanted his stuffed animal dog—something that resembled a golden retriever, which she called Sparky. When squeezed, Sparky said—in a high-pitched little boy's voice—one of three things: "I love you!" "That feels good!" or "Will you play with me?"

"No, sweetie, Sparky stays in the car," Laurie said over Joey's protests. She shut the backseat door. "We'll crack the window for him."

She adjusted the backpack straps and then glanced through the window into the front passenger seat. A box full of Brian's football trophies sat on the car floor. The cabinet Brian had jokingly used as a trophy case had been wrecked during the break-in Thursday. Brian never had much sentimental attachment to the dozen or so faux-gold cups, plaques, and figurines. But Laurie couldn't imagine throwing them away. Still, she didn't want to lug them to Seattle either. She checked with Detective Eberhard to make sure she wasn't removing evidence from a current crime scene.

The police hadn't found Tad's accomplice yet. Three women and another man were living with Ryder McBride at the farm outside Cle Elum. All of them had alibis, none of which were airtight, according to Eberhard. They all had police records, too—everything from possession to shoplifting. Two of Ryder's women had the same shoe size as the second intruder.

Laurie and Joey were still at the Hampton Inn while the investigation continued. Eberhard had registered them there under a different name—in case Ryder wanted to make good his threats. It took Laurie a while to figure out why her alias, Melanie Daniels, sounded so familiar, until she remembered it was Tippi Hedren's name in *The Birds*.

Though they were still searching for Tad's partner in the break-in, Eberhard saw no reason Laurie couldn't give Brian's awards away. She phoned the university's athletic department, and asked if they wanted the trophies for one of their display cases. She figured it was a fitting place for them. The head coach, Curt Reynolds, agreed, and thanked her for the donation. Brian had always been one of his favorite players.

Laurie had told him she'd drop off the trophies this afternoon. He and the assistant coach wouldn't be around, but Reynolds had said she could leave them in his office in the Nicholson Pavilion. The other assistant coach, Gordon Poole, would be there. Laurie had last seen Coach Reynolds and his assistant at the City Hall ceremony when the army had given Brian a posthumous award. She'd never met this Gordon Poole person.

The Nicholson Pavilion always reminded her of a circus tent—with a dozen tall, angled masts and suspension cables protruding along the front of the huge brick edifice that housed the basketball stadium. The athletic staff had offices in a long, rambling one-story structure connected to the stadium. The wall in front was all honeycomb-shaped windows.

Laurie stood in the parking lot next to the building. She decided lugging Joey and the trophies might be a little too much—especially since she wasn't quite sure where the coach's office was. Maybe she could get this Gordon Poole to carry the box inside for her.

"C'mon, Joey," she said, heading toward the building. He started to quiet down. "Wave good-bye to Sparky. That's my good boy."

Laurie thought back to her phone conversation with Coach Reynolds. She remembered he'd sounded a bit distant and cool. Maybe he secretly didn't approve of her giving away Brian's awards. Or maybe the coach just didn't like her too much right now. Not many people in town did.

Everyone knew about the naked dead man in her apartment and her dalliance with him back when Brian was fighting in Afghanistan. Never before had so many customers at the restaurant tried to peek into the pass-through window for a look at the chef. Of course, that was to be expected since she was in the news. But many of them had that look of disapproval and disdain. Her coworkers seemed tolerant and nonjudgmental—except for a new waitress nobody could stand. Her name was Celia. She was skinny, with long, dirty blond hair and terrible posture. She was usually a pill to Laurie anyway. Yesterday had been Laurie's first day back after the incident.

"Y'know, I don't care what you do with your personal life," Celia had told her. She'd been leaning against the kitchen counter, waiting for her order. "But when it affects me, I need to say something. Ever since you got your name in the papers, my tips have been terrible."

"And you're blaming me?" Laurie had asked, hovering over the stove. She'd tried her damnedest to sound like she didn't care. "Maybe you're just a terrible waitress."

"Well, one thing I know, you're a terrible mother. That's what everyone's saying."

Laurie had swallowed hard. "Celia, I've never punched a woman. And I don't want to now. So you need to shut your mouth and get the hell out of this kitchen right now."

"Don't push your luck, Celia," one of the other waitresses had chimed in. "Just look at what happened to the last person who crossed her."

Celia had made a hasty retreat out the saloon doors. Laurie's waitress friend had seemed to think it was pretty funny. But Laurie had been shaking inside. With her head down, she'd focused on her cooking.

Maybe Brian's old coach thought she was a terrible mother, too. Then again, she was hypersensitive lately. She felt onstage all the time, so certain everyone was judging her. She could hardly wait to move to Seattle, where no one knew her. She could keep a low profile for a while and then start all over. She just wished she had a job waiting for her there.

A navy blue Wildcats banner was stretched across the ceiling in the long corridor of the athletic department. Laurie could hear a basketball bouncing and feet stomping on the court next door. Between every other office door was a trophy case. Laurie stopped in front of the one that had Brian's photo in it. In the eight-by-ten he wore his muddied football uniform, and carried his helmet under his arm. His brown hair was matted down with sweat, but he was smiling. Laurie couldn't help tearing up as she looked at him. Attached to the photo, a label with black calligraphy was starting to curl at the edges:

Brian Patrick Trotter
1988–2014

A copy of the certificate that came with the Distinguished Service Cross was beside the picture. Laurie figured there was room in the display case for a few of his trophies.

"Look, Joey, there's Daddy," she said, pointing to the photograph.

Brian had never uttered those words, "I forgive you," to her, but he'd let her know in gestures. The way he'd held and nuzzled Joey didn't change at all in those last three days of his furlough. The doctor had been able to put a rush on the test results, and they'd gotten proof of paternity the day before Brian had left. He'd never even looked at the document. *I know whose son he is,* he'd said.

He'd spent two nights sleeping on the couch. The evening before he shipped out, he'd set up the sofa again with his pillow and a throw from Restoration Hardware. But within minutes, he'd wordlessly returned to their bed. Laurie had clung to him and cried. They'd fallen asleep in each other's arms. The next morning, they'd made love—for what would be the last time.

Four months later, he was dead.

He'd volunteered for a reconnaissance mission to locate a group of rebel insurgents in some place called Sangin. A sniper's bullet had gotten him in the throat.

Despite his endearing letters and e-mails, the love talk during their phone calls, and the Skype sessions with him happily tearing up at the sight of his baby boy, Laurie couldn't help wondering if somehow, a lingering disappointment in her had made Brian volunteer for that dangerous mission. That uncertainty would probably gnaw away at her until she was dead, too.

"There's your dad, sweetie," she said again, a little quiver in her voice.

Laurie moved on down the hall in search of Coach Reynolds's office. She found his name on a plate beside an open door. Poking her head in the doorway, she saw two desks, side by side, in the little room. A thirtysomething baby-faced man with a crew cut and a goatee sat at one of the desks. He wore a tight Izod knockoff polo shirt that revealed a slightly paunchy build. He was arranging hole-punched pages into a ring-clip binder. Behind him was a wall of floor-to-ceiling bookcases with books, binders, and trophies. Over to the right, Laurie noticed the door to another room ajar, which must have been the head coach's office.

Joey let out a little yelp, which made the man look up from his work.

"Hi," Laurie said. "Are you Gordon Poole?"

He smiled. "Yeah . . ."

"I'm Laurie Trotter. I think Coach Reynolds might have told you I was coming by."

The smile withered on his face. "Oh, it's you," he said. Then he went back to his work with the ring binder, papers, and the hole puncher. He nodded to an empty, hard-backed chair in one corner. "Well, have a seat. I'm going to be another couple of minutes here."

"Well, ah, I can't really sit down with this," she explained, with a thumb pointing to Joey. "I'm carrying precious cargo."

Gordon Poole didn't even look up. He stayed intent on his work. Laurie watched him insert—with painstaking deliberation—one slim stack of pages after another into the ring binder. Joey started to fuss a little. But Poole didn't look up. He punched holes in a new group of pages. Then he started to empty out the paper puncher.

Laurie finally cleared her throat. "Listen, I can come back when you're not so *terribly* busy."

At last, he gazed up at her, a bored look on his face. "You had some trophies for us?"

"Yes, they're in the car," she said, over Joey's babbling. "I'd have carried them in myself, but the box is pretty heavy. And I've already got twenty pounds strapped to my back. I was hoping you might help me."

He put two more sections of pages into the binder, and closed it. Then with a sigh, he got to his feet. "Parked out front?" he muttered.

"Yes, thanks," Laurie said. He brushed past her, and she followed him out the door. She thought about saying, "It's nice of you to do this for me," but then she thought, *Why?* The guy was a total jerk, making her stand there and watch him do mindless busywork for nearly ten minutes.

He walked a few steps ahead of her down the corridor. Without looking back, he pointed to Brian's photo in the display case. "There's your late husband," he said, and then he muttered, "Not that you give a shit."

"What?" Laurie said, stopping dead. "What did you just say?"

He kept walking. "Nothing," he grumbled with his back to her.

Laurie trailed after him. Sometimes it still took her by surprise when people were rude or nasty toward her. Her first thought was always, *What did I do to you?* And then she'd realize what all the nastiness was about.

He slowed down as he approached the exit, and let her go first. Laurie figured he just didn't want to hold the door open for her.

She went through the doorway and headed to her car. She didn't look back at him. Pulling out her keys, she pressed the device to unlock the Camry's doors. She opened the back door, where Joey's car seat was. Then she reached inside and locked the front passenger door. She unfastened the clasps to the backpack and took her sweet time transferring Joey to his car seat.

"Are those the trophies in there?" Poole asked, nodding at the box on the passenger side floor. He tapped his foot impatiently.

"Yes," she said, barely looking at him. She buckled Joey into his car seat. "I'm going to be another couple of minutes here."

He reached for the passenger door handle and gave it a tug. "It's locked."

"Yes," she said. Laurie brushed past him with the empty backpack in her hand. She moved to the other side of the car, opened the back door, and set it on the floor.

"You think I could collect those trophies now?" he asked, an edge in his voice. He tapped on the car window.

Laurie opened the driver's door. But she stopped to look at him. "Please tell the coach for me that I changed my mind."

"What?" he growled.

"You see, I do care about my late husband, Mr. Poole," she said coolly. "I do *give a shit*. And I don't want to entrust his awards to an asshole like you."

He shook his head at her, and started to back away. "Fine," he muttered. "Goddamn smart-ass slut . . ."

One hand gripping the top of the car door, Laurie stared defiantly at him. She tried to keep from shaking. She didn't feel victorious. She felt degraded. And worse, a part of her figured she deserved everything she got. She waited until Poole turned and retreated into the pavilion. She still had the jitters from confronting him, and her heart beat wildly.

She heard Joey making a fuss again.

"Okay, honey," she said, a tremor in her voice. She climbed into the driver's seat, then reached back to hand him Sparky.

When she turned around again she noticed something taped to the middle of the steering wheel. It was a close-up photograph of Tad McBride on the morgue slab. A sheet had been pulled down just below his chest. His eyes were closed, and there was a black-and-crimson gash in his neck.

Laurie let out a gasp. For a moment, she couldn't breathe.

In a panic, she looked around the parking lot for whoever had left this grisly photo. She expected to see the beat-up silver minivan parked nearby. But there was no sign of it. How had they broken into her car? Hadn't she locked it?

She knew it must have been Ryder. Who else could have had access to his brother's body in the morgue? She wondered if he was still around, watching her reaction.

"Will you play with me?" Sparky said, twice in a row.

Laurie anxiously dug into her purse and took out her

cell phone to call Detective Eberhard. But all at once, the phone rang in her hand. She let out a startled little cry, which prompted Joey to imitate her.

He tossed Sparky aside and banged his fists on the sides of his car seat.

Laurie clicked on the phone. Somehow, she knew it was Tad's brother. "Yes?" she said into the phone.

"Hi, is this Laurie?" a woman asked.

"Yes," she said, her heart still racing. She reached back and rubbed Joey's shoulder to quiet him. All the while, she kept looking toward the pavilion and around the parking lot.

"This is Cheryl Wheeler in Seattle," the woman said. "You sent me a delicious orange cake about ten days ago—"

"Yes," Laurie said numbly. She found herself nodding—even though Cheryl couldn't see her. She kept stroking Joey's arm. He began to quiet down.

"Well, I've started a catering business," Cheryl said on the other end. "I need a good cook working with me. I have a very prestigious job coming up before the end of the month. It's a seven-week commitment. I was wondering if you could come to Seattle, so that we could meet in person."

"Yes," she said once again. "Yes, of course, I could do that."

Laurie didn't feel elated—just dazed and still scared. She kept looking around the lot and the surrounding area. She was convinced Ryder was here somewhere watching her. She glanced once again at the photo of Tad on a slab in the morgue.

Cheryl Wheeler was throwing her a lifeline. Yet Laurie couldn't feel safe until she got out of Ellensburg.

Joey started crying again, louder this time.

"Well, I've got your e-mail address," Cheryl said, raising her voice to compete with Joey. "I'll get in touch, and we'll set up a meeting here in Seattle." She chuckled. "Sounds like I might not have caught you at a good time . . ."

"It's—it's okay," Laurie heard herself reply. With a shaky hand, she kept stroking Joey's arm. "Actually, your timing's perfect, just perfect . . ."

CHAPTER TEN

Saturday, June 14, 2:55 P.M.
Seattle

"**D**on't screw up," Laurie whispered to her reflection.

She stood in front of the mirror in the washroom at the Elliott Bay Café. The wood and brick coffee bar was near the back of a huge bookstore on Capitol Hill. It was the meeting spot for her job interview with Cheryl Wheeler.

She'd just driven nearly two hours, and then spent another fifteen minutes trying to find a parking space near the bookstore. Joey had slept in his car seat most of the time, but he'd become a bit cranky in his stroller as she'd pushed him the two blocks to Elliott Bay Book Company. She'd found Cheryl waiting for her at a four-top table in the café.

Thank God the café had a high chair—and vanilla pudding in the food display case. She'd figured bringing a ten-month-old along for a job interview would be a recipe for disaster. Hell, some people maintained even salting your food before tasting it during a lunch-interview could cost you the job. And here she was in-flicting a toddler on her prospective boss. But Krista and Nathan hadn't been able to babysit—and this was her only day off from the diner this week.

Fortunately, Cheryl was crazy for Joey. Outside of some get-acquainted talk while Laurie had gotten Joey situated, they hadn't really started the interview yet. She'd needed to pee since exiting I-90 forty-five min-utes ago. So Cheryl had volunteered to feed Joey his pudding while Laurie used the lavatory.

She felt a bit hesitant leaving her baby with someone she'd just met. But she knew it was Cheryl Wheeler, and she didn't want Cheryl thinking she didn't trust her with her son. It was almost like the salt test during the lunch interview.

While in the bathroom, she kept imagining Joey spitting pudding in Cheryl's face or loading his diaper in honor of the occasion. Then it occurred to her that she could very well botch the interview herself, with-out Joey's help.

So far, it hadn't come up yet that she'd killed an in-truder in her home a little over a week ago. The news had made the *Seattle Times,* but they'd buried it near the back pages. Cheryl might not have known about it. Laurie kept wondering if she should tell her. That meant explaining to her about Ryder McBride, too. On one hand, it had nothing to do with her capabilities as a job candidate. But there might be court dates coming up. Plus, this was a catering business, and they'd be working closely together. She could be putting Cheryl's life in danger—if Ryder tracked her down here.

Detective Eberhard had hauled Ryder into the police station to question him about the morgue shot he'd left inside Laurie's car. But Ryder had claimed to know nothing about it. They'd had to let him go.

One reason Laurie needed this job was to make a new start. Did she really want to tell her potential employer about this trouble she was running away from? As long as she kept a low profile and made sure no one besides Eberhard knew where she was, she didn't see a reason to tell Cheryl anything, at least not now.

Still, she felt a little guilty about it, because Cheryl seemed quite up-front in regards to the Grill Girl food truck explosion. While Laurie had set Joey in the high chair, Cheryl had told her that the blast had been caused by a faulty gas line. "At least, those are the official findings from the police and the insurance company. But I still don't believe it. I'd just had an inspection two weeks before it happened. Anyway, I wouldn't blame you if you have some concerns about that."

Cheryl was leasing-to-own a new food truck, which would be ready in time for the catering job in two and a half weeks. "As I mentioned on the phone, the job is a seven-week stint, after which time the food truck will be serving the downtown lunch crowd until the next catering gig comes along. So the work will be steady."

Laurie had wanted to ask her for more specifics about this catering job. But she'd wanted to use the restroom even more.

Now, as she washed her hands at the sink, she was kicking herself for not showing more interest in what might be her very first assignment with Cheryl. She looked a bit haggard in the mirror. Then again, appearing tired and slightly frayed came with the territory lately. At least her sleeveless, dark blue wraparound dress was free of wrinkles and baby puke.

"Don't screw up," Laurie said again. She grabbed her purse from the sink counter—along with the restroom key, which was attached to a plastic spatula.

Returning the key to the front counter, she caught a look at Cheryl and Joey. Her potential boss was making goofy faces at Joey while she maneuvered a spoonful of pudding in his mouth. He seemed delighted. Cheryl caught her looking. "Get yourself a coffee or something," she called. "Take your time. We're fine. In fact, I'm in love!"

When Laurie sat down at the table with her cappuccino, Joey didn't even seem to notice her, which was a little unsettling. "I can take over from here," she said.

"Oh, no, please, let me," Cheryl begged. "You just sit back and enjoy your coffee."

She shrugged awkwardly. "I've never seen him take to anyone quite as quickly as he's taken to you."

"Well, the feeling's mutual," Cheryl said, spooning up another dollop of pudding. She was smiling, but had tears in her eyes. "He's an angel. I—I had a little boy of my own for a while, but I lost him." Her smile waned.

"I'm sorry," Laurie murmured. She decided it was best not to ask about it.

Cheryl took a deep breath. "So, Gil Garrett is your godfather," she said, her eyes on Joey as she fed him. "You know, I'd love to land a catering gig for him and Shawna Farrell some day. It would be a real feather in my cap. They're always entertaining A-list types at their big house in Medina. I'll even take a gig at their seven-bedroom 'cabin' on Kitsap Peninsula. Have you ever been to either one?"

Laurie hesitated. "Oh, no . . . I . . ." She didn't want to admit that outside of the one time when Gil had held her as a baby, she'd never really met him. "Well, it—it's been a while since I've seen him."

Cheryl turned away from Joey for a moment to squint at her. "So, is he a blood uncle or a family friend or . . ."

"Uncle Gil and my grandmother were childhood sweethearts back in Boulder, Colorado."

Growing up without a dad, Laurie had focused instead on the famous producer who was her godfather. He became her father figure. The chances of ever meeting "Uncle Gil" weren't much better than her chances of a father-daughter reunion. But at least Gil Garrett had been in the news once in a while. And she'd felt a genuine connection to the handsome, middle-aged moviemaker.

But now, talking to Cheryl, she felt like a big liar.

"Well, I hope you'll put in a good word for me with your Uncle Gil," she said.

"I'll do my best," Laurie replied, forcing a smile.

Cheryl went back to feeding Joey. "Listen, you should know. About ten days ago, I drove to Ellensburg and had myself a pretty fantastic dinner at the Superstar Diner. I called ahead of time to make sure you'd be cooking that night. I had that wonderful grilled sandwich with the marinated chicken and provolone on rosemary bread . . ."

Laurie was amazed she'd driven almost a hundred

miles to sample her cooking. She put down her coffee cup and nodded. "The Rosemary Clooney Chicken Sandwich."

"If that's your recipe, I want it on our menu." Cheryl turned and grinned at her. "That's right, I said, *our.* I'd love to have you working with me, Laurie. I think it's going to be a good fit."

Laurie let out a stunned little laugh. "Well, so do I . . ."

Cheryl made a buzzing-airplane sound, and glided the spoonful of pudding into Joey's mouth. He waved his arms with glee. Cheryl gently dabbed his face with a napkin. "So, two questions, Laurie," she said. "How soon can you move here? And have you found a place to live yet?"

Laurie couldn't believe her luck.

Cheryl already had an apartment recommendation for her—if she was interested. It was on Capitol Hill, walking distance from the bookstore, and two blocks away from a place called Lullaby League Daycare. Plus Trader Joe's, Quality Food Center, and Group Health Hospital were all nearby.

Cheryl had walked to the bookstore. So Laurie offered to drive her home. "That would be terrific," Cheryl said. "The apartment I told you about is just across the courtyard from me. You can get a gander at the outside. If you move in, we'll be neighbors."

When they pulled up in front of the place, Laurie switched off the ignition and stepped out of the car for a better look. She didn't want to take Joey out of his car seat again, so she just stood beside her open door and checked out the apartment setting. The rambling 1930s-era, Spanish style complex housed eight units that surrounded a charming little courtyard. The tall wrought iron gate in front provided a sense of security.

"It's a one-bedroom," Cheryl said, climbing out of the Camry's passenger side. "They haven't placed an ad for it yet. I can tell the apartment manager to hold off until you've taken a look inside. The bedroom is on the second floor, with an annex that would make a perfect little nursery. You've got a full bath on the second floor and a powder room on the first. Best of all the kitchen has been totally updated—including a gas stove. It's practically move-in ready, partially furnished, too. And get this. If you need a sitter, there's this darling couple here who used to babysit for their grandson five days a week—until their daughter moved to Boston last month. They probably wouldn't charge you much to look after Joey. In fact, they might jump at the chance . . ."

Laurie gazed at the quaint apartment complex, and listened to Cheryl go on about the place. It all seemed too good to be true.

And maybe it was.

Laurie had a tiny nagging doubt about Cheryl Wheeler, and she wasn't sure why. Maybe it was because she hadn't been completely honest with Cheryl. "I'm headed back to Ellensburg today," Laurie said, still standing by the open driver's door. "But I hope to make the big move here at the end of the week."

"When you return, I'll have the manager give you the official tour."

"Well, this is incredibly nice of you, Cheryl. Thank you so much."

"Oh, I'm doing it for myself, too. The sooner you get moved in, the sooner we can start working together. We have to figure out the menu for our first catering job."

"My God, I'm such a goof." Laurie rolled her eyes and let out an embarrassed, little laugh. "I've been so overwhelmed by all this, I didn't even ask. Who's the client?"

"I guess I can talk about it now that you're on board. We, my dear, will be catering for Atlantis Film Group. They're shooting a movie here, starring Paige Peyton."

Dumbfounded, Laurie stared at her. She was trying to process it. Paige Peyton? Her boss at the Superstar Diner would flip. Laurie couldn't pass a magazine rack without seeing Paige Peyton's sultry-pouty face on the cover of at least two or three periodicals. She'd starred in one of those hard-hitting TV crime investigation dramas before recently moving on to the big screen.

Suddenly, it dawned on Laurie that this was indeed too good to be true. Here she was, hoping to maintain a low profile in her new city, and her first job would be catering a movie shoot with one of the highest-profile stars around. "Will there be a lot of press on the set, a lot of media coverage?" she asked.

Cheryl frowned at her from the other side of the Camry. "You seem worried."

"Oh, I just don't much like having my picture taken, that's all." She imagined Ryder seeing her there in the background during an *Entertainment Tonight* report on TV or on some movie-gawker website.

Cheryl laughed. "Well, I hate to tell you, but they'll be snapping photos of Paige Peyton, not the two broads inside the food truck." She shook her head. "Anyway, I wouldn't worry about it. They're trying to keep this shoot under wraps as much as possible, which means they don't want the press and a lot of other people around. That's why I couldn't tell you about it until now. And that's why I need to ask you to keep it hush-hush for the duration."

Laurie shrugged. "All right, but why all the secrecy?"

Stepping back, Cheryl closed the passenger door and sighed. "The movie is based on a real murder case here in Seattle years back. They're shooting at all the actual locations. They don't want to attract a lot of attention while they're filming. It could become a real three-ring circus if word got out. Anyway, whatever happens, it's not going to affect you or me as long as we stay in the food truck and do our jobs."

"What murder case?" Laurie asked.

"You're probably too young to know about it," she replied somberly. "It's from 1970. In fact, that's the title of the movie, *7/7/70*."

"That's a strange title . . ."

"They're doing it with the numbers—and slash marks," Cheryl explained. "It's the date of the murders: *7/7/70*."

Baffled, Laurie just shook her head.

"Look it up online," Cheryl said. "Maybe you already know about it, maybe you don't. Like I say, either way, it shouldn't affect how we'll serve up food to the cast and crew."

She tapped on Joey's window, and waved to him. "See you in a week, cutie-pie . . . I hope!" Then she backed away—toward the wrought iron front gate of the apartment complex. "It was wonderful meeting you, Laurie. Be careful driving home. I'll talk to you this week."

"Thank you, Cheryl!" she called, watching her unlock the front gate.

"Let me know if you change your mind about the job!" she replied, barely looking over her shoulder. The gate let out a squeak as she opened it.

Laurie wondered why she would say that now. Why would she change her mind? Did it have anything to do with this murder on 7/7/70?

Cheryl disappeared behind some tall shrubs bordering the apartment complex.

With a clank, the tall wrought iron gate swung shut behind her.

CHAPTER ELEVEN

In the Google Search box, she typed: *July 7, 1970.*

Laurie sat hunched over her laptop computer at the desk in her room at the Hampton Inn. From her "interview" dress, she'd changed into a black T-shirt and jeans. On the desk were the remnants of her dinner, red curry chicken and a Diet 7UP, carryout from Sugar Thai. The food was cold now, but she was still picking at it with a pair of chopsticks. Joey was asleep—at last—in the portable mini-crib she'd bought at Target in Yakima, back when they'd first checked in to the hotel. She'd even managed to attach his farm-animal mobile to the headboard. The radio in her room picked up a decent oldies station from Seattle. So Joey had nodded off to the Beach Boys.

Even with the clean, pleasant décor and terrific shower pressure, her stay in the hotel room had gotten old fast. She missed cooking in her kitchen, something she'd do when restless. Here, she just had TV, and out the window, a rather dreary view of the parking lot one story below. Her Camry was down there.

She wondered if Ryder McBride had seen the Camry. He knew her car. He'd even broken into it—God only knew how. What was to keep him from checking the various hotel lots in the area? Or maybe he'd followed her and Joey here from Nathan and Krista's one night. Obviously, he'd tailed her from home the other day, when she'd gone to the Nicholson Pavilion. She couldn't help wondering if he was watching her now—from the bleak, dark landscape beyond the hotel's parking lot.

She couldn't wait to move to Seattle. She had some concerns about the first catering assignment with Cheryl. But really, she was a lot less vulnerable inside a food truck on a crowded film location than practically alone at the Superstar Diner near closing time.

Still, durng the two-hour drive home this afternoon, she'd had her reservations. She'd wondered about the actual murder case on which this *7/7/70* was based.

Dusty Springfield was singing "Son of a Preacher Man" on the radio. Laurie took a sip of her Diet 7UP, and she focused on the Google Search line on her laptop screen: *July 7, 1970.* She hit the return button, and the list of results popped up. The first two were horoscopes for anyone born on July 7 of any year, apparently. The third result looked promising:

History Geek—What happened on July 7, 1970?
www.historygeek.com/070770/events
History Geek provides a complete reference page of historical events, birthdays, deaths and other milestones for Tuesday, **July 7, 1970** . . .

Laurie clicked on the link. Her eyes immediately went to the only "News Event" listed:

Seattle, Wa: Actress Elaina Styles Among
3 Dead In Grisly Cult Slaying

"Oh, my God," she murmured. "Of course . . ."

The murders may have occurred long before she was born, but Laurie still knew about them. Paige Peyton was perfect casting as the beautiful, red-haired film star. While in Seattle shooting an occult film, Elaina Styles and her singer-songwriter husband had rented a mansion. Laurie couldn't remember the husband's name, but he'd written and sung the hit single, "Elaina." Every time Laurie's mom had heard it on an oldies station, she'd shake her head, click her tongue, and say how sad it was—what had happened to them. "Oh, such a glamorous, beautiful couple," she'd say. "And listen to his voice." Laurie still recalled the tune, and part of the lyric: *I'm just insane for Elaina . . .*

They had a child, not much older than Joey. They also had a live-in nanny, a girl barely twenty. She was the third victim.

Laurie remembered reading that the baby had died, but not in the rented house with his parents and his nanny. The police had found the body somewhere else several days later.

She back-paged to the Google Search, and typed in the box: "Elaina Styles murder." Before she hit the return key, she wondered just how much Paige Peyton looked like the late-sixties star. Laurie clicked on the Image link, and a page full of photos came up. In the very first row were several glamour shots of the beautiful, slain actress—and then one of her dead.

Laurie grimaced at the horrific black-and-white shot, which confirmed the stories she'd heard about what they'd done to her.

She glimpsed the other small photos, too. Many of them were slightly faded color shots of the bloody crime scene. There were black-and-white individual morgue shots, too—close-ups of Elaina, her husband, and the young nanny on their respective slabs. The pictures reminded Laurie too much of the color photo of Tad that she'd found in her car. She wondered how these gruesome crime photographs had become available for the public. Then again, the murders had occurred nearly forty-five years ago. She shouldn't have been surprised that some of these photos had leaked onto the Internet.

There were also pictures of What's-his-name Hooper, the failed actor and cult leader of a group of hippies responsible for the murders. Laurie couldn't remember his first name. With his mustache, long blond hair, and those crazy, intense eyes, the oddly handsome creep was sort of a minor-league Charles Manson. Maybe he'd even aspired to be like Charlie by leading his crew in killing a glamorous film star. No one would ever know. Hooper and his tribe of followers would all be dead in a mass suicide by the time the police got to them.

Laurie's eyes kept coming back to the small black-and-white image of Elaina Styles as she'd been discovered on the living room floor of that mansion. It was true what people said. The killers had snapped her neck, and turned her head completely around. Her lovely face—mouth and eyes open, her long hair half-covering the neck—peered out at an impossible angle above her shoulders. A gaping knife wound appeared by her right shoulder blade. The photo cut her off at mid torso. She was naked.

Laurie remembered now. They'd found her skimpy, bloodied nightgown dangling from the mansion's front gate. Perhaps the killers had left it as a calling card.

She didn't click on the gruesome picture to see a larger image. She'd seen enough.

She didn't want to read anything about the murders— or remind herself of the details. She couldn't quite remember the circumstances of the baby's death. But right now, with Joey sleeping in his crib just across from her, she didn't want to know.

What it all boiled down to was that the subject matter of this movie would be pretty morbid. Laurie reminded herself of what Cheryl Wheeler had said: *It shouldn't affect how we'll serve up food to the cast and crew.*

She wasn't changing her mind about the Seattle job. There was nothing left for her in Ellensburg—except a lot of people who loathed her for cheating on her hero-husband. And there was someone else here who hated her so much he could end up killing her—or Joey. She had her own version of What's-his-name Hooper and his tribe, and they were out for blood.

Laurie clicked on the mail icon and found Cheryl's last e-mail. She pulled it up, and hit reply. She put in a new subject line, Great Meeting You Today, and started typing:

Dear Cheryl,

Thanks so much for meeting with me this afternoon, and for being so sweet to my son. I've never seen Joey warm up to anyone as quickly as he warmed up to you.

I'm really looking forward to working with you, Cheryl. I'd also like very much to take a look inside that unit in your apartment complex. If I may lift a line from Casablanca, I think this is the beginning of a beautiful friendship . . .

Wednesday, June 18, 6:55 P.M
Ellensburg

Laurie had four entrées in the oven, five sandwiches on the grill, and in the deep fryer, French fries, onion rings, and four pieces of chicken. But her mind kept going somewhere else.

It was her last night of work at the Superstar Diner. She felt nostalgic, sad, and scared. Funny, she'd thought she'd be so elated to put in her last night here. Instead, she just wanted to cry.

She felt the same homesick pangs with every visit she made to the Bancroft Townhouse apartment lately. She kept collecting things she needed for the move. So the place became emptier and emptier, until all that remained were big pieces of furniture she couldn't move herself. All evidence of Brian and Joey was gone, and without those personal accents, she saw how ugly the apartment really was.

Detective Eberhard didn't want a crew of movers coming in and traipsing all over what was still technically a crime scene. Laurie was in no hurry to get the big pieces out of there anyway. Besides, a moving truck in front of the duplex would have been a dead giveaway to Ryder and his group that she was relocating.

Right now, Joey's and her room at the Hampton Inn looked like a storage locker. Laurie had hired a couple of CWU students to come by the hotel Saturday morning and load up a small U-Haul with all the boxes, suitcases, and knickknacks she'd smuggled out of the apartment. Cheryl had recommended a storage facility close by where they could unload the stuff. Meanwhile Laurie and Joey would check into the Loyal Inn near the Space Needle for what she hoped would be a short stay.

Most of the staff at the Superstar Diner knew this was her last day—except, of course, for that bitch, Celia. No one was supposed to talk about it or make a fuss. Laurie didn't want Ryder or any of his pack to catch on that she was leaving for good. It would be just like any other day at the diner for her and everyone else. After three life-changing years at the place, it was sad to leave there without even a modicum of fanfare.

She was on automatic pilot, plating one entrée after another while she wondered about the locales for the movie shoot. They certainly weren't going to be filming inside the Seattle mansion where the murders had occurred on 7/7/70, were they? Most likely, they'd film exterior shots of the murder house—if it still existed. But she knew enough about moviemaking to assume they'd do all the interior scenes on a sound stage—in a replica of the living room where those three mutilated bodies had been discovered.

Laurie was removing the basket of chicken pieces from the fryer when Duncan rushed into the kitchen. "Hey, Laurie!" he said, out of breath. "Laurie, this woman's going crazy in the parking lot, and she keeps screaming your name . . ."

She couldn't see anything from the pass-through window. She quickly pulled two entrées from the oven. Everything on the grill looked okay for another minute or two. She followed Duncan out the saloon doors to the dining area. The restaurant was about two-thirds full, and a strange quiet had fallen over the place. A few people were murmuring or laughing uncomfortably. There wasn't the usual clanking of silverware. Most of the customers had stopped eating to stare at the woman in the parking lot. Even people at the counter were completely turned around in their stools.

"Well, I hope you're happy," Celia muttered, brushing past her.

From the kitchen door, Laurie gazed out the front window. A young woman stood in the middle of their parking lot. "Laurie Trotter is a murderer!" she screamed. Her voice was cracking. "She's a cheating whore and a murderer! How can you eat the food she's cooked? How can you eat food she's touched? What's wrong with you people?"

Laurie glanced over at Paul, behind the counter. Her boss was a burly, middle-aged man with a full head of wavy white hair. He was working the register tonight, and was talking on the phone: "Yeah, can you send someone right away? She's out there screaming at the top of her lungs . . ."

It took Laurie a few moments to recognize the crazy

woman. She had long brown dreadlocks and several piercings on her face. She was the one who had come into the diner a couple of weeks ago to drop off that creepy, filthy-looking sailor doll for Joey—"from his dad and his uncle." She was Ryder's errand girl. Laurie remembered the tattoos all over her arms. But her arms were covered today—in an airy, flower-print, floor-length dress with long, draped sleeves. As she screamed, she flayed her arms around—like a choir director gone mad. "You're eating dead animals served up to you by a murderess! Laurie Trotter is getting away with murder! She killed her lover! Do you hear me?"

A few people stood at the edge of the lot—keeping their distance from her, watching the bizarre tirade.

"Great food, Paul!" one of the regulars said in a loud voice. "But I'm not so sure about the floor show . . ."

A few people laughed.

Laurie remembered what she'd been thinking just a few minutes ago—that this would be just like any other day at the diner for her and everyone else.

It wasn't until the woman bent down that Laurie noticed the camouflage-pattern knapsack at her feet. She reached into the bag.

For a moment, Laurie's heart stopped. She thought the young woman was about to pull out an assault weapon. In seconds she could wipe out everyone sitting near the window.

But instead the woman took out a large canteen. "How many more people have to die before you all realize Laurie Trotter is guilty of murder?" she yelled, her voice cracking again. She unscrewed the top of the canteen, raised it over her head and dowsed herself with its contents.

A few people in the restaurant laughed as she soaked her hair and that flowery-print dress. The gown clung to her skinny frame. "You're all responsible! You have to do something!"

"I'm going to put a stop to this," Paul muttered, stomping toward the door.

The young woman reached into her bag again. She held something in her hand and waved it in the air above her head. It took Laurie a moment to realize the girl was waving a box of matches. Then it dawned on Laurie—the canteen hadn't contained water.

"This is for you, Tad!" she cried.

The woman struck the match and held it to her chest. But the flame first caught onto the wide, gas-soaked sleeve of her dress. The fire shot up her arm toward her shoulder—and her thick dreadlocks. Her hair ignited like old straw. All at once, her head was engulfed in flames.

Customers in the restaurant started screaming. Paul had gotten as far as opening the door, and now, the young woman's agonized shrieks were heard above everyone else.

It was as if she suddenly realized what she'd done. She began to swat at her arms and hair, and frantically ran in circles. But it only fanned the blaze. Her dress—from the floor-length hem to her neck—burst into flames. From above the waist, she was swallowed up in black smoke, fire and bits of flying, incandescent ash.

Laurie could barely see her anymore. The young woman was just a whirling incendiary mass in the middle of the parking lot. Laurie turned and rushed past the saloon doors. She grabbed a small fire extinguisher off its mounting bracket on the kitchen wall. She rushed back into the dining area and headed for the door. Paul stopped her, and took the extinguisher.

But by now, the woman had fallen to her knees—almost in the same way a piece of charred kindling snapped and broke in two. Past all the smoke, Laurie saw the soot-covered smoldering thing crumple to the pavement.

Paul hurried toward her with the extinguisher. With a loud whoosh, a white plume shot out of the tank, the billows swathing what was left of Ryder McBride's errand girl.

The restaurant was utter pandemonium—with customers screaming and children crying. Someone knocked over a table to flee to the other side of the dining area, one of many people desperately trying to get away from the window. Some customers had even run out the side door.

Amid all of the chaos, Laurie could smell scorched meat. It wasn't Ryder's girlfriend. Paul had closed the door after him. Laurie realized what she smelled were several orders burning on the grill.

She heard a police siren, faint at first, then louder and louder—until she could see the red strobe through the hazy gray curtain between the restaurant's front window and the parking lot.

She glanced over toward the counter, with only one customer left. The others had all moved to another part of the restaurant or run out the side door. She saw the place settings and the plates of half-eaten food left behind.

And at one setting, she saw a singular illicit cigarette left smoldering on a saucer—and beside it, an empty salt shaker with the cap off.

He'd been there the whole time, watching one of his followers go to her death for him.

Before sneaking out the side door during all the commotion, Ryder McBride had left his calling card—a little white mountain of salt on the counter.

CHAPTER TWELVE

Thursday, June 26, 5:22 P.M.
Seattle

One of the first things she'd bought Joey in Seattle was the toddler seat/desk unit. On the desk was a soft plastic phone that lit up, alphabet blocks that spun on a horizontal rod, an oversized pad of numbers that lit up and played a note every time he pressed one, and a steering wheel, which had dried beans or something inside that rattled whenever he turned it. The gizmos fascinated him. He'd been happily sitting at his "work desk" in the kitchen for the last half hour.

Laurie was getting ready to line the drawers and cabinets with blue-gingham patterned shelf paper. "You're So Vain" was playing on the radio's oldies station she'd become addicted to while they'd stayed at the Hampton Inn.

This was her second day at her new home—Unit 3, La Hacienda Apartments. The place was everything Cheryl had promised—with charming built-in hutches, nooks, and crannies. There was even an old-fashioned fake fireplace in the living room.

Except for Ryder's gruesome surprise on her last day at the diner, Laurie's escape to Seattle had gone pretty much as planned. Still, she hadn't completely recuperated from the shock of that sickening self-execution. The girl was a nineteen-year-old runaway named Simone Hahn. Her family in Billings, Montana, had been trying to locate her for over two years. Ryder McBride was brought in for questioning about the incident, and he claimed he barely knew her. She'd been a friend of Tad's, he'd said. Simone Hahn died in the ambulance on the way to Kittitas Valley Hospital.

At 6:50 on Saturday morning, two CWU students quietly packed into a U-Haul everything Laurie had been storing in her room at the Hampton Inn. They followed her and Joey in the Camry, all the way to Seattle. Everything got unloaded and locked up in a storage facility on Lake City Way. Laurie and Joey checked into the Loyal Inn—under her real name.

Once she'd seen the unit at La Hacienda, she didn't want to look anywhere else. She'd balked when the manager had wanted last-job and last-residence references from her. Laurie needed to cut all ties to Ellensburg—for a while at least. Detective Eberhard was the only one who knew how to reach her. Cheryl had saved the day. As Laurie's new employer, she vouched for her. The manager even let her move in a few days early.

The furniture in the place was decent, and clean-looking. One of her favorite pieces was here in the kitchen: a small, 1950s yellow "cracked ice"–pattern dinette set. There were even a few pictures on the walls—including a framed print of the Eiffel Tower in the living room that she liked. Yesterday, while Cheryl babysat Joey, Laurie had rented a U-Haul and moved her things from Lake City Storage into the apartment. This morning, she'd put the first coat of butter-yellow paint on the walls of the upstairs annex, which would be Joey's room. There was even a small window in there. It was perfect for him—at least for another couple of years.

Laurie still had unopened boxes in every room. But right now, her new kitchen—and shelf paper—were a priority. All the appliances were new, stainless steel, but the cabinets and drawers were probably original— with green glass knobs and pulls.

Joey pressed several numbers on the desktop in front of him, and each note he played competed with Carly Simon. Then he turned the purple plastic steering wheel and laughed at the rattling noise.

"They have you working at least three people's jobs there, Joey," Laurie declared, sitting on the laminated-wood floor with a kitchen drawer out of its sleeve. She wanted to give each drawer a quick soap-and-water clean before slipping in the shelf paper. "Whatever they're paying you isn't enough. You should . . ."

Laurie trailed off as she noticed something scribbled inside at the back of the drawer: *2-16-47*.

Was it a birthday or a lock combination or what? Obviously, it was something one of the previous tenants had needed to remember—and keep secret, since it was written on the back of a drawer. Laurie tried to wipe it away, but they must have used a fine-point laundry marker, because the set of numbers didn't fade at all. So Laurie just left it. Then she pulled out the next drawer in the stack and started cleaning that.

The doorbell rang. All at once, she tensed up. She

might have left Ellensburg nearly a week ago, but she couldn't shake a sense of foreboding. She still expected Tad's brother to show up at her door one day.

Getting to her feet, she told herself that it was probably just Cheryl. She patted Joey's mop of curly brown hair and headed to the front door. She checked the peephole. The glass distorted things slightly. She saw a dark-haired man with glasses, smiling and nodding—as if he knew she was looking at him. He even gave her a little wave.

Taking a step back from the door, she glanced toward the kitchen. She couldn't see Joey, but heard the music tones from the numbers he was pressing. She turned toward the door again. "Yes?" she called. "Who is it?"

"Hi, this is Vincent Humphrey, your neighbor in unit five!" she heard him call back cheerfully.

Laurie took another glimpse at the peephole and saw that he was still smiling and waving. It was almost as if he were trying too hard to convince her that he was just a friendly visitor.

With uncertainty, she fixed the chain on the lock and opened the door a crack.

"Hi, neighbor!" he said, grinning at her.

Within the narrow space, Laurie saw he held a small, potted African violet plant in his hand. He was a handsome man in his mid-forties, but he had a bad haircut—like he'd cut it himself. His glasses were Clark Kent style, and a bit nerdy-looking. The short-sleeve checkered shirt he wore was neatly tucked into his cargo pants, which—as she looked down and noticed—rode a bit too high over his black Converse sneakers.

"I want to welcome you to La Hacienda," he said. "I hope I didn't catch you at a bad time . . ."

Reluctantly, Laurie unfastened the chain lock and opened the door wider. She worked up a smile for him. "Hi, I'm Laurie," she said, still a bit wary.

"I bought you this," he said, thrusting the African violet plant at her. "It's a housewarming, welcome present. I got it on sale at Safeway and saved two dollars."

"Oh, well, thank you," Laurie said with an uncomfortable laugh.

"Looks like you're painting," he said, eyeing her paint-stained shirt. "Let me know if you need any help. I'm pretty good at painting—only not right now, because I have to go fix my dinner."

Laurie nodded a few more times than necessary. "Well, I might just take you up on that offer sometime, thank you."

Joey let out a cry.

From the doorway, her visitor tried to peek in at the kitchen. "Is that a baby I hear? Do you have a baby? Can I see it?"

Laurie hesitated.

"I won't touch her—or him," he said. "I promise. I know you might not like it."

Laurie didn't know how to answer him.

"See, once at Safeway—" he continued, "that's where I work. I'm a bagger. I've been Employee of the Month nine times. Anyway, once this little girl was running around near my checkout station, and I didn't see the mother anywhere. So the little girl fell—like, *bam*— and she started crying. Well, I went to help her up, and suddenly her mother came out of nowhere, screaming at me. It was really scary. I think the whole store heard her. I couldn't figure out what I'd done that was so bad. Anyway, later, my friend who used to live in this apartment here, she told me that it makes certain people uncomfortable for someone like me to get near their kids or pet them or anything like that. So I—I've learned my lesson. I'd never do that. I just want to look at your baby, that's all."

Laurie's heart broke for him. She managed a smile, but still stood in front of him, blocking his path toward the kitchen. Joey let out another cry. She didn't want to be like the bitch in the supermarket, yelling at this developmentally challenged man for coming to the aid of her unsupervised child. At the same time, she couldn't help wondering if he might be a friend of Ryder's—and this was all an act.

"Ah, he's a little hungry and cranky right now," Laurie said at last. "But I'd love for you to meet him some other time, maybe over the weekend . . ."

"What's his name?"

"Joey."

He nodded. "That's a good name." Scratching his head, he took a step back. "Well, I'm going to fix my dinner now, mac and cheese. My friend who used to live here, she used to make me dinner all the time. Maureen was a professional cook. She worked with Cheryl—y'know, the woman in apartment eight. They had a food truck, but Maureen got killed when it blew up."

Her mouth open, Laurie stared at him. "You mean this was her apartment?"

"Yes, that's all Maureen's furniture," he said, with a

nod at her living room. "She didn't have any family, and neither do I. So she left everything to me, but I only took a few things—some lamps I've always liked, you know, nothing too frilly-girly, and her picture albums, her TV, and stuff like that. Anthony, our manager, he said I could give all the rest to charity or he'd pay me two thousand dollars for it. So I took the money and put it right in the bank."

Standing in front of the doorway with the African violet in her hands, Laurie tried to process this revelation. Why hadn't Cheryl told her? It was unsettling. Cheryl had set her up in her dead predecessor's place— complete with the poor woman's furniture. Laurie kept thinking about the horrible way she'd died. Now, she was literally in that unfortunate soul's place.

"I miss Maureen a lot," the man said. "She was my best friend."

"What about Cheryl?" Laurie asked. "Aren't you friends with her, too?"

He sighed. "Well, Maureen said I should be polite to her, but not try to be friends with her or anything."

"Did she say why?"

Vincent shrugged and shook his head. "So, can I come by and see Joey tomorrow or Saturday?"

"Of course," Laurie said. She managed to smile again and hoisted the small African violet a little. "Thanks so much for the plant, Vincent, and thanks for stopping by . . ."

"Well, it's time to make my mac and cheese," he said, waving at her as he started up the courtyard's paved walkway. "Bye, Laurie!"

She heard a clank, and glanced over at the court-yard's wrought iron gate. Someone was entering the apartment complex. She noticed Vincent briefly look-ing that way, too. But he kept moving, and then pulled a key out of his pocket. He unlocked his apartment door, opened it, and ducked inside.

The woman breezing into the courtyard wore black slacks, and a pale blue sweater set. Her dark blond hair was pulled back in a ponytail. She carried a grocery bag. As she passed the fountain in the middle of the courtyard, she looked over and seemed to catch Laurie staring.

"Oh, swell!" the woman announced. "My day is made!"

Laurie set the plant on a table by the door. "I beg your pardon?"

The woman approached her, and Laurie could see she was about forty. "I said, 'Oh, swell,'" the woman replied, with a half smile. "I was hoping a cute, hot, single guy would be moving in next door. And I get you."

Laurie laughed. "Oh, it's a lot worse than that. You're getting a toddler, too. I'm Laurie . . ."

The woman nodded. "Brenda, in number two," she said. "That's my life, number two. So how old is the lit-tle nipper?"

"Almost eleven months," Laurie said. She noticed that Joey had quieted down and gone back to playing his music-tone number pads. "Let me know if he ever gets too loud for you."

"Will do," Brenda replied. "I see you've met Forrest

Gump. He's a sweet guy. But if you want my advice, don't get too friendly with him, or he'll be over here all the time. He won't leave you alone . . ."

Laurie didn't say anything. She was a bit taken aback by the insensitive Forrest Gump crack.

"Anyway, don't say I didn't warn you," Brenda shrugged. "The manager mentioned you're working with Cheryl Wheeler—in a brand new food truck."

Laurie nodded. "Yes, in fact, I just found out from Vincent that this used to be her former coworker's place."

"Cheryl didn't say anything to you?" Brenda laughed. She set down her grocery bag. "Well, that's typical of her. Yeah, Maureen lived here. She and old Vincent go way back. I think they've been here longer than anyone—or rather they *were* here longer than anyone. I should get my tenses right, now that Maureen has gone on to that great food truck in the sky." She let out a sad, little laugh. "Actually, she was a nice lady, a good neighbor. I liked her."

"So, Maureen lived here in the complex before Cheryl?"

"Oh, yeah, years before," Brenda answered. "Cheryl's been here only a few months. Her old place was going condo or something, so Maureen used her pull to get Cheryl into Unit Eight when it went vacant. You want to hear the funny part? She barely knew Cheryl at the time. I think she'd just started working in the food truck with her. And even after cooking alongside her for—what, three months?—Maureen never really trusted her."

"Why do you say that?" Laurie asked, frowning.

Brenda shrugged. "That's just the impression I got. I

mean, look at what Cheryl *didn't* tell you about this apartment. Did she mention that the cops were here recently?"

Laurie shook her head. "No. What for?"

"A couple of teenagers disappeared about two weeks ago. The last person to see them was a friend of theirs. They'd told him they were coming here—to peek inside this apartment."

Laurie just stared at her.

"Apparently, they'd heard about the food truck explosion, and were curious to see where the victim used to live. The kids are still missing—as far as I know. The police came by here asking all of us if we saw anything. I can't believe Cheryl didn't mention it to you. Well, like I said, typical."

Bewildered, Laurie kept staring at her. She didn't know what to say.

Brenda waved her hand as if to dismiss it, and then picked up her grocery bag. "Anyway, don't listen to me. God, you have to work with the woman. I should just zip it. I'm sure your luck with her will be a lot better than Maureen's."

"Well, I hope so," Laurie murmured—considering what had happened to her predecessor.

"Are you breast-feeding?"

Laurie blinked at her. The question, so out of the blue, threw her for a loop. "Ah, I—I switched to a bottle about six weeks ago."

"Good, because I make a mean Cosmopolitan," Brenda said. "I'll have you over for cocktails and a *Real Housewives* marathon sometime soon. Knock on the wall if you need anything . . ."

"Well, thanks," Laurie said, watching her neighbor amble toward the next doorway down. "Nice meeting you," she added. But she wasn't sure if that was really true.

Laurie closed the door. Past the radio and Joey's musical interludes, she could just detect the sound of a door closing in the next unit.

She turned toward the partially furnished living room. She focused on the framed Eiffel Tower print, which up until a few minutes ago, she'd liked.

Now it would be one of the first things Laurie would replace—if she decided to stay.

CHAPTER THIRTEEN

"Well, it wouldn't have been a very good sales strategy to tell you the apartment belonged to someone who had just been killed," Cheryl said. "I wanted you to rent the place, for God's sake, not talk you out of it. And it's a wonderful unit. They just repainted four months ago, there's all new carpeting upstairs . . ."

"I know," Laurie said, trying to smile and keep her tone light. She didn't want to come across as ungrateful. "You don't have to sell me on the place, you already did. I just—I just wish you'd been more up-front with me about it, that's all."

She sat across from Cheryl at a small café table in her kitchen, which had a huge refrigerator and an array of the latest food-prep machines. While rocking Joey to sleep in her lap earlier, Laurie had watched Cheryl at work, effortlessly moving around the kitchen, cutting up a small chicken, blanching vegetables, and soaking rice paper. Cheryl had on a sleeveless polka dot blouse and khakis. Her feet were bare, which gave her a certain earthy, bohemian air.

All Laurie really knew about Cheryl was from a *Seattle Times* fluff piece on The Grill Girl and its owner. It mentioned that Cheryl grew up in several different foster homes in Washington State. By her early twenties, she was homeless, begging for money on the streets, and spending it on drugs. She got into a rehabilitation program, which included cooking classes with a local chef. After that, she worked her way up from eat-cheap diners to fancy restaurants, and eventually saved enough money to start her own food truck business.

The Grill Girl was around for a few years, the best-kept secret in Seattle. Then her truck was profiled on the Food Network, and it became enormously popular. According to the article, Cheryl never forgot her beginnings, and she cooked for a homeless shelter once a week.

There was nothing in the *Times* piece about Cheryl ever having been a mother. Yet Laurie remembered her mentioning that she had a little boy at one time, who had apparently died—or been taken away from her.

Maybe that was why she was so crazy for Joey.

He was asleep in his portable crib in Cheryl's living room by dinnertime. Cheryl had prepared a Thai chicken wrap with spring vegetables—a possible selection for their catering menu next week. Laurie had eaten two wraps, and resisted a third.

As much as she admired Cheryl's culinary skills, Laurie was still leery after what her new neighbors had told her earlier tonight.

"About those kids who disappeared," Cheryl went on, leaning back in her café chair with a glass of Chardonnay in her hand. "The police were here, and talked to all of us. But no one in the complex saw or heard anything. I asked the cop if we should be concerned, and he said no. He said they were merely following every possible lead. I really didn't think it was worth mentioning to you."

Laurie felt uncomfortable putting her on the defensive like this. She just nodded.

"As for dear Maureen," Cheryl continued. "She was my friend, and I don't think of her as this *dead person*. And it's not like she died *in the apartment*. But yes, you're right. I apologize for not telling you the whole story. I just wanted that place for you and Joey."

Shifting restlessly in her chair, Laurie looked down at her plate. She still hadn't told Cheryl a single thing about what had happened in Ellensburg. Who the hell was she to criticize anyone for lack of *full disclosure*?

"It's fine," she said, at last. "It's a terrific apartment. I didn't mean to sound ungrateful." She got to her feet and started to reach for Cheryl's plate.

"No, no, leave it," Cheryl said. "I have my own system for washing up. Sit. Tell me what else you're wondering about. Ask away, and you'll get the whole truth and nothing but." She swilled down the rest of her wine.

It had been her third glass. Laurie figured she was a bit drunk at this point. She put Cheryl's dirty plate back down, and sat in the café chair once again. "Well, all right," she said with an awkward shrug. "You said you and Maureen were friends. But when I talked with

Vincent and Brenda this afternoon, I got the impression . . ." Laurie hesitated, uncertain how to phrase her question.

"Oh, Lord, don't listen to anything Brenda tells you," Cheryl said, dismissing it with a wave of her hand. She started to sip from her wineglass again, and seemed to realize it was empty. "Hell, Brenda has elevated talking behind people's backs to a whole new art form. She's hated my guts ever since I moved in. I have no idea why. Maureen never liked her much. But what did Vincent say? I'm interested . . ."

"Just that . . ." Laurie hesitated. She didn't want to offend her new boss any more than she already had. "Well, he indicated Maureen told him not to become too friendly with you."

Cheryl didn't seem hurt or surprised. She nodded. "Yes, I know. Maureen relayed that to me. So here's the thing about Vincent. As independent as he is, he can also be a little clingy. Maureen didn't want him glomming on to me. But I think it went to the opposite extreme, because now Vincent seems a bit afraid of me. He hasn't really gotten the chance to know me, and vice versa . . ."

Laurie wondered if *anyone* really knew Cheryl.

"Vincent and Maureen were tight, like mother and son," Cheryl went on. "I know he's hurting right now. I'd like to reach out to him, but well, I'm not sure I'd be able to give him the time he'd demand from me—not now, with this big job coming up. How's that for being brutally honest?"

Laurie didn't say anything. She was thinking about

earlier tonight. Now she wished she'd let Vincent come in to see Joey.

Cheryl got up, wandered to her huge Frigidaire, and pulled out the Chardonnay bottle. She weaved a bit as she walked. After topping off Laurie's glass, she re-filled her own. The bottle clanked on the table top as she set it between them. "Anyway," she said, sitting down again. "Outside of cooking a casserole and drop-ping it off for him, I haven't done much for the poor guy." She sipped her wine. "What else do you want to know?"

Laurie had a ton of questions—about her back-ground and the baby she lost. But she'd already come close to offending her new boss tonight, and decided not to push her luck any further. She shook her head. "No, nothing else. But thank you for clearing that up."

"Oh, don't thank me yet," Cheryl said. "I need to ask you for a favor, a big one. I'd really like for you to bake one of your marvelous desserts and send it to your Uncle Gil for me. I've tried my damnedest to connect with him and Shawna, but so far, I haven't gotten anywhere. I'm afraid I'll come across as a pest if I try to contact them again. You're Gil's godchild. He'll respond to you. Let him know you've partnered up with someone in a new catering company in Seattle, and that you'd love to cater a party for him and your Aunt Shawna."

Laurie's back stiffened up. She wanted to tell Cheryl that Shawna Farrell wasn't her aunt. And she barely even knew Gil Garrett. She couldn't help wondering if her frail *connection* to the one-time film producer was the only reason Cheryl had hired her.

"Just don't mention me or the Grill Girl food truck," Cheryl went on. "It's time for some covert action with them. Keep my name out of it." She reached across the table and took Laurie's hand in hers. "Will you do that for me? I'll pay you for the dessert ingredients—and your time, of course."

Laurie figured she had this coming—for exaggerating about her relationship with Gil in her first note to Cheryl. She worked up a smile, and gently pulled her hand away. "Sure, no problem," she said. She figured she'd send the damn dessert and the note. Cheryl couldn't blame her if Gil didn't respond.

She felt so uncomfortable. Of course, it was no help that her host was half hammered. She was trying to think of a polite way to collect Joey and call it a night. "Listen, I should—"

"Thank you," Cheryl interrupted, raising her glass as if toasting her. She took a swig. "You don't happen to have relatives with any pull at Evergreen Manor, do you?"

Laurie shrugged. "I don't even know what that is . . ."

"It's kind of a rest home. I'm trying to get a gig with them, too—you know, some special occasion or party or whatever. I want to do something for the old folks there."

"Sorry, I—I can't help you there."

"Well, if you can get me Gil Garrett, that's enough. I shouldn't ask for anything more." She took another sip of wine. "Oh, and of course, don't mention to Gil you're catering this movie. I don't think that'll score us any points with him."

"Why not?" Laurie asked.

"He's probably not too enthusiastic about a film focused on his former lover's brutal murder."

"You mean, Gil and Elaina . . ."

"You didn't know?" Cheryl asked. "I thought being his godchild, you'd know. He's the one who discovered Elaina Styles. He produced her first two movies. Before Shawna came along, your Uncle Gil and Elaina were a very hot item. Your godfather was quite the playboy. I couldn't pick up a copy of *Rona Barrett's Hollywood* without seeing a photo of Gil with some gorgeous starlet hanging on his arm." She laughed. "Of course, all this happened way before you were born, so I don't know why you'd know about it. I'll bet you've never even heard of *Rona Barrett's Hollywood,* have you?"

Laurie shrugged. "I'm afraid not."

"It was a movie gossip magazine with lots of pictures." Cheryl leaned forward. "Speaking of magazines and gossip, did you see the article in the new *Entertainment Weekly*?"

Laurie shook her head. At this point, she just wanted to go home.

"Oh, Lord, you need to see it . . ." She got to her feet and almost tipped over the chair. After ducking into the living room, she came back with a copy of *Entertainment Weekly* that had Julia Louis-Dreyfus on the cover. She searched through it, and then folded back the magazine to one particular page. "Just so there are no more surprises," she said, standing over her.

She held the magazine page for Laurie to see, but her thumb partially obscured the headline. The first thing Laurie noticed was the photo of Paige Peyton with big, tawny red hair, thick, sixties-style eye makeup, and coral frost lipstick.

DEAD RINGER, said the caption. *Peyton as 7/7/70 murder victim, Elaina Styles.*

Laurie took the magazine from her and stared at the headline:

'CURSED' PRODUCTION
Tragic Deaths and Eerie Occurrences Plague
Filming of Notorious 7/7/70 Murders

"Are they serious?" Laurie murmured.

"They seem to be," Cheryl said. "Go ahead and take the magazine home to read. I'm done with it." She patted Laurie on the shoulder. "At least now you can't say I held anything back from you."

Thursday, 9:55 P.M.

Even with all the windows open, it still smelled like wet paint on the second floor. At least, that was Laurie's excuse. So she had Joey asleep in his portable crib in one corner of the dimly lit living room. She would crash on her dead predecessor's sofa tonight. She had the Restoration Hardware throw and a set of sheets folded up in one corner of the couch—along with her pillow.

Though she hadn't painted yesterday, this would be their second night in the apartment, and their second night sleeping down here. There was nothing wrong with the bed she'd inherited. She'd thoroughly checked the bare mattress for the telltale specks of dried blood that bedbugs left behind, and it was clean. As much as she liked the notion of having their sleeping quarters on the second floor, Laurie couldn't help worrying that if someone broke in, she and Joey might be trapped up there. She imagined hearing footsteps on those stairs in the middle of the night, and having nowhere to run. For now, it just seemed safer downstairs, where she and Joey could always slip out the kitchen door or climb out a window. It was silly, she knew. Ryder McBride and his crew had no idea where she and Joey were.

She sat on the other side of the sofa from her folded bedding, beside a small "frilly-girly" lamp that Vincent must not have liked. She had her stocking feet up on the coffee table and her computer notebook on her lap. The Julia Louis-Dreyfus issue of *Entertainment Weekly* was at her side.

According to what she'd read online tonight, Elaina Styles and Gil Garrett had indeed been lovers. Elaina had dropped him because he couldn't stop screwing around. But they'd remained friends. Among the many photos she'd seen on Google Images was a color shot of Gil, Elaina, Hugh Hefner, and Joe Namath at a party at the Playboy Mansion in 1968. Another shot was from two years later, showing Gil and his new wife, Shawna Farrell, looking somber on some church steps as they left the memorial service for Elaina Styles and her husband, Dirk Jordan.

There were no gruesome photos like the ones Laurie had found online when she'd first looked up "Elaina

Styles Murder" nearly two weeks ago. Since then, she'd ventured on Google again and read bits and pieces about the events surrounding the murders on 7/7/70.

The Wikipedia entry for Trent Hooper was on the computer screen in front of her now.

She kept thinking about how Joey was the same age as Elaina and Dirk's baby son, Patrick. When the child wasn't found in the house with his slain parents, a nationwide search ensued. There were candlelight vigils and church prayer services for "Baby Patrick." The search ended on July 13, when police found the remains of a baby boy fitting Patrick's description wrapped in a blanket in a shallow grave. The burial site was in some woods near a rundown farm outside North Bend, Washington. The cause of death couldn't be determined because the baby's body had been badly burned.

The farm had belonged to a fifty-eight-year-old widow named Ernestine Biggs, who may or may not have been involved with Trent Hooper. The blond-haired nomad and failed actor was thirty-two years younger than her. "Ernie" allowed him and his friends to do whatever they wanted on the place. According to one visitor at the Biggs Farm, Trent often shared her bed. And when Trent and his followers went skinny dipping in a pond on the property, Mrs. Biggs was right in there splashing around with the others.

The police determined that between three to five intruders had broken into the rented mansion on Gayler Court on the night of July 7, 1970. They jumped the fence surrounding the house. Then one of them climbed in through a kitchen window—and let in the others. They rounded up Elaina, Dirk, and their live-in nanny for the summer, a twenty-year-old Seattleite named Gloria Northrop. The three were bound and gagged, then stabbed repeatedly.

At first, the police suspected that Gloria's boyfriend, a college dropout named Earl Johnson, may have had a hand in committing the murders. But he was soon exonerated.

A few days after the slayings, nineteen-year-old Susan "Moonbeam" Morkel, who had lived at the Biggs Farm for four months, wrote to a friend in Sacramento, describing the killings.

Laurie looked at a portion of the letter in the Wikipedia article. "Trent, me, and two others killed those people in Seattle," Moonbeam wrote.

I had no idea they were movie stars. I thought we were going there to rob the place. We cut the phone lines. They were all asleep upstairs. We were checking out the first floor for stuff to steal when Trent went to the stereo cabinet, and found the album, Immortal. He played "Elaina" real loud. The husband came down, and Trent hit him over the head so he was unconceous [sic]. Then we went up and got the two women. The music was still playing by the time we finished tying them up. Trent killed them, but he wanted us all to stab each one. I just stabbed the guy. I could see he wasn't breathing anyway. When we were finished and they were all dead, Trent told me to take off the woman's nightgown so we could hang it

from the front gate. Then he did that thing to her neck.
He said he wanted to do something that would really
freak people out . . .

Moonbeam never mentioned Elaina Styles's baby
son—or what they'd done with him. Perhaps it was
something she couldn't be quite so casual about.

When local police descended on the Biggs Farm
early on the evening of July 14, they discovered Trent,
Ernestine, Moonbeam, and nine others—all dead, in
what appeared to be a mass suicide. Among the nine
were Jed "JT" Dalton and Brandi Milhaud. Police investigators determined that both of them had partici-
pated in the killings on July 7.

The group—which also included another adult male,
three more women, and three children—had drunk
cyanide-laced lemonade. It appeared that Trent had shot
JT in the head before turning the gun on himself.

Between a mountain of forensic evidence in the
house on Gayler Court and Moonbeam's blithe confession in her letter to her friend, there was no doubt who
had committed the murders on 7/7/70. However, the
"why" behind the killings remained a mystery. One
theory was that the unsuccessful actor was jealous of
Elaina and Dirk's rising stardom. Another possible motive
had to do with Elaina filming an occult film at the time, a
subject that fascinated Trent. The fact that her head had
been completely turned around in death seemed to vali-
date this hypothesis. Rumors that the baby was used in
some sort of sacrificial rite fueled the occult angle as
well. Still, others maintained he was just a Manson
copycat.

Strangely, Trent became a cult figure for some. Even now, forty-four years later, T-shirts with his likeness continued to sell. People had chiseled off pieces from his tombstone in a cemetery near his San Diego birthplace—until the stone was replaced with a plain marker. A five-minute video some Trent Hooper "fan" had created on YouTube had—at last count—racked up over four million views. It showed early "actor" portraits of Trent—along with footage of his bit parts and wordless walk-ons in such TV shows as *The Invaders, Mannix, Get Smart, Gunsmoke,* and *Gomer Pyle, U.S.M.C.* He also had a few lines—and no billing—in two forgettable late-sixties, low-budget features: *Attack of the Wolf* and *The Grave Robbers.* Accompanying the YouTube clip was a heavy metal score that somehow—at least to Laurie—sounded disturbingly reverent.

Reading about Trent Hooper and his hippie disciples, Laurie saw troubling, obvious similarities to Ryder McBride and his tribe. She'd seen how one of Ryder's brood had even been manipulated into committing suicide at his whim. What was to stop any of the others from committing murder under his command?

Laurie had to remind herself again that Ryder was clueless as to where she was. Just yesterday, she'd phoned Krista and then the diner to make sure everyone was all right. They were fine. Nothing unusual had happened and no one had asked about where she'd disappeared to. They were safe—and for now, so was she.

Yet, at her side was a magazine with an article that seemed so ominous. On Tuesday, just five days from now, she'd start work catering for this film shoot at the actual locales where events surrounding Elaina's murder had taken place.

'CURSED' PRODUCTION
Tragic Deaths and Eerie Occurrences Plague
Filming of Notorious 7/7/70 Murders

Before **7/7/70** was even given the green light by producers, **Dana and Robert Gold** of Atlantis Film Group, the project had already seen one grim fatality. Screenwriter **Lance Taylor**, 30, had claimed his account of the murders of **Elaina Styles, Dirk Jordan**, their baby son, and his nanny would "rip the lid off the case" with revelations that would "stun even police investigators." But shortly after selling his closely guarded screenplay to the Golds for $950,000, Taylor perished near his home in Maui. He'd slammed his BMW Grand Coupe into a phone pole. A near-lethal combination of drugs and alcohol were found in his system. Once on board for a supporting role in the film, veteran actor and Oscar winner, **Darren Jager**, 63, suffered a debilitating stroke, and had to be replaced by **George Camper**. Filming in L.A. needed to be stopped for two days when a set mysteriously caught fire. Another day of filming was lost when **Shane White** (playing Jordan) rushed to his 14-year-old daughter's hospital bedside after she was severely injured in a horseback riding accident. Several strange mishaps during the L.A. shoot have caused expensive delays—

including an injury to a boom operator that resulted in a broken collar bone. When asked if he believed there was a curse over the film shoot, director **David Storke** balked: "Considering how many people are involved in making a movie, odds are that some of them will be touched by various tragedies within the three months of filming." Still, extra security surrounds the shoot, in some part to keep the potentially explosive script a secret, but also to protect the players. **Paige Peyton** (cast as Styles) has been receiving death threats. A small group of protesters calling themselves Hooper-Anarchists (after killer **Trent Hooper**) managed to disrupt and shut down a night shoot on Sunset Boulevard. Newcomer **T. E. Noll** (in **Revisiting Limbo**, on screens now) plays Hooper. "It's a little scary," he said. "I don't believe in curses, but I do spend a lot of time looking over my shoulder lately."

Laurie wondered what the hell she was getting herself into.

Her predecessor had died in a food truck explosion. And here she was, about to start work in a food truck on the set of a jinxed, accident-prone film shoot. She couldn't help thinking that Joey might end up an orphan before this film wrapped production—or, much worse, something could happen to him.

A loud clank outside startled her. It sounded like the front gate closing.

Laurie quickly set the laptop and the magazine aside, and got to her feet. Moving to the window, she glanced out at the shadowy courtyard. She stood there for at least a minute, but didn't see anyone.

One of Trent's followers had climbed into the kitchen window of the house on Gayler Court. Tad and his cohort had tried to enter her Ellensburg apartment the exact same way. She remembered seeing the screen pried off that kitchen window.

Laurie hurried into the kitchen, weaving around some boxes she hadn't yet unpacked. She made a bee-line to the back door, and double-checked that it was locked. She glanced inside the powder room and the pantry closet on either side of the short corridor by the entry. She checked the locks on the two kitchen windows. The screens were still in place.

She remembered the windows upstairs were all open. It was ridiculous, she knew, but she thought about the Lindbergh baby kidnapping. A makeshift ladder had been used to gain entry into the child's room. What was keeping Ryder and his tribe from trying something like that?

From the kitchen Laurie headed around a corner to the stairway. She switched on the light to the upstairs hall, and then scurried up the steps. Though it was dry by now, the paint smell was more prominent on the second floor. It was also cold and drafty. She kept rubbing her arms from the chill as she closed the windows in her bedroom, the bathroom, and then the annex that would be Joey's room.

She knew she was being paranoid, but it wasn't un-justified. After all, last night had been her first time sleeping somewhere other than a hotel room since Tad had broken into the townhouse.

Coming back downstairs, she heard something that made her stop in her tracks.

"Will you play with me?" he asked in a singsong voice.

For a moment, her heart stopped, too.

But Laurie let out a skittish laugh when she realized it was just Joey's stuffed dog, Sparky. She'd put it in his crib with him earlier.

She checked on him. Joey was asleep, half-covered by his blue blanket. Sparky was trapped under his little arm. Laurie pried the stuffed animal out from under Joey's elbow and set it in one corner of the crib. She didn't want the damn thing scaring the crap out of her again—in the middle of the night.

Laurie went to the living room window and gazed out at the moonlit courtyard once again. She thought about those teenagers who had disappeared trying to get a look inside this very apartment. In their quest, how far had they made it before they'd vanished? Had they gotten inside the apartment—only to meet their end here?

Laurie's mind was reeling with thoughts of forty-year-old murders, curses, and that missing baby boy. She imagined people holding candlelight vigils and prayer services for the safe recovery of Baby Joey.

Most of all, she wondered what was beyond that wrought iron front gate right now.

She couldn't help picturing a beat-up silver minivan out there.

CHAPTER FOURTEEN

Thursday, 10:32 P.M.
Ellensburg

Duncan could feel the rain on his hands as he steered his blue moped up Main Street. It was just a light drizzle. Heavy showers always made a tat, tat, tat on his bike helmet, and then water would start sliding down the back of his neck. Right now, the rain was tolerable. But he still had about three miles to go until he was home. He took the bike up to thirty-five miles an hour, and the motor roared.

He probably should have jumped on Tony's offer to drive him home. Tony was the new cook, Laurie's replacement. Together, they'd closed the diner tonight. Tony drove a Chevy pickup, and had room in the back for Duncan's "Blue Bomber." But Duncan liked riding his bike, and said no thanks, figuring he'd get home before the rain started.

Now he wondered if maybe Tony hadn't been concerned so much about the precipitation when he'd offered him a lift home. Maybe it was something far more serious.

Paul had warned the staff they needed to keep an eye out for a 2004 silver Town & Country minivan. The owner of the van had been harassing Laurie, and the police suspected he might have persuaded that wigged-out girl to set fire to herself in the parking lot last week. It baffled Duncan how anyone could talk somebody else into doing that to themselves. The guy must have been a hypnotist or something.

A silver minivan had pulled into the restaurant's lot earlier tonight during the dinner rush. A short, bosomy woman with greasy brown hair climbed out of the vehicle and wandered into the restaurant. She asked Duncan's least-favorite waitress, Celia, if Laurie was working there tonight. Celia told her that Laurie had quit and moved away. That was all anyone at the diner really knew. If Paul had any idea where Laurie had moved to, he wasn't talking.

Once she'd gotten her answer, the woman left the diner, climbed into the Town & Country, and drove away. As far as Duncan could see, she'd been the only one inside the vehicle. But the minivan returned at around 8:40. It parked in the far end of the lot, near the Blue Bomber. After a while, when no one came into the restaurant, Duncan stepped outside to make sure they weren't trying to steal his moped. His bike looked safe. When the minivan pulled out of the lot five minutes later, Duncan ran outside again to make sure the Blue Bomber was still there. To his relief, it was.

He called Paul at home, and told him about it. His

boss seemed slightly annoyed, but advised him to call again if the minivan returned. Then Paul asked him to put Tony on the phone.

Duncan wasn't sure what he'd said to Tony. Maybe he'd asked Tony to drive him home. Maybe Paul had been worried about something bad happening if the minivan came back.

Duncan checked his rain-speckled side mirror. He didn't see any sign of the silver minivan on Main Street. In fact, he didn't see another car behind him. He'd be home in less than ten minutes. He always used to bring home a piece of Laurie's dessert of the day (if any was left) and eat it in front of *Modern Family* re-runs he'd DVR'd. Now he had to settle for whatever the other cooks came up with for dessert, which was only just so-so. Tonight, he didn't take home anything. He'd have to watch *Modern Family* with a Coke and Cheetos.

He missed Laurie's desserts—almost as much as he missed Laurie. He'd always had a little crush on her. He didn't believe any of those hateful rumors people were whispering about her.

All at once, his bike seemed to buckle. Duncan pan-icked. Clutching the handgrips tighter, he felt the entire front pull and tilt to one side. The steering mechanisms seemed to lock up on him, and he heard a loud thump-ing sound. It felt as if the Blue Bomber might go com-pletely out of control and slip out from under him. Wincing, he slowed down and tried to maneuver to-ward the shoulder of Main Street.

As he came to a stop and caught his breath, Duncan realized his front tire had blown. "Damn," he muttered, hopping off the moped. He could feel the rain dripping off his helmet and down the back of his neck now. He stared at the tire's underside, flat against the roadside gravel. He was shaking.

He had a cell phone. But he couldn't call his mom, because she was asleep and had work in the morning. Plus she kind of had a drinking problem, and was better off not driving at night. He really didn't have a close friend he could call. He thought about the cook, Tony, but he was probably already home by now.

Duncan grabbed the handlebars and started walking the crippled Blue Bomber along the roadside. He kept the headlight on—in hopes some Good Samaritan might see him and stop by. But that didn't seem likely. Outside of a strip mall that was closed, this stretch of Main Street was mostly residential. The houses were a bit run down, too. From the looks of it, hardly anyone was still awake. At least, he didn't see many lights.

Pushing the bike was awkward. The wheel rim made a gnawing, crunching sound against the gravelly shoulder. Rain had gotten into one of Duncan's sneakers, and now his sock was wet. He figured at this rate, he probably wouldn't get home until midnight.

He suddenly felt so alone. He couldn't help thinking that those guys at school who called him a loser were sort of right.

Duncan knew his head was bobbing, the way it did when he got nervous. He felt a tightness creeping into his throat. Tears stung his eyes. But he told himself he wasn't going to start bawling.

A car sailed by, its headlights sweeping over him for a moment. He tried to keep his head still and continued to push his bike in the rain.

He wondered if someone in that minivan during the second trip to the restaurant had done something to his front tire to cause the blowout.

The rain was getting heavier. Duncan heard another car approaching, and glanced over his shoulder. Squinting at the headlights in the distance, he thought it looked like a minivan. He felt a pang in his stomach. His shakes got worse. Pushing the disabled moped even harder, he tried to pick up the pace. He thought of hauling the bike into the ditch near the shoulder and hiding there until the minivan passed. The headlights loomed larger on the rain-slicked road. As the vehicle came closer, he could see it was a black SUV.

Duncan let out a sigh of relief. He wondered if they had room for his moped in the back. Biting his lip, he stopped and waved at the SUV. The vehicle didn't even slow down. He felt a wet breeze as it sped past him. Dejected, he started pushing the Blue Bomber again.

But then he heard a screech. Up ahead, he saw the SUV's brake lights were on. Someone poked a head out the backseat window. "Hey, do you need a lift?" a woman called.

"Yes!" Duncan answered, so grateful he was a little breathless. "Yes, thank you!" He pressed forward with the moped, which suddenly seemed heavier and harder to move than before.

"You look like you're in trouble," the girl said, stepping out of the car.

"I was. Thanks for stopping." In the darkness, Duncan couldn't quite see her.

"Where can we drop you?" she asked.

"I live on Okanogan Street," he said, still catching

his breath as he neared the SUV. He saw her now, a skinny blond girl, not much older than him. He figured she was a college student. With her black, slightly tattered clothes, and heavy eye makeup, she had the "goth" look a few of them went for. But she had a nice smile.

"Okanogan?" she repeated. "That's no problem. Get in. We'll take you there."

He hesitated. "Would you mind if I loaded my bike in the back?"

"Sorry, but that's not going to work," the girl answered. "We've got a big crate back there. Tell you what. Okanogan is only five minutes away. Leave the bike, and we'll take you home. If you don't have a car there, you can help us unload the crate. Then we'll come back here and load up your scooter." She leaned in toward the car. "Is that okay with you?" she asked the driver.

"Fine," Duncan heard the driver say. It was a man's voice.

"Sounds like a plan," the girl said, smiling at Duncan. "C'mon get in . . ."

He hesitated. He didn't want to leave his Blue Bomber on the roadside in this sketchy neighborhood, not even for ten minutes. Plus he couldn't see who was in the SUV with her. What if there were a bunch of people in there, ready to pull some kind of prank on him? It happened to him at school a lot, people pretending to be his friend, and then suddenly doing something to humiliate the hell out of him.

"Well?" The girl impatiently drummed her fingers on the SUV. "Is that okay with you?"

Duncan was still uncertain. He glanced back toward the center of town, and didn't see any cars approaching.

"Is he coming or not?" the driver called. "Tell him to make up his mind. You're letting the rain in!"

"Did you hear that?" the girl said. "Y'know, we're just trying to do you a favor here, guy."

Duncan could see her blond hair was in wet tangles. "Yes, I'm coming! Sorry!" he said, pushing his Blue Bomber toward a tree at the roadside. He hoped no one would notice his moped under the big elm's low, sagging branches. He switched off the headlight, gave the seat a good-bye pat, and started toward the SUV. "This is really nice of you," he said. Tugging at the strap, he took off his bike helmet. "Thanks very much . . ."

"No worries!" the girl said, holding the door open for him.

He was scooting across the backseat when he noticed the two men in the front. The one on the passenger side quickly opened his door. "I'm making sure this guy doesn't try any moves on Amber," he announced, stepping outside and shutting his door. Then he opened the back door and got inside.

Duncan balked. He was just about to move into that spot. Now he suddenly found himself squeezed between this man who looked too old for college, and the girl. She shut her door.

"Next stop, Okanogan Street," she told the driver.

Duncan could see only the back of his head—and his eyes in the rearview mirror.

The SUV started moving. Its windshield wipers

squeaked. Clutching the wet bike helmet in his lap, Duncan listened to the rain on the roof. "Um, thank you for doing this, you guys," he said nervously.

He glanced at the man beside him. He was about thirty—with heavy beard stubble and messy, black hair. Something about him looked familiar—especially his dark eyes, intense and intimidating. Duncan tried to remember where he'd seen him before.

"What's your name?" the girl asked.

"Duncan."

"Well, Duncan," said the man, pressing his shoulder against his. "That pretty thing beside you is Amber. You can look, but don't touch. I'm Luke. And the man at the wheel, driving us to our destination, is Hans."

Duncan let out a nervous chuckle. Luke and *Hans*? All he could think about was *Star Wars,* Luke Skywalker and Han Solo. Were they putting him on?

"So, Duncan, do you get high?" the man asked.

"No, not really." His head started to shake a little.

The girl put her hand on his knee. "Oh, I'll bet you'd be a lot of fun if you just loosened up, Duncan."

"Yeah, he looks like a regular party animal," the man said. He leaned forward toward the driver. "Doesn't he look like a serious party animal to you, Hans?"

"A wild man," the driver snickered.

"Really, I'm not," Duncan murmured, squirming.

"Then what are you doing out so late?" the man asked.

"I was coming back from work," he answered. "I— I'm a dishwasher at a restaurant."

The SUV seemed to pick up speed. He heard the

tires humming louder and splashing water on the wet road. He couldn't even read the street signs, they were going so fast.

The man slung his arm around the back of the seat. "What restaurant do you work at?"

"The Superstar Diner."

"Isn't that the place where the cook murdered that guy in her house?" the girl asked.

"It was an accident," Duncan murmured. "That wasn't her fault. The guy was stalking her."

He caught the driver's eyes studying him in the mirror. "Shit, guys, look at the way his head keeps bobbing up and down. We ought to shrink him and set him up on the dashboard."

The girl laughed, and squeezed his knee. "He's just kidding . . ."

"Yeah, we'd never shrink you, Duncan," the man said. "You're our pal. So, I forget—what's the cook's name again?"

Duncan realized his street was coming up. "Hey—ah, you—you need to slow down. This is me. This is my street . . ."

"*This is me!*" the driver repeated, bobbing his head up and down in an exaggerated way. He and the girl started laughing. The car sped past his street.

"Could you please stop?" Duncan asked. "I—I need to get out here."

"He's just taking a shortcut," the girl said.

Panic-stricken, Duncan glanced over his shoulder, and past the man's arm. The back of the SUV was empty. There wasn't any crate. "Listen, you guys, thank you for the lift," he said, a tremor in his voice. "But—but you can drop me off here . . ."

"Hey, relax and enjoy the ride, Duncan," the girl said, rubbing his thigh. "I mean, what's the hurry? Don't you want to have some fun?"

The man cleared his throat. "Quit pawing him," he said. "You did your job. You got him into the car. Now, just sit back and shut the fuck up. Duncan and I were having a private conversation . . ."

The girl took her hand off his thigh, and folded her arms. She turned toward the window.

Duncan gazed at the man beside him. Now he re-membered when he'd seen him before. It was a month ago. The man had come into the diner when he and Laurie were about to close. *"Go back to your mopping, Einstein. Laurie and I are having a private conversa-tion . . ."*

"So, you were about to tell us the name of the cook," the man said.

The vehicle slowed down, but only to turn onto North University Way. They were driving farther away from his house.

Duncan could feel his heart racing. He stared at the man—almost defiantly. "You know her name. It's Lau-rie. I've seen you in the diner. You own a silver Town & Country . . ."

"That's right," the man said. "Go to the head of the class. This is a rental. I got it just for you. So, where is she? I know she skipped town. Where'd she go?"

"I don't know," Duncan said. It was hard to talk—or even breathe—he was so scared. He tried to muster up some courage. "And even if I did know, I wouldn't tell you."

The man's hand slid down from the top of the car seat, and gripped Duncan's shoulder. It hurt a little. Duncan figured the guy was just getting started. "Hans is going to take us to a dead end road off Old Highway Ten," he said. "Do you think you'd tell us where Laurie is—after we strip you naked and tie you to a tree? Amber might like it. She's curious to see how well hung you are, aren't you, Amber?"

"I'm not talking to you," she muttered, staring out the window.

"Tell him, sport," the driver said. "Ordinarily, I wouldn't mind beating the shit out of you, but it's a nasty night out there, and I don't feel like getting wet."

The man grabbed Duncan by the back of the neck. "C'mon, where the fuck is she?" he whispered. "Think about it, Duncan. The bitch isn't worth the beating you'll get. Before we tie you to that tree, we'll take away your shoes and your clothes. We might just have to leave you there for the critters to nibble on . . ."

Duncan felt him squeezing tighter. Because of his head tremors, the talon-like grip on his neck hurt even more. Tears filled his eyes. They weren't far from Old Highway 10. "I don't know where she moved to!" he cried. "I swear. Nobody knows, not the boss, not her neighbors, nobody! That's the truth, I swear! Now, please—please, let me out of here . . ."

"Stop the car," the man said in a low voice.

Duncan felt the pressure slacken on the back of his neck. The car skidded a bit as it came to a halt. They were on Old Highway 10. Duncan didn't see any other cars around—no one to save him.

The man pulled his arm away. "This loser doesn't know shit," he grumbled. Then he opened his door and stepped out of the car. He bent forward and gazed in at Duncan. "Okay, get out . . ."

Tears streaming down his face, Duncan stared at the man, uncertain what they were going to do to him. For a few moments, he was too afraid to move.

"C'mon, you wanted out, so get out," the man barked. "Only you aren't telling anyone about this. Because if you do—if the cops so much as ask me one question about taking you for this little joyride—then you'll regret it. I know where you live, Duncan. And I can have my friends pay you and your mother a visit there on Okanogan Street."

Duncan wondered how the man knew that he lived at home with his mother. He must have had someone ask at the restaurant—or maybe he'd had someone following him around. "I won't tell," he promised, scooting toward the door.

As he stepped outside, the man grabbed him by the front of his shirt. "What the hell? Aren't you going to thank us for the lift?"

Duncan was so rattled, he dropped his bike helmet. "Thank you," he murmured.

The man sneered, and gave him a little shove before he let go of his shirt. Duncan staggered back, away from the SUV. He regained his footing, and looked up in time to see the man ducking into the front seat. He shut the door, and the vehicle took off with a screech.

A few pebbles from the road shot up and hit Duncan in the leg.

With the rain pelting him, he stood there in the middle of the lonely highway. He watched the SUV pull away, and felt as if he'd just cheated death.

Suddenly, the vehicle's brake lights went on. He heard the engine roar as the SUV backed up at a high speed. The tires let out another squeal and the car abruptly stopped. Duncan watched the man hop out of the passenger side. Brandishing a shotgun, he marched toward him.

Paralyzed with fear, Duncan watched helplessly as the man raised the shotgun and pointed it at him. Duncan couldn't move or even scream. The shot rang out.

He thought he was dead.

He heard a thump, and swiveled around to see a raccoon lying on the roadside. A pool of blood started to bloom under its furry body.

Duncan glanced back at the man.

"Why don't you scrape that thing off the pavement, cook it, and serve it up to your customers at that piece-of-shit diner you work at?" he yelled. The man laughed, and then climbed back inside the SUV. With another squeal from the tires, the vehicle sped away.

His head shaking, Duncan watched the taillights disappear in the darkness.

He took a few deep breaths, but it didn't do any good. He was still shaking. He managed to pick up his bike helmet. He turned and gazed at the dead raccoon. Clutching the bike helmet to his stomach, he started to walk along the roadside. The rain on his face mixed with his tears.

He wasn't sure how far he was from his house. He guessed it was at least two or three miles. And he had no idea what he'd do about his moped. Maybe he'd take his mother's car and go pick it up—if the bike was still there. It might be another hour or two before he could do that. He wasn't certain.

Duncan wasn't certain of anything—except that he'd never ever tell a soul about any of this.

CHAPTER FIFTEEN

"So is there anything safe to eat here—and vegan?" the short, pudgy twentysomething bleached-blond man asked. He had a cell phone mechanism on his ear, and wore black nail polish. He stood at the window of the food truck—one of several trucks, vans, and trailers parked in a lot by the beach at Golden Gardens in Ballard.

It was Laurie's first day on the *7/7/70* set. The weather had cooperated beautifully with mild temperatures and an overcast sky—perfect for filming, she was told. They were shooting a scene with Paige Peyton and Shane White—as the doomed Elaina and Dirk—walking barefoot along the beach. A cameraman shot the scene from the top of a big crane attached to a small tractor on the sand. Crew members were holding up reflectors and microphone booms. About thirty people were standing near the shoreline, working on the "intimate" scene. Apparently, the small lapping waves were just loud enough to create problems for the soundman.

There was a wide clearing in some bushes between the beach and the parking lot. But Laurie hadn't been able to see any of the filming from inside the food truck. All she could see were the other trucks, an open-sided tent, and the trip hazard, thick black power cables running along the pavement. Between the street and the parking lot, the security team kept scores of on-lookers at bay, many of them with cell phone cameras out and ready.

Besides the food, Laurie's main concern today was the very real possibility of having her photo end up on TV, in the newspaper, or online. She didn't want Ryder or any of his clan finding out where she'd gone. The absurdity of hiding out on a movie set didn't escape her.

Obviously, those onlookers behind the security barricade didn't give a damn about the women in the food truck. They wanted to see Paige or Shane. A still photographer and a cameraman were recording all the on-set activity for a *Making of 7/7/70* documentary that would end up on the DVD and Blu-ray. The only press person they let through was Dolly Ingersoll, the seventy-ish entertainment reporter for CNN. She was caustic, bitchy, and enormously popular. Apparently, she was writing her own book about the murders, and the making of the movie. Perhaps that was why she and her cameraman had acquired near-exclusive coverage of the film shoot. At least it seemed that way. They were all over the set. Fortunately, the women in the food truck didn't seem to interest Dolly one iota.

From inside the truck, Laurie had caught fleeting glimpses of Dolly—as well as Paige and Shane on their way in or out of their trailers. She got reports and updates from Cheryl about everything happening on the set. Before the lunch rush, Cheryl had stepped out of the truck a few times, leaving Laurie alone to do the prep work for several minutes at a stretch. That had been fine with Laurie, giving her more room to move around inside the tiny, hot space for a while. So far, she and Cheryl had worked well together. They'd had a practice run the day before, parking the new food truck by South Lake Union to serve the Amazon lunch crowd. Laurie had felt as if she'd been thrown into rough waters to learn how to swim, but she'd survived. There had been four other food trucks competing for business, and Cheryl was pretty certain Grill Girl II had drawn the most customers.

As the lunch break on the film shoot drew near, Laurie and Cheryl had started cooking and wrapping up sandwiches and burgers to accommodate the rush. They'd tried to anticipate every potential problem. "I hear these film people are notoriously finicky. We're talking food restrictions a-go-go," Cheryl had declared. So they'd put three vegan items on the menu: a grilled portobello mushroom sandwich on gluten-free bread, a tofu wrap, and a spinach salad.

They'd also been briefed—by the laid-back, lanky, handsome production assistant, a Brit named Danny—on how to interact with the VIPs, specifically Paige Peyton. "You must never address her personally—unless she talks to you first," Danny had warned them—in his

British Received Pronunciation accent. "She has an assistant, this viperous, smug little toad with bleached-blond hair. You'll know him when you see him. If you have anything to say to Paige—even if Paige is standing right there in front of you—say it through the obnoxious assistant. So it's, 'Would Ms. Peyton like a salad today—or perhaps a small child she'd like to boil in her cauldron and eat?' Never talk to her directly."

"Is it safe to look at her?" Cheryl had asked. "Or should we put special viewing boxes over our heads, like the ones you use when there's a total solar eclipse?"

Danny's description of Paige's assistant was spot-on. Standing at the food truck's order window, he seemed distracted by someone talking to him on that earpiece phone device.

Laurie started to tell him what was "safe" and vegan. "We have a grilled portobello mushroom—"

With annoyance, he dismissed what she was saying with a wave of his little hand. Then he held up his index finger to indicate she should shut up for a minute while he listened to whoever was on the phone. Laurie figured it was Paige—in her trailer. It didn't seem to matter to the guy that people were waiting in line behind him.

"Ms. Peyton would like a salad," he announced at last. "Do you think you could handle that?"

"Would Ms. Peyton prefer spinach or arugula?" Laurie asked.

"Spinach," he said, taking out another mobile device and looking something up on it.

"Our vegan salad comes with sliced pears, sun-dried

cranberries, red onion, toasted walnuts, and a tahini maple dressing," she explained loudly, so that Paige could hear. "Would that be all right?"

Apparently, Paige heard, because her assistant nodded. "Forget the onions," he said, not looking up from his mobile device. "Dressing on the side."

"I'll have it for you right away," Laurie said. She turned toward the small salad station, and started loading up a recyclable container with spinach and the proper ingredients. "VIP," she said to Cheryl, so her boss would know she had stopped everything to work on an order for a VIP. This was Cheryl's cue to pick up the slack at the order window with the people waiting behind Paige's assistant.

Laurie's hands shook as she put the salad together. Though Paige sounded like a bitch and her assistant with the black fingernail polish was an absolute worm, it was still important to Laurie that she get the order right—even if it was just a salad. She didn't want to disappoint Cheryl.

After those initial doubts during her first couple of days at La Hacienda, Laurie had finally settled in. She and Joey had even slept upstairs the night before last, and yes, she'd had Brian's baseball bat at her bedside. But she'd slept soundly—and so had Joey.

His babysitters, the retired couple, Hank and Tammy Cassella, couldn't have been nicer. Their place was baby-proofed from taking care of their grandson. They still had his crib and playpen. They'd invited her and Joey over to dinner on Sunday night. Tammy made an exceptional chicken marsala. Joey seemed to take an instant liking to them both—and vice versa.

Laurie had already applied to Lullaby League Daycare, which had a rating of four and a half stars (out of five) on Yelp. They didn't ask for any background information on her, thank God—just Joey's immunization and birth records. They'd assured her that once everything checked out Joey could start spending his days at Lullaby League. In the meantime, she had this kind neighbor couple looking after her son.

She'd already called the Cassellas twice today, and both times, they'd put Joey on the phone to babble cheerfully into it. All the while, she'd heard Tammy coaxing him, "Say hello to Mommy!" She knew Joey was in good hands.

It was all thanks to Cheryl—her new life, and this second chance.

Laurie didn't want to let her down by screwing up a simple salad order for a very temperamental star. She filled two small containers with dressing, and made sure the lids were snapped on tight. She set them inside with the salad, closed the top, and put a rubber band around the container. She slipped three napkins and a plastic fork under the rubber band, and then returned to the window. She handed the container to Paige's assistant. "Did you want anything for yourself?" she asked.

He barely glanced up from his mobile device. "From *here*?" he said. "*Please*. I don't think so."

"Well, let me know how Ms. Peyton likes that tahini dressing," Laurie said.

"Oh, yes, I'll make it a priority!" he said sarcastically. Then he wandered off, his mobile device in one hand, the salad in the other.

There was no time to ruminate over what a creep he

was, because they still had crew members to feed. The good news was that a lot of people came back to say how much they liked the food. The director sent his assistant over for a second order of Cheryl's Thai chicken wraps. He got the last two.

Things seemed to be winding down when Laurie noticed Paige storm out of her trailer. She looked even more angry-crazy with her big, teased-out mane of long red hair. She had facial tissues around the collar of her mod-print sixties blouse, and in her hand was the open salad container—the attached lid flopping up and down as she flounced toward the food truck.

Laurie glanced at Cheryl. "Oh, God, I don't think Paige Peyton liked her salad . . ."

"What?"

Laurie turned toward the window again to see Paige barreling toward her.

"What the fuck is this?" Paige hissed. With a flick of her wrist she hurled the container's contents at Laurie. Walnuts, pears, and dressing-soaked spinach leaves hit her in the face. "I told you, no walnuts! How stupid are you?"

Stunned, Laurie gaped at her. Her left eye was stinging, and she automatically started rubbing it. A bit of salad dressing must have gotten in there. She was too bewildered to say anything. But she wanted to scream, *Are you insane?*

"What part of 'no walnuts' don't you understand?" Paige yelled.

"Your assistant didn't say a thing about holding the walnuts!" she argued, a tremor in her voice. With annoyance, she picked a piece of spinach off her forehead. "He said, 'no onions and dressing on the side,' that's all. Maybe if he wasn't on his iPad while he was talking to you and giving me the order—"

"We're terribly sorry for the mistake, Ms. Peyton," Cheryl cut in, gently pushing Laurie aside. "It won't happen again. Is there something else we can prepare for you?"

"Forget it," Paige snapped, throwing down the empty salad container. "Fuck it." Then she spun on her heels and headed back toward her trailer.

The meltdown had gotten the attention of several crew members by the tent—as well as some of the on-lookers on the other side of the lot. Among the witnesses there was an awkward, dumbfounded silence—and then a quiet murmuring. Finally, someone laughed, and everyone started chattering.

Laurie kept rubbing her eye. She couldn't stop shaking. "I'm so sorry," she whispered to Cheryl. "I gave that snotty creep the salad exactly the way he ordered it, I swear . . ."

Cheryl picked a walnut off her shoulder. "You don't try to tell these people they're wrong, not even when they are." She rinsed out a dishtowel and handed it to her. Then she patted her on the back. "Like she couldn't have just eaten around the damn walnuts . . ."

Laurie wiped off her face. She noticed salad dress-ing splattered on her apron. Fortunately, she had her hair in a ponytail today, so at least she wasn't picking walnuts out of her hair.

"Hey, you two . . ."

Laurie looked over toward the order window. It was the production assistant, Danny. "I wouldn't take it personally," he said. "She flips out like this at least twice a week. We all hate her guts. If it's any consolation, she left her trailer door open, and I could hear her screaming. She's ripping that weasel-assistant of hers a new one."

"So, you don't think we're in trouble?" Cheryl asked.

"Oh, God, no," he said. "Even if she had the power to get you guys fired—which she doesn't—there'd be a riot. A lot of people are saying this is one of the best lunches they've had on any set. Just keep on serving up that fantastic food." He started to walk away.

"Thank you!" Laurie called.

She went to the sink and washed her face, splashing water on her eye. She glanced over her shoulder. No one was at the order window. Cheryl was putting food away in the refrigerator.

"So, do I still have a job?" she asked meekly.

"Of course," Cheryl said, pausing in front of the open refrigerator. "After what just happened, I should be asking if you still want to work here. I'm sorry I didn't stand up for you. But I just thought it better to defuse the situation . . ."

"No apologies necessary." Laurie started to dry her face off with some paper towel.

"Which one of you ladies got the spinach salad in the kisser?" someone asked.

Laurie glanced over toward the window. Dolly Ingersoll peeked back at her. Nipped and tucked many times over, the CNN gossip queen had big, square glasses and blond hair that was probably a wig. She pointed at Laurie. "You're the one . . ."

Laurie shook her head and backed into the sink.

Dolly stepped aside, revealing the cameraman behind her. "Get a shot of her," she urged him. "I want her just like that, with her face still wet . . ."

Horrified, Laurie turned away and darted into the corner of the truck, out of his camera range. "No, I'm sorry," she said. "Please, leave me alone . . ."

"Don't be silly! You're going to be on TV!" Dolly exclaimed.

But Laurie wouldn't even look at her.

Dolly must have turned to her cameraman. "I can't believe we had a celebrity meltdown right here, and we didn't capture it on camera," she said. Then she must have turned away and called to the people by the tent. Her voice was raised, but slightly muffled. "Did anyone get that on their iPhone . . . anyone?"

Laurie stayed in the corner of the food truck, her head turned away. She held the paper towel to her face. "Please, get her out of here," she whispered.

"My God, what's wrong?" Cheryl asked.

"I don't want to be on TV," she said under her breath. "I don't want to be online. This can't happen. I—I had a stalker in Ellensburg, a very dangerous man. I'm scared he'll find out I'm here." She started to cry. "He'll come after Joey and me. I'm sorry I didn't tell you before . . ."

Cheryl stroked her arm. "Don't worry about it."

"Hey!" Dolly called, poking her head in the order window again. "Listen, I want to interview you! A major meltdown by Paige Peyton, this is gold! What's your name?"

Laurie just wanted a hole to open in the floor so she could drop down into it and disappear.

"I'm the one who was waiting on Ms. Peyton," Cheryl said, moving toward the window. "My name's Cheryl. This is my truck and catering service, Grill Girl. It's really a thrill to meet you, Ms. Ingersoll. I'm a big fan . . ."

"You're a big liar, too," Dolly replied. "Nice try. I'm not blind, you know. I could see your partner in there had a wet face and a splattered apron. Now, I heard Paige Peyton threw a salad at one of you, and obviously it was her."

"Well, I'm sorry, but you heard wrong," Cheryl said. She stood at the order window and blocked Dolly's view inside. "Ms. Peyton came back here to—to hand me her empty container so it could be recycled. And I accidentally dropped it. That's all."

Laurie noticed the door to the food truck was unlocked. She imagined Dolly's cameraman, any minute now, flinging the door open to get her on film.

"Okay, so if that's really how it went," Dolly was saying. "I want to confirm it with your coworker there. Why won't she talk to me? Is she an illegal?"

Laurie dared to inch over to the door and lock it.

"No. She'd just rather not be on TV. I hope you'll respect that. But *I* don't mind being on TV at all. I'll talk to you . . ."

All at once, someone started tugging at the food truck door. With her back pressed against the refrigerator, Laurie watched the door handle jiggling.

"Listen," she heard Cheryl say in a cool, businesslike tone. "I want to keep my job here, Ms. Ingersoll. Wouldn't you like to continue here, too—as a welcome presence on the set? Is it worth alienating the producers to cover a silly little incident that will be forgotten the day after tomorrow? No one even has it on video. Think about it, Ms. Ingersoll. Why don't we just stick to my side of the story? No one threw anything at anyone. Paige Peyton returned a container to be recycled and I accidentally dropped it. That's all, end of story. No big deal."

The truck's door knob kept clinking. No one said anything for a few moments.

"Charlie!" Dolly bellowed. "Forget it!"

Suddenly, the doorknob stopped twitching. He'd given up.

Laurie let out a grateful sigh. She couldn't believe Cheryl's gutsiness, talking to Dolly Ingersoll that way. If she hadn't stood up for her with Paige earlier, she'd certainly made up for it now with Dolly. But a part of Laurie still felt it wasn't over yet.

"You think you're really clever, don't you?" she heard Dolly growl. "Well, like I said, *Cheryl,* Miss *Grill Girl,* I've had my eye on you this morning. I've seen the way you've been snooping around, hanging out by the stars' trailers. I saw you trying to sneak a look at the associate producer's copy of the script when you thought no one was looking. You aren't fooling me for a minute. You're not here just to serve up food. You're after something. I can tell."

Laurie watched Cheryl take a step back. She wondered if Dolly had hit a nerve.

Cheryl was shaking her head. "I don't know what you're talking about."

"I'm wise to you, honey," Dolly said. "You're the one

whose food truck blew up the same day you signed on to cater this movie. Talk about a curse. Didn't someone die in that explosion? You're bad news, honey."

Laurie heard Dolly's voice fade a little, as if she were walking away. "I'm going to get the goods on you if it's the last thing I do . . ."

CHAPTER SIXTEEN

Thursday, July 3, 4:40 P.M.

Though exhausted, Laurie still wanted to spend some time with Joey. So she put him in the car with his stroller, and they drove the nine blocks to Volunteer Park. The shoot had wrapped early for the July 4th holiday weekend. A lot of the cast and crew were catching afternoon flights back to Los Angeles.

For the last two days, she'd managed to duck out of sight whenever Dolly Ingersoll and her cameraman passed the food truck. Cheryl seemed to be avoiding her, too. Cheryl took over the order window both yesterday and today when Paige's snooty assistant came by to pick up the actress's lunch. The witch must have liked the spinach salad after all, because she'd ordered it again—both days, along with the tofu wraps today. No walnuts and no onions, of course.

As far as Laurie was concerned, the true "curse" on the *7/7/70* film shoot was Paige Peyton. She wouldn't have been surprised if those death threats Paige received were from former colleagues.

Any concerns she'd had about Paige getting her fired had been quelled by quitting time yesterday. After wrapping up the lunch service, she and Cheryl had set out three big trays of her lemon bars on a table in the tent. The bars had disappeared within forty-five minutes. Laurie had even spotted Paige's assistant stuffing his face with one, and wrapping up two more in a napkin to take with him. The slices of orange cake this afternoon had gone just as fast. Between the lunch menu and the specialty desserts, everyone seemed happy.

Laurie should have been happy, too. She was fond of Cheryl, but like the poor woman who last held this job, Laurie couldn't completely trust her. Dolly had been right. Cheryl seemed to be up to something. Before the lunch rush both yesterday and today, she had once again stepped out of the food truck for several minutes at a time. She'd explained that she just wanted to stretch her legs.

At one point this morning, Danny had stopped by the truck, and called to Cheryl, hovering over the grill. "Hey, I've asked around, and there's no way I can get you a copy of the script. You know, it's a big, guarded secret. The crew just gets what we're shooting the next day—and nothing more. Even Paige and Shane are only getting sections of it at a time . . ."

"Just a sec," Cheryl had said. "Hold on . . ." She'd left several sandwiches on the grill and hurried out of the truck to talk with Danny privately. Laurie had abandoned her prep work to make sure the sandwiches didn't burn.

When Cheryl had come back inside the truck, Laurie had asked, "Why did you need to see a copy of the script? I thought we were working from the shooting schedule. Isn't that enough?"

"Oh, I was just curious, that's all," Cheryl had answered. "Could you cut up some more avocados for the chicken burgers?"

Laurie had let it drop. How do you press your boss for a truthful answer when she was being deliberately evasive? Cheryl hadn't pressed her about her stalker situation in Ellensburg. Laurie figured she had no right to point fingers. She still hadn't been totally honest with Cheryl about her relationship with "Uncle Gil" Garrett. But yesterday, she'd sent him a container of lemon bars—along with a note about her new catering job in Seattle:

> *Dear Uncle Gil,*
> *It's been a while since I've been in touch. I'm*
> *glad you enjoyed the treats last Christmas.*
> *Thanks so much for the lovely card. I've recently*
> *moved to Seattle, and am working at a catering*
> *business with a marvelous, versatile chef. I hope*
> *you'll keep us in mind the next time you throw a*
> *party. For my famous godfather, I'll see you get a*
> *discount! I hope you like the lemon bars.*
>
> *Affectionately,*
> *Your goddaughter, Laurie*

She'd written her e-mail and phone number at the bottom of the note, which had gotten Cheryl's thumbs-up.

Though they probably wouldn't get a reply, Laurie had sent the dessert package out overnight mail. She figured it was the least she could do—after Cheryl had done so much for her. She'd been right about the apartment. It was ideal for Joey and her. Still, Laurie couldn't help feeling a bit disconcerted whenever a stray bill or piece of mail for Maureen Forester ended up in her box. And the police never did find those two missing teenagers.

For now, she wasn't going to think about it. She wasn't going to think about the movie shoot or the Elaina Styles murders or Ryder McBride. She had the next three days to spend with her son and work on getting the new apartment looking the way she wanted it. Maybe then it would seem more like Joey's and her home—and not some dead woman's place.

The weather was beautiful outside, sunny and in the high 70s with a light breeze. After spending most of her morning in that cramped, hot food truck, she relished the outdoors. She felt reenergized pushing Joey in his stroller along the park's winding paths. She'd dressed Joey for July 4th—one day early—in blue shorts with a red-and-white striped T-shirt. Kicking and cheerfully babbling in his stroller seat, he looked so cute with the sun shining on his curly hair. Nearly everyone who passed him waved or made a fuss over him, and Joey waved back. He lapped up the attention, and so did she.

"Look at the dog, Joey!" she said, pointing to a man playing fetch with his golden retriever on the lawn beside the park's thirties-era Asian Art Museum. People were sunning themselves on beach blankets. Two teenagers tossed around a Frisbee. On the other side of the museum, the old, round, dark-brick water tower loomed over the sprawling park.

She took Joey around to the promenade in front of the museum. "Look at the big donut, honey!" she said, pointing to a modern, nine-foot-tall ebony granite sculpture. According to the plaque on the pedestal, it was called *Black Sun*, by Isamu Noguchi. Several people were sitting on the pedestal. A teenager was helping his friend curl up inside the sculpture's donut hole. This was the heart of the park, with cars cruising by and people strolling about. Laurie stood near the pedestal, looking over a large man-made reservoir—and beyond that, in the distance, the Space Needle, Elliott Bay, and the Olympic Mountain range.

She took it all in, and told herself that she was doing all right. This was a big improvement over Ellensburg. She still felt homesick—but mostly for Brian. Her memories with him were there—and in Europe.

Laurie wasn't sure how long she was standing there, staring at the beautiful urban vista, but Joey started to kick and make a fuss. He wanted to get moving again. Pushing the stroller, she started down a path to a large, round fish pond nearby—with lily pads and goldfish. The pond was surrounded by a circular gravel walkway. Bordering that was a neatly trimmed hedge. Laurie hoisted Joey out of the stroller and kept her arms around him while he perched on the edge of the pond. He got a thrill looking at the various sizes and colors of goldfish swimming by. He kept pointing to them, and babbling happily. After a few minutes, Laurie was about to put him back in his stroller, but he started to cry. So even though her arms were tired, she propped him back on the edge of the pond and let him look at the fish some more.

She glanced up toward the ebony granite "donut" sculpture again. A skateboarder zoomed past several people milling around near the pedestal. One of them was Cheryl.

Laurie almost didn't recognize her, because she was wearing sunglasses. She'd changed from her work clothes into a pale blue top with beige slacks. Laurie tightened one arm around Joey and started to wave at her boss. But then she balked.

Cheryl was deep in serious conversation with a tall, handsome, thirtysomething man in a business suit. He wore sunglasses, and had neatly styled salt-and-pepper hair. Laurie didn't recognize him. She was pretty sure he hadn't been on the movie set.

He didn't look too happy with Cheryl. He shook his head, and even started to jab his finger in the air at her.

Laurie wondered if it was some secret lovers' quarrel. She was too far away to see if the man wore a wedding ring.

Cheryl was glancing around—apparently to see if they were attracting attention. She looked embarrassed. She gently put her hand on the man's arm. She began to lead him down the path to the fishpond.

Laurie immediately moved Joey from the pond's edge into his stroller seat. He let out a loud wail of protest. "Hush now, honey," she whispered. Then she stole a glance at Cheryl and the mystery man. She glimpsed them just long enough to see Cheryl freeze in her tracks. From the look on Cheryl's face, Laurie could tell she didn't want to be seen. So Laurie quickly turned away, trying to act as if she hadn't noticed her.

Once she got Joey situated in the stroller, she peeked up toward the start of the pathway again. Cheryl and the man were gone.

She took her time pushing Joey in his stroller around the hedges and up the pathway. He'd stopped crying. As she reached the promenade by the Black Sun sculpture, Laurie casually glanced around. She decided to pretend she hadn't noticed Cheryl until now.

But she didn't see Cheryl or the younger man anywhere. Obviously, they'd gotten the hell out of there once Cheryl had spotted her. But why? She didn't care if Cheryl had a boyfriend.

Pushing Joey's stroller, Laurie headed for her car. She decided to pretend she never saw Cheryl here this afternoon. After all, it was none of her business. She wasn't going to ask Cheryl about any of this.

She probably wouldn't have gotten an honest answer anyway.

The thin, pale woman with raven hair sat alone at the wheel of a dark blue SUV. The vehicle was parked across from the Asian Art Museum. She looked out at the "donut" sculpture. With a telephoto lens, she'd snapped several photographs of Cheryl Wheeler and Dean Holbrook, Jr., during a clandestine meeting.

The two had ducked down a path that led toward the water tower.

Dean Holbrook, Jr., was on her client's list of "potential" candidates.

The woman had figured it would be only a matter of time before Cheryl approached him. And sure enough, she'd followed Cheryl here to the park ten minutes ago for this rendezvous.

It hadn't looked as if Holbrook was willing to talk with her. But that hadn't stopped Cheryl before. Hell, Cheryl's food truck and her work partner had been blown to pieces, and even that hadn't stopped her. Now she was on that film set every day, trying to dig up a lead.

No, Cheryl wasn't giving up.

She had to be stopped. But she was still too high-profile right now. The food truck explosion remained a topic of interest for the police and the general public.

The woman would have to wait at least a few more days until she could scratch Cheryl's name from the top of the list. Cheryl was the only *definite* amid the short roster of *potential* candidates—until now.

Working her mobile device, the black-haired woman sent an e-mail to her employer with the photos she'd just taken attached. She had a pretty good idea how her employer would respond. There could be no more meetings between Cheryl Wheeler and Dean Holbrook, Jr.

It would be impossible for Cheryl to get any information from a dead man.

The woman in the blue SUV noticed Cheryl's new employee also happened to be in the park—with her child in tow. She was in apartment number three. Her name was Laurie Trotter.

That name was on the list now, too.

The poor, dumb thing probably had no idea what she'd gotten into.

CHAPTER SEVENTEEN

Sunday, July 6, 5:05 P.M.
Seattle

Dean Holbrook, Jr., saw a strange, naked woman in his basement window.

He and his wife, Joyce, lived in a beautiful, old brick house in Washington Park, one of Seattle's most desirable neighborhoods. With three bedrooms and a separate basement apartment, the house was too big for just Joyce and him. But Dean hoped to remedy that soon. They'd been trying to conceive for almost four years, and now they were looking into adoption.

They were certainly perfect candidates. He was thirty-five, and the youngest partner in one of Seattle's most prestigious law firms, D. B. Donahue & Associates. Joyce was on the board of Northwest Ballet and several nonprofits. And they had this impressive home.

Dean was proud of the large, well-manicured front lawn. Their house was one of few on the block that had a fence—with big, potted geraniums atop the posts on either side of the driveway gate. Going in, they used the automatic openers in their cars. Going out, there was an electric eye to open the wrought iron gate. The mailman, *Seattle Times* delivery, FedEx, and UPS all had the pass code.

Dean had used the pass code to get in moments ago. He'd just finished a round of golf with some business associates at Broadmoor Golf Club, which was walking distance from his house. The older guys in the golf clique envied his youthful vitality for hoofing it to the clubhouse. Too bad he hadn't been able to impress them on the course today. He'd played miserably. An off day, he'd told himself. But it was more than that. He'd been *off his game* in so many ways since Thursday afternoon, when he'd met with that bitch, Cheryl Wheeler.

A postgame martini had helped his disposition a bit. But he'd still been moody and on edge, hauling his golf clubs the seven blocks home. Ordinarily, Dean would have gone in the front door. However, earlier today he'd turned on the backyard sprinkler. So he'd needed to switch it off.

That was why he'd continued down the driveway, past the side of the house toward the backyard. And that was how he'd noticed the well-built, naked brunette in his basement window.

He and Joyce rented the basement apartment to his younger brother, Adam. Dean figured he was doing his only sibling a big favor, because the rent was dirt cheap: seven hundred a month for a spacious one-bedroom in one of Seattle's best neighborhoods. Adam was thirty years old, and a "starving artist." He'd won some awards at the Gage Academy of Art, and had some rinky-dink gallery in Belltown that carried his paintings. But it wasn't a real living yet. So Adam supplemented his income as a cashier/checker at the Trader Joe's about a mile and a half up the hill on 17th and Madison.

The nude woman glanced up over her shoulder at Dean, and seemed totally blasé about the whole thing. She didn't try to cover herself or hide. She just stood there with one hand on her hip, and went back to talking to Adam. Dean couldn't see who was in the living room with her, but he assumed it was Adam, who was probably naked, too.

He didn't stop and stare, but he saw enough to notice she had a back tattoo and a rather voluptuous ass. Then he made a beeline for the backyard. He switched off the sprinkler system, let himself in the kitchen door, and unloaded his golf bag in the coat room. All the while, he shook his head in disgust. Adam drove him crazy sometimes. Could he possibly be more indiscreet? He could have lowered his blinds, at least. Did he even know this woman? They gave Adam a place to stay, and he was treating their beautiful home like it was a flophouse.

Joyce wasn't home. But what if she were? What if one of those adoption agencies happened to come by here for a surprise visit—and they got an eyeful of that sideshow in the basement window?

Dean thought about going down there and giving his brother a talking-to. But he decided to wait until Miss Back Tattoo left the premises.

He went upstairs and took a shower, hoping it might

mellow him out a little. He was getting dressed in the bedroom when he heard a car—and the mechanical hum of the front gate yawning open.

It was Joyce. She'd been visiting this gay couple who were friends of hers. They'd recently adopted a baby from a private agency. It was part social call, part research. "Include me out," Dean had told her.

As Joyce's Jetta pulled into the driveway, it passed the brunette woman—now clothed in jeans and a striped top. She was on her way out. The woman waved at Joyce, who stopped the car. They spoke briefly. Then the woman moved on through the open gate while Joyce parked the car in back.

Dean finished dressing, and hurried down the stairs. He caught his wife as she came in though the kitchen entry. She had close-cropped brown hair, and wore white slacks and a brown top that showed off her trim, athletic figure. "Hey, honey, how's it going?" he said. And then without skipping a beat, he asked, "So what did Adam's girlfriend say to you?"

Joyce set her purse on the breakfast table. "She said, 'Hi, I'm Adam's friend, Frieda.'"

"I came home and passed his window and there she was, standing in his living room, stark naked."

"Well, good for Adam," Joyce said, opening the refrigerator. "Though I didn't know he was cougar bait. What do you want for dinner tonight? I still have all this food left over from the Fourth . . ."

"What do you mean, 'cougar bait'?" he asked. Sometimes, Joyce's laissez-faire attitude drove him nuts.

"She was at least forty-five if she was a day. So, we

have all these hamburgers drying up. I guess I could make a casserole or spaghetti . . ."

"We'll go out," he said, dismissing the dinner discussion. "It doesn't bother you that he's bringing strange women into our home?"

Joyce closed the refrigerator door, and turned to him. "Honey, that basement apartment isn't our home, it's his. Aren't you going to ask me about Stafford and David and their baby girl?"

"What if that woman was a prostitute?" Dean asked.

"Your brother's really cute. I doubt he'd need to pay a prostitute—"

"I'm going to talk to him," Dean said, marching to the kitchen door.

"Oh, leave him alone," he heard Joyce groan, but he was already outside.

The house's previous owner had sealed off one set of basement stairs, making the apartment totally separate from the main house. He and Joyce had access to the downstairs furnace room, laundry, and storage from a stairwell off the kitchen. He had to walk around the corner of the house to a set of outside steps that led down to Adam's front door. Dean knocked on it—loudly. He almost expected to see his brother answer the door in just his underwear or in a towel. He was pretty sure Adam didn't own a robe.

His brother came to the door in jeans and a paint-smeared white T-shirt that hung loosely on his wiry frame. He was barefoot. As usual, his wavy brown hair was a mess, and he needed a shave. But it was a look girls seemed to go for. "Hey, what's up, Peeping Tom?"

he grinned, leaning in the doorway frame. "Frieda said she saw you . . ."

"You know, I don't care what you do with your life," Dean said. "But at least have a little discretion. If you're going to be screwing strange women in this apartment in the middle of the afternoon, at least lower the blinds so the neighbors don't see."

"What are you talking about? This place is surrounded by bushes and a fence. No one can see in here . . ." He stepped back into the apartment, which was reasonably neat—except for his painting easel, a mess of rags, soaking brushes, and paint in one corner of the living room.

"Well, I saw what was going on down here," Dean said, following him inside. "What if Joyce was having friends over—or holding one of her board meetings here? What's she supposed to say to them? *'Oh, that's just my bohemian brother-in-law fucking some stranger . . .'*"

Adam shook his head. "God, you're such a horse's ass—and so full of shit. You say you don't care what I do with my life, but you do. You're always rushing to judge me." He took the canvas off the easel and turned it around to show Dean a half-finished painting of the brunette. "I'm not screwing Frieda. She's married, and has a son in college. She's an artist's model. I'm painting a life study, you moron. I kept the blinds open for the natural light." He put the picture back on the easel. "Boy, I'm glad as hell you didn't pass by the window two weeks ago when Jeff was posing for me. The shit would have really hit the fan."

"Well, you should have told us—*warned us*—that you'd be bringing people in here to pose nude for you,"

Dean retorted. He was still angry—and now, a little defensive. "Show a little responsibility, why don't you? I'm
giving you a real break with the rent here. The least you
could do is conduct yourself with some degree of . . ." He
threw his hands up in resignation. "Oh, the hell with it.
You're thirty years old. I thought by now, you'd have
grown up and maybe amounted to something. But you
haven't. You have no respect for me or this house.
Meanwhile, I'm the one who's keeping a roof over
your head. And I'm paying the bills for Dad at Evergreen Manor. When's the last time you chipped in for
that, huh?"

Adam stared at him, his pale green eyes filling with
hurt. He stepped back, shucked his T-shirt over his
head, and stomped into the bedroom. A few moments
later, he came back into the living room wearing a blue
Polo shirt that Dean recognized as one of his hand-me-
downs. Hell, he even kept his loafer of a kid brother
clothed.

"When's the last time you visited him, huh?" Adam
shot back. "I'm there every day. And I'm not asking for
any medals. I want to go. I want to see Dad. I want to
see him while he can still remember who I am." He
plopped down on the sofa, reached underneath it, and
pulled out a pair of beat-up sneakers. He put them on
over his bare feet. "On the rare times you visit him,
you're so uncomfortable that you make Dad uncomfortable, too. Jesus, why do you hate him so? You're
such a hypocrite. You always act like you're such a
great son, because you pay his bills at Evergreen Manor.
But all the while, you can't stand him."

"I know the old man a lot better than you do," Dean

said quietly. He didn't want to tell Adam what he knew—and what had happened that had soured him on their father. He couldn't help thinking again about that meeting with Cheryl Wheeler on Thursday afternoon.

He sighed. "Adam, you have no idea how much I'm protecting him—along with our good name."

His brother finished tying his shoelaces, and looked up at him. "You're right. I don't know what the hell he ever did to deserve your contempt or indifference or whatever. I just know he was a great father to me." Adam reached for his cell phone on the end table by the sofa. "Maybe when you *deign* to visit Dad next month—*if your schedule permits*—you can talk it out with him, and actually have a meaningful conversation . . ."

Adam looked as if he were about to phone someone on his mobile device, but then he glanced up. "You know what Dad told me last week? He was having one of his more lucid days, and he said he knows how much you hate visiting him. So he pretends to be out of it. He said he sings 'Bye Bye Blackbird' to himself, pretending you're not there in the room with him—just so you'll leave, so you'll hurry up and go."

Dean slowly shook his head. But he realized what Adam was talking about. His father's semi-catatonic rendition of "Bye Bye Blackbird" had always prompted him to make a quick exit. He couldn't fathom that on some of those occasions—maybe even all of them— his father had been faking it.

"So, who really knows the old man better, huh?" Adam asked. He started punching numbers on his cell phone.

"Who are you calling?" Dean asked.

"Orange Cab," Adam said, with the phone to his ear. He was obviously on hold, because he was still glaring at Dean. "I'm going out and getting shit-faced while I figure out a new living arrangement—preferably some-place where the landlord won't be reminding me every chance he gets about what a huge favor he's doing me. I'm not taking my car, because I don't want to be driv-ing drunk later . . ." He turned away. "Yes, Orange Cab, I need a pickup in the Washington Park area . . ."

With a sigh, Dean turned and lumbered out the door. As he started up the concrete stairwell, he thought about his brother calling a cab in anticipation of get-ting drunk later.

It was about as responsible as Adam would ever get.

Climbing into bed shortly after midnight, Dean didn't realize that on this day—almost to the hour—forty-four years ago, Elaina Styles, Dirk Jordan, and their child's nanny were murdered.

Tonight, he and Joyce had gone out to eat at Luc, a French restaurant just up the street. He probably shouldn't have had the third glass of wine. He'd nod-ded off in front of the TV with the remote in his hand. Joyce had tried to wake him, but had finally given up and gone to bed without him. He'd woken up around 11:45, switched off the TV, the lights, and the overhead fan, and then he'd lumbered upstairs. He'd stripped down to his undershorts, brushed his teeth, and climbed into bed.

Now he was wide awake, damn it.

Dean heard a car motor, and then the front gate opening. He tossed back the covers and hurried to the window. He saw an orange taxi on the street, and his drunken younger brother weaving up the driveway. Adam disappeared around the corner of the house, and a few moments later, Dean heard the apartment door open and then slam shut.

"What's going on?" Joyce asked sleepily. She half sat up in their bed.

"Adam's home," he grumbled. "Sorry he woke you. Talk about inconsiderate . . ."

"He didn't wake me. You did—when you jumped out of bed."

"Sorry," he muttered, crawling back under the covers.

"You're too hard on him," Joyce said, reclining again. She turned her back to him and tugged the sheets up to her neck. "He's a sweet guy and he loves you. Promise me you two will have a boys' night out tomorrow, talk things over, and smoke a peace pipe."

Dean blindly reached over and patted her hip. "We'll see," was all he said. He didn't want to make any promises. He wasn't too hard on Adam. His brother had it easy. His brother was doing what he wanted to do, and living in a dream world. He had no idea about their father's reprehensible past. Dean was doing him a big favor by keeping it secret.

How exactly Cheryl Wheeler had found out about it was beyond him. But one thing made sense now. The explosion of her food truck was probably no accident. If she went around asking people what she'd been asking him Thursday afternoon, she was as good as dead.

Dean was pretty certain no one had seen them to-gether. She hadn't tried to call him again, thank God. So maybe he'd seen the last of her.

He heard the gate humming again.

He glanced at the digital clock on his nightstand: 1:43 A.M. He must have drifted off. Dean quietly crawled out of bed and crept to the window. He wondered if Adam had gone out again. But when he looked outside, he saw the gate was closed. There was no sign of any-one on the moonlit lawn. He told himself the humming noise could have been anything. It wasn't necessarily the gate. Sometimes a car passing by had that same mechanical purr.

Dean started back toward the bed, but stopped sud-denly. He heard a clanking sound downstairs—like silverware. Adam had a key to the house. Had he let himself inside? Maybe he'd run out of booze, and was going after their supply now.

Dean could hear floorboards creaking.

He ducked into the closet and switched on the light. He grabbed a pair of sweatpants off a hook and put them on.

"What's happening?" Joyce murmured, squinting at the closet light.

"Someone's downstairs," he whispered.

They always left the front entrance hall chandelier on when they went to bed. It made a dim light in the up-stairs hallway. Dean moved toward the bedroom door.

There was a distant click.

He stopped again. His heart was racing.

Orchestral music began to swell, with chiming bells. It was the beginning of some oldies song. It sounded like "Cherish." Someone was tinkering with the music system in his study. Dean was almost certain Adam was down there. What burglar would break into a house and put on music?

A man with a velvety voice started to sing on the recording: *"I'm just insane for Elaina . . ."* The music got louder.

"What's going on?" Joyce asked. "Dean?"

Baffled, he stood there with his bare feet rooted to the carpet. Drunk or not drunk, why would his brother be doing this? It made no sense.

The song kept playing—Dirk Jordan singing about his wife, Elaina Styles.

Dean remembered someone telling him that the song had become even more of a hit after Dirk and Elaina were murdered.

Past the music, he heard the floorboards creaking again. The sound was closer now. He stared out at the hallway, and watched a shadow sweeping across the wall.

"Jesus, honey, call nine-one-one!" he said, swiveling around.

He saw Joyce in bed, in her pale blue nightgown, fumbling for the cell phone on the bedside table.

All at once, he felt something hit him hard against the back of his head.

Then he didn't hear the music anymore.

Adam Holbrook woke up from his drunken slumber to the sound of music blaring in the room above him.

He squinted at the clock on his night table: 1:51 A.M.

His head was pounding. He tried to ignore the throbbing pain—along with that stupid music. What the hell was happening up there? Sometimes he could hear the TV if Dean had insomnia. Maybe his brother had one of the music channels on. It sounded like Solid Gold Oldies. Was Dean doing this to torture him? He had to be waking up Joyce, too.

It stayed cool in the basement apartment, even during the summer. But Adam staggered out of bed and switched on the oscillating fan in the corner of the room—just for white noise. Still, it was no competition for the loud music upstairs.

He ducked into the bathroom to pee. He wore only a pair of boxers with smiley faces on them, which someone had given to his brother as a joke. After he flushed the toilet, Adam slurped some water from the faucet. He hoped a little hydration might subdue what seemed like one awful hangover in the making. He knew he was still a little drunk.

Retreating back to bed, he pulled the sheet over his ears to help mute the music from upstairs. He tried to convince himself that he was listening to the radio. He started to doze off.

But then a loud thud woke him again. It was directly above him—in Dean and Joyce's living room. He heard footsteps. It sounded like more than two people up there, at least three, and something was dragging across the floor. All the while that melody kept playing. Were Dean and Joyce having an argument? Muffled voices rose over the music, but he couldn't tell what they were saying.

"Oh, my God, no!"

That, he heard. It was Joyce.

One of them was stomping their feet.

Adam ducked his head under the pillow again to block out the racket. They were having a major knockdown-drag-out up there. He'd heard them during a few skirmishes before—just not at this crazy hour or set to music, no less. And it almost sounded *physical,* which had never happened before.

A part of him wanted to go up there and put a stop to it. But he was just drunk enough to take a swing at his brother. He really liked Joyce. God only knew how she put up with Dean. His brother could be a pain in the ass sometimes, but he'd never hit Joyce—ever. Of course, Dean couldn't afford to. He was always acting like it was a big sacrifice to pay for their father's care at Evergreen Manor. But it was Joyce's money. She was an heiress from one of those old Seattle families. They'd owned one of the TV stations. Her parents were dead, and she had no siblings. Joyce and Dean bought the house with her money. She was the one who had invited Adam to move into the apartment. He'd offered to pay rent. Joyce had said no. But Dean had thought it was a good idea.

Adam slipped the pillow back under his head. They'd gotten quiet now. All he could hear were footsteps—two sets this time. He figured he must be really drunk, because he could have sworn earlier that at least three people had been up there. As for the music, some crooner—maybe Sinatra or Tony Bennett or Bobby Darin—finished up the last song. Adam could hear murmuring now, serious and solemn in their tone. But strangely, it didn't sound like either his brother or his sister-in-law. Was it the TV?

All of it made a weird kind of sense to him. They'd put on the music so he wouldn't hear their bickering. Now Joyce had gone to bed and Dean had switched on the TV.

With the fan blowing on him—and offering that steady, assuring white noise—Adam started to drift off again. The voices and footsteps seemed to fade in and out.

The next thing he heard was a click.

With a start, he sat up in bed. He wasn't sure how long he'd been asleep. He didn't even have time to look at the clock on his nightstand. He knew someone was at his door. There was the unmistakable sound of the key in the lock, and then the knob rattling.

Adam stumbled out of bed and made his way to the living room. There was just enough moonlight through the windows to see the doorknob twitching back and forth. He'd set the bolt lock earlier when he'd come back from the Comet Tavern on Capitol Hill. The flimsy bolt was hardly the ultimate in security. One fierce kick and the thin little mechanism screwed to the door would have broken off, and whoever wanted to get inside could indeed get inside.

Staring at the door, Adam braced one hand on the wall to keep himself from teetering over. He was con-vinced it was Dean trying to get inside the apartment. Though his brother had a set of keys, the bolt worked only from the inside. Dean had come down here in the past, after a fight with Joyce—so he could gripe.

Well, Adam didn't feel like talking with Dean right now.

Joyce had come down here to kvetch, too, on a few occasions when she was mad at Dean. She knew she had an ally in him. What if it was her at the door?

Whoever it was, they weren't giving up. The door-knob kept clicking and twisting back and forth. The bolt rattled.

Why the hell didn't they just knock?

Adam moved closer and glanced out the peephole. It was black. Someone was covering it on the other side. His brother did that sometimes—just to be funny. But not at this hour and not right after a serious fight.

Adam backed away from the door. The knob stopped shaking.

He stood there paralyzed, listening. He heard some-one retreating up the cement steps. He kept waiting for the sound of the kitchen door as it opened and closed. He kept waiting to hear footsteps above again.

Except for the hum of his oscillating fan, it was deathly quiet. All that music and noise, and now, noth-ing.

Adam grabbed his cell phone out of the bedroom. He called Dean and Joyce's home line. He could hear a muted ringing in the kitchen above him. The machine clicked on: *"Hi, you've reached the Holbrooks,"* Joyce announced cheerfully in the recording. *"We can't come to the phone right now, but if you leave a message after the beep, one of us will get back to you. If you're trying to reach Dean, his cell phone number is . . ."*

Hanging on the line, Adam moved to the window. He couldn't see anyone outside. He finally heard the beep on the other end of the phone line. "Hi, you guys, it's me," he said. "What's going on up there? Was one of you just at my door? I'll try your cells. Call me back right away. If I don't hear from you, I think I'll call the cops."

He clicked off. He tried Dean's and Joyce's cell phones, leaving a message with both of them. Then he threw on his clothes. He found the house keys, and stashed them in the front pocket of his jeans—along with his cell phone. Before heading out the door, he grabbed the first thing he could think of to use to defend himself—a painter's knife.

He unfastened the bolt on the unlocked door and stepped outside to the cement stairwell. The cool night air—and his heart pumping—sobered him up a little. He glanced down the driveway, and spotted something wrapped around a spoke on the front gate. It looked like a small tattered flag, flapping gently in the breeze. He was too far away to discern what it was.

As he moved down the driveway toward the gate, Adam heard a twig snap. He stopped dead, and glanced around. Was someone hiding in the bushes or behind one of the trees on the front lawn?

He noticed some of the first-floor lights were on inside the house, but the curtains were all drawn. Dean's BMW and Joyce's Jetta were still parked in the driveway. Why weren't they answering their phones?

Adam didn't see anyone skulking on the front lawn. With uncertainty, he approached the front gate for a better look at the thing fluttering from one of the spokes.

It was a pale blue nightgown, splattered with blood.

Adam turned around and stared at the house. He felt sick to his stomach. With the painter's knife clutched in his shaky fist, he started back up the driveway. He headed for the kitchen door. It was how he usually entered their house.

He kept his eyes glued to the bushes alongside the driveway. The leaves quivered in the breeze—like that awful, bloodstained thing on the gate. He didn't know his sister-in-law's sleepwear. He prayed the nightgown wasn't hers.

He was just drunk enough that he didn't trust his own judgment. He thought about calling the police. But what if he was wrong? And the cops would see he was intoxicated. Dean would be furious.

The kitchen door wasn't locked. As he opened it, the hinges squeaked. "Dean? Joyce?" he called tentatively. The overhead light was on. Adam noticed a few of the drawers were open—one of them, the utensil drawer. The phone message light was blinking.

As he moved through the kitchen, he heard a scratchy *click-click-click* sound. It came from Dean's study, just down the hall. The desk lamp was on, and two drawers were open. He saw Dean's music console was on. He was a vinyl and old LP collector. A record album had been left on the turntable. Adam pressed the power button, and the turntable stopped. He saw the record that had awoken him earlier:

IMMORTAL
The Legendary DIRK JORDAN Sings
"Elaina" and Other Hits

Without the noise from the record skipping, the house was suddenly quiet.

Adam started down the hall to the living room. "Dean?" he called again. He rounded the corner, and then halted. What he saw sucked the breath out of him. It was as if someone had suddenly punched him in the gut.

He saw his brother curled up on the floor with his hands tied behind him. The plush, beige Persian rug beneath him was soaked with blood. He wore a pair of sweatpants. Adam could see the puncture marks on his naked back.

There were too many to count at a glance.

Monday, July 7, 2:31 A.M.
Seattle Police 911 recording

911: *Seattle Police. What's the nature of your emergency?*

CALLER: *They're dead, they're both dead . . . My brother and my sister-in-law . . .* [Crying, indistinguishable] *. . . They're here on the living room floor, and there's blood everywhere . . .*

911: *Can I have the address?*

CALLER: *They've been stabbed . . . someone . . .* [Crying, indistinguishable]. *Dean, I'm so sorry . . .*

911: *What's the address there, sir?*

CALLER: *517 Prescott in Washington Park.*

911: *Is there anyone else in the house? Do you think you might be in danger?*

CALLER: *I don't think so . . . Whoever was here, I'm pretty sure they're gone . . . the—the front gate . . .*

911: *Are you hurt?*

CALLER: *No . . . I'm . . .* [Crying] *I didn't see who did it. I didn't see anything. They—they must have broken in. They tried to get into my apartment—in—in the basement . . .*

911: *You said there are two people dead?*

CALLER: *My big brother . . .* [Crying] *. . . Dean Holbrook. They stabbed him. And Joyce, his wife, my sister-in-law. Joyce—she's naked. They took her nightgown . . .* [Indistinguishable] *And they did something to her neck. Her head, it's completely turned around.*

CHAPTER EIGHTEEN

Monday, July 7, 5:50 A.M.
Seattle

Laurie and Cheryl were driving across the Magnolia Bridge, on their way to the house on Gayler Court where the murders had occurred exactly forty-four years ago. Cheryl had assured her earlier they'd be working in the food truck the whole time. It would be parked in the driveway. She'd said neither of them would have to set foot inside the house.

Now all that had changed.

Cheryl had subcontracted with a woman named Bonnie to set up a food table on location every morning with donuts, croissants, and bagels, and three big urns with coffee, decaf, and hot water for tea. Bonnie also provided coolers of soft drinks, bottled water, and packaged snacks for the cast and crew. She'd told Cheryl she wouldn't have any problem doing the job when the shooting locale moved to the "murder house."

But Bonnie had phoned Cheryl just an hour ago.

She'd loaded up the minivan with everything, and she'd gotten as far as the front gate at the Gayler Court address. Because it had started to rain, one of the production people had told her that she'd have to set up the breakfast spread inside—on the kitchen counter. But Bonnie couldn't even make herself drive up to that house. She'd turned around the minivan and headed to Cheryl's place.

Cheryl had woken Laurie with a distress call at 5:20. She needed help setting up the breakfast spread. Laurie had gotten a hold of the Cassellas next door, and they'd agreed to take Joey. Thank God they were morning people. And thank God Joey had slept through the whole handoff process.

"Bonnie said she'll get someone else to handle the breakfast deliveries for the rest of the week while we're at Gayler Court," Cheryl said. Clutching the steering wheel, she watched the road ahead. She had the windshield wipers on delay. The rain wasn't too heavy, but it kept the dawn sky a dark gray.

Laurie squirmed in the passenger seat and remained quiet. Earlier, she'd been too rushed to think about anything beyond getting dressed and getting Joey over to the Cassellas. It had just started to sink in where they were headed.

"She's lucky I don't fire her ass," Cheryl went on. "Then again, she was pretty shaken up and apologetic. And after all, actually going inside the house wasn't in her job description."

It wasn't in my job description either, Laurie wanted to say. But she stayed silent.

"We should be out of there this morning by eight,"

Cheryl continued. "Then we'll head to the barn, load up Grill Girl II, drive back this way and be on schedule for lunch . . ."

Yesterday, they'd spent their afternoon at Cheryl's making potato salad and noodle salad, cutting up chicken to marinate, and doing other prep work for today. Laurie also baked chocolate chip "blond brownies" and frosted cookies. It was fun. Cheryl had *The Best of Bruce Springsteen* playing. Joey was at his busy desk, rocking along with the music. Then while she fed Joey his dinner, Cheryl cooked them up an impromptu dinner—delicious salmon tacos and dirty rice.

Laurie was having such a good time she didn't dare spoil the momentum by asking Cheryl what she'd been doing on Thursday afternoon with that thirtysomething, silver-haired man in Volunteer Park. She figured it was none of her business anyway.

She returned with Joey to their apartment last night, feeling content. After putting him to bed, she sat on the living room sofa with the laptop in front of her and the baby monitor on the end table. It was a novelty having him sleeping on a different floor. Laurie had decided to read up online about the "murder house," though at the time she hadn't figured on having to set foot inside the place.

Now she sort of wished she hadn't done the research. It probably would have been less stressful going into the house knowing very little about it.

While Cheryl drove, Laurie gazed out the window at the incredible view of the twinkling city lights and Elliott Bay from Magnolia. Even in the rainy dawn it was impressive—as were the homes in the area.

"Turn right on Gayler Court in approximately five hundred feet," the navigation system announced.

Laurie felt a nervous twinge in her stomach. She wished it were lighter out.

Hunched close to the wheel, Cheryl seemed to be searching for the street. "Remember, there will be at least a dozen technicians in the house when we get there," she said, almost as if she read her mind. "It's not like the two of us are going into this spooky old mansion alone with a couple of flashlights. Oh, here it is . . ."

She turned onto the narrow side street. Laurie didn't see any other houses, just trees and bushes. Up ahead, parked along the roadside was a white sedan with SE-CURITY printed on the back. Someone had set up orange cones.

"Your destination is on your left," the navigation system announced.

Cheryl slowed down. A heavyset black woman in a guard's uniform climbed out of the security car. Laurie rolled down her window. The guard had a plastic rain cover over the top of her guard hat. She gave them a big smile. "Here's breakfast!" the guard laughed. "We weren't sure we'd see this truck again. Your friend took one look at the place, turned around, and hightailed it out of here. Go on in. You'll have to lug everything in through the front. They have a truck blocking the back way. What's for lunch today?"

"The pulled pork is the best thing on the menu," Cheryl said. Then she pointed to Laurie. "And just wait until you try this one's blond brownies."

Laurie tried to work up a smile. But she kept staring

at the big, open metal gate—the same one Elaina Styles' bloodied nightgown had been tied to.

"By the way, just a heads-up," the guard said. "There might be more of us security folk when you come back here with the Grill Girl truck. We're expecting trouble."

"What do you mean?" Cheryl asked.

"Those nutty Hooper Anarchists or whatever they call themselves," the woman said. "They posted something online about how they were going to congregate around here today and do their damnedest to make noise, raise hell, and screw up the film shoot."

"Oh, Lord," Cheryl sighed. "Spare us . . ."

Laurie had read some more about the Hooper Anarchists that the *Entertainment Weekly* article had alluded to. A dozen to twenty idiots donning ski masks and Trent Hooper T-shirts had created a disturbance at two different shooting locations in Los Angeles. So far, they hadn't shown up at the Seattle locales. Laurie wondered if they really had enough clout to organize something here. Probably. If they could get themselves on TV or on the Internet—even with their faces covered— all sorts of morons would show up and create a disturbance for the sheer fun of it.

And then, of course, there were the ones who were dead serious.

"Save me one of those blond brownies," the guard said.

Laurie nodded at her. "I sure will."

She braced herself as Cheryl started down the driveway. Ahead, she saw two big trucks parked in a turnaround in front of the white, sixties-modern estate.

Even in the muted dawn light, Laurie could see that the lawn had been mowed, and the trees and hedges had been trimmed back. They'd spiffed up the house, too. Obviously, the filmmakers had tried to make the place look as it had in 1970.

She knew about its history. She'd seen photos of the place before the movie people had come along to give it a face-lift.

The owner back in 1970 had moved to Brentwood, and used the house as a rental. But once the murders occurred there, no one in their right mind wanted to lease the place. Besides, the house remained a crime scene—and uninhabitable—for well over a year. During that period, the police had a tough time keeping out adventurous high school and college kids.

According to the online article Laurie had read called "Haunted Seattle," this was when the house went from being a macabre landmark to something "truly evil and cursed." In 1971, a UW student snuck into the house through a kitchen window—the same window Trent Hooper's disciple (most likely Jed "JT" Dalton) had used to break into the place the year before. Once inside, the young man went upstairs, where he tied a rope around the railing that overlooked the spacious foyer. With the other end of the rope, he fashioned a noose, slipped it over his head, and made the fatal, aborted jump toward the foyer's tiled floor.

In 1972, a seventeen-year-old high school dropout stabbed his girlfriend to death—in the living room, where Elaina, her husband, and their nanny had been slain.

People who broke into the house for fun or on a dare

later talked about "cold spots" in different rooms. One girl, who managed to sneak into the mansion with two friends on a warm July night, swore they could all see their breath when they stood in a certain spot in baby Patrick's nursery. There were other reports—of strange, "almost human" sounds, and doors shutting on their own.

The trespassing got so bad that the Seattle Police put a patrol car on guard duty in the turnaround outside the house. Stories emerged from the cops that they'd seen and heard someone walking around inside the mansion when no one was really there. One officer, who refused to perform guard duty again, said he could hear what sounded like a baby crying inside the house. Another cop claimed the swing set in the backyard would go back and forth on its own, when there was no wind at all.

Laurie wasn't sure how much of this was truth or urban legend. The stories were hard to substantiate.

In 1977, the owner in Brentwood finally sold the Gayler Court property to a Phoenix millionaire named Conrad Ellison. He restored the place to its original opulence and amped up security. Ellison made it into his summer retreat, and according to a friend, he held séances there every July 7. By 2002, he was bedridden and died peacefully in his sleep at age eighty-six. His bedroom was the one Elaina and Dirk had occupied on the last night of their lives. Ellison willed the place to his nephew under the proviso that it not be torn down. Apparently, the nephew was given an allowance to maintain the estate.

But from the recent photos Laurie saw online, she

figured the maintenance money must have been spent somewhere else. The mansion had looked terribly neglected, even sinister. Then again, whoever posted the article online had probably wanted to create an impression that the place was indeed haunted. Under the comments section, someone wrote:

3/19/14, from Brad Reece, Seattle:

Good article! Last month, an unidentified homeless man was found inside the house (the living room, I think) with his throat slit. They said he'd been sleeping there for a while. As far as I know, the police are still investigating it. Sounds kind of strange to me. We don't get too many homeless people in that part of Magnolia. Anyway, the haunting continues. I wouldn't spend the night in that place for a million dollars.

The "murder house" didn't look quite as ominous now, with two big trucks parked outside, the lights blazing inside, and several technicians moving around. Still, there was a sort of somber quiet among the workers. And the morning mist gave the place an otherworldly glow.

Along with the dull rain, a night chill lingered in the air as Laurie helped Cheryl unload the boxes of pastries and baked goods from the minivan. Even when she saw the crew setting up lights and power batteries on the living room floor, Laurie still felt ill at ease crossing the threshold into the foyer. She thought of the violent murders in that room, and remembered the photo she'd glimpsed of Elaina—with the stab wounds in her back and her head completely turned around.

Laurie glanced up at the railing at the top of the curved staircase, and imagined the troubled UW student who had hung himself from there.

"The kitchen's thataway!" one of the technicians called to her. He pointed to a corridor on the other side of the stairs. "Need any help?"

"We sure do!" Cheryl replied, a little out of breath. "If you'll carry in one of the coffee urns, I'll see you get the first cup. Do the outlets work in there?"

"Tested and approved," he replied, brushing past them as he headed outside.

Laurie followed her into the kitchen. The house was drafty, with a musty smell—probably from being closed up for so long. She figured Conrad Ellison must not have been completely faithful to the original design when he'd had the place restored. The kitchen looked more like 1990s than the late sixties. The cabinets were a natural dark wood, and all the appliances were white. They must have worked, too, because she could hear the refrigerator humming. Laurie noticed two separate alcoves off the kitchen: one was a back stairwell and the other was a short hallway toward the back door. It looked like someone had given the place a thorough cleaning.

"I think this is a good place for the pastries," Cheryl said, setting two boxes on the counter. She still seemed to be out of breath. "We—we'll just leave everything in the boxes and put out plenty of napkins . . ."

As Laurie set down her two boxes, she noticed Cheryl—with a hand on her heart—glancing around the kitchen. She seemed to focus on the window by a built-in breakfast booth. Laurie wondered if that was the window the killers had used to enter the house that night exactly forty-four years ago.

She looked at Cheryl, whose face had turned white as chalk. "Are you okay?" Laurie asked.

She sighed. "I don't think I got enough sleep last night. I—"

A sudden, loud clatter interrupted her.

Startled, Laurie almost jumped out of her skin. She swiveled around and saw the technician in the kitchen entryway, holding one coffee urn. He'd dropped a second one.

The stainless steel urn rolled back and forth on the floor. The lid had flown off, and the pieces inside had spilled out.

Laurie caught her breath. "My God, you stopped my heart!" she laughed.

But then she turned to Cheryl, who had tears in her eyes. She held a hand over her mouth. She looked as if she were about to be sick.

"Cheryl?" she whispered.

She just shook her head and ran toward a little hallway off the kitchen. Laurie trailed after her, but Cheryl ducked into a bathroom. She slammed the door shut.

"Jesus, I'm really sorry," she heard the technician say. "I didn't mean to scare you guys. I don't think it's broken . . ."

Laurie watched him set the one urn on the counter. Then he started to pick up the pieces to the second one.

"It's okay," she said. She went to help him, but hesitated and glanced back at the bathroom door. Cheryl probably needed her help more.

Laurie wondered what was wrong with her. But she couldn't help being more concerned about something else.

How in the world had Cheryl known where the bathroom was?

CHAPTER NINETEEN

Monday, July 7, 11:08 A.M.

Adam heard the tires screech as he took another curve along Lake Washington Boulevard. He realized he was going forty-five miles per hour, fifteen miles over the speed limit. He wiped the tears from his face and told himself to slow down. His poor dad had already lost one son and a daughter-in-law today. That was enough.

His father didn't know about Dean and Joyce yet. As much as he dreaded telling him the news, Adam needed to be there when his dad found out.

The windshield wipers of his secondhand Mini Cooper whisked back and forth in the light rain. Adam eased up on the accelerator and maneuvered another curve in the winding, tree-lined road. He had the local news station on the radio—extra loud to keep him alert and focused. He was emotionally and physically exhausted. For the last seven hours, he'd been grilled by the police—first at the house, and then at the East Precinct on Capitol Hill.

Adam wasn't too familiar with details of the Elaina Styles murder case, and he didn't know anything about a film shooting in town. He'd never heard of the Hooper Anarchists. So when the police asked if he had any idea why his brother and sister-in-law had been chosen for these copycat murders, he didn't know what the hell they were talking about. Someone had to explain it to him. The police didn't say anything, but Adam had a feeling they considered him a suspect— maybe even their only suspect. He answered their questions as candidly as possible, and tried not to get testy when they asked the same questions again and again. He did break down and cry a few times under the grilling.

They let him call Evergreen Manor shortly after eight o'clock this morning. He asked the doctor in charge to make sure no one told his dad the news. He also asked if they could please keep him away from the TV or radio. He pictured his poor widowed father, confused and devastated—without anyone there to comfort him. He'd been a "resident" there for four months, and he still considered the doctors and nurses strangers and the other patients as "old geezers and loony cases." He was in the beginning stages of dementia. Shortly before Dean had moved him to Evergreen Manor, he'd fallen down the stairs at home and broken his leg. He was out of his cast, but still hobbled along with the help of a cane. Adam's dad was only sixty-nine years old, but in the last year he'd aged terribly. Today's news wasn't going to help any.

A patrolman had driven Adam home and told him that his basement apartment was part of the crime scene.

Adam found four squad cars parked in front of the house and about thirty onlookers in the street. To his surprise, there was only one TV news van—with a reporter and a cameraman beside it, sizing up the scene.

One of the cops by the front gate said he needed to clear it with one of them before he took anything out of his place. They'd already searched the Mini Cooper, and gave him the okay to take it and visit his dad. He told them he'd come back to pick up some of his things later.

He was still wearing the clothes he'd had on when he'd found Dean and Joyce on the living room floor. One glance at poor Joyce, and he'd seen she was dead. But he'd felt his brother's neck and his wrist for a pulse. He'd sobbed on his brother's shoulder once he'd verified that he was gone, too.

He wished like hell he and Dean hadn't fought. The last thing he said to his big brother had been a jab about how Dean made their father uncomfortable during his rare visits to Evergreen Manor.

Dean and Joyce had indeed been footing the bill for the rest home, and it obviously wasn't cheap. They had a top-notch professional staff, a cafeteria, a notions store, a gym, and a movie and game room. Since they catered mostly to the elderly, infirm, and early dementia patients, their security staff was always on the alert— not only for patients who might wander out of the building, but also for scam artists preying on the residents.

Evergreen Manor was about four blocks from University Village shopping mall. It was a sprawling, two-story redbrick building with white shutters. Except for a garden courtyard area, they didn't offer the residents much in the way of outside diversions—except some benches by the entrance. In nice weather, at least a dozen of them would congregate out there—in their wheelchairs and with their walkers that had the tennis balls fitted on the bottom back tips. They'd be dressed in anything from their pajamas and robes to their Sunday churchgoing best. Adam knew a lot of them by name—even though his dad still didn't.

As he pulled into Evergreen Manor's parking lot, Adam cringed at the mob scene by the building's front entrance. He pulled into a spot, shut off the Mini Cooper, and climbed out from behind the wheel. He watched a security guard arguing with one of the TV news van drivers. The poor guard was probably trying to get the driver to move out of the emergency zone. "Oh, shit," Adam murmured, counting one, two, three—four TV cameramen. The old-timers in their usual spot, protected from the rain under the front entrance canopy, seemed to enjoy the excitement and attention.

Adam stood in the drizzling rain for a moment, and took it all in. Now he knew why there had been only one TV news van in front of Dean and Joyce's house. The rest of them were here. They'd tracked down his poor, feeble dad, and wanted a statement from him.

His father had probably already been told that his older son and daughter-in-law were dead. Adam realized he was too late to be there and help cushion the blow for him.

With his arms crossed in front of him, he trotted toward Evergreen Manor's entrance. He tried not to make eye contact with anyone. He hoped to keep moving fast enough so that no one would notice the blood on his shirt.

"That's him!" said Dave, one of the residents. The old man in a cardigan and ugly golf pants was talking with a reporter near the entrance. "That's the brother, Adam . . ."

All at once, Adam found himself face-to-face with a small, smartly dressed, nipped-and-tucked, seventy-something blonde with a mic in her hand. It took him a moment to recognize Dolly Ingersoll, the show business gossip maven. She had a cameraman at her side. "Adam!" she said. "Why do you think your brother and his wife were targeted by these copycat killers?"

He just shook his head in her direction and kept moving through the crowd to the front door.

"What do you think of the Elaina Styles movie they're shooting here in town?" she called. "Do you think it prompted the murders?"

The other TV reporters zeroed in and fired questions at him, too. They were talking over one another when Adam ducked inside the building. He hurried to the front desk, and recognized the stout, copper-haired nurse on duty. She was around his father's age. "Hi, Jodi," he said, picking up the pen to sign the visitors' book.

"Adam, I'm so sorry to hear about your brother and sister-in-law," she murmured.

"Thank you." He signed in, and then looked at her warily. "Does—does my dad know?"

She winced. "Yes, I'm afraid so. We were trying to keep a lid on it, but that was kind of tough with the three-ring circus going on outside. One of the other residents told him."

Adam sighed. "Oh, God, how is he? Do you know?"

"He's in his room. One of the therapists was in there with him a while ago."

Adam thanked her and hurried down the corridor to his father's room.

There were touches of home in the small unit, which had a hospital bed in the middle of it. Framed family photos adorned the dresser and nightstand—including his parents' wedding portrait, and Dean and Joyce's wedding photo. His father had insisted on having a couple of Adam's paintings on the walls. There wasn't enough room for his dad's big screen TV, so he had to settle for a twenty-nine-inch model. But he'd managed to squeeze in his own Barcalounger from home. He sat there now, in a plaid shirt and navy blue pants that showed a bit of his white legs over the sock lines. He was still a good-looking man. His wavy white hair needed a trim, but it was carefully combed. He had the TV on mute, but was staring out the rain-beaded window at the garden.

There was no sign of the therapist. Adam couldn't tell whether or not his dad was fully functioning right now. "Pop?" he said, stepping inside.

His father grabbed his cane and got up from the chair. "Aw, poor Adam," he said. "You poor guy, they said you're the one who found them . . ." He hobbled over to him, opened his arms and fiercely hugged him. The old man still smelled of Mennen Speed Stick. He patted Adam on the back. "Isn't it awful?" he whispered.

Adam had hurried here to help his senile father through this. But his dad was lucid, and comforting him. Adam didn't expect this, and he didn't expect to start weeping again. He clung to his dad. "I don't understand it," he cried. "Why Dean and Joyce? I don't understand why this happened . . ."

His father kept patting him on the back. "I think they were getting even," he said.

Adam pulled back to stare at him. His father looked clear-eyed and cognizant. "Who's 'they'?" Adam asked. "What are you talking about, Dad?"

In response, the old man tenderly put a hand to Adam's face and wiped the tears away. He gave him a sad smile. Then those clear, old eyes of his seemed to glaze over. Leaning on his cane, he made his way back to the Barcalounger and sat down.

"Dad, what are you talking about?" Adam asked. "Who's getting even—and what for?"

His father gazed out at the garden.

"Dad?" Adam said,

He seemed unreachable now, in his own little world.

"Looks like the rain stopped," the old man murmured—as if talking to himself.

CHAPTER TWENTY

"Look at those bloody morons," said Danny in his crisp accent. He wore jeans and an untucked striped shirt with the sleeves rolled up. Holding an umbrella over his head, he stood about a third of the way into the driveway of the Gayler Court house.

Laurie and he were watching a demonstration by at least thirty Hooper Anarchists outside the front gate. Most everyone in the group wore scarves over the bottoms of their faces or ski masks. About half of them sported Trent Hooper T-shirts or sweatshirts. They'd started gathering out there at ten o'clock. Cheryl and Laurie had returned in the food truck around the same time. The rowdy group screamed and chanted. Some brought tin lids from garbage cans to bang together— anything to make noise so they could screw up the film shoot. One of them even yelled through a bullhorn— until a cop took it away from him. The protestors were nearly matched in their numbers by policemen, security people, and TV reporters on the scene.

"They wouldn't be carrying on like this if the television news people weren't here," Danny pointed out. "They're feeding off each other."

So far, the demonstrators hadn't interrupted much. The crew had spent most of the morning setting up lights and sound while the director rehearsed with Paige and Shane and other people in the scene. They hadn't shot anything yet. That was scheduled for after lunch. By then, they'd hoped the idiot protestors would get tired of standing out there in the rain.

After Cheryl's little breakdown at the start of the day, the rest of the morning had gone pretty smoothly. She'd spent about five minutes in the bathroom, before emerging with her face washed and her eyes slightly pink. "Sorry about that," she'd said, getting back to work on the breakfast spread. "I was trying to act so nonchalant. I guess I was a little more squeamish about this place than I wanted to let on. How's the coffee urn? Did it survive the crash?"

Later, between the meal services, while returning to Gayler Court in the food truck, Laurie had tried to think of a casual way to ask Cheryl about something that had been bothering her most of the morning.

"Well, at least we won't have to work inside that house again," she said, watching Cheryl at the wheel. "You must be almost as relieved as I am . . ."

"Actually, we'll have to go back into the kitchen to set up your blond brownies and the cookies—and make sure there's enough coffee and soda," Cheryl replied, eyes on the road. "But you don't have to worry about that. I'll handle it alone."

"Are you sure you'll be okay? I mean, earlier this morning, when we first stepped into the kitchen—"

"I'll be fine," Cheryl said, cutting her off.

"I wanted to ask you something about that. How did you know where the bathroom was?"

Cheryl had shot her a look. "What are you talking about?"

"When you ran to the bathroom, you seemed to know just where it was. Yet that was your first time inside the house, right?"

Cheryl said nothing for a moment. She kept her eyes on the road. "I got a look at the layout ahead of time," she finally replied. "I asked for a diagram of the house so Bonnie would know where to set up this morning. You know, Isernio's makes a good chicken bratwurst. I was thinking about adding a bratwurst sandwich this week—maybe with some melted provolone on a potato bun . . ."

The not-too-subtle subject change wasn't lost on Laurie, who decided to drop it. But she knew Cheryl was lying. The original plan had been to set up breakfast in a tent outside, but the rain had made them move it inside to the kitchen.

Once they'd finished with the lunch rush, Laurie told Cheryl she needed to stretch her legs. What she really wanted to do was talk with the production assistant, Danny, to see if there was any truth in Cheryl's diagram story.

She'd found him here in the driveway, watching these obnoxious protesters. She figured the TV news cameras were focused on them—and not her. She was far enough away that no one would take her picture.

A few protesters were really laying it on thick for the cameras, too—yelling and shoving their fists in the air. One of them hurled a rock at a policeman, which erupted into a small skirmish. Two cops grabbed him and wrestled him to the ground—amid outcries from several of the rock-thrower's fellow anarchists.

"God, what a mess," Danny sighed. "We better hightail it out of here, before they start throwing things at us."

Huddled beneath their umbrellas, Laurie and Danny headed back toward the house. "Cheryl mentioned that someone gave her a diagram of the house," Laurie said ever so casually. "Was that you or one of the other production guys?"

He squinted at her. "A diagram of this place? You mean a layout of where the rooms are and all that?"

Laurie nodded. "Cheryl said somebody gave her one so the breakfast woman would know where to set up the coffee and pastries."

He shook his head. "You must have misheard her. Besides, we didn't know until early this morning that we'd be using the kitchen. Good thing they cleaned it ahead of time. Anyway, as far as I know, the only thing close to a diagram we have is a rough sketch of the grounds—so we could figure out where to park the trucks. Maybe that's what Cheryl was talking about."

"No, she said she had a diagram of the kitchen and the bathroom in back."

He shook his head again. "The set designer came up with some sketches and maps of the house, but there's no reason Cheryl would be getting those. Anyway, the kitchen area isn't even in there."

Laurie stopped walking for a moment. "It isn't?"

"The kitchen in this house is a remodel from the nineties," he explained. "They built a set in L.A. to match the original 1968 kitchen. We shot all the kitchen scenes in the studio three weeks ago. That's the set that caught on fire. Anyway, we don't have any kind of diagram showing the kitchen in this house, because we're not using it. I don't know what Cheryl's talking about."

Laurie said nothing.

Danny gave her a nudge. "Are you all right?"

She nodded. "Ah, I must have misheard her. Could you do me a favor and not say anything to Cheryl about this? I wouldn't want her to think I wasn't listening to her when she's telling me something."

Before Danny could answer, his cell phone rang. Under her umbrella, Laurie stayed beside him while he answered it.

"Hello, this is Danny," he said into the phone. Then he listened. "I'm here about halfway down the drive-way chatting with Laurie . . . yes, Laurie from the food truck . . ." The noise from the protestors swelled. "What?" he said into the phone. "Oh, God, that's terrible . . . Are they connected to the film? Anyone we know?" He paused. "Uh-huh . . . Well, I doubt they'll shut down for the rest of afternoon. It would cost them about thirty thousand dollars. That much respect for the victims they don't have . . . Yeah, well, okay. I'm on my way there now. Bye." He clicked off and shoved the cell phone back inside his pants pocket.

"What happened?" Laurie asked.

He slowly shook his head. "A Seattle couple was murdered last night, a copycat killing—just like Elaina and Dirk. The wife's nightgown was found on the front gate of the house. The killers snapped her neck and twisted her head around."

The protesters started screaming louder and banged their garbage can lids. Danny glanced back at them with annoyance. "I wonder if any of those assholes are responsible . . ."

Laurie shuddered. "Were there—were there any children?"

"No, just the husband and wife," he said. "A couple named Holbrook. They're not connected to the movie . . ."

Laurie closed her umbrella and shook off the excess water. Then she stepped inside the food truck to find Cheryl had practically everything put away and cleaned up. Her boss was giving the food-prep area a final wipe down with a spray bottle of Lysol countertop cleanser and a sponge.

"I'm sorry," Laurie said, standing in the doorway. "I could have helped take care of that. I didn't mean to ditch you during the cleanup."

"Hey, you needed the walk," Cheryl replied, not looking up from her work. "Believe me, I know what it's like to start feeling cooped up in here." She glanced out the order window. "What's going on?"

Over Cheryl's shoulder, Laurie could see several people gathered under the canopy of a large half-tent pitched beside them on the driveway. One of the crew-men hurried past them.

"Hey, what's happening?" Cheryl called.

"There's a report on TV about the copycat murders!" he replied, looking over his shoulder at them.

Cheryl turned to Laurie. "Do you know what he's talking about?"

Wincing a little, Laurie nodded. "I just found out about it. A couple was killed—just like Elaina and Dirk. They even broke the woman's neck and twisted her head around."

"Oh, Lord," Cheryl murmured. "That's awful . . ."

"Danny said he was pretty sure they weren't connected to the filming. I think he said the last name was Holbrook."

"What?" Cheryl whispered, her eyes widening. She took a step back and bumped into the counter. The Lysol spray container slipped out of her hand.

"Did you know them?"

"No, I—" Cheryl shook her head again. Her face turned ashen.

"Danny thought maybe one of those crazy Hooper Anarchists might be responsible," Laurie said. "Or maybe it has something to do with the anniversary . . ."

Cheryl shot a quick glance out the order window again. Tossing aside the sponge, she almost knocked Laurie over as she hurried out the door.

Stepping over cables, Laurie followed her to the half tent, where at least a dozen members of the crew had gathered. They huddled around a TV monitor on a tall metal stand. Over the tops of several heads, Laurie saw Dolly Ingersoll on the monitor.

"Well, that explains why Dolly wasn't hanging around here today," she heard one of the crew people say. "But what's she doing covering real hard-hitting news?"

"It's show business," another one replied. "Or at least, show-biz-related . . ."

Laurie tried to keep under the canopy, but she was edged out by the crowd. She felt the drizzle on the back of her neck. Cheryl was in the same predicament, but she didn't seem to notice the precipitation. She was gazing at the screen.

"I'm told Adam Holbrook has just arrived," said Dolly into a handheld mic. *"He is the younger brother and brother-in-law of the two victims. He discovered them dead in their home early this morning . . ."*

The picture switched to a thin, handsome man who looked haggard as he made his way through a crowd of reporters and bystanders. The shirt he wore was smeared with blood.

"Adam!" Dolly said, lunging at him with the mic in her hand. *"Why do you think your brother and his wife were targeted by these copycat killers?"*

He shook his head and moved on.

Laurie turned to Cheryl. "Are you sure you don't know these people?" she whispered. "Because when I said Holbrook, you went white as a—"

Cheryl shushed her. "I'm trying to watch this."

On the TV screen, Dolly faced the camera. Laurie noticed several of the bystanders surrounding her were elderly. *"That was Adam Holbrook, here to console his widower father. Adam Holbrook, once again, is the brother of Dean Holbrook, one of the victims of the Styles-Jordan copycat killing. Holbrook and his wife,*

Joyce were brutally murdered in their home early this morning . . ."

Then the image changed to a photograph of an attractive couple, which must have been taken at a swanky party. Both were dressed semiformally, and they had cocktails in their hands as they smiled for the camera.

"I'm told Dean and Joyce Holbrook were quite active in Seattle social circles," Dolly was saying in voice-over.

The wife was pretty with short brown hair. But Laurie barely noticed her. She was staring at the doomed husband. That good looking man with the salt-and-pepper hair had been in Volunteer Park with Cheryl four days ago. Laurie could still see them arguing by the donut sculpture.

She turned to Cheryl again. "You *do* know them," she whispered. "I saw you talking to that man in Volunteer Park on Thursday . . ."

Cheryl frowned at her. "No, you didn't."

"But I did. I think you saw me, too—"

"No, you're wrong," she hissed, eyes still narrowed at her. "I don't know what you're talking about. I've never seen that man before. You're mistaken, Laurie. Now would you please quit interrupting? I'm trying to watch this, for God's sake."

Cheryl turned, folded her arms, and focused once again on the TV screen.

Laurie studied her stern profile, and noticed she was trembling a bit.

She glanced around to see if anyone else had caught

Cheryl snapping at her. They were all too busy watching Dolly Ingersoll on TV. She remembered what Dolly had said to Cheryl last week: *"You're not just here to serve up food. You're after something, I can tell . . ."*

Laurie took a step back—to put some distance between her and Cheryl. She knew her boss was lying. But she'd been silenced.

So she stood there in the rain and didn't say another word.

CHAPTER TWENTY-ONE

Monday, 3:47 P.M.

Laurie stopped at the mailboxes just inside the courtyard entrance. In the box marked number 3, she found her first bill to the new address—from Visa. There was also something that looked like junk mail for Maureen Forester. Laurie was too tired to mark it *No longer at this address—Deceased.* Or maybe just writing *Deceased* on the envelope was enough. Whatever, this one was going into recycling. She treaded toward her apartment. The surprise early wake-up call, the ten hours of work, and dealing with Cheryl today had taken their toll on her.

She remembered her mother had once quit a job after only six days. She seriously considered doing the same thing today.

Cheryl had dropped her off at the front gate, because she'd needed to gas up the food truck. Laurie was glad to get the hell away from her for a while. She was still upset over that news report on the copycat killings. She wasn't mistaken about the man who was murdered.

Cheryl was lying—and about something that was deadly serious. Laurie had seen her in the park on Thursday with Dean Holbrook. Cheryl denying it and snapping at her didn't change the truth one bit. It merely shut Laurie up.

So, for the last two hours, including what seemed like an excruciatingly long drive home, she hadn't said another word to her boss about the copycat killings. She'd barely said anything at all. She'd remained icily polite to Cheryl. Her boss had punctuated the awkward silence in the truck by mentioning every few minutes something about this week's menu items or their work schedule. But all the while, Laurie had sensed her anxiety. She'd wanted to tell her: *I understand what a shock this is for you. Someone you know was just murdered—and it's connected to the movie we're working on. Or maybe the connection is a lot deeper, only you won't tell me. I'd help you if I could, but you're shutting me up and shutting me out. So screw you . . .*

Now she knew why Maureen never trusted her. And Dolly Ingersoll sure had Cheryl pegged: *"You're bad news, I can tell."* People around Cheryl were dying. Laurie wondered if she was better off taking her chances with Ryder and company in Ellensburg.

She wished there was someone she could talk to. She wasn't about to call the police. Besides, what could she tell them? She'd seen her boss talking with Dean Holbrook four days before his murder. It was hardly incriminating—just unsettling in the way Cheryl had vehemently denied it.

She didn't want to get Cheryl into any trouble. Cheryl had given her this break, hired her, and found her a nice place to live. If that wasn't enough, she remembered how Cheryl had run interference for her with Dolly Ingersoll—and she'd never asked for any explanations.

Inside the apartment, Laurie tossed the mail on a table in the living room and headed upstairs. She peeled off her clothes, which at this point stank of grease and cooked meat. As she stood in the tub under the warm shower, she imagined her predecessor, Maureen, in this exact same spot, washing off the food truck stink, too.

Her hair was still damp when she went three doors down to pick up Joey. She brought a Tupperware container of cookies and brownies for the Cassellas. She paid them to look after Joey, but it wasn't much.

Tammy met her at the door with Joey in her chubby arms. Laurie heard the TV on in the living room, just around the corner from the vestibule where they stood. She gave Tammy the container of goodies as an apology for dumping Joey on them so early in the morning. Tammy insisted he wasn't any trouble.

All the while, Joey tugged at the gold locket Tammy wore on a chain around her neck. She was a stout woman with short, layered gray-auburn hair. "Well, we almost got it on video," Tammy said, handing Joey off to her. "He took a step and a half today."

"Oh, no, and I missed it!" Laurie moaned. Not being there for so many of Joey's little milestones broke her heart. And right now, having him kick and fuss as she took him from the sitter didn't help her disposition any either.

"How was your day?" Tammy asked.

"Not terrific," Laurie replied. She figured Tammy didn't expect a long answer to her polite question. But Laurie couldn't help it. "You know, I have to tell you," she said, gently bouncing Joey in her arms so he'd quiet down. "I've been working alongside Cheryl for over a week now, and—well, I like her, but she's hard to get to know. I keep wondering if it's just me. You were friends with Maureen. How did she and Cheryl get along?"

Tammy gave an awkward shrug. "Well, we don't know Cheryl very well either. Then again, she's always terribly busy. I think when Maureen first started working with her she was in the same boat as you are now. In fact, when Cheryl moved in across the courtyard, Maureen asked Hank and me to let her know if she acted peculiar in any way. I remember thinking that was an odd request—especially since Maureen was responsible for her getting the apartment . . ."

Laurie kept rocking Joey in her arms. She thought about how Maureen had warned Vincent not to get too close to Cheryl. It certainly was odd that she'd bring someone into the apartment complex—and then caution the neighbors about her. Why would she do that? The only thing Laurie could think of was silly—a line from one of Brian's favorite movies, *The Godfather II*: "Keep your friends close, and your enemies closer."

"Do you . . ." Laurie hesitated. "Do you think Maureen might have wanted Cheryl as a neighbor so she could keep an eye on her or something?"

Tammy let out a puzzled laugh. "You got me. But that's an interesting question. I think they got to be better friends as time passed. Just earlier this month, I mentioned as much to Maureen. She said it was funny

I should bring that up, because she'd recently found out something about Cheryl which made the two of them *almost like family.* I don't know what it was, but—"

"Laurie, are you still here?" Hank called from the living room—over the TV noise.

"Hi, Hank," she called. "Thanks so much for rescuing us this morning—"

"Get in here," he said. "I think you're on TV!"

Laurie balked. A twinge of panic tugged at her stomach. She held Joey a little tighter as she followed Tammy into the living room. Hank Cassella sat in his recliner with both feet up. He wore plaid shorts and a gray sports shirt that matched the color of his receding hair. An ice pack rested on one knee. "Sorry I can't get up," he said. The big flat-screen TV was reflecting off his glasses and he held the remote in his hand. The image on the screen was frozen—and slightly blurry. The Hooper Anarchists were putting on their show for the cameras in front of the house on Gayler Court. The CNN logo was in the right bottom corner of the screen.

"I think I just spotted you on your movie set," Hank explained. He pressed the remote, and the image on the big screen went into reverse. Laurie saw him skip by a shot of the house. "Here it is," he said. The image froze, and then went to normal speed again with a lingering look at the "murder house." Huddled under their umbrellas, she and Danny stood in the driveway. The shot was just close enough and lasted just long enough for Hank to recognize her—Hank and anyone else who might be looking for her.

"Isn't that you?" he asked.

"Yes," she said, swallowing hard.

"Did you see Mommy on TV?" Tammy asked Joey in a cheery, excited tone.

"Sit down, take a load off," Hank said. "This is running right now on CNN. Let's see if they show you again . . ."

But Laurie remained standing. She rocked Joey in her arms and stared at the TV.

"*. . . a production plagued with protests and catastrophes,*" Dolly Ingersoll announced. "*And today, on the anniversary of the slayings . . .*"

It wasn't the same broadcast from a couple of hours ago. Dolly must have updated it—and procured from someone else the footage shot during the demonstration.

"Look at those creeps," Hank said. On-screen, the protestors were confronting police. "They won't even show their faces, so you know they've come to make trouble . . ."

"Honey, please, we're trying to watch this," Tammy said.

The picture switched to a shot of a stately brick house—with squad cars and onlookers outside the big gate in front. "*Here, in this beautiful home, in one of the most desirable neighborhoods in Seattle, Dean and Joyce Holbrook were brutally slain . . .*"

"That's Washington Park," Hank said. "It's barely a mile away . . ."

"I'm double locking our doors tonight," Tammy murmured.

"*. . . found Joyce's bloodied nightgown hanging from the front gate,*" Dolly continued. "*Inside the house, on a turntable in Dean Holbrook's study was Dirk Jor-*

dan's LP 'Immortal,' just as forty-four years ago, police found the same record album on the stereo in the living room where Dirk, Elaina, and their baby boy's nanny were murdered." The image on-screen switched to the same shot Laurie had seen earlier—of Dean and Joyce Holbrook dressed to the nines at a social function. *"Most horrific of all similarities was what the copycat killer—or killers—did to Joyce Holbrook. Like Elaina Styles, her neck was broken, and her head turned completely around . . ."*

"I wouldn't have thought the police would allow her to give out all these details," Hank remarked.

"We should turn this off," Tammy said. "This can't be good stimulation for the baby . . ."

"Oh, for Pete's sake, he doesn't understand," Hank retorted. "Besides, I want to see if they show Laurie again."

At the moment, they showed the brother, trying to dodge Dolly as he entered a building. It was the same footage Laurie had seen a couple of hours ago. She winced at his blood-smeared shirt. *"The bodies were discovered by Holbrook's brother, Adam, a local artist, who lives in the basement apartment of their home,"* Dolly went on. *"Adam Holbrook told police that loud music and screams woke him some time after two o'clock this morning. I tried to speak with him here outside Evergreen Manor, where he came to break the disturbing, tragic news to his father, a resident at the retirement facility . . ."*

"You can tell Dolly's had work done," Tammy commented.

But Laurie wasn't listening. She was trying to remember where she'd heard the name Evergreen Manor before. Was it from Cheryl?

On the screen, Dolly stood with a handheld mic in front of the house on Gayler Court. "The Seattle Police are currently following leads, but they're without a suspect in this morning's brutal copycat slaying. Meanwhile, here at the actual Styles-Jordan murder house, the cameras continue to roll for the film *7/7/70* on this forty-fourth anniversary of the slayings. This is Dolly Ingersoll reporting . . ."

"Thank you for that special report, Dolly," the handsome anchorman said. *"I understand you're writing a book about the murders of Elaina Styles and Dirk Jordan . . ."*

The picture switched back to Dolly, still in front of the Gayler Court house. There was obviously a slight delay in the feed, because she just stared blankly at the camera for a moment, before replying: *"Yes, Tyler, my book, 'Slain Star, The Elaina Styles Story,' will be out this fall, months before the film release of '7/7/70.' It's a serious piece of investigative journalism, and some might say a real departure for me. But I promise you, my book will rip the lid off the Styles-Jordan murder case. I wouldn't be a bit surprised if police reopen the case and some arrests are made. Of course, there will also be exclusive coverage of the movie-in-the-making, and this disturbing new development today with the copycat killings."*

The anchorman came back on the screen. *"That was CNN correspondent Dolly Ingersoll in Seattle,"* he said. *"In Phoenix this morning, a deadly five car pileup—"*

"Well, I guess they won't show you again, at least

not until they rerun this in a couple of hours," Hank said, putting the TV on mute.

Laurie was barely listening to him. She was still thinking about Evergreen Manor. Cheryl had talked about the place. It was after the chicken wraps dinner that night when Cheryl had gotten pretty tipsy: *"You don't happen to have relatives with any pull at Evergreen Manor, do you? It's kind of a rest home. I'm trying to get a gig with them, too . . ."*

Was that the reason for the meeting with Dean Holbrook in the park on Thursday? Maybe she was asking for his help in getting her a catering gig at the rest home where his father resided. Or was it something more than that? It had to be. Why else would she so hotly deny ever talking to him?

"Laurie?" Tammy said.

She turned to her and blinked. Joey let out a tired, hungry cry.

"You left us for a little while there," Tammy laughed.

"Oh, I'm just a bit battle-fatigued from work," she said, rocking Joey again. "I should scoot. Thanks for letting me drop off Joey so early today. It should be the regular time tomorrow." She worked up a smile for Hank. "Thanks for letting me know about my TV debut."

"Want us to DVR it next time it comes on?" he asked.

"No, but thanks anyway." She nuzzled Joey's cheek. "Wave good night to Hank and Tammy, sweetie," she said.

He obliged her, and the older couple made a big deal out of saying good-bye to him. He kept waving at Tammy as she walked them to the door and handed Laurie her baby bag full of supplies.

Laurie stepped outside, but then turned to Tammy in the doorway. "You know when we were talking earlier? You mentioned Maureen had found out something about Cheryl that made them almost like family. Did you ever find out what it was?"

Tammy shook her head. "No, I didn't."

"Do you know if she ever talked to Cheryl about it?"

"I have no idea." With a sad look on her careworn face, Tammy gave a helpless shrug. "I'm afraid you'll have to ask Cheryl. You see, just a couple days after Maureen and I had that conversation, she died in the explosion, the poor thing."

"Oh, I see," Laurie murmured, rocking Joey in her arms. She gave her a pale smile. "Well, thanks, Tammy."

"See you tomorrow," her neighbor said. "Take care."

With her face pressed against the top of Joey's head, Laurie retreated toward home. She heard the door close behind her—and then the lock clicking.

CHAPTER TWENTY-TWO

Monday, 5:35 P.M.

"Oh, Adam, no . . . my God, no . . ."

The woman on the other end of the line was Adam's cousin, Judy, and she was crying. She lived in Milwaukee with her husband and three kids. Along with his dad, they were Adam's only living blood relatives. Her mother and Adam's mom had been sisters. Adam hadn't talked with Judy in at least two years, and now he was on the phone telling her that his brother and sister-in-law had been murdered.

"I'm—I'm so sorry, Adam," she wept. "Can you—can you please hold on for a minute? I can't . . ."

There was a thump. She'd obviously put the phone down, but he still heard her muffled sobs. There was nothing he could say or do to console her. There was no silver lining to any of this. Dean and Joyce had died horribly. He remembered Joyce's terror-filled scream directly above him. He'd seen what they'd done to her.

Earlier tonight, he'd gone back to the house to pick up some of his things. The cop on duty had also let him copy down some phone numbers from Joyce's address book. Though nice enough, the cop had also been pretty tactless, mentioning offhand that early reports indicated Joyce had been stabbed thirteen times, and Dean, twenty-eight times.

Apparently, that had been the exact same number of stab wounds inflicted on Elaina Styles and Dirk Jordan.

Adam had found a temporary place to stay courtesy of his Capitol Hill friends, Dave and Stafford. They'd recently adopted a baby girl, Thea. In fact, Joyce had just been at their house yesterday to talk with them about the adoption process. Adam had studied art with Dave, who had a combination art studio/guest apartment above their garage—complete with a bathroom, kitchen area, and a sofa bed. They were happy to let Adam stay there—especially since they were headed out of town in a day, and needed someone to look after the house, collect the mail, and water the plants while they were away.

It was just what Adam needed, a place to be alone where the TV news people couldn't find him. Right now, he sat on the sofa with two suitcases in front of him, and a view out the window of treetops. He was running on about two hours of sleep and no food. He figured he'd eat something after he made these calls.

He'd already broken the news to Dean and Joyce's friends, the ones whose numbers were in Joyce's address book. A few of them had already heard about the murders, but for others, it was a shock—and there were tears, even hysterics in a couple of cases. Adam also had made calls to several old family friends, some who hadn't even known about his dad's dementia. So it had been a double dose of bad news.

He had one more family friend to call after Judy, and he dreaded it. His uncle Marty and aunt Doris were Dean's godparents. His dad and Marty went way back. Marty drove up from Tacoma once a week to visit his father at Evergreen Manor. Adam was putting the call off for last.

He heard another little thump on the other end of the line. "I'm sorry, cuz," said Judy, her voice a bit scratchy from crying. "It's such a blow about your dad's condition, too. I had no idea . . ."

"Neither did we until just a few months ago," Adam said.

"Does Uncle Dino—does your dad understand what happened to Dean and Joyce?"

"Yes, he was comforting me, which is typical. I just left him about a half hour ago. He's doing all right—considering. They're keeping a close eye on him tonight." With the phone to his ear, Adam squirmed on the sofa, and hunched forward. "Listen, I feel funny bringing this up, Jude. But my dad said the damnedest thing. I asked him why anyone would do that to Dean and Joyce. Why this copycat killing? I wasn't really expecting an answer or anything. But Pop said, 'I think they were getting even.'"

There was silence on the other end.

"I couldn't help wondering what he meant," Adam went on. "I mean, *getting even* for what? Had my dad done something? Anyway, it got me thinking. Dean was always saying that I really didn't know our dad. He gave me the impression that my dad had done something really awful at one time . . ."

"Your sweet father? My uncle Dino? Are you serious?"

"I know, it's crazy," Adam said. He hated having to ask her about such things. Dean had held it over his head for so long. Now his brother was taking that old family secret to his grave. Adam doubted he'd ever get anything out of his dad. Even if his father could remember past the dementia, if this secret was as shameful as Dean had let on, then their father wasn't about to tell him.

"I thought my mom might have said something to your mom," he explained. "You know, a secret between the sisters . . ."

"We have some fairly juicy scandals on our side of the family, but I never heard a bad word about your father, Adam."

"I just keep thinking about what he said, 'They were getting even.'"

"Well, maybe it was the dementia talking," his cousin offered.

"Maybe," Adam granted. But his father had seemed lucid when he'd said it.

Adam had asked a couple of his dad's buddies about it when he'd phoned them. But like his cousin, they didn't seem to know what the hell he was talking about. Adam figured he probably shouldn't have brought it up—not even to close family friends. Maybe it was better off staying buried. Yet if this family secret had something to do why Dean and Joyce were murdered, he needed to know what it was.

"Have you made the funeral arrangements yet?" Judy asked.

"No, not yet," he said. "They have to do the autopsies first. The funeral probably won't be until next week."

"Well, I don't think Bill and the kids can make it, but I'd like to be there for you . . ."

"That's sweet, but I don't want you going to a lot of expense—"

He heard a beep on the line. Adam quickly straightened up on the couch. "Judy, can you hold on?" he asked. "I have another call . . ." He glanced at the caller ID on his device: CONNELLY, MARTIN 360-555-1708. His uncle Marty must have received the news from someone else. Adam got back on the line. "Judy, I'm sorry, I need to take this. I'll send you an e-mail when I figure out the funeral arrangements, but please, don't feel under any obligation, okay?"

"We'll talk in a couple of days, cuz. You take care." From the cracks in her voice, he could tell she was starting to cry again. "Give my love and condolences to your dad."

"I will," he said. "Thanks, Judy."

He got to his feet, and clicked onto the other call before it went to voice mail. "Uncle Marty?"

"How are you holding up, kid?" he asked.

"I'm hanging in there," Adam replied, but he started to tear up. Marty always had a kind of likable gruff manner. It threw Adam for a loop to hear him sounding so uncharacteristically tender. He wiped his tears away, and paced back and forth in front of the window. "I was just about to call you and Aunt Doris. I had a list of people to phone with the news, and kept shoving you guys farther down to the bottom. I knew you'd take it the hardest. I'm sorry. How did you find out?"

"From one of the guys higher up on your list," Marty replied. "Your aunt Doris is in the can right now, having herself a good cry. She'll call you back in a few minutes. But right now, I need to speak to you alone before you call anyone else . . ."

Uncle Marty's gruff manner was back. In fact, the old man sounded as if he were annoyed with him.

"Okay," Adam said tentatively. He stopped pacing.

"I know you've had a big shock and a rough-as-hell day, but you need to be a little more careful about what you're saying to people."

"I'm not sure what you mean."

"This talk about a dark secret in your dad's past, and someone 'getting even' with those copycat killings, it's kind of reckless, kid. You're better off keeping a lid on that. Your dad isn't in any shape to defend himself against any accusation or explain things. So, just let it go. Leave it alone."

"Leave *what* alone?" Adam asked. "Uncle Marty, I don't know what it is Pop was supposed to have done. That's why I'm asking around. Dean often alluded to something, but he wouldn't tell me. If it has anything to do with what happened to Dean and Joyce, don't you think I have a right to know?"

"Like I said, just leave it alone," he replied. "You can't keep asking people about this. You ask the wrong person, and you'll end up like your brother."

"Then there's a connection," Adam said. "This wasn't just some random killing. Uncle Marty, the police don't have any suspects right now—except maybe me. Obviously, you know something—"

"I don't know a goddamn thing," Marty growled. "I'm just saying family secrets should stay inside the family. Quit asking stupid questions. People are grieving. Now, I don't want to hear another word about this."

"Listen, I can't pretend like—"

"What the hell did I just tell you?" Marty cut him off. "Doris will call you in a few minutes, and I don't want you bothering her with any of this bullshit. Got that?"

"So there's this—*thing* hanging out there, and it may have something to do with why Dean and Joyce were killed. But I'm supposed to forget about it. Is that right?"

"Exactly. I'll drive up to see your dad tomorrow morning. And I don't want you bothering him about this either. Believe me, it's all for your own good. Otherwise, how are you holding up, kid?"

Adam let out a dazed, pathetic laugh. "I'm lousy."

"Same here," he said. "Hell of a thing. I'll talk to you tomorrow. You can expect your Aunt Doris to call in a few minutes. Expect some waterworks, too. She's taking it pretty bad."

"Okay," Adam said. "Thanks, Uncle Marty."

"I mean it about keeping your mouth shut," he said. "If you don't, you better start watching your back, kid."

Adam heard a click on the other end of the line, and then it went dead.

CHAPTER TWENTY-THREE

"**D**o you have a couple of minutes?" Laurie asked. With Joey in her arms, she stood at Brenda's door. She'd been getting ready to make cupcakes for tomorrow. But when she'd heard Brenda come home from work, she'd scooped up Joey and hurried outside to the next door down.

Brenda seemed a little reluctant to let her in. She stood in the doorway with one hand on the knob. Her dark blond hair was pulled back into a ponytail again, and she wore a maroon top with khaki slacks. "You aren't going to ask me to look after your child, are you?" she said. "Because I'm not good with kids. They don't like me."

"Oh, no," Laurie said. "I've been thinking about something you said to me the other day about Maureen and Cheryl . . ."

"Well, if we're going to talk about the neighbors, you better step inside." Brenda opened the door wider. The apartment layout was similar to Laurie's, and the furnishings looked like Pottery Barn's finest. But Brenda was a slob. A pillow from the bedroom was propped on one end of the sofa, and nearby, within reaching distance, were two TV tables full of glasses and old dirty plates. The big screen TV was on mute. A litter box sat in the middle of the living room—and it needed cleaning. The apartment smelled. "That's Mr. Darcy," Brenda said, pointing to an orange tabby parked in an easy chair, which had a T-shirt slung over one arm. "Mr. Darcy, this is Laura . . ."

"Laurie," she gently corrected her, "and Joey."

Brenda reached into her purse—on a side table stacked with old junk mail. She pulled out a pack of Winstons. "So, after a week of working with Miss Thing across the way, I guess you must have some issues." She lit a cigarette. "If you're one of those anti-smoking Nazis, feel free to open the door."

"That's all right," Laurie said. Brenda hadn't asked her to sit down, and Laurie figured she wouldn't stay long. She'd get Joey in the fresh air again within a couple of minutes. "Actually, Cheryl and I are getting along all right. But I keep remembering what you said about Maureen not really trusting her . . ."

"No farther than she could throw her," Brenda said, sitting on the sofa arm. She took a long puff on her cigarette. "I suppose you want an example. Well, maybe things changed over the months, but when your boss first joined our happy little La Hacienda family, Maureen pulled me aside. She told me on the Q.T. that if Cheryl came around here asking questions about her and her background, I should let her know."

"Did she think Cheryl was trying to spy on her or something?"

Brenda shrugged. "Beats me. Anyway, Cheryl never grilled me about Maureen, so it was a nonissue. In fact, Cheryl has said a total of maybe twenty words to me since she moved in four months ago. Talk about stuck-up . . ."

"Is she close to any of the neighbors?"

Brenda let out a stream of smoke. "Now that Maureen's toes-up, I guess she's closest to the Cassellas— or maybe the Teds, that's the gay couple next door to her, Ted Something and Ted Something Else. They're hardly ever here. They live on Whidbey Island."

Laurie shifted Joey from one hip to the other. Brenda wasn't kidding about not having any interest in kids. It was rare that Laurie talked with another woman for any length of time without the other woman asking to hold Joey. At the moment, he seemed fascinated with Brenda's cat, yawning and stretching on the chair. He pointed at it and jabbered away in baby talk.

"Do you know how Maureen and Cheryl met?" Laurie asked over his chatter.

Brenda nodded. "Maureen started going to Cheryl's food truck for lunch. She became a regular, and started suggesting recipes . . ."

"Did she work nearby?"

Brenda considered it for a moment, and then let out a little laugh. "As a matter of fact, she didn't. I think the food truck was over near Second and Pike at the time. And Maureen was working in the bakery at Whole Foods near South Lake Union. That's quite a hike, almost a mile away."

Laurie wondered why Maureen would go that far to wait in line at a food truck when her workplace offered a huge variety of delicious ready-to-eat foods, which she probably got at a discount. It made no sense, unless Maureen had an ulterior motive.

She rocked Joey in her arms, and he quieted down. "Did Maureen ever say anything to you about wanting to switch jobs?"

"No. Until Cheryl offered her the job at Grill Girl, I thought she was pretty happy at Whole Foods."

"Did Maureen ever share with you any—*discoveries* she'd made about Cheryl?"

"I'm not sure what you mean."

"Well, according to Tammy Cassella, Maureen said she'd found out something about Cheryl that made the two of them *almost like family.* Do you know anything about that?"

"First I've heard of it." With a sigh, Brenda moved from the sofa arm to stub out her cigarette. For an ashtray she used a plate with a half-eaten taco on it. "So, how are things on the movie? Is Shane White as gorgeous in person as he is on the screen?"

"He's very handsome," Laurie answered, working up a smile, "and nice, too, very down-to-earth. But then, I've only waited on him twice."

"What's the deal with all those creepy Trent Hooper disciples? That would totally freak me out to have them hanging around my workplace. Aren't you afraid some of them will figure out where you live? I mean, they could easily follow the food truck here . . ."

Laurie winced a little, and held Joey tighter. "I really hadn't considered that."

"Well, I for one am bolting my door tonight," Brenda said. The cat leapt down from the chair and up to the sofa. Brenda picked him up and stroked him. "Thank God I have Mr. Darcy to protect me. Did you hear about the copycat murders just down the hill from here? I wouldn't be surprised if those Trent Hooper followers are behind it. Did you see the house on TV?"

Laurie nodded soberly.

"Their front gate, where they found that woman's bloody nightgown, it's just like ours. Did you notice?"

"No, I hadn't," she murmured.

"Speaking of things that are kind of scary," Brenda said. "I have a confession. You're going to think I'm horrible. But Vincent gives me the creeps sometimes. I mean, it's kind of bizarre, because he's actually pretty cute, but then he opens his mouth and starts talking . . ."

"I think he's very nice," Laurie said, hoping to shut her up.

"Now, don't get all offended. I'm just saying, at times I'll come around a corner or I'll step inside the gate—and he's right there, almost as if he's waiting for me. And then he'll smile, and I'm not sure what he's thinking. I've never seen the inside of his apartment. I can't help imagining what it's like in there. I know it sounds crazy, but every once in a while, I wonder if he's faking the whole Boo Radley routine."

"I don't think he's faking," Laurie said coolly. She shifted Joey around so he was astride her other hip. "Well, I asked for a couple of minutes and we've stayed much longer than that. We should get going."

"You know, we should work out a signal," Brenda

said. "Our living rooms and bedrooms are right beside each other. If one of us is in trouble, we should knock four times on the wall. What do you think?"

Laurie nodded. "Knock four times, sounds like a plan . . ."

"One more time than the Tony Orlando song," Brenda said.

Laurie just nodded again and turned toward the door. "Wave good-bye, Joey," she said.

Brenda didn't move from the sofa arm; so Laurie let herself out.

She didn't like Brenda very much. There was a tiny, irritating grain of truth to what she'd said about Vincent. But for Laurie, the strangeness was only there because she didn't really know him yet. So far, he seemed like a sweet man. After all, on his first visit, he'd brought her an African violet plant, now on her kitchen windowsill. He was a hell of a lot more neighborly than Brenda.

Vincent had stopped by again on Saturday. Laurie had forgotten that she'd told him he could meet Joey then, but Vincent had remembered. The visit had lasted a mere fifteen minutes. They'd sat in the kitchen, and he'd watched Joey eat his lunch of chicken roll, cheese, and peeled, cut-up fruit. Laurie had offered Vincent a glass of milk and couple of leftover lemon bars, which he devoured. He'd spent most of the time talking about his job at the Safeway. Before leaving, he'd mentioned coming by again the following day. Laurie had felt guilty putting him off, but she'd suggested he wait until later in the week. She'd seen he was a bit crestfallen.

But she just didn't want to get into a situation where Vincent—or anyone else—felt free to drop in every day.

In that sense, she didn't feel much more neighborly than Brenda.

Back inside her apartment, with her door double locked, she started to get Joey's turkey and carrots dinner cooked and chopped. But all the while, she was haunted by what Brenda had said about the Hooper Anarchists—and their possible role in the copycat killings. The CNN coverage reminded her that she'd stood there in the driveway of the Gayler Court house in plain sight of that group. She hadn't seen any of their faces—thanks to their scarves and ski masks.

What if Ryder and his tribe had been among them?

Once she had Joey fed and parked in his playpen in front of a DVR'd *Sesame Street* episode, Laurie phoned Don Eberhard in Ellensburg. He picked up after three rings: "Hello?"

Since moving to Seattle, Laurie had a new cell phone with a blocked number. Eberhard was the only one who had her phone number, but it still didn't come up on his caller ID whenever she called him. "Hi, Detective Eberhard, it's Laurie," she said.

"Hey, Laurie, how are you doing?"

"Okay, I guess," she said, competing a bit with Cookie Monster on TV. She was sitting at one end of the sofa. "I hope I didn't get you during your dinner . . ."

"Nope, I was just getting in my car to head home," he said. "I haven't even started the engine yet, so your timing's perfect. Say, you've certainly had a lot going on there in Seattle—between the protests on your film set and those copycat killings . . ."

"Yes, it's pretty disturbing," she said. "And I'm the one who came here to get away from trouble."

"From the frying pan, right into the fire," he said. "How are you coping? You really okay?"

"Well, actually I'm worried, because CNN showed a brief glimpse of me at the movie set today. It was during a report on the copycat murders. So much for my keeping a low profile . . ."

"Was that the report Dolly Ingersoll did?" he asked.

"Yes, did you see me? It was near the beginning of the report. I was standing in the driveway with an umbrella. I was talking to someone . . ."

"Yeah, we had that on the break room TV. I'm sorry I didn't notice you."

"No, don't be sorry. I'm glad you didn't see me. That's good. I was worried Ryder or one of his cronies might have seen that report and recognized me."

"Well, I didn't, and I knew you were working on that set. So I don't think you have anything to be concerned about."

"Thanks, that's what I needed to hear," she said. Maybe it was just a fluke that her neighbor, Hank, spotted her. But she still wondered about the mob of masked protesters on the film set. "Ah, listen, do you know if Ryder is still there in Ellensburg?"

"As of this morning he was," Eberhard answered. "In fact, I was going to call you. We picked him up for questioning. Someone set fire to your old townhouse last night."

For a moment, Laurie was dumbstruck. "My God,"

she finally murmured. "Was—was anyone hurt? My neighbors a couple of doors down, Krista and Nathan Aronson, do you know if they're all right . . ."

"No reported injuries," Eberhard said. "We questioned McBride, and he had an alibi. But that doesn't mean one of his followers didn't torch the place. Anyway, Ryder was making all sorts of protests about police harassment. We had to let him go."

"What about the restaurant?" Laurie asked anxiously. "Is everyone there okay? Have you heard anything?"

"Well, they had a strange thing happen there on Friday morning. Your boss went to open up the place at five-thirty, and he found a dead raccoon in front of the door. Someone had shot it. I don't know if it was a calling card from McBride or just a prank by some kids with nothing better to do."

Laurie's money was on Tad's son-of-a-bitch brother.

"Anyway, I'm pretty certain Ryder and his gang still have no idea where you are," Detective Eberhard assured her. "Outside of me, there's just one other guy on the force who knows you're in Seattle, and he's keeping it under his hat. You haven't told anyone. So I think you and your little boy are safe there as long as you don't make any more TV appearances."

Laurie studied Joey sitting in his playpen, staring through the bars at *Sesame Street*.

"Thank you, Detective Eberhard," she said.

"You're welcome," Don Eberhard replied.

He was still parked in front of the police station in his white Chevy Impala. People could tell at a glance it was an unmarked police car. They didn't have to peek inside at all the technical apparatus attached to the dashboard to figure it out. Whenever he merged onto the highway, most other cars around him would slow down. His unmarked car didn't fool anybody.

He phoned his wife, Gretchen, and asked if she needed anything while he was downtown. They lived about fifteen minutes away—in the "boonies," Gretchen liked to say. The drive always seemed longer, because a long stretch of it went through acres of apple orchards. At night, the road was just blackness for miles, but then he'd take a turn and pull into their little development—with a dozen big, beautiful new homes. During the day, they had a view of the orchards and the Stuart Mountain Range. Gretchen and their daughter, Erin, were a bit isolated out there. But he'd never worried about their safety—until recently, when he started making an enemy of Ryder McBride.

Gretchen reported that she didn't need a thing, and they were having spaghetti for dinner tonight.

Don started the car, cracked a window, and backed out of his parking spot. As he headed down Main Street, he was thinking that he hadn't had a cigarette in over two weeks. According to what he'd read online, he was supposed to be feeling more energetic and less edgy from withdrawal. But his cigarette while driving home from work had always been one of the best of the day—and he still missed it terribly.

He was so busy fighting his craving that he didn't notice—until several blocks down Main—that a silver minivan was following him. It was two cars behind him—just far enough back that he couldn't tell whether or not it was Ryder's Town & Country.

He kept checking in his rearview mirror for the next four blocks, and finally pulled over in front of a Kentucky Fried Chicken. He waited for the minivan to pass, but it turned right at the cross street before the restaurant. Don didn't get a good look, but he was pretty sure it was Ryder's beat-up Town & Country.

Hunched close to the wheel, he pulled back onto Main Street and headed for the edge of town. He kept an eye on the rearview mirror. The last thing he wanted to do was lead Ryder and his friends out to the house.

As he got close to the orchards, the damn minivan showed up again. "Shit," Don muttered, tightening his grip on the wheel. The vehicle was at least a dozen car lengths behind him—and the only other one on the road. Don slowed down to twenty in the thirty-five-miles-per-hour zone—just to see if the silver minivan slowed down, too. It did. They were keeping a distance behind him. So far, Ryder—or whoever was driving—hadn't done anything illegal. There wasn't much Don could do. Because of the distance, he wasn't even sure it was the same minivan.

After taking a curve in the road, he drove for another minute, and then pulled over on the shoulder. Don waited. He touched his gun in the shoulder holster. In his nine years on the force, he hadn't fired it once in the line of duty.

He kept waiting for that minivan to come around the curve. But there was nothing. It must have turned down another side road—or maybe turned around completely.

Don still couldn't breathe easy as he continued toward the orchards and Taylor Canyon Way, the long, monotonous stretch of road before home. He kept checking the rearview mirror. No one was behind him.

He turned onto Taylor Canyon Way. After driving about a mile, he still hadn't encountered a single car—which was typical. The roadway was empty behind him.

The breeze came through the open window. He was starting to crave a cigarette again when he spotted something up ahead. A car had pulled over to the side of the road. Its hazard lights flashed. Don eased off the accelerator. As he came closer to the vehicle, he could see it was a black Honda Civic. Its driver was a young brunette, nicely dressed in jeans and a pink, tailored oxford shirt. She stared down at something in the middle of the road. A shovel was propped up against her car.

Don pulled up behind her and parked. This close, he could see it was a dead German shepherd on the pavement.

The woman waved at him. Don stole another look in the rearview mirror. Seeing nothing back there, he climbed out of the car.

"Thanks for stopping!" the woman called to him, a little breathless. Up close, Don saw she was pretty and in her early twenties. She took hold of the shovel handle. "This poor pooch, I don't know how long it's been lying here, dead. I was going to bury it, but then I'm not sure about touching it . . ."

He glanced at the dead thing on the road. There wasn't any blood. Its hair was wet and shiny. Don noticed it wore a collar. He wondered what the dog was doing all the way out here, where there was nothing but orchards.

"Anyway, I thought maybe at least I'd push it to the side of the road," the woman said. "But it's heavy—and that seems so uncaring . . ."

"I'll call the city and they'll come pick him up," Don said, crouching down beside the fallen animal. The tail was curled up, bent slightly as if frozen in rigor mortis. The tongue drooped out of its mouth. Don reached for the collar to check the tag for its owner's contact information. His fingers brushed against the dog's ice cold, wet hair. Then he touched its neck—frozen solid. He could see the half-melted ice crystals in the dog's hair. Someone must have had the thing in a freezer.

"What the hell," Don muttered. He glanced back and noticed the silver minivan approaching in the distance.

Then he looked up to see the pretty young woman holding the shovel over her head.

Before Don could straighten up or reach for his weapon, she brought the shovel down. It hit the top of his head with a loud clank.

He let out a groan, and crumpled to the roadway—right beside that dead dog.

He was woken by something that sounded like a gunshot, following by a loud screeching.

As soon as he opened his eyes and saw Ryder McBride grinning at him, Don knew he was a dead man. Ryder would never let him walk away after this. Don's only chance for survival was to escape.

That didn't seem very likely. Don couldn't move and

his head throbbed so horribly, he was nauseous. They'd stripped him down to his undershorts. He was sitting in a hard-backed chair with his wrists tied behind him. His ankles were tied to the legs of the chair—and for good measure they'd tied two cords of rope around his waist to the back of the chair. It pinched at his naked skin, and kept him from wriggling around.

Another loud pop resounded outside—followed by more high-pitched squeals.

Don guessed he was in an abandoned farmhouse. It smelled rotten. Garbage and a few broken crates littered the bare wood floor of the darkened room. Dressed in a black T-shirt and jeans, Ryder stood in front of him with his arms folded. The pretty girl in the pink shirt leaned against the wall, fascinated by something on her mobile device.

On the other side of a cracked, dirty window, Don could see the sun was setting over the mountains. It looked like a beautiful night out there. One of Ryder's buddies, Lester Heinemann, paced back and forth. He occasionally tossed a lit firecracker in the air at some bats. Don realized that was what all the noise was about. He also realized there was no one nearby to complain about it. So if he yelled out for help, nobody would hear him.

Except for the creatures he was frightening, Les seemed to be alone out there. The Impala was parked beside Ryder's minivan. There was no sign of the girl's Honda Civic. Don figured they must have stolen it and then abandoned it on the roadside.

He opened his mouth to speak, but his throat was so dry that he broke into a coughing fit. It made his head pound worse. He finally caught his breath. "I see you found yourself a new recruit, Ryder," he said.

Scratching his beard stubble, McBride smirked at him. "That's Jacy," he said. "Jacy, meet Detective Eberhard, one of Ellensburg's finest."

"We've met," she said, barely glancing up from her mobile device.

Don cleared his throat again. "Did you know, honey, that Ryder's last recruit—the one you're replacing—he talked her into setting herself on fire. She burned to death. Are you ready to die for him, too?"

Across the room, her eyes met his for a moment. Then she giggled and focused on her mobile device again.

Don flinched as another firecracker went off outside. "Where'd you guys get the German shepherd?"

"Ryder accidentally hit him with the minivan earlier this week," Jacy answered. "He said maybe we could use him for something. So we put him in the big freezer in the garage. I think it'll be another couple of days till he's completely thawed out . . ."

"If Ryder hit him, you can be sure it was no accident, honey."

"All right, enough chitchat." Ryder sighed, glaring down at him. "You know why I brought you here. You know what I want . . ."

"A fourth for bridge?" Don replied.

"Go ahead and make with the bad jokes for now, piggy," Ryder said. "In about a half hour, you'll be begging me to kill you. So cooperate, and maybe I'll go easy on you. On your cell, I saw a bunch of incoming calls from a blocked number, and you took them.

I'm guessing that's your girlfriend, Laurie Trotter. So, where is she?"

"She's not my girlfriend," Don said, tugging at the rope around his wrists—to no avail. "She was your brother's girlfriend—two years ago for about two weeks. Then she dumped him, which if you ask me, was a really smart move. That's the only crime she ever committed against the McBride brothers. And yet you're so hell-bent on punishing her, you helped put your brother in his grave—along with that piece of kindling who used to be one of your girls. And now you're going to kill me, too—all so you can hunt down someone who never did a thing to hurt you."

"That's right," Ryder said. With a sudden jerk of his leg, he set his foot on the chair—so his boot was directly in front of Don's crotch. He pulled a jagged-edged knife from a sheath inside the boot. "She's got my brother's kid. That kid has my blood flowing in his veins. I'm going to take him and raise him as my own. But first, that bitch is going to pay for what happened to my brother . . ."

He leaned forward and gently brushed the tip of the knife against Don's cheek. "Now, if you don't tell me where she is, maybe your wife, Gretchen, will be more helpful. Maybe she knows. After we dump your body, we might just pay Gretchen a visit tonight. I like your house. The little red mailbox in front is a nice touch. Your girl, Erin, she's a real cutie. She goes to Ellensburg High, right? I believe Ms. Neff is her homeroom teacher. I just may have to pop Erin's cherry for her—that is, if Daddy hasn't gotten to her first . . ."

If his throat weren't so dry, Don would have spit in

Ryder's face. "You're so full of shit," he muttered. He told himself McBride's threats to his family were all bluff. He figured he'd been unconscious for at least an hour—maybe two. Gretchen would have caught on that something was wrong and called the station by now. There were probably a couple of cops at the house at this very minute. He was almost certain his girls were safe. They'd be well provided for, too.

"I'd say things are looking a lot more shitty for you, detective," Ryder replied. He tickled Don's earlobe with the point of the blade. "It's getting dark in here and there's no electricity. If you won't voluntarily tell us where that bitch is hiding, I'll have to torture you in the dark. Why prolong your agony, huh? You're going to die tonight either way . . ."

Another loud pop outside interrupted him.

"The question for you is how long do you want to hold out for her sake?" Ryder went on. "I mean, what is she to you?"

As Ryder lightly manipulated the knife point inside the crevices of his ear, Don tried not to flinch.

"Hey, did you ever see that movie *Reservoir Dogs*? It's one of my favorites, especially that scene where the guy cuts off the other guy's ear. It really cracked me up when he's holding the severed ear in his hand and he starts talking into it." Ryder chuckled. "How about if I did that to you?"

"Fine," Don grumbled. "Just do me a favor and cut off both ears so I won't have to listen to you anymore, you moron."

Ryder glared at him. He moved the knife to Don's throat. "I'm looking at a dead man," he whispered.

Don knew it was the truth. He hated the fact that his eyes started to water up. He didn't want Ryder to know he was scared. He took a deep breath.

"If that's the case," he said, keeping his voice steady. "Maybe one of you assholes can spare a cigarette . . ."

Monday, 9:43 P.M.
Spokane, Washington

"Hotel Davenport," the switchboard operator said. "How can I direct your call?"

"Yeah, you have a new cook there in the kitchen," the man said. "She goes by the name of Melanie Daniels. Can you connect me? Tell her it's Detective Don Eberhard calling, and it's urgent."

"One minute, please" the operator said. She put him on hold and rang the kitchen.

"Room service, how can I help you?" the woman answered.

"Is this Rosie or Stella?" the operator asked.

"It's Rosie. Midge, is that you?"

"Yeah," the operator said. "I have someone who wants to talk to a new cook there in the kitchen, Melanie Daniels."

"Melanie Daniels? That name sounds familiar, but she's not one of our cooks," Rosie said. "We haven't hired any new kitchen staff since the beginning of the year. Hey, you know why I recognized that name? I just figured it out. It's from *The Birds,* the character played by that blond girl . . ."

"Tippi Hedren," the operator said.

"Yeah," Rosie said. "Sounds like you're on the butt end of a joke."

"I guess. Thanks. Talk to you later, Rosie," the operator said. She switched back to the caller. "Sir? I'm afraid there's no Melanie Daniels on the kitchen staff."

"Well, she would have been hired within the last week or two," the man on the other end of the line said. "She also goes by the name Laurie Trotter. She's got to be there . . ."

"Sir, we haven't had any new kitchen staff since the beginning of the year," the operator explained.

"Check your records!" he insisted.

Midge couldn't help thinking the caller was the one at the butt end of a joke. "We don't have anyone working here named Laurie Trotter either," she said. "And I'm sorry, but the only Melanie Daniels I'm aware of is the character Tippi Hedren played in *The Birds.*"

There was dead silence on the other end.

"Sir?"

"That son of a bitch," the man muttered.

Then he hung up.

CHAPTER TWENTY-FOUR

Laurie woke up so disoriented she didn't know where she was. At first, she thought she was in her bed at the apartment in Ellensburg. It took her a few moments to realize she was on the sofa in her place in Seattle.

She had stretched out on the sofa, thinking, *Just ten minutes, a little catnap.* According to the digital clock on her TV cable box, that had been nearly two hours ago. She had the TV on low, waiting to see if CNN reran Dolly Ingersoll's report. Right now, they were showing a commercial for some antidepressant that had about fifty near-deadly side effects the narrator was describing in a casual, no-worries tone.

After putting Joey to bed, she'd phoned Krista and Nathan—as well as Paul from the diner. Everyone was okay. Paul had mentioned that Duncan seemed a bit unnerved by the dead raccoon in front of the diner's entrance. "But you know how easily rattled he gets," Paul had said.

Laurie had baked and frosted 140 cupcakes, twenty more than Cheryl needed for tomorrow. She figured she'd give ten to Vincent and ten to Hank and Tammy. All the while, she'd thought about Cheryl—and Dean Holbrook, Evergreen Manor, and Dean's artist brother, Adam. She'd scribbled down the Holbrook brothers' names on a memo pad with the intention of surfing the Web for information about them. But then a quick cat-nap on the sofa had seemed so inviting.

She sat up and rubbed her eyes. Dolly Ingersoll was on TV, but it wasn't the report from earlier today. She stood on a lanai in front of a beautiful swimming pool. Dolly didn't have a handheld mic or a somber expression here. This was some sort of fluff piece.

Laurie grabbed the remote and pressed the Info button. The show's description came up across the bottom of the screen:

44—CNN, 11:00–11:30: *DISHING WITH DOLLY* (repeat)
Dolly Ingersoll visits the Seattle area home of actress
Shawna Farrell and husband, film producer Gil Garrett.

Laurie let out a stunned little laugh. On the screen, Dolly sat poolside with "Uncle Gil" and Shawna Farrell. Ensconced on a patio sofa, Gil wore sunglasses, a long-sleeve white shirt, and an orange kerchief around his neck. His white hair was slicked back and he was tan. But he looked old and unhealthy. *"Oh, don't ask me what she puts in those smoothies,"* he said in his gravelly voice. *"I have them every morning. They taste great, but I think a little vodka in there would help."*

"Oh, you're such a devil," said Shawna at his side. She tossed her head back and laughed. With her tawny, shoulder-length hair and big sunglasses, she looked every bit the retired movie queen. She wore something obviously from her Shawna Chic collection, a vibrant, shimmery blue-and-green sweat suit. Thanks to some excellent plastic surgery, she looked more like fifty than seventy. *"He's a bigger health nut than I am,"* she said. *"Every morning he's in this pool, swimming his laps. When I married him, I didn't know he was part fish . . ."*

"Tiger shark," Gil cracked.

Laurie wondered if Cheryl knew this was on. But then, she'd probably gone to bed hours ago.

On TV, three little yelping Pomeranians joined Shawna, Gil, and Dolly at the poolside. Shawna fawned over the dogs while Gil ignored them.

Laurie heard the front gate clank. She got to her feet and went to the window. She didn't see anyone in the courtyard. Had somebody just left? It was a strange time for someone to be stepping out.

Then she noticed the lights were on in Cheryl's apartment across the way. Cheryl was awake after all. Her blinds were closed, but Laurie could still see the light through the slats. She couldn't help wondering if it was Cheryl who had just stepped out at this late hour. And if so, whatever in the world for?

"Oh, look at this closet!" Dolly was saying on TV. *"How many shoes do you have?"*

Shawna laughed. *"Dolly, a woman stops counting after two hundred pairs . . ."*

"Dolly, I think our waitress wants to go home," said her editor, Gary Korabik.

"Well, I don't want to go home yet, so it looks like she's shit out of luck," Dolly said with a glass of wine in her hand.

They were the last customers in Daniel's Broiler. The restaurant's beautiful wood and stone interior seemed cavernous. It was so quiet without anyone else in the place. From their booth, Dolly and her editor had a view of the boats docked in the Lake Union marina. Dolly was enjoying herself. It helped that Gary was a lean, handsome forty-year-old with wavy black hair. He wore a black suit with a jazzy tie. He'd flown in from New York to wine and dine her and discuss her book.

Dolly was still on a high from the amazing day she'd had. She'd shown everyone that this old gossip queen had the journalistic chops to cover a hard-hitting news story. The copycat killings were a gold mine for her. She would include the new murders in her book—along with behind-the-scenes coverage of *7/7/70*. She'd play up the "cursed production" angle, too. She'd already made it known that she didn't intend to treat screenwriter Lance Taylor's car smashup as just an ordinary accident. This was going to be a definitive study of the Styles-Jordan murders and their aftermath.

"Do you know that right now, they're rerunning the interview I did in May with Gil and Shawna?" Dolly pointed out, ignoring the fact that the restaurant had turned off the background music and undimmed the lights. "I'm going after Gil Garrett for an exclusive interview about Elaina Styles. He discovered her, you know. They were lovers—only she couldn't tolerate the way he went around screwing anything that moved." She shook her head and clicked her tongue against her teeth. "But you know, despite his roving ways, Gil was crazy about Elaina. I don't think he ever really got over her. He was furious at her when she married Dirk. In fact, between you and me, I think he married Shawna on the rebound."

"Well, that's fascinating," Gary said, sounding distracted. He took a sip of his decaf. "Listen, Dolly, I hate to harp on this. But Legal needs to know exactly what you've uncovered that's going to have the police reopening the case. I mean, before you 'rip the lid' off these killings, you need to run it past us. We could be looking at some potential lawsuits, or subpoenas, or God knows what other kind of trouble. Can you at least give me a clue as to what you've found? Throw me a bone that I can share with Legal."

"I'd like another Merlot," Dolly said. In one gulp, she drained what was left in her glass.

"The bar's closed," Gary said.

"For me, they'll reopen the bar," Dolly declared. Every restaurant she set foot in had to bow to her whims—or she'd Twitter that the place was terrible. She had that kind of clout. The people here knew it, too.

"Dolly, I have a confession," Gary said, slumping against the seatback. "I'm still on East Coast time, which makes it about a quarter to three for me. I've been without sleep for twenty-two hours and I'm exhausted. I really need to call it a night. But first, could you please give me an answer on this? Can you tell me *anything* about the new information you've uncovered?"

She glared at him. "I'll reveal my findings when I'm good and ready. If you—or *Legal*—object, well, I'm quite willing to dissolve our contract and find another publisher."

The truth was she didn't have any groundbreaking, lid-ripping news about the forty-four-year-old murders. Despite all the hype, neither did the movie. She had the goods on *7/7/70*'s "happily married" director, David Storke, who was once arrested for soliciting a cop in a public restroom. His studio at the time had managed to sweep the whole mess under the rug. But Dolly had used her knowledge of the incident to coax him into letting her see the heavily guarded screenplay. It was hard-hitting and well written, but there were no big revelations.

For her book, *Slain Star, The Elaina Styles Story,* Dolly had hired a couple of peons to research all the police files on the case. She didn't expect them to come up with anything new either. But she had her old interviews with Elaina and Dirk. She also planned to include some postmortem photos in the book—for shock value.

Though disingenuous, all her talk about the book's "shocking revelations" seemed to be working. In fact, Dolly had even received a few death threats about it— some untraceable texts, and a couple of letters. She'd had her share of hate mail and death threats before. But this time she thought about hiring a bodyguard, and of course, making her publisher pay for it. If nothing else, it would be nice to have someone to run errands and fetch things for her twenty-four/seven.

"You're killing me here, Dolly," Gary said. "If something in that book turns out to bite us in the ass, we really need to know about it in advance so we can be prepared. Help us help you."

"I'll think about it," she sighed. "And I can't believe you're paraphrasing *Jerry Maguire* to me. Now, if you won't buy me another glass of wine, you can at least walk me to my car . . ."

The parking lot, right off the marina, was nearly empty. Gary escorted her to her rented Cadillac ATS and opened the car door for her. But he didn't wait around after that. Dolly was still setting up her navigation system to direct her back to the Fairmont Olympic Hotel when Gary ducked inside his own rental and took off.

Dolly knew she'd had at least three glasses of wine. So she popped in a breath mint—just in case a cop stopped her. Then she started for the parking lot's exit. Her phone rang, and she reached for it, figuring it was Gary. "Yes?"

"How much do you really know about the Elaina Styles murder case?" a woman asked on the other end.

"What?" Dolly said, annoyed.

She was still at the lot exit—with the nose of her Cadillac ATS in the empty street. She glanced at the caller ID, and saw the number was blocked. Whoever it was, they had a lot of nerve calling her this late.

Dolly pulled out of the lot. "Who is this?" she barked. "How the hell did you get my number?"

For a moment, there was no response.

"Hello?"

"Who am I?" the woman finally said. "You don't know me, Dolly. But I work with the man who's in the backseat of your car right now."

Dolly squinted in the rearview mirror. A man sat up in the backseat.

She let out a startled cry and dropped her phone. She started to swerve, and the car's left front tire skidded against the curb. Dolly slammed on the brake.

The man grabbed her shoulder. "Calm down," he said quietly. "If I wanted to kill you, old lady, I would have done it by now . . ."

"What do you want?" she asked. Her heart was pounding.

"First, I want you to take your foot off the brake and get this car moving again," he said.

Dolly glanced around, and spotted only one other car in the area—about a quarter of a block ahead in the oncoming lane. She kept a steady grip on the steering wheel so the man couldn't see her hands shaking. She pushed down on the accelerator, and stole a glance in the rearview mirror again. With a streetlight glaring in back of them, his face was swallowed up in the shadows. Dolly took a couple of deep breaths. "My—my purse is right up here on the front seat," she said, a tremor in her voice. "I have about two hundred dollars and my credit cards . . ."

"I don't want your money," he replied. "I want you to pick up the phone—if you can reach it . . ."

Dolly noticed her cell had landed on the passenger seat, beside her purse. With a trembling hand, she grabbed it. "Okay, now what?" she asked, feeling sick to her stomach.

"Put it on speaker mode, and then set it down there in the cup holder." He patted her shoulder.

She took her eyes off the road for a few moments while she switched her phone to speaker mode. Then she placed it in the console's cup holder. "What— what's going on?" she asked. "What do you want?"

She'd been addressing the stranger in the backseat. But it was the woman on the other end of the phone who answered: "What we want, Dolly, is for you to tell us what you know about the Styles-Jordan murders. What's this big discovery you've made?"

"I haven't discovered anything," Dolly admitted.

"You said there will be arrests."

"I was just trying to drum up interest in my book."

"What exactly have you uncovered? You said the police will have to reopen the case."

"I was hyping my book, for Christ's sake!" Dolly insisted, tears in her eyes. "I swear, I don't know anything—"

"Turn right here at the light, just after the Eastlake Market," the man said.

Biting her lip, Dolly was obedient. They started up a steep hill. Ahead, just past another traffic light, there was a freeway wall and a cross street.

"Take another right," the man said. "And then stay on the road. It'll veer left and go under the Interstate."

She did what she was told and navigated the curve in the road. Emerging from under the freeway, Dolly spotted a grassless, hilly park beneath I-5—with stairs and winding trails around the tall concrete support beams for the highway. Though clean and well lit, the colonnade still had a stark eeriness to it. "Where are you taking me?" she asked nervously.

"Right here," said the woman on the phone.

"Pull over, and park it," the man told her, his hand on her shoulder once more.

Dolly steered over to the curb and came to a stop. Shifting into park, she glanced at the pockets of darkness in the dirt-and-concrete park. There didn't seem to be another soul around.

"Lower your window," said the woman on the phone.

It was too much, having these two barking orders at her. Dolly was used to being the one issuing orders. Frazzled, she reached for the switch on the armrest. The descending window hummed. She looked in the rearview mirror again. "I've just about had enough of this," she said. "Goddamn it, what's going on . . ."

"We're going to take a little walk . . ."

Dolly swiveled toward the open window. A pale, homely, long-faced woman with black hair was staring back at her. She had her hand on the car door. A long leather cuff covered her arm—from her wrist halfway up to the elbow. "Get out of the car, Dolly," she said, past the noise from the highway above them.

Opening the car door, she reluctantly climbed out from behind the wheel. "I've already told you, I don't know anything. I don't have any new information, I swear . . ."

The woman took hold of her arm and led her across the street—toward a slope covered with trees and shrubs.

Dolly noticed a small stairwell that wound up the hill through all the foliage. "I demand to know where you're taking me," she said.

The woman said nothing, and kept pulling her toward the bottom of the steps.

Dolly glanced over her shoulder at the man following them. She finally got a good look at him. The black V-neck T-shirt he wore hugged his muscular frame. His arms were covered with tattoos. He was about thirty, and swarthy. His black hair was cut so short—with a hairline so perfectly straight across—it almost looked drawn on with a magic marker. His shadow-stubble handlebar mustache had the same painted-on effect. He looked a bit silly, trailing after them with her purse in his hands. But then he started rummaging through it.

Dolly suddenly realized who these people were. She mustered up her courage and turned to the woman. "So where are your ski-masks and Trent Hooper T-shirts?"

The horse-faced woman said nothing. She just nodded toward the stairs.

Dolly had thought it was just a short stairwell, but now she looked up at a seemingly infinite six-foot wide concrete stairway that ascended through the lush woods. She couldn't even see the top of it. "Come on, walk off your dinner," the woman said finally.

Dolly hesitated. "Are you insane?"

"Move it, old lady," growled the man behind her.

She took a deep breath and started up the stairs. "What the hell is the point to all this?" she asked. "Just how far do you expect me to go? What is this?"

"These are the Howe Street Stairs," the woman said, still clutching Dolly's arm. "They're a landmark around here. There are three hundred and eighty-eight steps. But if you answer my questions, you won't need to go all the way to the top."

"I've already told you—"

"You've said on several occasions that Lance Taylor's car accident in Maui was no accident at all." The woman's grip tightened, almost cutting off the circulation in Dolly's arm. "What did you mean by that?"

"I was talking about the cursed movie production," Dolly explained, already feeling winded. "He was the first—*calamity* associated with the film. It's good press, more hype, that's all."

"*Calamity,*" the woman said, with a tiny smile. "I like that word."

"She's got a little stun gun in her purse," the man behind them announced. "Actually not so little, it's got three-point-five million volts."

"Give it to me," the woman said, pausing on the steps.

Dolly tried to catch her breath. Ahead, there was a small landing with a light post and a park bench. "Can't we—can't we sit down?" she asked meekly.

The woman pocketed the stun gun, and then forged on, pulling at her arm. "What do you know about Cheryl Wheeler?" she asked.

"Who?"

"The woman who runs the food truck, she's catering the movie shoot."

"Oh, her," Dolly said, her throat going dry. She still couldn't see the top of the stairs. They seemed to disappear in a black gap between the shadowy trees and shrubs. "I hardly know her. Why? Are you—are you friends of hers?"

"Something like that," the woman said. "Has she been talking to you?"

"I—I had a run-in with her last week," she answered, her voice weak. She struggled for a breath. "Other than that, I haven't talked to her—"

"I have her hotel key card," the man interrupted.

Dolly glanced over her shoulder and saw they'd climbed at least a hundred steps. She clutched the banister to combat her vertigo—and sheer exhaustion. She could now see the cityscape and the headlights of the cars on the freeway.

The woman kept dragging her up to the next step and the next. She was relentless. "Is your computer in your hotel room?"

Dolly just nodded. She was too winded to talk.

"Room five-nineteen, at the Fairmont Olympic, right?"

Dolly nodded again. She wondered how they knew her room number. She realized these two weren't part of that Hooper Anarchist mob. They were much smarter than that. Were they someone Cheryl Wheeler had hired?

She noticed another landing—and another bench— a few more steps up. She was sweating, and her perfectly coiffured blond wig was slightly askew. "We—we've got to stop up here," she panted. "You're giving me a heart attack . . ."

"Maybe that's the point," the woman replied, tugging at Dolly's arm again.

But Dolly grabbed hold of the banister with her free

hand, and she held on. She wasn't going to take another step. With what little strength she had left, she resisted.

"Move it," the man said.

"Screw you," Dolly gasped, her lungs burning. "Screw both of you. You don't—you don't scare me. You two are ridiculous . . ."

The man chuckled and moved aside.

Clinging to the banister, Dolly gazed down at the seemingly endless row of steps she'd just climbed.

"You're the one who's ridiculous," the woman whispered, "with your bad plastic surgery and that crooked wig. You look like a frail, old clown." She finally let go of her arm. "One good push is all it will take, Dolly. Just imagine your brittle bones shattering against each one of those hard concrete steps. And if that doesn't kill you, believe me, bitch, you'll wish you were dead. You'll be begging me to come down, snap your neck, and end it for you."

Dolly shook her head defiantly. "You can't kill me here," she said, her voice a bit stronger now. "You can't kill me until you've double checked my room and my computer. How can you be sure I haven't been lying to you all this time?"

"You know something, Dolly?" the woman said. "I trust you."

"What?"

She looked at the stun gun in the woman's hand. Before Dolly could recoil, the woman shoved the device against the side of her neck.

Dolly heard it hum, and she smelled her flesh burning. She was helpless. She couldn't even scream. All the breath was sucked out of her again. It felt as if some monster had grabbed her by the throat with its talons. The pain was excruciating. She wasn't aware of anything else.

Dolly didn't realize she'd let go of the railing. She didn't even know she was tumbling down the long, endless stairway—until her body slammed against the concrete step.

Then she felt one of her brittle old bones crack.

That was only the first step. And it was a long, long way down.

CHAPTER TWENTY-FIVE

Tuesday, July 8, 4:08 P.M.
Duvall, Washington

"Look at these gorgeous beets, all the different shades," Cheryl said. "We need to put a beet salad on the menu this week."

Laurie admired the vegetables on display at the farmer's market. There were baskets full of butternut squash, asparagus, beets, red potatoes, carrots, radicchio, and nearly every kind of salad staple. As they perused the vegetables, Cheryl seemed the happiest Laurie had seen her all week. She was in her element.

Or was she just happy because Dolly Ingersoll was dead?

Laurie couldn't help remembering how Dolly had practically threatened Cheryl: *I'm going to get the goods on you if it's the last thing I do . . .*

Dolly's death was all they'd talked about on the film set this morning—until the Hooper Anarchists had started showing up around eleven o'clock—with recruits. At least a hundred of them had gathered out there by noon. Making all sorts of racket, they threw things over the fence—and at the police. There were several arrests, and for a while, it looked as if a full-scale riot might break out. All of it was utterly pointless—just a bunch of jerks with their faces covered, acting up for the TV news cameras.

Laurie made sure to stay out of camera range today.

If the atmosphere on the set weren't tense enough, things between her and Cheryl hadn't changed since yesterday. They got through the day being polite to each other, but there wasn't much camaraderie. When the news broke about Dolly, they didn't discuss it with each other. And Laurie didn't dare bring up the fact that Dolly Ingersoll wasn't one of Cheryl's favorite people. Laurie kept getting updates from Danny and other crew members about Dolly's death, which seemed to give some credence to the "curse" plaguing the *7/7/70* production. Sometime last night, TV's reigning gossip queen had fallen down a long stairwell between North Capitol Hill and Eastlake. She'd broken her neck. Laurie didn't share any updates with Cheryl.

The protestors had dispersed by the time she and Cheryl had gotten out of there. They hadn't even hung around to see if her cupcakes were a hit. After lunch, they'd set the cupcakes out on the kitchen counter of the "murder house," and then left. Once in the truck, Cheryl had announced that she wanted to buy some produce. So they'd driven directly here to this farm in Duvall. And once there, Cheryl's whole demeanor changed. She seemed so relaxed. She even looked younger.

"This is one of the things I love best about cooking,"

she said, examining some asparagus. "Seeing where the food is grown and talking with the people who grow it, I feel so lucky. And you can see the pride they take in what they're doing. It really inspires you to become a better cook, don't you think?"

Laurie found herself smiling at her boss for the first time all day. She nodded. "This reminds me of my cooking classes in Paris. They took us on a field trip to a farm about ninety minutes outside the city, and we got all these fresh ingredients for the dishes we were cooking. You're right. It makes such a difference."

"Oh, I'm so jealous," Cheryl sighed. "I've never been outside the United States or Canada. My cooking classes were with a bunch of other kids who needed re-habilitating. Half of them you wouldn't trust with a carving knife. But we had a great teacher and chef." She picked up a head of butter lettuce. "I think we should get a dozen of these, and of course, we'll need arugula . . ."

Laurie wanted to ask Cheryl about that time in her life. She wanted to ask her about the little boy she'd lost. But whenever she started to feel a connection with Cheryl, a wall went up. The sad thing was she liked Cheryl and admired her. She was grateful to her for this job. And even if the apartment had belonged to her dead predecessor, Laurie still thought it was a great place for her and Joey—especially when she stacked it up against the dumpy townhouse in Ellensburg.

She hated not being able to trust Cheryl. But it was clear Cheryl was lying to her about a number of things. Yet none of those things concerned Laurie directly. To explain how she knew where the bathroom was in the

Styles-Jordan murder house, Cheryl had claimed to have seen a diagram of the place—when no such diagram existed. Was it possible that during her misspent youth, she'd been one of the scores of teens to explore the closed-up mansion? Maybe Cheryl just didn't want to admit that. And perhaps she didn't want anyone to know she'd met with Dean Holbrook days before his murder, because that might mean having to talk with the police. She'd had enough run-ins with the law when she was younger. She'd probably been asking Holbrook to use his clout and connections to get her a catering gig at the rest home where his father lived.

Still, she couldn't press Cheryl on these issues, not without pissing her off.

While Cheryl placed her produce orders, Laurie wandered over toward the food truck and a hand-painted sandwich board sign for the farmer's market. She checked her mobile device for the latest update on Dolly Ingersoll's death. Through Google, she found a *Los Angeles Times* article that was twenty-two minutes old:

GOSSIP ICON DOLLY INGERSOLL, 76, DIES IN FALL

Laurie skimmed over the first few paragraphs, searching for some new details. She found something six paragraphs down:

Ingersoll had dined at the Seattle restaurant, Daniel's Broiler, earlier on Monday night with Gary Korabik, her book editor at Matterhorn Publishing. According to Korabik, they left the restaurant separately at around 11:45. The

restaurant is approximately half a mile from Seattle's Howe
Street Stairs, the 388-step hillside stairway where
Ingersoll's body was discovered. Her rental car was parked
near the bottom of the steps. Police have been combing the
wooded area surrounding the stairs for Ingersoll's purse . . .

Laurie remembered hearing the front gate clank at
around 11:20 last night. And Cheryl's apartment had
been the only other one with any lights on. It was about
a ten-minute drive to those stairs from their apartment
complex. This was the second night in a row that someone Cheryl knew had been killed—and both deaths
had occurred just minutes away from La Hacienda.

"Laurie, can you give me a hand here?" Cheryl
asked, approaching the food truck with two bags full of
vegetables.

Startled, Laurie put her mobile device in her pocket
and quickly opened the back door of the food truck.

"We have six more where these came from," Cheryl
said, handing her the bags, which were heavy.

Once Laurie loaded them in the truck, she caught up
with Cheryl on her way back to the vegetable stand for
the other sacks. "Boy, I don't know where you get your
energy," she said, catching her breath. She was trying
to sound as casual as possible. "You should be totally
pooped after the day we had yesterday. Plus I noticed
you were still up when I went to bed around midnight
last night. Did you get any sleep at all?"

Cheryl stopped and gave her a baffled smile. Then
she retrieved two more bags. "I don't know what you're
talking about. I was in bed by ten-thirty."

"Well, your lights were on," Laurie said.

Cheryl seemed stumped for a moment, but then she nodded. "Oh, yeah, I was so tired I forgot to turn them off before going to bed. C'mon, grab a couple of bags. We're going to have two new sides on tomorrow's menu—beet salad and garlic green beans."

Laurie picked up the sacks of produce and caught up with her again at the food truck.

She wasn't sure if she believed Cheryl or not. But she wanted to.

"Once we get home," Cheryl said, "how would you and Joey like to come over and help me with some prep work?"

"Ah, I have a couple of things to take care of first, if that's okay," Laurie said.

"That's perfect. I'll cook us some dinner." Cheryl set the sacks down by the truck. "You stay put. I'll get the last couple of bags."

Laurie watched her trot toward the produce stand. She was thinking of Dolly Ingersoll's "accidental" death.

And she just couldn't get over how happy Cheryl seemed.

Dear Adam,

I'd like to extend my condolences. I was so sorry to learn about the deaths of your brother and sister-in-law. I didn't know them, but I have a friend who did. At least, she knew your brother, Dean. Please forgive me for intruding on your privacy during this very difficult time. But I'm wondering if

you could spare a few minutes to meet with me this week.
If you name a time and place that's convenient for you, I'll
be there. It's rather important. Otherwise I wouldn't intrude
on your grief like this. Thank you very much.

Sincerely,
Laurie Trotter
206-555-0607

Hunched over the laptop on her desk, Laurie hesitated before sending the e-mail.

The TV was on. Joey sat in his playpen, mesmerized
once again by the same *Sesame Street* episode she'd
played for him last night.

Earlier today, Laurie had searched the Internet, and
found that *Adam Holbrook, Artist,* had a Web site—
with a contact page. He also had a bio page—with his
photo. When she'd seen him on TV yesterday, it certainly hadn't been the best of circumstances. From his
laid-back good looks—the unkempt hair and cute
smile—she'd expected his work to be pretty unconven-
tional, nothing to take seriously. But his paintings and
drawings impressed Laurie. They reminded her of
Edward Hopper with the beautiful use of color and
shadow.

Contacting Dean Holbrook's brother had been one
of the things she'd had to "take care of" before meeting with Cheryl again. She wasn't sure how much good
it would do—or how much Adam Holbrook knew about
his brother's activities. She hated bothering him right
now, but she had to know what Cheryl was up to—before someone else died.

Taking a deep breath, Laurie clicked on the Send icon.

She figured she had a snowball's chance in hell of hearing back from him.

She heard the front gate clank, and glanced out the window. In his white short-sleeve shirt and black tie, Vincent started up the courtyard path. He had his red Safeway apron folded and tucked under his arm.

A brief visit with Vincent was the other thing she needed to "take care of."

"Hey, Joey," she said, switching off the laptop. "We're going to pay a call on our neighbor. C'mon, let's say go say hi to Vincent . . ."

"Hey," Vincent said, with a surprised smile as he opened the door. His eyes lit up behind his glasses. "Hi, Laurie, hi, Joey . . ."

"You seemed to enjoy my lemon bars the other day," Laurie said. She held Joey in one arm and had a Tupperware container in her other hand. "So when I made cupcakes last night, I made a few extra for you."

"Wow, thank you." Vincent took the container from her, and opened his door wider. "Would you like to come in?"

"Sure, if we're not intruding," Laurie said, stepping over the threshold.

"You're not intruding yet," he replied. "*Big Bang Theory* isn't on until seven, so I still have some time to talk to you, then take my shower, and get dinner started before then. Tonight is Stouffer's Lasagna night."

"Well, we won't stay too long then." Laurie glanced around his living room. "I really like your place, Vincent."

It was clean, but cluttered looking, thanks mostly to the bulky antique furniture that seemed to belong in a big old house—not this small apartment. Plus he'd collected a lot of junk—the greater part of it related to U.S. presidents, including small bronze busts of Washington, Lincoln, and Kennedy, and a model of the White House. There were books on the presidents and framed presidential portraits in the tall bookcase. He didn't seem to have any political party preference either. There were portraits on the walls of Obama, Clinton, Reagan, FDR, and Eisenhower. Scattered among them were several framed family photographs.

"Is this you?" Laurie asked, pointing to a school photo of a gawky-cute boy in a turtleneck sweater. A mark above his eye looked like a flaw on the faded photo.

"Yes, that's me, looking like a nerd," he said with a laugh.

In one of the photos, he was a teenager, wearing his glasses and standing between a couple in their late sixties. "Are those your grandparents?" she asked.

"No, that's my mom and dad," he said, hovering behind her. "They're dead now."

Laurie figured he must have inherited the bulky, old furniture from them. "You look a little like your dad," she remarked.

"That's funny, because they adopted me when I was

four," he replied. "They were really nice people—to—y'know, take someone like me. Maureen used to say I was 'special,' but they were the ones who were special. Would you like a Coke or a root beer?"

She smiled at him. "Oh, no, thanks."

She couldn't help thinking about what a jerk Brenda was for insinuating that Vincent's apartment was probably some chamber of horrors—like Ed Gein's back parlor or something. Moreover, Vincent was a hell of a lot better host than Brenda was.

"Do you think I'd spoil my lasagna dinner if I had a cupcake now?" he asked.

Laurie laughed. "Oh, what the heck, go for it."

"Would you or Joey like one?"

"No thanks, those are all for you." Gently bouncing Joey in her arms, she studied the other framed snapshots. "Is this Maureen with you in front of the Christmas tree?" she asked.

Sitting on his sofa, Vincent had the Tupperware container in his lap. He was prying off the lid when he looked up at her. "Yes, that was taken last year."

"She has a kind face," Laurie murmured. She looked like a sweet lady, someone Laurie would have enjoyed having as a neighbor or a friend.

"I have all her Christmas ornaments now," Vincent said, carefully peeling the paper cup off a frosted cupcake. "Maureen had the best Christmas ornaments. I have her photo albums, too. They're right here . . ." He nodded at the clunky, oak, two-tiered coffee table in front of him. Three thick ring-binder books were stacked on the lower tier. "Would you like to see?"

Laurie hesitated. "Ah, sure . . ."

Vincent put down the cupcake long enough to move the books from the coffee table to the center sofa cushion. Laurie sat down on the other side of the couch. Joey shifted around in her lap and reached over her shoulder, which prompted Vincent to stick out his finger out. Joey grabbed it. Vincent laughed. "Hey, Joey . . ."

Laurie opened the first album, and noticed several faded color photos of two teenagers and a baby not much older than Joey. They were outside, smiling and squinting in the sun. It looked like they were in a park. From their bell-bottom jeans and the long hair, parted down the middle, Laurie guessed the photos were from the late sixties or early seventies. A young man with black hair combed over his forehead was in some of the shots, too. "Is this you?" Laurie asked, pointing to the baby.

"No, I don't know whose baby that is," he said. "But that's Maureen with the brown hair, and that's her brother. I don't know who the other girl is. I'm not in this book until near the end. You can skip ahead if you want to. Would it be okay if Joey let go of my finger now so I can eat my cupcake?"

"Oh, of course, I'm sorry." She moved Joey a bit lower into her lap, and he released Vincent's finger without a fuss. Laurie looked at the other girl in the photos—a brunette. She remembered what Tammy Cassella had said about Maureen, how she'd discovered something about Cheryl which had made them "almost like family." The dark-haired girl in these photos looked nothing like Cheryl. Laurie figured she was grasping at straws.

"Did Maureen and Cheryl know each other long before Maureen started working for her?" Laurie asked.

"I don't think so," Vincent said, reaching over and turning several pages of the album. "Here's where I am . . ."

Laurie glanced at the brownish-tinted photos of a teenage Vincent—with his parents and Maureen, who looked about thirty years old. It appeared to be an intimate Thanksgiving dinner. There were shots of a cooked turkey on a table with a centerpiece arrangement of foldout crepe-and-paper pilgrims and pumpkins. Another man was in the photos with them: a balding, brawny-looking guy with an affable smile.

"That's Maureen's husband, Jim," Vincent said, pointing to the man. "He was a sheriff in this small town outside Spokane. He and Maureen were good friends with my parents. Only he died of cancer. Our neighbors, Mr. and Mrs. Blankenship, were there that Thanksgiving, too. But I don't think we got any photos of them. This picture was taken in 1984, when Ronald Reagan was president . . ."

Laurie glanced around the room—at all the presidential portraits. "You'd know, of course."

Nodding, he took a bite out of his cupcake. "Jim died in 1990, when George H. W. Bush was president," he said with his mouth full. "Jim and Maureen didn't have any kids. And she didn't have any family. My dad died from Parkinson's when Clinton was president in 2000. After that, my mother got cancer, and Maureen helped take care of her. Mom died when the other Bush was in office in 2004. Anyway, since both Maureen and I didn't have any family, we decided to look after each other. We moved here to Seattle nine years ago. This cupcake is really good. Pardon me for talking with my mouth full." He took another bite.

"That's okay," Laurie said. "You know, I was thinking about something you said the other day. You mentioned that Maureen told you to be polite to Cheryl, but not to get too friendly. Do you know why she said that?"

He finished up his cupcake with one final bite, and shook his head.

Joey started to squirm a bit, and she shifted him around on her lap again. "I know Maureen helped Cheryl get the apartment here, but I get the impression she—well, it seems to me Maureen did that in order to keep an eye on her."

Vincent frowned. "I'm not sure what you mean. Are you talking about like when Maureen did her homework on Cheryl?"

Laurie gazed at him and blinked. "She did *homework* on Cheryl?"

He nodded. "Yeah, Maureen collected a whole bunch of homework on Cheryl."

"You mean she was doing research on her? Did she have documents about Cheryl's background?"

He nodded again, and then scratched the back of his head. "It was a secret, but I guess she wouldn't mind me telling you, since she's dead. Maureen kept it all in a blue folder. But after she died and I went through her stuff, I couldn't find the folder anywhere. I guess she must have thrown it away." Vincent winced a little. "Um, I'm going to need to take my shower pretty soon . . ."

Laurie closed the photo album. "Oh, of course, I'm sorry. I didn't mean to stay so long . . ."

"You're welcome to come back and watch TV," he offered.

She got to her feet, and shifted Joey around so he was astride her hip. "Thanks, but I'm due over at Cheryl's. We have to cook some food for tomorrow . . ."

"Maureen used to do that, too," Vincent said, walking her to the door. He opened it for her. "Well, thanks for the cupcakes, Laurie. Bye, Joey!"

"Thanks for your hospitality," Laurie said, stepping outside. "Wave good-bye, Joey."

It took him a moment to catch on—and he finally waved at Vincent.

She stole a look at Cheryl's unit across the courtyard. The lights were on. Laurie figured she'd get through the next couple of hours with Cheryl if she didn't talk about anything beyond tomorrow's menu.

"Laurie?" Vincent called to her—in almost a whisper.

She turned around. "Yes?"

"Y'know that stuff I told you about Maureen's homework?" he said. "Maybe you better not tell Cheryl. She might not like it."

Laurie nodded. "Don't worry, Vincent. I wouldn't dream of telling her. Thanks again."

Joey waved good-bye once again.

Then Laurie turned and started for home.

She didn't have to wonder what had happened to that blue folder full of "Cheryl homework." It had probably gone up in smoke—just like Maureen.

* * *

She heard a knock on the door just as she was getting Joey ready for Cheryl's.

With him wiggling in her arms, Laurie checked the peephole. Through the slightly distorted glass, she saw Cheryl waiting outside. Laurie unlocked the door and opened it. "Hi, I was just on my way over . . ."

Cheryl leaned against the doorway. She looked tired. She held one of the bags from the farmer's market. "Are you going to hate me if I cancel on tonight?"

Laurie shook her head. "No, not at all," she replied. "Are you okay?"

"Physically, yes," Cheryl sighed, setting down the bag. "My mental state is another story. I'm in kind of a funk."

"What happened? You seemed in a good mood at the farm."

With a melancholy smile, Cheryl reached up and caressed Joey's cheek. "I'm always in a better mood when I'm out in the country like that. But then I got home and switched on the news." She shrugged. "They were talking about Dolly Ingersoll, and the reality of it finally sunk in. I guess I'd been in denial all day about it. She wasn't one of my favorite people, but she certainly didn't deserve to die."

"Do you think she was murdered?" Laurie asked.

"From the news report, the police seem to think she was mugged and tossed down those stairs."

"And what do you think?" Laurie pressed.

Cheryl gave her a pale smile. "I think I should head back home and get those beans cut." She nodded at the produce bag on Laurie's threshold. "I meant to ask earlier, what are you going to make with all these Granny Smith apples?"

"Eva Marie Saint's Apple Pie. I figure six of them should be enough."

"Oh, one of your Superstar Diner specials," Cheryl said, nodding. "Well, I'm sorry to leave you alone with all those pies to bake."

"It's no problem. Are you really sure you want to be by yourself tonight? It might help if you talked about what's bothering you."

"No, that wouldn't help at all," Cheryl said. "Right now, what I need is some alone time with my work—and maybe an extended consult with Dr. Chardonnay. That would make me feel better. Anyway, I apologize for backing out of our plans tonight." She patted her shoulder. "Laurie, if I seem to—to shut you out at times, I hope you don't take it personally, because it has nothing at all to do with you. I happen to think you're pretty terrific. I mean that."

"Thank you, Cheryl," she said. She took a deep breath and tried to choose her words carefully. "I really like working with you. But—well, I keep thinking of what happened to Maureen, and then the copycat murders—and now Dolly Ingersoll. I think you know something, and you can't tell me or just don't want to. But you need to tell me this much. Are Joey and I at risk?"

Cheryl's eyes wrestled with hers, and she didn't say anything for a moment.

"Please, don't act like I'm crazy," Laurie whispered. "We both know what I'm talking about."

"Joey's safe," she finally replied. "Starting tomorrow morning, I think it would be best if I loaded up the food truck by myself. That'll give you more time in the morning. You can drive yourself to and from the set. You should be all right."

"What are you saying? Do you think someone's coming after you?"

Cheryl shook her head. "I'm just being cautious, that's all. Please, don't ask me anything else. And please don't quit on me."

She touched Joey's cheek again. Then, before Laurie could say anything, she turned around and hurried across the courtyard.

Joey wouldn't fall asleep. She ran out of the usual lullabies and ballads to sing to him. He finally nodded off during her slow, quiet rendition of Lady Gaga's *Bad Romance*. The Eva Marie Saint Apple Pies were a breeze in comparison. It was the actress's recipe, which Laurie had found in *Bon Appétit* magazine. It was easy, because the crust didn't have to be rolled, and came out like shortbread. Customers at the Superstar Diner loved it.

While the pies baked, two at a time, Laurie checked on Google and Craigslist for Seattle restaurants now hiring cooks. Cheryl had just asked her not to quit. But she'd also finally confirmed Laurie's suspicions that being around her just wasn't safe. Maybe that was the real reason Cheryl had canceled tonight. Laurie thought

about the mornings they'd loaded up the food truck—
when it wasn't even light out. She realized how vulnerable they'd been on their pickup route from the bakery
to the butcher to the film locale. If someone were to
come after them, that would have been an ideal time.
Obviously, Cheryl realized that.

The job market looked pretty dismal. So were her
prospects of ever hearing back from Adam Holbrook.
But she kept checking her e-mail anyway. If Cheryl refused to tell her what was happening, maybe Adam
Holbrook could. Perhaps between Dean's brother and
her, they could figure it out.

While all six pies rested, she poured herself a glass
of wine and started to look up cooking jobs in Portland. An e-mail notification clicked on the corner of
her computer screen.

Laurie told herself not to get excited. It was probably junk mail. She clicked on her mailbox and looked
at the short list of incoming e-mail. It was at the top:

**7/8/2014 gil@gilgarrettproductions.com Thanks
 & Catering Work**

"Oh, my God," she murmured. She clicked on the
Read icon, and gazed at the note:

Thank you for the delicious dessert. I'm glad to have such
a talented goddaughter. I'm planning a casual dinner party
in early September to celebrate my wife's birthday. If
you and your catering associate are free this Saturday

afternoon, I'd like to meet with you and discuss. Please keep all this confidential, as the party is going to be a surprise.

All Best,
Gil

Do not reply to this e-mail. Please send your e-mail response to my assistant, Rachel Porter (Rachel@gilgarretproductions.com—425/555-9074)

Gil Garrett Productions, Inc.
P. O. Box 22
Bellevue, Washington 98008
Phone: 425/555-9073
Fax: 425/555-9075

CHAPTER TWENTY-SIX

"I'll have the Reuben. But could you hold the sauer-kraut and Thousand Island—so it's just a plain corned beef with Swiss and it's grilled?" Adam's father handed the menu to the waiter. "One of these days some smart restaurant will put 'Grilled Corned Beef and Swiss on Rye' on their menu and save me from going through this whole rigmarole every time I order."

Sitting across from his dad in a booth at the Deluxe Bar and Grill, Adam could tell he was pretty lucid right now—at least, lucid enough to order a corned beef sandwich the way he liked it. In moments like this, Adam felt like he had his father back. But then he noticed an old tomato juice stain on the front of his dad's plaid shirt, and it was a reminder that his father's clarity was just temporary. His dad used to be such a sharp dresser, and here he was in a dirty shirt.

They were having a late lunch. Adam wore a thin tie with a striped shirt and khakis. They'd just come from

Bonney-Watson Funeral Home, where they'd made arrangements for Dean and Joyce's burial. Adam hadn't wanted to put him through any of it, but his father had insisted on coming. Once there, he'd gotten confused. He'd thought they were planning the funeral service for Adam's mother, and kept asking where Dean was. At one point, he'd even told Adam, "You remind me of my younger boy, Adam. Are you a friend of his?"

Adam had managed to get them both through the whole ordeal, but by the end of the consult with the funeral parlor associate, he was exhausted. He also wondered how the hell he was going to pay for everything. He knew Dean and Joyce had a lot of money put away, and it was probably going to him. But there was no telling how long that money would be tied up.

Adam ordered the cheapest thing on the Deluxe menu, the soup of the day: chicken gumbo.

His dad was with it enough to wait until their server left, and then he remarked, "She'd be a pretty attractive gal if it weren't for those rings in her nose."

"Different strokes, Pop," Adam said, reaching for his water glass.

"These kids with their pierced this and pierced that, and all the crazy tattoos," his father lamented. He nodded toward a skinny young man and his girlfriend at a table by the window. "Look at that idiot, sitting at the table with his hat on. You go to a nice restaurant, you take off your hat when you sit down to eat. What's with these kids and the backward baseball hats anyway?"

Adam chuckled. "Dean used to do a pretty good imitation of you carrying on about eating-out etiquette and 'these kids today.'"

His father gave a tired, melancholy smile. "Yeah, poking fun at the old man was about the only thing you two ever saw eye to eye on."

It didn't slip by Adam that his dad was talking about Dean in the past tense. Yesterday, Adam had tried to find the right moment when his father was cognizant enough to ask him about this deep, dark family secret. Dean and Uncle Marty knew about it. And there was every indication it had something to do with Dean and Joyce's deaths. But the opportunity never presented itself—until now.

"Well, I think Dean was kind of hard on you, Pop," Adam said, setting his napkin in his lap. "He could be such a tight-ass at times. He expected you to be perfect. But you know, you could tell me anything, Pop, and it's not going to change how I feel about you."

His father shifted a little in his seat, and then he moved his cane so it leaned against the side of the booth at a different angle. "Well, thank you, son. That's good to know."

"Dean used to make out like he knew something about you, Pop, something you were ashamed of. He never told me what it was. He always acted like he was protecting me from some terrible secret . . ."

The waitress with the nose rings returned with their sodas, and Adam turned quiet.

"Sure takes awhile to get a drink around here, doesn't it?" his father said, once the waitress left.

Adam leaned forward. "Pop, you know what I'm talking about," he whispered. "I wouldn't bug you about this, only I can't help thinking there's a connection between this old secret and what happened to Dean and Joyce."

Adam's dad sipped his Coke, sat back, and sighed.

"Pop, why would somebody be 'getting even' by killing Dean and Joyce that way? You said that the other day. If you have any idea who might be behind the murders, you need to tell me . . ."

His father nodded, and then cleared his throat. "The best corned beef is in New York City—or maybe Chicago. You know what we should do? We should load up the minivan and take off on a cross-country, a family road trip, you and Dean and your mother and me. Dean can spell me on the driving. He has his driver's license, doesn't he?"

With resignation, Adam slumped back in the booth. He worked up a smile, and then raised his glass. "Here's to family road trips, Pop," he sighed. "And family secrets . . ."

Joey was a hit with the old folks on the benches in front of Evergreen Manor—especially the ladies. They took turns holding him. Laurie kept close by, one hand ready to catch him if he slipped out of someone's frail, uncertain grasp. But none of the elderly ladies let him go, and the looks on their faces as they nuzzled up to him were so remarkable. Just holding a baby seemed to take years off each one of them. And Joey was golden, too. He didn't squirm or cry. He loved being the center of attention.

Laurie had come there looking for Dean Holbrook's father. But she hadn't been able to get past the nurse at the front desk—a stout, copper-haired sixtyish woman with lipstick on her teeth. "Mr. Holbrook's son signed him out at ten-thirty this morning," she'd explained. "I don't know when they're coming back. It might not be until after dinner."

Laurie had asked if she could wait in the lobby.

"I'm sorry, but no," the nurse had replied, slowly shaking her head. "All guests have to be cleared with the resident or their immediate family, no exceptions. I hope you understand. We've had quite a few media people trying to get in to talk with Mr. Holbrook."

"Can I wait out front?"

The nurse had sighed and nodded. "Suit yourself."

From the residents out by the front entrance Laurie had learned that Adam Holbrook had taken his father to a funeral home on Capitol Hill. Most of them were certain Mr. Holbrook would be back in time for dinner, because it was Salisbury steak tonight—apparently a big thing around there. So Laurie waited outside with them. She was one of few people in front of the rest home without a walker or a cane.

While a spindly woman with blue rinse in her hair and a pink fleece robe held Joey in her arms, Laurie glanced at her wristwatch. It was three-thirty. She'd been out here for about twenty minutes now. She'd gotten out of work early today.

Driving herself to and from the set had made for a much shorter workday. Alone in her own car, she kept thinking how tense the drive would have been if she were with Cheryl in the food truck. Now that her boss had acknowledged Laurie might be at risk associating with her, how could the two of them just ignore it?

Yet somehow today, Cheryl had managed to do just that.

When Laurie had first gotten to the food truck this morning and started unloading her apple pies, she found Cheryl slicing up a ham. "It was strange driving myself here this morning," Laurie said. "I have to admit, I was worried about you all alone on that pickup route . . ."

"Well, I'm here," Cheryl replied, not glancing up from her work. "I managed okay."

"Looking over your shoulder the whole time, no doubt," Laurie replied.

Cheryl said nothing. Again, she didn't even glance up at her.

"So are we going to talk about what's going on?" Laurie asked.

"I got the word that they're breaking for lunch a half hour earlier today, so we need to get cracking. The good news is we'll probably get out early. How did the pies turn out?"

They kept busy and kept it all business as they fixed lunch in the food truck. Laurie felt safe there on the set—with a strong police presence outside the gate of the "murder house." It wasn't necessary. Only a handful of protestors showed up in the morning. Dolly Ingersoll's death had bumped them off the TV newscasts yesterday, and the cameras and TV news vans weren't there today. So, without anyone to perform for, most of the Hooper Anarchists stayed home.

After lunch, Laurie and Cheryl sliced up the apple pies and set them on the kitchen counter. It was then she told Cheryl that Gil Garrett wanted to see them this Saturday.

Cheryl was ecstatic. Immediately, she started talking about how they needed to make an assortment of dishes Gil could sample. "And we have to make sure we're meeting and dealing with Gil—and not some underling," she said. "We need to get that across to him in our e-mail response when we set up the meeting. It should just be us and him. I don't want a lot of other people around to muck up his decision-making . . ."

Laurie promised that tonight she'd send her a draft of the e-mail reply for her approval—before sending it to Gil's secretary.

She didn't tell Cheryl about her other plans for tonight.

She was going to start packing.

She couldn't keep working for Cheryl in this constant state of uncertain dread. She figured Joey was indeed safe with Tammy and Hank, and he was scheduled to start at Lullaby League Daycare next week. The setup there was ideal. After some initial misgivings, she loved her apartment, too—such an improvement over the dumpy Bancroft Townhome in Ellensburg.

But she felt like a sitting duck working alongside Cheryl. *Talk about a curse,* the late Dolly Ingersoll had said to her boss. *You're bad news, honey . . .*

It wasn't just paranoia either. Cheryl had admitted that there was cause for concern.

But she wouldn't elaborate. If perhaps Laurie had gotten some sort of explanation, she might not have been so anxious to get the hell away from Cheryl Wheeler and her food truck.

Unless Cheryl could give some sort of assurance that she was safe working at her side, Laurie figured she'd be crazy to stay there. She planned to go online and start looking for a new apartment tonight. It would be tough to get a new place without a job or references. Still, she was determined to make a clean break from Cheryl. If she couldn't find a place that was move-in ready by next week, she'd check back into the Loyal Inn.

Still, before she pulled the plug on La Hacienda and Cheryl, Laurie figured she owed it to herself to visit Evergreen Manor. Maureen Forester may have had a whole file on Cheryl, but the only lead Laurie had was the rest home where Cheryl longed for a catering gig. Dean Holbrook's father was a resident there. Bothering him with a bunch of questions while he was grieving was pretty tactless. But it seemed quite possible Dean's meeting with Cheryl had something to do with his death. Why else would Cheryl be so reluctant to talk about it? If in the days just after Brian's death, someone had come to her with information about why and how he'd died, Laurie would have welcomed it—painful as it might have been. A part of her still wanted to know why he'd volunteered for that reconnaissance mission.

She didn't have any answers for Mr. Holbrook, but between the two of them, maybe they could figure out why his son and daughter-in-law had died that way.

The lady with the blue rinse was named Shirley, and according to Shirley, Mr. Holbrook was in the early stages of dementia. They hadn't seen much of his older son, Dean, but the daughter-in-law ("*a lovely girl . . .*") had visited every week. The younger son, Adam ("*oh, he's a charmer . . .*") came by almost every day.

Laurie wondered if Mr. Holbrook was in any frame of mind today to answer her questions. So that left Adam, who still hadn't replied to her e-mail. From the buzz on the set the last two days, Adam Holbrook was the only potential suspect in the copycat murders that the police had so far. After all, he'd discovered the bodies; he'd claimed to have been sleeping in their basement while the murders had occurred, and he was in line to inherit a ton of money. But according to what Laurie had read online, the police hadn't charged him with anything—at least, not yet.

"There they are," Shirley said, bouncing Joey on her knee and nodding toward the parking lot. "That's Adam and his father. The father isn't much for socializing." She stretched her withered neck and called out: "Yoo-hoo, Adam, there's someone here who wants to meet you!"

Laurie collected Joey from her, and then stood up. Adam Holbrook wore khakis and a casual shirt with a skinny tie. His hair was messy, but somehow it looked right that way. He waved back at Shirley and smiled. Most everyone by the front entrance seemed to know him, and he knew them: "Hey, Ruth, how's your hip feeling today?" and "Hi, Bob, I like your shirt."

He was so disarming and cute it was hard for Laurie to think of him as a potential suspect in a brutal double-murder. Then again, she remembered Tad, and figured her first impressions of men couldn't be trusted.

His father, a handsome older man, leaned on a three-prong cane as he hobbled alongside him. He nodded distractedly at the others.

"Hey, Shirley," Adam said. He stole a glance at Laurie. "How's the vertigo today?"

"Not so bad at all," Shirley said. "Listen, Adam, this is Laurie, and the little one is Joey."

"Excuse me," Mr. Holbrook cut in. "Nice to see you, but I have something that can't wait." He shuffled toward the front doors. "Adam, come by the room later!" he called over his shoulder.

"Sure thing, Pop!" he replied. Then he smiled at Laurie and shook her hand. "Hi. Sorry about my dad. He's not being rude. He just had two Cokes at lunch, and it was a long drive back here. So, are you Shirley's daughter or her sister?"

"Oh, listen to him!" Shirley said, patting Adam's shoulder. "We just met, silly. She came by to see you. I'll leave you kids to talk alone . . ."

While Shirley stopped to caress Joey's cheek and say good-bye to him, Laurie caught a glimpse of Adam. The smile had vanished from his face. He crossed his arms in front of him.

"By the way, how are you holding up today?" Shirley quietly asked him.

He nodded. "I'm doing okay, thanks."

She patted him on the shoulder again, and then ambled inside. Adam seemed to have been waiting until she was gone before he frowned at Laurie. "So you came here to see me?" he asked, stepping a little farther down the walkway—out of earshot of the old folks.

Laurie followed him. "Yes, I thought—"

"Whose baby is that?" he asked, cutting her off.

Her eyes narrowed at him. "Well, he's mine, of course. What kind of question is that? I'm not a reporter if that's what you're thinking. My name's Laurie Trotter. I e-mailed you last night."

"You and about a hundred other people," he replied. "Suddenly a lot of folks want to buy my paintings, or they just need to talk to me. I've even had a few women—and men—who would like to date me. So, which category do you fit into?"

Laurie switched Joey around so he was straddling her other hip. "Listen, I don't want to bother you or harass you—and I certainly don't want to *date* you. If you just give me a minute, I'll explain. You see, a friend of mine knew your brother—"

"Yeah, I've had a lot of people contacting me whose friends knew Dean or they claim to have known Dean themselves. And I was stupid enough to take them seriously at first." He shook his head. "I've just come back from a funeral parlor where I made arrangements to bury my brother and my sister-in-law. This was followed by lunch with my father in which he became disoriented, and then broke down and cried for fifteen minutes. So you'll pardon me if I don't feel like talking to you."

"Listen, I'm sorry," Laurie said. Joey began to fuss, and she caressed the back of his head. "I know this is a terrible time for you . . ."

"Your baby's tired," he interrupted. "Why don't you take him home, okay? Take him home to his dad." He turned and started to walk away.

"His father's dead," Laurie snapped. "He was killed six months ago on a recon mission in Sangin. That's in Afghanistan."

Adam stopped and gazed back at her. "I'm sorry," he muttered.

Laurie took a deep breath. "No, I'm sorry. My—my husband's death has nothing to do with why I'm here. I didn't mean to use it as some kind of comeback line to put you in your place. I don't usually do that. I've never done that."

"Well, it worked," he murmured, slipping his hands in his pants pockets, "because I feel like a first class heel. And now you've got me standing here, ready to listen to whatever you have to tell me."

"Can we start over again?" Laurie asked, holding Joey with one arm while she extended her free hand to him. "I'm Laurie Trotter, and this is my son, Joey. And I'm really sorry for your loss . . ."

He shook her hand. "Hi, Laurie, hi, Joey," he said.

"It's nice to meet you, Adam." Laurie could see that they still had the attention of the old-timers gathered outside the front door. She backed away and Adam followed her. "Here's the thing," she said, her voice dropping to a whisper. "I'm helping to cater the film that's being shot here in town, *7/7/70*. It's about the Styles-Jordan murders. Last Thursday afternoon, I was in Volunteer Park with Joey and I happened to see my boss—her name's Cheryl Wheeler. Do you know her? Does that name sound familiar?"

Adam shrugged. "No, I'm sorry . . ."

"She owns and operates a food truck called Grill

Girl. Last month, it blew up in the middle of down-town."

He nodded. "Oh, God, yes, of course. I heard about that."

"Well, now Cheryl's catering for this movie," Laurie continued, ignoring Joey, who grabbed at her hair. "I'm working for her. On Thursday I saw Cheryl in the park, having what seemed to be a heated discussion with a nice-looking man. On Monday, when it came on the news about your brother and sister-in-law, I recognized him. He was the one in the park, talking to my boss. I said as much to her, and she flatly denied it. But I know she's lying. And I keep thinking it's too much of a coin-cidence that we're working on this movie about the Styles-Jordan murders—and your poor brother and sister-in-law were killed exactly the same way."

His mouth twisted over to one side, Adam stared at her and shook his head. "I'm sorry, but I don't recall my brother ever mentioning a Cheryl Wheeler to me. And I had no idea this movie was even being shot here until the police asked me about it on Monday. Dean never said anything to me about it either."

Joey kept tugging at her hair, and she finally took hold of his chubby, little arm and pulled it away. "Honey, please . . ."

"You sure it was my brother she was talking to?" he asked.

Laurie nodded. "Yes, positive. And three days later, he was dead."

"Have you talked to the police?"

"No. Right now, it's her word against mine. I don't

want to get Cheryl in trouble. She's been really good to me and my little boy. But I know she's lying when she says she didn't meet with your brother. Only last week, she was asking if I knew someone here at Evergreen Manor. She said she wanted to cater an event here. But something tells me it's just an excuse to get her foot in the door."

"Why? What for? What would she want at this place?"

"Maybe she wants to talk with your father," Laurie said, grasping at straws. "I don't know. The security in this place seems pretty tight. Catering an event here would be one way of getting inside—especially if your brother wouldn't allow her to see your dad. He didn't seem too happy with her when I saw them on Thursday afternoon. Do you think your dad might know who Cheryl Wheeler is?"

Adam hesitated. "Well," he finally said, "let's go in and ask him."

The dark blue SUV was parked in the lot in front of Evergreen Manor. The woman sitting at the wheel watched Laurie Trotter and Adam Holbrook in deep discussion. And now they were heading inside the rest home together.

The woman figured this was the result of the blunder with Cheryl Wheeler five weeks ago. Had Cheryl been killed in that food truck explosion, these two people wouldn't be talking right now—and they wouldn't have to die. The father would have to go, too. Her client would want it that way, a clean sweep.

One thing bothered the woman sitting alone in the SUV.

She told herself it wasn't really necessary. But then these things happened—collateral damage. She had to prepare herself for the very real possibility.

She'd never killed a baby before.

"Are you sure you've never heard of Cheryl Wheeler before, Pop?" Adam asked.

Sitting in a Barcalounger with the cane standing beside it, his father shook his head. "Nope, I'm sorry, son. That name doesn't sound familiar at all."

Laurie sat at the end of Mr. Holbrook's bed with Joey in her lap. He was getting more and more restless.

Adam had been pacing, but now he pulled a hard-backed chair close to his father and sat down across from him. "Pop, Laurie here is working with this Cheryl person on a movie. It's about the Styles-Jordan murders. Do you know what I'm talking about?"

"It happened in 1970," Laurie said. "Elaina Styles and her husband, Dirk Jordan, were murdered here in Seattle . . ."

Mr. Holbrook looked at her, clear-eyed. He nodded soberly. "Yes, I remember that. It was a terrible thing, a real shame . . ."

"We were talking about this earlier, Pop," Adam said, leaning forward in his chair. "Dean and Joyce were killed by someone who was copycatting those murders."

Joey let out a bored cry.

Mr. Holbrook squirmed a little. He nodded at Adam.

"Yes, of course, I remember. Someone was imitating Trent Hooper and his clan."

"That's right. You said they were getting even by killing Dean and Joyce," Adam whispered. "What did you mean by that, Pop?"

Laurie stared at them. She didn't know what he was talking about. Joey cried again, and she bounced him on her knee to quiet him. She wanted to hear what Mr. Holbrook had to say.

But the old man squirmed in his chair again, and he just shook his head.

"Is there some kind of connection between us and those killings back in 1970?" Adam pressed. "Pop, c'mon, please, think back. Don't fade out on me now . . ."

Joey kept crying. Laurie tried to shush him.

Mr. Holbrook seemed to be getting more restless. He started to tremble. He reminded Laurie of poor Duncan with his head tremors. He finally turned toward her. There were tears in his eyes. "You've got to keep the baby quiet," he whispered. "For God's sake, they'll hear it. Please, keep the baby quiet . . ."

"Oh, I'm really sorry," Laurie whispered. "Maybe we should go—"

"No, it's okay," Adam sighed with resignation. "We've lost him. He's somewhere else right now. He's gone back in time someplace."

Mr. Holbrook kept shaking his head at her over and over. "Please, they'll hear the baby," he whispered. A tear rolled down his cheek. "You need to keep him quiet . . ."

Laurie couldn't help wondering if he'd gone back to 1970.

CHAPTER TWENTY-SEVEN

Wednesday, July 9, 4:40 P.M.
Seattle

Holding Joey with one arm, Laurie reached into her mailbox by the front gate and pulled out three pieces of mail—all of them addressed to Maureen Forester: a flier from Trader Joe's, a sale announcement from Macy's, and something that looked like a bill from a place called E-Z Safe Storage.

She tucked all three pieces of mail under her arm and glanced over at Cheryl's unit. She couldn't tell if anyone was home or not. She carried Joey through the courtyard toward her apartment, careful about how she handled him. He'd loaded his diaper during the ride home from Evergreen Manor.

Once inside, she got him cleaned up, changed, and in his playpen. Never one to resist a bargain, she put the ads for Trader Joe's and Macy's aside for later. Then she scribbled on the front of the envelope for the bill: *NO LONGER AT THIS ADDRESS—DECEASED.* She would put it out by the mailboxes tomorrow. She

didn't want some storage facility to keep sending her
bills for Maureen Forester.

She started for the kitchen, but suddenly stopped in
her tracks.

Laurie turned and hurried back to her desk in the
living room. She snatched up the envelope and tore it
open.

"E-Z Safe Storage, how can I help you?"

"Hi," Laurie said into the phone, a little breathless.
She was sitting at her kitchen table with the bill in front
of her. Across from her on the counter was a drawer
she'd pulled out of its sleeve. She'd lined it with blue
gingham shelf paper last week, and she'd discovered
those numbers on the back of the drawer: *2-16-47*.

"My name is Maureen Forester, and my account
number is S-5-163," she said, consulting the bill. "I
have a couple of storage lockers, and I'm trying to remember if this one has a combination lock on it or if it
has a key."

"Depends on the type of lock you used," said the
woman on the other end. "If you've forgotten your
combination or can't find your key, we'll break off the
lock for a twenty-dollar cash fee, no checks or credit
card. And of course, we require an ID for that."

"I have the address of the storage facility here,"
Laurie said. "That's up north, isn't it?"

"Right off Aurora, near Shoreline," the woman said.

"And there's something else. I've forgotten what
my locker number is. Would you be able to look that up
for me?"

"You just gave it to me. It's your account number."

Laurie glanced at the bill again. "S-5-163?"

"South Yard, Building Five, Locker 163."

"Will someone be there to let me into the building?"

"There's twenty-four-hour video surveillance, and a guard on duty until ten—if you need any assistance. The keypad combination for the entry into the building is there on your bill, the last four digits in that series of numbers at the bottom left corner."

Laurie glanced at Maureen's bill once again.

"I show you have a current balance due for this billing quarter of ninety-seven dollars and twenty-two cents," the woman said. "Would you like to pay that with a credit card over the phone now—or would you rather pay by mail, Ms. Forester?"

"Oh, by mail, thank you," Laurie said. "Thank you for all your help."

Once she clicked off the line, Laurie immediately made another call. It rang three times, and then someone picked up: "Hello?"

"Hi, Tammy, it's Laurie. Something's come up. Would it be a huge imposition if I asked you and Hank to look after Joey for the next hour or two?"

"Jesus, what's with the traffic in this city?" Laurie muttered.

She was catching every stoplight on Aurora Avenue, and inching along between them. It started to drizzle, and Laurie switched on the wipers. She'd been in the car nearly an hour and had driven only nine miles. She hadn't factored in rush hour when she'd impulsively jumped into the Camry and started for Maureen's storage locker in North Seattle.

Ever since leaving La Hacienda, Laurie couldn't shake the feeling that someone was following her. She kept checking her rearview mirror, but didn't see a silver minivan in back of her. Perhaps she was still on high alert, because she'd had a false alarm earlier—after pulling out of the lot at Evergreen Manor. A silver minivan had followed her for at least two miles, but she'd lost them turning down Lake Washington Boulevard.

She had to remind herself once again that Ryder McBride had no idea where she was. She had Detective Eberhard keeping tabs on the situation. If anything had gone awry in Ellensburg, she would have heard from him by now.

Laurie felt she might now have another ally in Adam Holbrook. And it wasn't just because she found him attractive either.

The visit with Adam and his father had helped her realize something. The food truck explosion, the copycat murders, Dolly Ingersoll's death, and whatever Cheryl was hiding—all of it had seemed connected to the movie being made. At least, that had been what she'd thought. But why would Maureen Forester be doing "homework" on Cheryl months before they'd even signed on to cater the movie? If Maureen's blue folder was indeed in locker number 163, there couldn't be anything about the *7/7/70* movie in it.

The killings had started before the movie had even gotten the green light. Lance Taylor had promised that his screenplay would "rip the lid off" the Styles-

Jordan murder case, and "stun even police investigators." Soon after he sold that script, he wrapped his sports car around a phone pole. Dolly Ingersoll had used that exact same expression when she'd announced on CNN that she would "rip the lid off the case." The night that broadcast aired, she broke her neck falling down the Howe Street Stairs. How many of the "accidents" on that "cursed" production were really accidents—and not sabotage?

Someone was trying desperately to keep the lid *on* the Styles-Jordan murder case.

People weren't dying because of a movie. They died because they claimed to know something new about those old murders from forty-four years ago. Dean and Joyce Holbrook didn't have anything to do with the movie being made. Did Dean have some inside information about the Styles-Jordan murders? Was that why he was meeting with Cheryl?

Laurie thought about this afternoon, when she and Joey had left Evergreen Manor. Adam had walked them to the door, and then out to her car. "I think my dad might have been involved in something shady a long time ago," he admitted.

"By a long time ago, do you mean like in 1970?" Laurie asked.

"Maybe, I don't know. I'm not certain. Dean used to carry on like he knew something pretty sordid about our father. But—well, I shouldn't even be telling you this. I just met you. Hell, I barely know you."

"I'm taking a chance with you, too," Laurie said, stopping beside her Camry. "You could rat me out to my boss—or worse, rat my boss out to the police."

"Looks like we're just going to have to trust each other," he said with a hint of a smile.

"What were you talking about back there when you said someone was *getting even* killing your brother and sister-in-law that way?"

"I didn't say it, my dad did—a couple of days ago." Adam shrugged. "It could have been his dementia talking. I'm not sure. I've been trying to get an explanation out of him. If I find out anything, I'll call you . . ."

They exchanged phone numbers, and he helped her secure Joey into his car seat. It was so much easier with two people doing it.

Laurie remembered looking at him in her rearview mirror as she'd headed toward the lot exit. He'd ambled back toward the rest home entrance, and started talking with the old folks gathered out there.

The sky grew darker, and the rain began to come down heavier. Laurie turned the wipers to high speed while she waited at another traffic light on Aurora. In the rearview mirror, all she could see was a blur of headlights beyond the water cascading down the back window.

"Turn right ahead on One Hundred Eighteenth Street," her navigation system announced. Laurie could barely hear it past the rain beating down on the roof.

Tightening her grip on the wheel, she took the turn. A crack of thunder startled her. They didn't get thunderstorms or lightning too often in the Pacific Northwest. She slowed down. She could barely see anything. The hammering on the car roof became even more intense. White icy pellets bounced off the windshield and hood. Her headlight beams caught them as they covered the road. She felt the tires skidding.

This was a first for her. She'd never driven in a hailstorm before.

"Your destination is on your right in approximately one hundred feet," the navigation system said.

Laurie maneuvered the turn, and came to a gate in a tall, chain-link fence—with a coiled roll of razor-serrated wire along the top. There were security cameras mounted on either side of the gate. With the rain and hail pouring down so hard, Laurie could just make out the long, sprawling, one-story, windowless buildings—one after another. The place resembled photos she'd seen of POW camps in World War II—everything but the guard towers. By the gate, on the driver's side, they had a little station with a callbox. She flicked the switch on her armrest, and the window descended, letting the rain and hail in.

Laurie squinted at the callbox contraption and saw a keypad and a screen with the message repeatedly running across it: Press # to Access Entry. Laurie hated these things. They never worked for her.

"Shit," she muttered, getting her hand wet as she reached out and pressed the pound sign.

Another message came up on the little screen: Using keypad, enter the first three letters of last name.

For a moment, she blanked out on Maureen's last name. The woman on the phone with E-Z Safe Storage didn't tell her she'd have to do any of this. Laurie's entire arm was now drenched. She could barely make out the letters corresponding with the numbers on the phone keypad. Her wet hand was shaking as she pressed 3-6-7 for *F-O-R*.

Enter account number, said the message running across the screen.

She nervously glanced at the bill on the passenger seat. Shadows of raindrops on the windshield fell across the document.

"Damn it," Laurie hissed. Rainwater and melting hail kept blowing through the open window, soaking her left side—from shoulder to thigh. The steering wheel was getting wet. Flustered, she hesitated, and then pressed 7 for the *S* part of Maureen's account number, and then the other digits.

Nothing happened for a few moments. The message running across the little rain-beaded screen said Please wait.

At last, Laurie heard a buzz. The message over the phone pad read Welcome, proceed ahead. To her utter relief, the chain-link gate in front of her began to slide open.

As she drove past the gate into the compound, Laurie couldn't help wondering what kind of ordeal she would have to go through to get the hell out of this place. She took a deep breath, and flicked the switch on the armrest to raise the window. The hail started to dissipate. Laurie checked the rearview mirror to make sure no one had followed her into the facility.

A sign up ahead pointed to the South Yard. Driving past the buildings—and the parking areas—she counted only three cars. She wondered where this guard on duty was.

Laurie found building 5, and parked beside the entrance. She hadn't brought along an umbrella. With Maureen's bill in her hand, she ran from the car to the door of the warehouse. The doorway was just deep enough to protect her from the downpour. A keypad with a little red light was on the door above the push handle. Squinting at the digits on the bottom of Maureen's bill, Laurie punched in the numbers.

A tiny green light above the keypad started blinking, and she pushed down the door handle. Inside, the rain patter on the roof echoed. The place had the damp, musty smell of a cellar. It was cavernous and dark, with only small pools of light from distantly spaced, single-bulb fixtures overhead. She could barely see anything. "They've got to be kidding," Laurie murmured. Then she noticed a light switch and a call button by the door.

She flicked on the switch. The number of lights on overhead suddenly doubled. But it was still gloomy in there—with shadowy pockets amid the rows of chain-link cages. Rain-soaked, Laurie shuddered from the cold as she started hunting for locker 163. She finally found locker 160 around a corner. But she saw something nearby that made her heart stop.

At first, it looked like a man standing in there behind the chain-link door.

Then she realized it was a life-size clown mannequin. This one was a bozo-type clown with a red-ball nose and a big, maniacal grin. Any minute now, she expected it to move.

Shuddering, Laurie hurried past it to locker 163 next door. She stopped to look at what Maureen had stored in the dim compartment: an old standing lamp, a big, stuffed chair, a file cabinet, boxes, and a couple of wardrobe bags. Laurie focused on the combination lock, and prayed this long shot paid off. Anyone could have written those numbers inside the back of the kitchen drawer: *2-16-47*. Even if Maureen had written them, the numbers could have meant a score of other things. Biting her lip, Laurie turned the dial on the lock and then gave it a tug.

Nothing. "Shit," she grumbled. She didn't want to call the guard on duty to come cut off the lock. She doubted he'd do it anyway—even if she tipped him extra. They wanted a photo ID. She doubted he'd settle for her just showing him Maureen's bill.

She gave the lock another spin and tried again. Then she held her breath and gave the lock a tug.

It opened. "Thank you, God," she whispered.

She found a switch just inside the chain-link door, and realized each locker had its own overhead. She flicked it on. The wardrobe bags hung on a pole that ran along near the top of the cage. It was silly, but she always thought wardrobe bags looked like vertical coffins—the perfect place to stash a dead body. To put her mind at rest, she unzipped the bags and found men's clothes—including a policeman's uniform. She remembered what Vincent had said about Maureen's husband—that he was a sheriff. A couple of the boxes were open on top. One had old Christmas decorations, and another held LPs. *The Best of Bread* was at the top of the stack.

Laurie eyed the file cabinet, and hoped it was unlocked. She also hoped her second long shot about this venture would pay off. She pulled the file cabinet's top drawer, and it stuck—but only for a second. Inside, she found folders of old letters and old income tax records for James Clark Forester and Maureen Johnson Forester that went back to 1980.

The next drawer down had more folders, crammed with clippings, glossy photos, and pages torn from magazines—all having to do with Barbra Streisand. The clippings went all the way back to the mid-sixties. But Maureen seemed to have gotten over her Barbra obsession sometime in the early eighties, because Laurie didn't see anything in there for *Yentl* or any of Barbra's later movies.

She started to get discouraged, and figured someone had destroyed the file on Cheryl. She opened the next drawer down and saw two thick files—in accordion-style pale blue folders. What stuck out among all the documentation was a copy of *Life* magazine. Laurie expected to see Barbra Streisand on the cover. But when she pried it out, she found the cover was dated July 17, 1970. It showed a slightly blurry black-and-white photo of the same gate Laurie had driven past today—and several times this week. A bloodied garment was tied to one of the spokes. All it said on the cover was THE SEATTLE MURDERS.

She wondered if both files were full of data about the Styles-Jordan killings. Maureen must have been collecting this data for years. And she'd only known Cheryl for a few months. Was this what Vincent thought was her "Cheryl homework?"

Laurie reached in the middle of the second file and blindly pulled out a sheet of paper. She winced at the old Xerox photo showing several people—mostly women, along with a couple of children—lying dead on the ground by a picnic table. Most of the women wore cutoffs and tank tops. Some were wearing body paint. They looked like hippies.

Laurie turned the paper over and read something scribbled on the back: *Biggs Farm—Hooper's Followers— 7/13/70.*

She remembered that most of them had drunk cyanide-laced lemonade. Trent had shot his friend, and then himself.

Past the rain patter on the roof, she thought she heard a door shut.

Laurie froze. She wondered if it was a distant clap of thunder. Or had someone just stepped inside the warehouse?

Rattled, she quickly stashed the *Life* magazine and the Xerox back into the thick file. Then she dug both accordion folders out of the drawer and set them on top of the box of LPs. Though she wanted to get out of there, Laurie couldn't leave without checking the next file drawer down. It squeaked as she pulled it opened. She found the drawer was full of high school and college yearbooks.

She heard someone whispering. Then a second person shushed the other one.

All at once, most of the overhead lights went off.

Laurie reached over and switched off the locker's individual light. She didn't want them to know where she was. For a few moments, she stood perfectly still.

She remembered the silver minivan that had been following her earlier. Had they caught up with her again?

She glanced around the storage space for something she might use to defend herself. But she didn't see anything. She spotted an ugly Christmas wreath sticking out of a Nordstrom bag. She carefully took the wreath out, set it aside, and loaded up the bag with the two files.

She heard footsteps. They seemed to be getting closer.

Poking her head out of the stall, she didn't see anyone coming down the corridor. She grabbed the Nordstrom bag, and crept out of the storage cubicle. The chain-link door yawned as she closed it. She fastened the lock in place, and gave it a spin.

She padded down the corridor—past the clown mannequin locker.

But then she came to a stop. Through the chain-link cages and over the piles of junk, she glimpsed someone moving up the other row of lockers. Laurie wondered if they could see her, too. She thought about making a run for the exit.

Then she heard a girl giggling. She smelled marijuana smoke.

Somebody let out a wolf cry, and it echoed throughout the warehouse.

The girl laughed again. "Shut up!" she said to her boyfriend. "You want us to get caught? Now, I know their locker is around here someplace."

"Shit, I can't believe your father has an old *Penthouse* collection in this place . . ."

Laurie let out a sigh, and then took a couple of deep breaths. She retreated toward the door. She thought about switching on the light—to give the kids a dose of the scare they'd given her—but decided to leave them in peace.

Her heart was still racing as she climbed back in the car. She placed the Nordstrom bag on its side on the passenger floor. The rain had eased to a steady downpour. Driving back to the compound's front entrance, she wondered once again exactly how she'd get out of there. But as she approached the gate, it opened automatically.

She passed through the gate, and glanced in the rearview mirror.

All at once, a van sped by on the access road ahead of her, its horn blaring.

Laurie slammed on the brake. The tires screeched.

Trying to catch her breath, she sat there under a streetlight with her Camry's nose in the road. The windshield wipers squeaked as they moved back and forth.

Laurie glanced down at the bag on the passenger floor. Some of the files had spilled out. The one on top had shadows of raindrops racing down it. The black-and-white photo was of a policeman standing over a shallow grave. He pointed down at a small, charred thing wrapped in a filthy blanket. Laurie didn't have to look at the back of the photo to figure out what it was.

She knew it was Baby Patrick, and the sight of it broke her heart.

CHAPTER TWENTY-EIGHT

Wednesday, July 9, 11:40 P.M.
Seattle

He was dead tired. But tonight—like the last couple of nights—Adam was afraid to fall asleep. He was worried he'd be woken by that music again, the same music they'd played while stabbing to death his brother and sister-in-law.

Stretched out on the sofa bed, he stared up at the ceiling of his friends' garage apartment/studio. He thought about Laurie Trotter. Adam liked her, and trusted her. But he didn't want to believe her theory about his dad possibly having a connection to the Styles-Jordan murders. Still, if it was true, that might explain why someone was "getting even" by killing Dean and Joyce that way.

Obviously, the secret from his father's past wasn't some private indiscretion or small misdemeanor. It had to be something pretty damn serious. But was he really involved in one of the most notorious crimes of the century? Uncle Marty had warned him: *"You can't keep asking people about this. You ask the wrong person, and you'll end up like your brother."*

His father was twenty-five when Elaina Styles and Dirk Jordan were murdered. From what Adam knew, his dad was single at the time, making a living in Seattle as a construction worker and going to business school at night. By his father's own admission, he was "scared as hell" he'd get drafted and sent to Vietnam. He was several years away from meeting Adam's mother and starting his own successful plumbing-supply business. Except for living in the same city where the Styles-Jordan murders had occurred, how could he be connected to those killings? Trent Hooper and a bunch of hippies had killed those people. The police had proven it, hadn't they?

Yesterday, Adam had gone online and looked up the murders that had inspired this copycat killer. He hadn't gotten too far in his research before finding photos of the crime scene from forty-four years ago. They were too sickening—and too damn similar to the scene he'd discovered in his brother's living room early Monday morning. Adam hadn't been able to look at any more.

He threw back the covers, and crawled out of bed. He figured if his father had something to do with those infamous murders, he needed to learn more about them—no matter how uncomfortable it made him.

But when he tried to start up his mobile device, he found it was out of juice. He got the cord out and plugged it in to recharge. His laptop was in the basement apartment, part of the crime scene—and inaccessible.

"Shit," Adam muttered, pacing around in his undershorts. He sat down on the unmade sofa bed, and glanced out the window at Dave and Stafford's house. Stafford had a desktop computer in his study.

Adam threw on his jeans, sneakers, and a *Family Guy* T-shirt Joyce had given him years ago. Grabbing the house keys, he headed out the door. "Eek, squeak, eek, squeak," he muttered to himself as he climbed down the outside stairs. He'd only been staying in the studio above the garage for three nights now, and the sound of these stairs was already a familiar sound to him.

He let himself in the front door, and then made a beeline to the alarm box and punched in the disable code. His friends were well-off and had a big, beautiful, three-story mission-style home. Stafford's study was on the second floor. They'd told Adam to please raid the refrigerator, because most of the food in there would go bad by the time they returned from their trip. So he poured himself a glass of milk, hoping it would make him fall asleep a little faster.

He drank it in front of the computer at Stafford's desk. He read the Wikipedia entries for "Elaina Styles Murder" and "Trent Hooper." He didn't see how his father was even remotely associated with the case. Trent Hooper and his gang were never tried for the murders. But if the group's suicide at the Biggs Farm wasn't an admission of guilt, the police had mountains of evidence placing Hooper and three of his followers in that house in Magnolia the night Elaina, Dirk, and their son's nanny were murdered. One of the killers even wrote a letter to a friend, bragging about what they'd done.

Adam started to nod off in front of the computer. He figured if he could fall asleep reading about this stuff, he could fall asleep anywhere. It was 12:36 A.M. according to the clock at the bottom right corner of the monitor. He clicked out of Internet Explorer, and picked up his empty glass.

That was when he heard the noise downstairs—a squeak, like a chair moving across a hardwood floor.

Suddenly, he was wide awake. Adam told himself that it could have just been the house settling. It was a big old house, it made noise. With the glass in his hand, he crept out to the hallway and glanced down from the top of the stairs. The foyer looked empty. He couldn't see any other room from where he stood.

He'd deactivated the alarm. He tried to remember if he'd locked the door behind him. It was on the catch, he knew that much. But it might not have been double-locked.

He heard a repeated *click-click,* the exact same sound his basement apartment door had made on the night of the murders.

Adam felt the hair stand up on the back of his neck.

He knew he was probably overreacting, but he couldn't help it. He remembered Stafford once admitted that they kept a gun hidden on the top shelf of the bookcase in his study. He hurried back into the study and set down the empty glass. Then he grabbed the straight-backed desk chair, and pulled it over to the bookcase. Climbing up on the chair, he reached his hand behind the row of books on the top shelf. His fingers brushed against a small box. Grabbing it, he heard it rattle. He found a dark gray box with *Atlanta Arms & Ammo* on it. He set it on top of the row of books and hunted for the gun. He hadn't handled a gun before, and wondered about the likelihood of it going off if he grabbed it the wrong way. *This was how the artist blew off his fingers.* Carefully, he took the gun by its muzzle and fished it out from behind the books. It was black—with Glock 19 imprinted along the top.

It sounded like floorboards creaking downstairs. Or was the noise coming from outside? He couldn't tell.

Any minute now, he expected the sound of romantic bells chiming, and Dirk Jordan singing about Elaina.

Clutching the gun and box of bullets to his chest, Adam jumped down from the chair and almost tipped it over. He returned to the top of the stairs, and glanced down at the foyer once again. He almost expected to find the front door open, but it was shut. He didn't hear anyone trying to get in. Had he imagined it before?

Or were they already in the house?

He heard a faint rustling. It seemed to come from somewhere between the side of the house and the garage. Then there was another sound: *Eek, squeak, eek, squeak, eek, squeak . . .*

He hurried to the guest room, where the window looked out to the garage. Catching his breath, he hid behind the curtain and peered out toward the apartment. He didn't see anyone on the stairs. Had they already ducked inside the studio? He was pretty sure he hadn't locked the door. He hadn't meant to stay here this long.

In the window across the way, he noticed he'd left

the light on. He could see the foot of the bed and, in the background, some of Dave's paintings leaning against the wall. A shadow swept over the room. Someone was in there, he was almost certain.

A small fogged window for the bathroom was near the top of the stairs. It was dark. Adam kept the bathroom door closed, because it blocked the entryway when open.

He watched a light suddenly appear on the other side of that fogged glass.

Someone had just opened the bathroom door to check if he was in there. They were looking for him.

"Jesus Christ," he murmured. Still clutching the gun and the box of bullets, he hurried back to Stafford's study. He didn't know the first thing about how to load and fire a gun. But he figured he'd have to learn fast. Once they realized he wasn't there next door, they'd probably try here.

Adam's hands were shaking as he set the gun and the box of bullets down on Stafford's desk. He grabbed the cordless phone off its cradle and clicked on the Talk button.

Then, for the second time that week, Adam called 911.

Thursday, July 10, 1:06 A.M.

Laurie woke up with a start. She heard Joey crying.

Laurie had nodded off on the sofa in the living room. She still had a stack of papers from Maureen's folder in her lap. Joey's wailing came over the baby monitor, which was propped up against the second folder on the coffee table. The documents, photos, and news clippings slid from her lap and scattered to the floor as she jumped off the couch. She staggered upstairs to the baby's room.

Standing up in his crib, Joey clutched the railing with one hand and banged at it with the other. Laurie rushed to him. He stopped crying long enough to catch his breath.

"What is it, sweetie?" she asked, picking him up. "Did you have a nightmare? Oh, and you have a wet diaper. C'mon, let's take care of that . . ."

Laurie stepped back into her bedroom. "Mommy's going to get you changed in just a minute," she said over his fussing. Meanwhile, she checked her closet and the bathroom. No one, they were alone up here. Joey crying out in the middle of the night was nothing novel, but tonight it unnerved her.

Joey continued to fuss after she'd changed his diaper. "Well, you're wide awake—unlike your dear mother," she murmured, picking him up again. "Let's go downstairs. Maybe you'll doze off down there. The couch worked for Mommy, it might work for you . . ."

Back in the living room, she stepped over the papers on the floor and made her way back to the sofa. Joey quieted down while she rocked him in her lap and quietly warbled "Sweet Baby James."

Laurie gazed down at the mess of documents and photos. She'd barely scratched the surface of what Maureen had collected.

By the time Laurie had gotten back home from E-Z Safe Storage—and then picked up Joey at the

Cassellas'—it was after seven. She'd just put him to bed when Cheryl called, asking if she had drafted her response to Gil Garrett yet. And what was she planning for tomorrow's dessert?

Desperate, Laurie went through her pantry, and found the ingredients for about three dozen Toll House cookies, which wasn't nearly enough. After that, she got creative. She made thirty oatmeal raisin cookies with some cereal and a packet of Ocean Spray Craisins. Finally some leftover Granny Smith apples from today's pie went into the forty cinnamon apple cookies.

Then she sat down and drafted her e-mail reply to Gil. She was exhausted and a bit peeved at Cheryl. After begging for help to get her an audience with Gil, suddenly Cheryl got picky about just who could attend this meeting. Laurie figured she should have told Cheryl to write the damn e-mail herself. It took her twenty minutes to compose just a few lines:

Dear Uncle Gil,

Thank you for getting back to me. I'm thrilled you're considering our company to cater your surprise party in September. Any time you'd like to meet on Saturday afternoon works for us. We will have food samples for you to taste. My partner requests that we meet with you alone in order to make sure the focus is on your reaction to the food, without any outside influences. I hope that will be possible. We want to make certain your individual tastes and wishes are met. And please, do let us know if there's any kind of food or theme you're leaning toward for this party. Thanks again for considering us, Uncle Gil!

I look forward to hearing from you about a meeting time
and place.

Sincerely,
Your Goddaughter, Laurie

She sent the draft to Cheryl, and got a response five
minutes later:

Hi, Laurie,

This is great! Just change the closing line to: **"I look
forward to hearing from you about the meeting time.
As we will be coming to you, please let us know if
there are any special instructions or directions
required for visiting your home."**

You never know with these multimillionaires . . . I don't
want a surprise strip search at his front gate.

Please send that e-mail (with the changes) out as soon as
you can.

Here's a great big thank-you for making this happen. See
you on the set tomorrow. Get some sleep!

Thanks again,
Cheryl

Laurie made the change Cheryl wanted, and sent the
e-mail to Gil's assistant.

By then, it was close to 10:30, and she just wanted
to go to bed. She looked at the two fat accordion-type
files on her coffee table, and told herself it could wait
until tomorrow.

But she couldn't. She poured herself a glass of Merlot and started rummaging through the files. She'd dreaded coming across photos of the murder scene in the Gayler Court house, but didn't see any. However, she found several more Xerox pictures of the group suicide by Hooper and his disciples at Biggs Farm. It was strange, to see them all sprawled out on the ground like that—some poor, misguided hippie girls, a middle-aged woman, and a couple of innocent children. There was no visible blood—except in the photos of Trent and his friend, Jed "JT" Dalton, who had been his accomplice in the murders of July 7, 1970. Both had taken a bullet in the head.

The Xerox pictures were in black and white, and obviously copied from official police crime scene photos. Maureen must have found them amid her sheriff-husband's files. Laurie imagined Maureen digging through a storage room for the photographs, then copying them at a Xerox machine in his office.

That must have been several years before she'd even met Cheryl.

Laurie wondered if Maureen had collected all this data out of a morbid fascination with the case. Or was she somehow personally involved in the murders? It couldn't be just a coincidence that Cheryl ended up working on the set of the *7/7/70* film. Had going after that movie catering job been Maureen's idea?

Laurie was beginning to think there was no such thing as a Cheryl file, but then she found a thin blue folder within the accordion-style file. In it were clippings and pages torn from magazines about Cheryl and the Grill Girl food truck. Laurie recognized a couple of the articles—from *The Seattle Times* and *Seattle Met* magazine. She also found old police records with mug shots of Cheryl at ages nineteen, twenty, and twenty-three. The name on the arrest records was *Charlene Anne Mundy,* though it was unmistakably Cheryl looking like a somber street urchin in the mug shots. The charges varied: drug possession, resisting arrest, shoplifting, and forgery.

In one of the articles Laurie had read a while back, Cheryl had admitted to having a drug problem and several brushes with the law in her youth. But Laurie didn't know that she'd gone to the trouble of changing her name to help erase her checkered past.

Cheryl had also said she'd grown up in several different foster homes. Laurie figured that was why Maureen had collected a listing of adoption agencies in Washington, Oregon, and Idaho. There were several letters from these agencies sent to Maureen Forester between 1979 and 1980, all of them basically form letters, all of them saying the same thing: *We have no record of the child you described in your letter.*

From what Laurie could tell, it seemed as if Maureen had been searching for Cheryl since 1979—maybe even earlier than that. And they finally connected five months ago? She wondered how the Styles-Jordan murders figured into all this. Why was Cheryl's folder tucked inside this file full of 7/7/70 research?

There was another police bulletin about Charlene Anne Mundy. It was a "missing child" flier, which paired her with another child. The blurry photo showed a young Charlene with her arm around a little boy. They stood in front of a swing set:

MISSING

CHARLENE ANNE MUNDY *JAY "BUDDY" MUNDY*
Age: 15	*Age: 3.5*
Eyes: Hazel	*Eyes: Blue*
Hair: Brown	*Hair: Brown*
Height: 5'2"	*Height: 3'4"*
Weight: 110	*Weight: 38*

Last Seen: Eugene, Oregon, on May 26, 1974

CHARLENE ANNE MUNDY and her brother, "BUDDY" MUNDY, disappeared from the residence of their uncle, Dorian Jefferson Mundy, at 718 Polk Street, Eugene, sometime in the afternoon of 5/26/74. Charlene is a freshman at Willamette High School. She has long light brown hair, parted in the middle, and was wearing a red sweater and blue jeans. "Buddy" has dark shaggy hair with bangs and has a birthmark over his right eye. He was wearing a green-striped short-sleeve shirt, red pants, and green sneakers. Anyone with information regarding the whereabouts of these two youngsters is urged to contact the Eugene Police Department at 458-555-1212.

Laurie wondered if this baby brother, "Buddy," was the child Cheryl had mentioned back when they'd first met for the job interview at the Elliott Bay Café. *I had a little boy of my own for a while, but I lost him,* she'd said.

There was nothing else in the Cheryl portion of the file. Laurie had dozed off with that "missing" flier in her hand.

And now Joey had finally dozed off, thank God.

Laurie carefully got up from the sofa and carried him upstairs to his crib. She tucked him in, and then wandered back down to the living room. It was after two o'clock in the morning, and she could barely keep her eyes open. But she had to look something up on Google, or she'd never fall asleep.

Laurie sank back down on the couch and set her computer notebook in her lap. She got onto the Internet, and pulled up Google. On the search line she typed: Charlene Anne Mundy. The first few results were Facebook pages for people with similar names. Laurie checked three pages of results, and didn't find anything about a girl that went missing in Eugene, Oregon, in 1974. Her luck wasn't any better with Jay "Buddy" Mundy.

Finally, she tried Dorian Jefferson Mundy. The first result was an obituary from the *Oregonian,* dated September 30, 1990.

> MUNDY, DORIAN JEFFERSON, 47, passed away peacefully in the home of his longtime friend, Lawrence Driscoll, of Portland. Mundy was part owner of Paws Salon Pet Grooming in Portland. He is survived by his many friends, both two-legged and four-legged. In lieu of flowers, donations can be made to Oregon Humane Society.

Laurie didn't know the man at all, but she started crying.

Maybe it was because she was so tired. Part of her was crying for herself, too, because all this research wasn't getting her anywhere. She should have been on-line looking up job opportunities—instead of trying to dig up something about Cheryl—or rather, Charlene.

She switched off her computer, then got to her feet and turned off the living room light. She glanced out the window at the courtyard.

There was only one other unit with a light on. It was Cheryl's. Was she still up? Or had she gone to bed and forgotten to turn the lights off again? Maybe she'd pur-posely left them on.

Laurie started up the stairs to bed, and realized that maybe one person in this apartment complex was even more scared than she was.

Thursday, 2:15 A.M.

"I'm really sorry," Adam said, standing outside the front entrance to Evergreen Manor. "It's just I couldn't sleep, and my dad told me the last couple of nights have been really rough for him. I think he'd feel better if I was there in his room with him."

He didn't know the middle-aged, East Indian nurse by name, but he'd seen her there before. She was on the other side of the door, which was held half-open by the stocky security guard next to her. "I am sorry, too," she said in her crisp accent. "But this is most irregular. I will have to check with the doctor on duty before I allow you to come in."

"Could you ask him to make an exception, please?" Adam said. "You might have heard my brother and sister-in-law were killed three nights ago. Anyway, my dad's still pretty traumatized. I'm just really worried about him right now . . ."

She nodded, and then retreated to the front desk in the lobby. The guard, whom Adam didn't know, stepped back, closed the door, and locked it. Looking at him through the window panel in the door, Adam worked up a contrite smile. But the husky man didn't smile back.

Adam wasn't lying. He was worried about his father. He figured if someone had come after him at his friends' garage apartment, then they might try to get at his father here. The security was good in this place, but not infallible.

A squad car had pulled in front of Stafford and Dave's house within six minutes of Adam's 911 call. But by that time, whoever had broken into the garage apartment was gone. The cops gave the studio the once over, and asked Adam if he noticed anything missing. The intruder hadn't touched Adam's iPhone. And his wallet—with all his money and credit cards in it—was still there on the kitchenette counter. It would have helped if he'd actually seen the perpetrator. But all he'd seen was what looked like someone opening his bathroom door.

Adam started to think the cops didn't believe him. Maybe they still considered him the only suspect in Dean and Joyce's murders, and thought he'd made all this up about someone breaking into the garage apartment just to throw them off.

But both cops were perfectly nice. They filled out a report, gave him a card with his case number on it, and suggested he keep the door double locked tonight. As soon as they left, Adam put on a pair of khakis, a nice shirt, and a light jacket. Then he drove here to Evergreen Manor.

In a way, it was reassuring to know they had the doors covered here. Still, Adam was worried about his father's safety. After what had just happened earlier tonight, Uncle Marty's warnings suddenly had a lot of credibility.

Through the glass panel in the door, Adam watched the nurse come back. She murmured something to the guard, and he opened the door all the way. "Dr. Mathias said it's all right—as long as you sign in," the nurse said with a polite smile.

"Thank you so much," Adam replied, stepping into the lobby.

"Are you planning to stay the rest of the night?"

Adam nodded. "Yes, if that's okay."

Ten minutes later, he was sitting in his father's room—on his father's Barcalounger. Adam listened to him snore.

He had his shoes off and a blanket tossed over him. His jacket was rolled into a ball, and tucked between the chair's cushioned armrest and his hip.

In the pocket of that jacket was his friend's Glock 19. It was loaded.

CHAPTER TWENTY-NINE

Thursday, July 10, 11:18 A.M.
Seattle

"Lord, are you three men blind?" Adam's aunt Doris said. She was scowling at his father. "Dino, you can't go out in that shirt. It's got one . . . two . . . three stains on it. Am I the only one to notice these things?"

Adam hadn't noticed. But he remembered the tomato-juice stain on the shirt his dad had worn yesterday.

"You can't go out looking like that, Dino," Aunt Doris went on. "Better take it off . . ."

Sitting on the edge of his bed, Adam's dad started to unbutton the shirt. "She just wants to see me with my shirt off," he chuckled. "Isn't that right, Dodo?"

"You wish," she muttered, opening up his father's closet. "Okay, what do you have in here?"

Aunt Doris was a tall, big, bossy woman with jet-black hair—which had to be a dye job, because she was about seventy years old. She was about two inches taller than Marty, who looked a bit like a bulldog, and had hardly any hair at all.

Marty was taking Adam's father to lunch and a Mariners game. They'd planned it two weeks ago, and Marty insisted it was probably just what Adam's dad needed right now. Doris came along for the lunch. She was skipping the game to shop at Pike Street Market.

She kept telling Adam how terrible he looked. Did he get any sleep at all last night?

He'd dozed for about three hours. He still had the gun rolled up in his jacket, which he'd stashed on the bookcase by the TV. Adam wasn't joining them for lunch. But before they took off, he hoped to catch a few minutes alone with Marty. While Doris tried to find a clean shirt for his dad, Adam leaned in close to his uncle. "Can I talk to you about something—in the hallway?"

Marty nodded, and then turned to Adam's dad. "We'll be right back. Dino, call me if she tries to make you take off your pants."

Adam checked the corridor to make sure they wouldn't have an audience. About six doors down, an elderly man in a robe stood outside his room with the help of his walker. He was out of earshot. Otherwise, the hallway was empty.

"So, what's going on, kid?" Marty asked. "You need help paying for the funeral?"

"Probably," Adam sighed. "But that's not why I wanted to talk with you, Uncle Marty. It's about this— *thing* Dad was supposed to have done at one time or another, this deep, dark secret. I think I have a right to know what it is—especially if it has something to do with why Dean and Joyce were murdered. After all, I—"

"Christ on a crutch, would you lower your voice?" Marty hissed. He glanced up and down the hallway.

Adam had been whispering. He couldn't help rolling his eyes.

"And don't give me that look," Marty growled. "Things that happened forty-some-odd years ago, before you were even a gleam in your old man's eye, you don't need to know about."

"You mean like *forty-four* years ago?" Adam asked in a hushed tone. "Was Dad somehow mixed up in the Styles-Jordan murders?"

"Just because some nutcase randomly picked your poor brother and sister-in-law, and decided to kill them that sick way, it doesn't mean—"

"Don't they have a laundry service in this place?" Doris called out. "All of these shirts are filthy!"

"He has some Izod sport shirts in the dresser!" Adam called back. Then he turned to Marty. "The other day you said that if I knew about this—*family skeleton,* my life might be in danger."

"That's right. I wasn't just saying that to hear myself talk, kid."

"Uncle Marty, last night, somebody broke into the apartment where I was staying. So, my life is already in danger."

Marty's dark eyes narrowed. "Have you been talking to anyone else about this *family secret* business—recently?"

Adam thought of Laurie Trotter. She was the only

one he'd mentioned it to since Uncle Marty had given him the gag order on Monday night. He looked at Marty and shook his head. "Listen, if you tell me, I promise not to talk about it. So, are you going to clue me in or what? I mean, I'm going crazy here, Uncle Marty. You say knowing about this could get me killed. But I think I'm far more likely to get myself killed by *not* knowing about it."

"Now is not the time," Marty whispered. "Maybe after the funeral, okay? For now, keep your mouth shut, and watch—"

"And watch my back," Adam interrupted. "Yeah, I know."

Marty gave his shoulder a gentle punch. "Wise ass," he muttered. Then he headed back into the room.

"It's plain and boring, but it's clean," Doris announced, gesturing toward Adam's dad, who sported a pale blue shirt she'd found for him. "Now, you won't look like a bum at lunch and the game, Dino. Adam, you need to go through his closet and get half that stuff cleaned." She leaned over the desk and scribbled something on a notepad. "You also need a girlfriend . . ."

"What?" he muttered. "Where's that coming from, Aunt Doris?"

"My friend Mary Agnes has a lovely daughter, Jill, single, pretty, and she lives right here in Seattle. You should call her up." She tore the page off the notepad and thrust it in Adam's hand. Then she turned and patted her husband on the shoulder. "I'm starved. Are we going to get moving or what?"

Adam was about to shove the piece of paper in his pocket, when Doris frowned at him. "Call her!" She nodded at the note. "I mean it. Look at that, and act on it!"

With a sigh, Adam glanced at the note—written in Doris's perfect penmanship:

> *Meet me at the big Ferris wheel*
> *on the Pier at 1:15.*
> *I'll tell you what you want to know.*

He looked up at her, and she just nodded.

"Okay, Aunt Doris," he said.

Thursday, 11:32 A.M.

"Don't these beets look beautiful?" she asked.

Cheryl held out the big, stainless steel bowl for Laurie to see. It was full of multicolored beets, fennel, and herbs.

"Gorgeous," Laurie muttered, barely glancing in the bowl. She stood at the stove, flipping the burgers they made ahead of time and kept warm for the lunch rush.

Maybe it was due to her lack of sleep last night, but she was cranky today—and not very patient with Cheryl's "food talk." Within the last few days, they'd had the copycat murders and Dolly Ingersoll's fatal "accident." Cheryl herself, upon her own admission, wasn't exactly a low insurance risk. All of these things were linked somehow—along with the Styles-Jordan murders. But Cheryl refused to talk about it.

"Friday, I'm going back to the farm," she said, stirring the beet salad. "I want everything we make for Gil to be fresh. I've been trying to land an audition with him for nearly a year now. That's what this is, an audition *with food.* Thanks to you, it's finally happening."

"The job here—with this movie," Laurie said, with a glance at her boss. "You had to work to land this job, too, didn't you? Was it Maureen's idea? I mean, did she have a special interest in the subject matter?"

"No, Maureen didn't even know about it," Cheryl replied, focused on her work. "No, when I heard they'd be filming here in Seattle, I thought it was a prestigious job and started campaigning for it. That was months back."

Laurie figured Cheryl had to be lying once again. Maureen had collected a mountain of documentation about the Styles-Jordan murders. Yet it was Cheryl who ended up catering the *7/7/70* movie—without Maureen having a thing to do with it. That was too much of a coincidence.

"So, how long have you been campaigning for a special catering gig at Evergreen Manor?" Laurie asked.

Cheryl stopped and stared at her. She shrugged. "A while . . ."

"Dean Holbrook, the man who was killed in those copycat murders on Monday, his father is a resident at Evergreen Manor." Laurie paused. "But then, you probably already knew that, didn't you?"

Cheryl didn't say anything. With a sigh, she turned and headed toward the refrigerator with the bowl of beets.

"I understand you ladies make some really good grub," said someone at the order window.

Cheryl turned toward the window.

Past the sizzling burgers and the vent whirling, Laurie heard her gasp.

The stainless steel bowl slipped out of Cheryl's hands and fell to the floor with a clatter. Beets spilled all over the rubber walking mat.

The young man at the window had dirty, shoulder-length blond hair and dark whisker stubble. His blue eyes were intense and haunting. There was something both oddly attractive and vile about him. For a moment, Laurie thought it was Trent Hooper grinning at them.

"God, I'm sorry!" the man laughed. "I didn't mean to scare you guys. Four stars for the makeup team, huh? I'm Tom Noll . . . T. E. Noll. I'm playing Trent Hooper, but I guess you already figured that out."

Laurie nodded. "Hi," she said, getting her breath back. "Are they—are they filming the murder scene today? They didn't tell us . . ."

"Yeah, the home invasion and the murders," he said. "It's on the docket for this afternoon, all day tomorrow, and the beginning of next week. Should be an intense few days." He squinted at Cheryl. "Are you okay?"

Cheryl didn't seem to notice she'd dropped the bowl full of beets. She backed toward the door, opened it, and hurried outside. She shut the door behind her.

"Jesus, I'm really sorry," T. E. Noll said. "I didn't mean to upset your friend. I was just having a little fun. I've scared a few people today with this makeup job, but she's the first one who seemed to take it personally."

"It's all right," Laurie said, working up a smile. "She's just on edge. She'll be okay."

"Will you apologize to her for me?"

She nodded. "Come on back at lunchtime."

As T. E. Noll wandered off, Laurie quickly returned to the grill and took off the burgers. They could go in the well-done stack. She stepped over the stainless steel bowl and opened the door. She found Cheryl sitting on the bottom step—of three that led up to the truck door. Her back was to Laurie. Hunched forward, she seemed to be rubbing her forehead.

"He apologized for upsetting you," Laurie said, staring down at her. She suddenly pitied Cheryl. But at the same time, she felt a lingering resentment toward her. She was tired of her boss's evasiveness and secrecy.

Cheryl didn't move. "I feel like such an idiot," she murmured.

"He gave me a pretty good scare, too," Laurie said. "He sure looks like the genuine article, doesn't he?"

Cheryl didn't answer.

Laurie folded her arms in front of her. "Then again, I never saw the genuine article in person." Her voice dropped to a whisper. "Have you, Cheryl? Something tells me you have."

Cheryl didn't turn around. She rubbed the back of her neck. "Could you see if there's anything left to salvage of the beet salad?"

Laurie gazed down at her. "For God's sake, what's going on here, Cheryl?"

"What's going on is we have to serve up lunch in twenty minutes," she said, finally standing up. "And we're nowhere near ready." She turned toward the door, but wouldn't look up at her.

Laurie sighed. "Listen, tomorrow's going to be my last day here. I'll work with you on Saturday, when we visit Gil, but that's it." She slowly shook her head. "I can't keep doing this. I have a child. I need to make sure he's safe . . ."

"He is!" Cheryl insisted, locking eyes with her at last. "Do you think I'd let anything bad happen to that little boy—or you?"

"It's kind of hard to believe that when people around you are getting killed—and every other thing you tell me is a lie. I'm sorry, but I think Dolly Ingersoll was right about you. You're not just here to serve food. You wanted this gig—you campaigned for it—with something else in mind, an ulterior motive . . ."

"It hasn't anything to do with you," Cheryl whispered. "You don't need to know . . ."

"And I don't need this job either," Laurie replied, "not when it puts Joey and me in harm's way. I'm sorry, Cheryl. Like I said, I'll stick it out with you through tomorrow and Saturday. Then we're done."

She glanced over her shoulder into the food truck. She stared at all those beautiful beets from the farm in Duvall, now scattered across the dirty rubber mat.

What a sad, horrible waste, Laurie thought.

Thursday, 1:13 P.M.

Aunt Doris had picked a lousy day to go up in the Seattle Great Wheel—if that was her intention. A misty fog hovered over Elliott Bay, and it had just started to drizzle. Only about twenty people waited in line to ride the huge Ferris wheel on Pier 57.

Doris wasn't in the line when Adam spotted her. Under a purple umbrella, she stood by a railing at the edge of the pier. Seagulls buzzed overhead. She waved at Adam as he approached her. "Hey, honey!" she called. "Do you think we'll be able to see anything from up there in all this rain?"

Before Adam could answer, she hugged him. Some water from her tilted umbrella dribbled down the back of his neck. "Did you notice anyone following you here?" she whispered in his ear.

"No," he said, confused. He didn't know he was supposed to be on alert for someone tailing him.

"Come on, let's get our tickets and grab a place in line," she said, wrapping her arm around his. "I'll see if we can get one of these pod thingies all to ourselves."

"You said you might be able to tell me something about my dad—"

"Wait until we're alone." She nudged his ribs with her elbow. "And keep your eyes peeled for anyone who might be watching us."

She was starting to sound like Uncle Marty with his "watch your back."

At the head of the line, Doris gave the employee her sweetest smile. "Could my nephew and I ride alone, young man? The cancer medication I'm on gives me vertigo sometimes, and he's here to talk me through it. I wouldn't want to make any other passengers uncomfortable . . ."

"Well, maybe you shouldn't be going on the ride, ma'am," murmured the young, blond man in the *Seattle Great Wheel* rain slicker. He looked concerned.

"Oh, but it's on my bucket list of things to do before I die. Please, honey, could we ride alone?"

The employee sighed. "Well, seeing as there aren't that many people here today . . ."

The gondola tilted and rolled a bit as Adam sat down across from his aunt. Once the employee closed the hatch, Adam frowned at her. "That poor guy, he thought you were dying, Aunt Doris."

"Hey, I've survived cancer twice," she said. "If that doesn't allow me to use the cancer card once in a while, I don't know what does. And it worked, didn't it? Besides, we could both be dead soon if it leaks out that we had this conversation."

The big wheel moved for a moment, then stopped as the gondola behind them was unloaded and took on new passengers.

"So, I'm not sure what you know," he said. "But Dean used to act like Pop had some kind of dark secret from his past. It kind of soured him on Pop, too. Anyway, I guess this thing about my dad is pretty damn serious."

"It is, honey," she said.

"Then you know about it . . ."

"Of course, I know about it." She sighed. "Lord, I've spent most of my life pretending to have my head in the clouds, not aware of a blessed thing. When you're married to a nice man who has some pretty shady business associates, you learn to act dumb. In some cases, it's better to know the score and act clueless than not knowing a damn thing. You keep your mouth shut and your eyes peeled for land mines. That's how I survived back when your uncle Marty was doing business with the mob."

Adam gaped at her. When they were younger, Adam and his brother used to joke about Uncle Marty possibly having ties to the mafia. *"Don't forget the cannoli, Marty,"* was Adam's twist on the *Godfather* line, which always got Dean laughing. Still, Adam was surprised to hear Doris admit it now.

"You know, I always kind of figured Uncle Marty . . ." He trailed off. "But Pop wasn't associated with them, was he?"

Doris nodded. "Yes, honey, your dear dad was working for them, too—about forty-five years ago."

The gondola swayed back and forth as the wheel rotated again for another loading. They were a bit higher now, looking down through the mist at the pier and the rain-dashed bay.

"I thought Pop had a construction job," Adam murmured.

"Who do you think owned the construction company?"

Adam wondered if this was the deep, dark family secret. Or was it worse than that?

"Pop didn't ever kill anyone, did he?"

She glanced down at the bay and sighed. "Your dear father is one of the sweetest men I've ever met. Back when all this started, he was supporting your widowed grandmother and paying for his night classes. Your grandfather wasn't exactly Mister Money Smarts, and he left them pretty broke. Dino borrowed money at work, and just got in too deep with the wrong people. But they gave him a break. They realized they had a good, hardworking kid in their employ, so they gave him extra work. They had your father running errands and driving people around, nothing else—nothing too heavy-duty. He got out from under them in 1971. He paid back his debts and kept his mouth shut."

They were still loading people on the big wheel. Adam shifted restlessly on the bench. "Did my father have anything to do with the Styles-Jordan murders?"

She nodded. "Yes, but only remotely."

"But how could he be involved? A bunch of hippies killed those people. The evidence was overwhelming . . ."

Suddenly, Adam felt his stomach lurch. The Ferris wheel was moving steadily now, taking them up over the water. Through the rain-beaded glass, they looked across at the Highway 99 viaduct and the city skyline. In the other direction was the Olympic mountain range. Down below, the people on the pier had shrunk to thimble size.

But Doris ignored the scenery. She gazed directly at him. "You're right, sweetie," she said. "That awful Trent Hooper character and his followers murdered those poor movie people. Your father didn't have anything to do with that part of it."

"Well, then what—"

"The group your father was working for started their own investigation of the case."

Adam squinted at her. "You're saying mobsters conducted an investigation into the Styles-Jordan murders?"

"Who better?" Doris replied. "Haven't you heard that old saying, 'It takes a thief to catch a thief'? Well, these local mob boys were hired by someone with a lot of clout down in L.A. to find Elaina Styles' killers.

And don't ask me who this big shot was, because I haven't a clue. But I can tell you this, the local mob guys found the killers before the police did. Your dad was on the team with three other guys. He was doing his usual grunt work, driving mostly."

"So, what happened?"

Doris sighed, and moved her purse into her lap. "What happened is everyone died."

"I know," Adam said. "They all committed suicide . . ."

She shook her head. "I'm not talking about Trent Hooper and his clan. I'm talking about the three men on the investigating team. Your father is the only one still alive."

"What are you talking about?"

She leaned toward him, and her voice dropped to a whisper. "Something happened at that farm where Hooper and his cronies died. Your dad and the other three showed up there a whole day before the police found that group dead. What exactly went on, I don't know. But I'm not sure I buy this 'group suicide.' I tried to get the truth out of Marty once, but all he could tell me was, 'Things got messy.' I have a feeling even he doesn't know any of the details."

Adam stared at her. He'd seen a photo on Wikipedia of the group suicide at Biggs Farm. Some of the victims had been children. Doris was telling him that his dad may have had a hand in that. He glanced down at tiny boats in the water below, and the people—like dots—on the pier. He felt sick. He couldn't breathe right. "Well, isn't there—" He swallowed hard. "Isn't there anyone who knows what really happened that day?"

"Your father," she said. "I'm guessing he must have broken down and told Dean at one point. That would account for the strain on their relationship. You don't look so good, honey. Your color's off. I've ridden this thing before. The trick is, don't look down. Keep focused on me . . ." She opened her purse. "Do you want a peppermint?"

Adam nodded. "Thanks."

She started searching through her purse. "Marty thinks your brother must have said something to the wrong person—or maybe he was seen talking to the wrong person. Something along those lines is probably what got him killed, God rest his soul . . ." She fished out a red-and-white swirled hard candy, and handed it to him. "Here you go, hon."

"Thanks," he murmured, peeling off the cellophane wrapper. "So what happened to the three men on the investigating team?"

"One of them was shot to death about ten years ago," Doris said somberly. "I don't know the details. The second one died of a heart attack last year—or at least, they said it looked like a heart attack. The third one on the team was a fellow named Freddie Rothschild. I didn't know him very well, but Marty did. He moved down to Phoenix last year, but never got completely out of the business the way Marty and your dad did. In that line of work, the walls have ears. There's always someone watching and listening—and willing to sell information they've picked up. That's why we're talking in here—in this space capsule thingee." She gave a nod to their surroundings. "How are you feeling, by the way?"

Adam sucked on the peppermint. "Better, thanks."

"Where was I?"

"Freddie Rothschild, and the walls had ears."

Doris nodded. "About four months ago, they announced this *7/7/70* movie was going to be made—with all sorts of shocking revelations about the case. Well, someone wasn't very happy about it. The writer of that movie script was the first to go. The police called it an accident, but anyone with half a brain could tell you it was a hit." She glanced out at the Olympics for a moment, and then sighed. "Not long after that, a couple of unsavory characters from 'the old gang' approached Marty, and asked just how far gone your father was with the Alzheimer's."

"It's not officially Alzheimer's, Aunt Doris. Technically, he's still in the early stages of dementia."

"Alzheimer's, dementia, whatever you want to call it," she said impatiently. "The point is, these guys had already checked up on your dad. Marty told them Dino wasn't doing well at all. If you ask me, I think that's what saved your father's life. That's why they left him alone. But Freddie Rothschild wasn't sick. His memory wasn't failing him. They started watching him. Your uncle Marty thinks they even bugged his home down in Phoenix. The story goes that about three months ago, a woman from Seattle met with Freddie and she grilled him about the Elaina Styles murders."

"Do you know the woman's name?" Adam asked.

Doris frowned. "No, and I have to admit, a lot of this is what the lawyers in their pinstriped suits call 'hearsay.' This is just what I've pieced together from tidbits I've gotten during lunches with a couple of the wives from the old days—and from whatever your uncle Marty has told me after a couple of martinis."

"Did anyone ever mention someone named Laurie Trotter?" he asked.

Doris frowned and shook her head. "No, that doesn't sound familiar. Anyway, I don't know what transpired between Fred and this woman from Seattle. But Fred was killed not long after their meeting. It was about ten weeks ago. The police called it a house robbery gone haywire. Somebody stuck a—a thing in his eye and it went right into his head . . ."

"What kind of a thing?"

She shrugged. "They said it could have been a very thin, long knife, or some kind of thick needle. Anyway, whatever it was, it killed him."

"What about this woman in Seattle?" Adam pressed. He was still thinking about Laurie—and her boss. "What have you heard about her?"

"Well, if she isn't already dead, my guess is she isn't long for this world." Doris reached across and took his hand in hers. "And sweetie, you're going to be in the same boat as her if you keep asking people questions about your father's past and the Elaina Styles murder case. Your uncle Marty believes that's why your brother and his dear wife were killed the way they were. He thinks it was—in part—a warning to anyone with any inside knowledge of the case to keep their mouths shut."

Adam scowled. "But that's kind of stupid. I mean, killing Dean and Joyce that way just stirred up even more interest in those old murders."

"Yes, among those people who don't have a clue

about what really happened," Doris said. "But to the few of us who know that those killings—and the suicides—weren't all they appeared to be, well, those people got the message loud and clear." She squeezed his hand. "That's why your uncle Marty is so worried about you, honey."

Adam had lost track of how many rotations the big wheel had made, but he was pretty certain they were now on the descent of their last round. He was still trying to fathom everything his Aunt Doris had just told him. "So, basically, you're saying the mob killed Dean and Joyce . . ."

"Someone very powerful is pulling the strings here," she whispered. "Maybe it's that big shot in L.A., if he's still around. Whoever it is, he probably hired a local mob hit man or a professional assassin. Your uncle Marty says what happened to Dean and Joyce was a professional hit. He also said the hit must have been carried out by someone who really loves their job . . ."

The wheel stopped to unload and reload people in the gondola in front of them.

"Promise me you won't talk about this with anyone else," Doris said. "Not only for your sake and your sweet father's sake—but also because your uncle Marty and I would like to stick around and enjoy his retirement for a few more years."

"I promise," Adam said. But already, he was thinking about comparing notes with Laurie. And as much as he loathed it, he'd need to talk with his father about this—during one of his dad's lucid moments. He still couldn't wrap his head around the very real possibility that his father had been involved in that "group sui-cide."

"So, take your aunt Doris's advice, honey," she said. "Act dumb. Keep your mouth shut and your eyes peeled for the land mines."

Adam nodded. "Thanks, Aunt Doris."

Their gondola was close to the ground now, next for unloading. Through the rain-beaded glass dome, he gazed at the people on the pier. Most of them were looking up at the Great Wheel.

But there was one woman who caught his attention. Dressed in black, she stood off by herself along the pier railing. She was a strange looking woman with tangled, raven hair and a long, pale face. She wasn't looking up.

She was staring directly at him.

CHAPTER THIRTY

Thursday, July 10, 6:41 P.M.
Seattle

"So the 'Seattle woman' who met with Freddie What's-his-name in Phoenix, that must have been Cheryl—or possibly Maureen."

Laurie sat with Adam in the kitchen at the yellow dinette set she'd inherited from Maureen. Joey was beside them in his high chair. He'd just finished eating his chicken with SpaghettiOs, much of which ended up on his bib, his high-chair tray, and the floor.

Laurie had thrown together some pasta carbonara for Adam and herself. This was the first time she'd sat down to dinner with a man since Brian died. It was hardly romantic with Joey there, but it felt good. His very presence in the apartment was reassuring—and seemed to break a sad, lonely hex on the place. Plus he was a nice man. Earlier, when Joey had hurled a fistful of SpaghettiOs at him, Adam had just laughed it off.

When she'd buzzed him in about ninety minutes ago, he'd seemed slightly shell-shocked. He'd admitted he was still bewildered over a long conversation he'd had with his aunt earlier in the afternoon. "I think my dad might have somehow been involved in what happened to Trent Hooper and his followers," he'd said.

"You mean the group suicide?"

"My aunt isn't so sure it was a suicide."

Then Adam had recounted everything his aunt had told him. They'd analyzed it all through dinner.

"It must have been Cheryl," Laurie said, pushing aside her plate. She'd hardly touched her carbonara. "Cheryl went down to Phoenix to talk to this Fred person, and he was killed. Not long after that, her food truck blew up—with Maureen in it. I think they were going after Cheryl and Maureen just happened to be in the wrong place at the wrong time. Look at Cheryl's pattern. She campaigned to get this film catering job, and it wasn't just so she could serve up food to movie stars. She was after something else. Dolly caught on to that early. Cheryl was trying to get her hands on the movie script, because it was supposed to have new information about the murders in it . . ."

Adam nodded. "My aunt Doris said the screenwriter was murdered because somebody didn't want that information coming out."

"I think Dolly Ingersoll was killed for the same reason. She was going to 'rip the lid' off the case, and look what happened to her." Laurie tossed her napkin on the plate. "Would you like some more?"

"Oh, no thank you, but that was incredible." He patted his stomach. "I can't believe I ate like I did. This is the first time I've had an appetite since Sunday."

Laurie took their plates to the sink. She wet a dishtowel and returned to the table and wiped off Joey's face and hands. "Anyway, as I was saying about Cheryl's pattern. She's been trying to land a special catering gig with Evergreen Manor, too. I think it's an excuse to get inside the place and talk to your father. I have a feeling that's why she met with your brother in Volunteer Park last week . . ."

"My aunt said Dean may have been killed because he was seen talking to the wrong person," Adam said. "Maybe someone else besides you saw them in the park that afternoon."

Laurie stopped swabbing Joey's hands. She turned to look at Adam. If his aunt was right, the same person may have seen her—with Joey.

"Are you okay?" he asked.

She nodded. "Listen, this Saturday we're going to Gil Garrett's mansion in Medina to audition for a catering job. That's been a goal of Cheryl's for almost a year. Now, I'm almost certain she has other reasons for going. That catering audition is just an excuse. The big shot down in L.A. who ordered the special investigation, who's to say it wasn't Gil Garrett? He was in love with Elaina. He discovered her."

"And you're going along with Cheryl to meet with Gil Garrett?" Adam asked. "Are you crazy?"

"I helped set it up. I promised her I would."

"Well, so what?" Adam retorted. "God knows what she's getting you into. Laurie, I don't understand why you're even still working with her."

"Tomorrow's my last day. Saturday I'm just helping out."

"With all this going on, I don't understand why you're

still here. If I were you, I would have packed up and moved somewhere else by now . . ."

She turned to wipe off Joey's tray. "This was my somewhere else," she said, her back to Adam. "This is where I packed up and moved away to. I really wanted this to work. I had a—a bad stalker situation in Ellensburg. He broke into my house, and I killed him. Now, his brother is after me—along with a tribe of his followers. The comparisons to Trent Hooper are a little scary . . ."

She felt Adam touching her shoulder. "Jesus, I'm really sorry . . ."

But Laurie couldn't look at him. Getting to her feet, she unsnapped Joey's messy bib and carefully carried it to the sink. She ran it under the hot water. "The story isn't as simple as that," she said, her back still to him. "The man who was stalking me, I'd slept with him a couple of times—over two years ago, while my husband was overseas. It wasn't really an affair, and I can't call it a fling, because that almost makes it sound fun. It was—just a bad mistake."

She shut off the water, grabbed a dishtowel, and finally turned to face him. "Anyway, I don't want to keep any secrets from you," she said, drying her hands. "I wanted you to know, because I like you, Adam."

"I like you, too, Laurie," he whispered.

She felt her face flush. Suddenly, she couldn't look at him again.

"I'm glad you told me about Ellensburg," he said. "But I still think you shouldn't go with Cheryl to Gil Garrett's house. Talk about bad mistakes. I'm really worried something terrible is going to happen there . . ."

Laurie knew he had a point. But it wasn't as if they were meeting someone in a dark alley at midnight. This was a Saturday afternoon at a mansion in Medina. She wasn't exactly sure what Cheryl was planning. But a part of her had to go there with her. She still felt a strange loyalty to Cheryl. And at long last, she was going to meet her godfather. Most of all, she had a feeling the resolution to all this was somewhere beyond the front gates of Gil Garrett and Shawna Farrell's estate.

She told Adam she'd think about what he said.

He needed to get back to Evergreen Manor before visiting hours ended. He was spending the night with his dad again. But before leaving, he asked if there were any photographs of the Biggs Farm suicide scene in those files she'd unearthed.

Laurie pulled some of the Xeroxed photos from Maureen's files and showed them to him.

It was strange to look at those photographs of dead women and children—while listening to Joey babbling happily in his playpen.

Adam had glanced at only a couple of shots before his face seemed to tense up. "Thanks," he murmured, handing the photographs back to her. For a few moments, he wouldn't look at her.

But he smiled when he waved good-bye to Joey. Laurie walked him to the door. "Listen," he said. "If you get scared or freaked out or anything, call me. I'm fifteen minutes away. I'll keep my phone on vibrate. You won't wake up my dad. And I probably won't get much sleep anyway . . ."

"Thanks," Laurie said.

"Could I see you tomorrow? I'd like another chance to talk you out of this thing on Saturday."

Laurie smiled. "Sure."

"Thank you for dinner," he said. "You're an amazing cook. In fact, I think you're amazing—period. G'night."

Then he turned and walked away.

Laurie didn't go back inside until she heard the front gate clank shut.

Thursday, 8:11 P.M.

"Are you spending the night again?" asked Jodi, the copper-haired nurse at the front desk. She reached for a visitor's badge.

The gun in Adam's jacket pocket left a bulge, and he tried to conceal it as he signed in at the desk. "Yes, I'm staying over. I hope that's not a problem."

"No problem. Let us know if you want a cot." She handed him his visitor's badge. "Did your friend get ahold of you?"

He was about to pin the badge to his shirt, but hesitated and stared at her. "What friend?"

"A woman called about ten minutes ago, asking if you were sleeping here again tonight or if she should try you at your friend's place." Jodi shrugged. "I told her I didn't know for sure."

Adam frowned. "Did this woman leave a name?"

Jodi shook her head. "I asked if I could take a message, but she said no."

"Well, um, thanks," he murmured. Scratching his head, he started to wander away.

"Don't forget to put on your visitor's ID!" Jodi called to him.

"Oh, thanks . . ." he called back. He pinned the badge to his shirt, and continued down the dimly lit corridor. He was wondering who this woman was who had called for him. Laurie knew he was here, and so did Aunt Doris. Besides, they both had his cell number. Why would they need to know where to reach him tonight? He tried to think of who might have known that he'd stayed at Stafford and Dave's garage apartment for the last few nights. Had he told anyone at work?

Adam remembered what Uncle Marty had told him: *"Watch your back."* He nervously patted the gun in his jacket pocket, and made a mental note to go online and read up some more on how to fire the damn thing. He wasn't even sure he'd loaded it correctly.

Stopping in his father's doorway, he found the old man in his Barcalounger staring at a Humphrey Bogart movie on TV. The three-footed cane stood within his father's reach. He had a small bag of Mini Chips Ahoy! in his hand, and cookie crumbs dotted the front of his shirt.

Adam couldn't imagine him having anything to do with that group suicide on Biggs Farm. It just didn't make sense.

"Hey, Pop," he said, stepping inside the room.

His dad glanced at him, and sighed. "Dean, where's your mother? I've kind of had it with this place. When's she going to come here and take me home?"

Adam sat down on the end of his father's bed. He didn't know how to answer him.

So he didn't say anything.

Thursday, 10:36 P.M.
Ellensburg

He waited outside the door of the darkened restaurant while Tony set the alarm.

Duncan felt funny asking for a ride home. Still, he really hoped Tony would offer him a lift—though there wasn't much chance of that happening. Tony had some stuff in the back of his pickup, and they'd have to move it around to make room for Duncan's Blue Bomber. Despite some rain earlier in the day, it had turned into a clear perfect summer night. There was no valid reason why he wouldn't want to ride home on his moped—except it was two weeks ago tonight that those creeps had taken him for a ride.

The next morning, they'd dumped the dead raccoon by the restaurant entrance. Duncan had gotten sick to his stomach when Paul had told him about it later in the day.

Since then, he'd gone online and ordered some pepper spray, but it still hadn't come in the mail yet. He'd also gone on sites teaching self-defense tactics. He'd learned how to surprise an attacker with a square blow to the nose or throat—or a kick to the groin. They called this sudden, fierce retaliatory action a *dry gulch*.

But Duncan was still scared. His mother didn't understand why he got so nervous at night. She didn't know that he'd just recently started keeping a steak knife between his mattress and box spring—within reach if he was awoken in the middle of the night.

He still hadn't told a soul about what had happened on that rainy evening two weeks ago.

He'd been anxious on these nights when he closed the restaurant. But last Thursday and tonight were especially bad, because they were the weekly anniversaries. Duncan was suspicious that way. He would probably never again wear the shirt he'd had on that night.

While waiting for Tony, he nervously glanced around the Superstar Diner's parking lot—and checked the access road for any cars headed this way. He didn't see anyone. He'd wheeled his moped closer to Tony's pickup. He didn't have any dessert to go tonight. He didn't want anything. He just wanted to get home—without anything bad happening.

Tony finally stepped out of the restaurant and locked the door. He was about forty, and looked a bit like Elvis in the later, fat years. Duncan often wondered if that was one reason Paul had hired him—in order to keep with the restaurant's retro theme. "You know, you don't have to hang around while I close up," Tony said, lumbering toward his pickup. "It's not like when that woman cook was here. I can do it by myself. It's no sweat."

"Well, Paul wants two people to be here when we lock up," Duncan explained. His head bobbed a little. "Just to be on the safe side."

"Whatever," Tony grumbled, climbing into his pickup. "See you tomorrow."

"Good night!" Duncan called. Then he hopped onto his Blue Bomber, turned the key in the ignition, and pressed the electric start button with his thumb.

Nothing happened.

Beside him, the engine of Tony's pickup let out a roar. The vehicle backed out of the parking space.

Duncan checked the moped's kill switch to make sure he had it in the "run" position. Then he tried the start button again and again, but to no avail. He turned toward Tony in the pickup. "Hey, wait!" he called.

But Tony must not have heard him. The pickup pulled away and headed onto the access road. Duncan helplessly watched its taillights fading in the distance.

He gave the moped's start button another try. Still nothing. He had this awful feeling in his stomach. Someone must have tinkered with his bike again.

With a shaky hand, he reached into the pocket of his cargo pants for his cell phone. But he wasn't sure whom to call. His mom? She was probably in no shape to drive. And it seemed like jumping the gun to call the police. He wondered what the phone number was for a taxi. And if they could pick him up, just how long would he be stuck out here waiting?

Duncan glanced toward the access road again, and saw a pair of headlights in the distance. He thought maybe Tony had come back for something. For a brief moment, he thought he was saved. But then he realized it wasn't Tony's pickup. It was a smaller car driving up the access road. As it came closer to the restaurant, the headlights went off.

In a panic, Duncan tried to climb off his bike, but he tripped. He hit the pavement hard, and the moped toppled over onto his leg. The phone flew out of his hand.

He heard the engine purring as the car approached. He glanced up and saw it was a maroon Honda Accord. It came to a stop right in front of him. Duncan desperately tried to untangle himself from the bike. He felt so trapped. Tears streamed down his face, and his head shook.

Over the sound of the idling engine, he heard the car door open. It triggered the open-door warning chime.

At last, Duncan crawled out from under his bike. He saw a scruffy-looking man standing by the driver's door. He had his hands in the pockets of his jeans. He was laughing.

When they'd taken him for that ride two weeks ago, he'd seen only the back of the driver's head and his eyes in the rearview mirror. But Duncan recognized the mean laugh. This was the guy who called himself Hans.

"Hey, Duncan," he said in a smug tone.

Duncan managed to get to his feet. He couldn't stop shaking. He clenched his fists.

"It's been two whole weeks, and not a card or a phone call thanking me for the ride," the man said, strutting toward him. "Have you heard from your girl-friend, Laurie? I'll bet you have. I'll bet you can tell me where she is . . ."

Duncan was so scared he couldn't move. "Leave me alone," he murmured.

The man laughed again. "You should see yourself. Your head's shaking so much it looks like it's gonna rattle right off your skinny neck . . ." With one hand still in his pocket, he reached out with the other one and grabbed Duncan by the front of his shirt. "Oh, and you're crying, too. That's precious . . ."

Duncan remembered how much they'd humiliated

him that rainy night two weeks ago. And he remembered the term he'd picked up on the Internet for a surprise attack: *dry gulch.*

All at once, he was enraged.

"Asshole!" Duncan cried, slamming his fist into the smug punk's throat. He grazed the bottom of his chin and punched him in the Adam's apple.

The man let go of him. He didn't gasp. All that came out of him as he staggered back was a strange, pathetic, choking sound. His hands came up to his neck.

Duncan punched him again—square in the nose. He heard something snap and blood spurted from the man's nostrils. Duncan felt some of it spray his face. He was about to hit him again.

But then the punk's legs seemed to give out from under him. He fell against the front of the car and crumpled to the pavement.

For a moment, Duncan was afraid he'd killed the guy. He stared at the Accord, expecting a group of the man's friends to jump out of it at any moment. But he took another step toward the idling car, and saw no one was inside. Hans had come alone.

Past the incessant beeping of the car door alarm, Duncan heard the man moaning. He sounded like a wounded animal. His face was covered with blood.

Duncan bent over him and felt his pockets. He found a switchblade in the pocket of his jeans.

"No, no, please . . . don't . . ." the man begged in a raspy, broken voice. Then he started coughing and sobbing.

Duncan backed away. He shoved the switchblade in

his pants pocket. Glancing around near his fallen Blue Bomber, he found his cell phone. He dialed 911.

While he waited for the emergency operator, Duncan could feel his head shaking. But it really didn't matter. He was still alive. He was still standing.

That miserable scumbag was curled up on the pavement, groaning.

And he'd put him there.

CHAPTER THIRTY-ONE

In the living room of the Gayler Court house, a chair and a tall plant had been tipped over, and three short coils of rope lay half-unwound on the carpeted floor.

Today they were shooting a scene in which Dirk Jordan was attacked—just as he'd been in that very room forty-four years ago. His own melodic composition and voice had woken him in the middle of the night. He'd come downstairs to investigate the music blaring on the stereo, and found his killers waiting for him there. A ficus plant and a cushioned chair had toppled over during the struggle. A Union Jack throw pillow was on the floor beside the fallen plant. The killers had already laid out the rope to tie up their victims.

Laurie remembered some of the same details in the crime scene photos she'd seen online.

She and Cheryl passed by the living room as they brought in the trays of lemon bars. Technicians were lighting the set while stand-ins—dressed in hippie garb—

were escorted into the living room by an assistant director.

Laurie noticed that Cheryl barely glanced toward the living room—or at any of the grubby-looking stand-ins. It was as if she'd made up her mind ahead of time to avoid looking that way. Cheryl's tray shook in her hands. She seemed relieved when she finally set it on the kitchen counter.

She'd been tense all morning, and even burned a couple of sandwiches. She'd said she was nervous about the meeting with Gil Garrett tomorrow. It was set for 2:30. Laurie had gotten the confirmation from Gil's secretary—along with directions to the house in Medina.

All Cheryl talked about was the menu for their "food audition." She never even mentioned the fact that this was Laurie's last official day. Maybe she didn't think Laurie had been serious about quitting. Or maybe it really didn't matter to Cheryl now that she had her appointment with Gil.

Laurie had made the lemon bars last night, after saying good night to Adam and putting Joey to bed. Before turning in, she went over Maureen's files again. Thanks to what Adam had told her, many of the pieces were starting to come together. But Maureen Forester was still a big missing section of the puzzle. Laurie couldn't figure out where Maureen fit into all of this.

Rummaging through Maureen's files, she glanced at a "missing" flier for Baby Patrick Jordan. The photo they used of the beautiful dark-haired boy looked airbrushed. Laurie figured some Hollywood photographer must have taken the picture. She started to read the description on the flier, but couldn't get past the first line when they mentioned the baby's yellow Snoopy pajamas. It just hit too close to home for her.

There were news clippings about false alarms in the search for Baby Patrick. A nanny, who happened to be African-American, was detained by police in Lake Oswego, Oregon, after someone spotted her in a neighborhood park with a white baby boy in her charge. A clairvoyant, claiming to know the whereabouts of Baby Patrick, led investigators to a section of woods in Seattle's Discovery Park. She claimed the baby was buried there. But all they unearthed were the remains of someone's dead cat. Some of the clippings were announcements from churches and synagogues all over the country about special prayer services for the missing child.

Maureen had saved articles from years later, too. One was from 1997, about a twenty-eight-year-old Dallas man who claimed he was Elaina and Dirk's supposedly dead son. There were several articles calling for the victims' graves to be exhumed so DNA testing could verify the identity of the child found in the shallow grave near the Biggs Farm.

The many photos and articles about Trent Hooper confirmed once again for Laurie that the makeup people had done a hell of a good job on that actor, T. E. Noll. Laurie remembered how traumatized Cheryl had been after seeing him outside the food truck.

She found articles about Gloria Northrop, the twenty-year-old nanny and often-forgotten victim of the murders on 7/7/70. For a while, her boyfriend, Earl Johnson, had been a suspect. Maureen had saved articles about him, too. From their photos, both Earl and Gloria looked slightly familiar: Gloria with her long dark hair parted down the middle, and Earl with his goofy grin and the dark bangs in his eyes. Laurie figured she must have seen similar photos of them online—during one of her many recent Google searches.

She was tired and blurry-eyed by the time she'd crawled into bed. Despite all the disturbing things she'd read that night, Laurie had fallen asleep just moments after her head had hit the pillow.

That didn't mean she wasn't tired today.

"I'm running on fumes!" her mother used to say when she was exhausted. And that was how Laurie felt now. She saw to it that the arrangement of lemon bars on the counter looked appetizing. Then she checked the urns to make sure there was enough coffee and hot water for the rest of the day. Laurie was taking a look at the supply of bottled water when her cell phone rang.

Only a few people had the number, so it always took her by surprise when someone called. She figured it was the Cassellas—or possibly Don Eberhard in Ellensburg. Laurie glanced at the caller ID: Ellensburg Police Dept. 509-555-1122.

Laurie clicked on. "Hello, Detective Eberhard?"

"Um, no, this is Mike Walter," the man said on the other end. "Is this Laurie Trotter?"

"Yes . . ." Something was wrong, she could tell.

"Laurie, I worked alongside Don Eberhard. You and I have met before."

"Yes, of course," she said. "Is Don okay?"

"Well, that's the thing. I'm afraid I have some bad news. Don went missing on Monday night. We found his car this morning—on the road to Mount Stuart, in the woods off Highway 97. His body was in a gully nearby. He'd been shot."

"Oh, God, no," she whispered. She braced herself against the counter.

"I'm sorry," the cop said. "He was very fond of you, Laurie."

Tears welled in her eyes. She felt responsible. She remembered he had a wife and a teenager daughter. "Do they—do they know who killed him?" she asked in a shaky voice.

She heard a heavy sigh on the other end. "Last night, after closing up the diner, your busboy friend Duncan McCarthy had a run-in with Lester Heinemann. He's one of Ryder McBride's crew . . ."

"Oh, no, poor Duncan," she murmured.

"'Poor Duncan' practically put the guy in the hospital. Turned out Heinemann was driving a stolen car, so we were able to haul him into the station and book him immediately. We found out this wasn't his first encounter with Duncan. Two weeks ago, he, McBride, and a girl named Amber Shapiro took Duncan for a little ride and tried to get information out of him concerning your whereabouts. I guess they threatened him and scared the holy hell out of the kid, because Duncan kept mum about it until last night. Anyway, we got a confession out of Heinemann. He said that he, Ryder, and another girl picked up Don on Monday and Ryder killed him that night . . ."

"Oh, God, it's all my fault," Laurie said, her voice cracking.

"Nonsense," the cop replied. "It was Ryder McBride who shot him. And Don knew the risks of this job. It's a hazard of our profession. Now, listen, Ryder and two of his girls have taken off. We believe they're on their way to Spokane. Don led them to believe you were there. We've notified the Spokane police and the Washington State Patrol. Ryder and his groupies won't get far. I think your best bet is to stay put in Seattle. We've given your case number to the Seattle P.D. Now, I have some numbers for you to call—here and in Seattle—in case anything comes up. Do you have a pen and paper handy?"

One of the sound men came in for a lemon bar, and Laurie borrowed a pen from him. She wrote down the phone numbers on a napkin. She also got the address of Don Eberhard's widow, so that she could send her a note.

"What happened?" Cheryl asked—as soon as Laurie clicked off with the Ellensburg policeman. "Are you okay?"

Grabbing another napkin, Laurie wiped her tears. "Someone who was very nice to me got killed," she replied with a tremor in her voice.

She was thinking it was nice of the cop to tell her that she wasn't to blame. But the truth was Don Eberhard would still be alive if it weren't for her. She retreated toward the little hallway, by the bathroom. She didn't want the film crew to see her crying.

Cheryl followed her. "Laurie, I'm so sorry. Is there anything I can do?"

She shook her head. She started to dial the Cassellas. She needed to check that Joey was safe. Then she would call Krista and Nathan—to make certain they were okay, too. She glanced at Cheryl. "Listen, do you need me for anything else?" she asked in a raspy voice. "I'd like to go home."

"No, we're fine here," Cheryl said. "Take off, go."

Laurie heard Tammy answer on the other end: "Hi, Laurie!"

"Hi," she said. "I'm just checking in. How's Joey? Is everything all right there?"

"Joey's fine," Tammy replied. "We went to the park this morning and had a great time. Are you okay? You sound funny."

"I'm all right," she said, rubbing her forehead. "Listen, I'll be by to pick him up in about a half hour or so."

"We'll be here," Tammy said. "Take your time. He just went down for his nap."

"Thanks, Tammy," she said.

When Laurie clicked off, she glanced at Cheryl, who was still hovering. She looked so worried and upset. It might as well have been a friend of hers who had been killed.

"What is it?" Laurie asked.

Cheryl bit her lip. "Will you still be able to go with me to Gil's tomorrow?" she asked.

That was what troubled her.

Laurie frowned. "Yes, Cheryl," she said.

Then she brushed past her and headed for the front door.

Friday, 4:04 P.M.
Ellensburg

"Duncan!" The night hostess, Stephanie, called from the other side of the pass-through window. "The phone's for you! Take it there in the kitchen, will you?"

He'd been loading a stack of dirty plates and silverware into the dishwasher. "Okay, thanks, Stephanie!" he called, pulling off his rubber gloves. Ever since he punched that man last night, Duncan had been worried Ryder McBride and his gang would come after him. The cops tried to assure him that he wasn't in any danger, but Duncan couldn't be so sure. No one ever phoned him here at the restaurant. He imagined it was Ryder or one of Ryder's friends calling to threaten him.

His head started to shake a bit as he walked across the kitchen to the phone on the wall. He wiped his hand on his apron and picked up the receiver. "Hello?"

For a moment, there was nothing.

Then he heard her voice. "Duncan? Duncan, it's Laurie."

"Hi, Laurie," he said, breaking into a smile. "God, I've really missed you . . ."

"I've missed you, too," she said. "Listen, I just wanted to thank you—and apologize. I spoke with the police, and I hear I caused you some trouble. I'm really sorry. I hope those creeps didn't hurt you . . ."

"You didn't cause me any trouble," Duncan said. "They did, but I'm fine. I didn't get hurt or anything. Did the police tell you I beat up one of Ryder McBride's buddies last night?"

"Yes, I hear you really flattened him," Laurie said. "Thank you, Duncan. You're my hero . . ."

With the phone to his ear, Duncan leaned against the kitchen wall. His head was shaking a little. But he had a triumphant smile on his face.

Friday, 5:09 P.M.
Seattle

His dad must have been pretty lucid, because he got up from his Barcalounger when Laurie came into the room. She was carrying Joey, her purse, and a Bartell Drugs bag.

Leaning on his cane, his father shook Laurie's hand. He said he remembered her from the day before yesterday. He offered Joey a Mini Chips Ahoy! Laurie tried to catch the crumbs as the baby gobbled it up.

"So, are you two going steady or something?" his dad asked.

Adam chuckled nervously. "No, Pop, at least, not yet." He led him back to his chair. "Remember, Laurie was asking you some questions the other day? We're hoping to pick up where we left off . . ."

This was Adam's idea. And Laurie had agreed to give it another try. She'd told him that if she seemed like a bit of a wreck when he saw her, it was because she'd had some bad news about a friend today. She didn't elaborate.

"I brought you guys some lemon bars," she said, handing him the plastic bag from Bartell Drugs. She sat down on the edge of the bed with Joey.

"Thanks, we'll eat them later," Adam said. "Laurie's a wonderful cook, Pop." He set aside the Tupperware container of bars, and found Laurie had also tucked the photocopies from the grisly scene at Biggs Farm inside the bag.

"Mr. Holbrook, I was asking you the other day—"

"Oh, call me Dino," he said with a smile, shifting a bit in his lounger.

"Dino, the other day I was asking you a lot of questions," Laurie said. She kept a hand on Joey's back as he crawled around the foot of the bed. "But I didn't get around to asking about a couple of people you might know or remember. Does the name Cheryl Wheeler sound familiar?"

Adam's father smiled and shook his head.

"What about Charlene Mundy . . . Charlene Anne Mundy?"

His lips moved as he silently said the name to himself. Then he shook his head again. "Nope, sorry."

"How about Maureen Forester?" she pressed.

He shrugged. "Sorry. Then again, Adam might have told you, my memory lately isn't what it used to be."

Adam pulled the straight-backed chair closer to his father and sat down. "You're doing great, Pop."

"The other day we were talking about Trent Hooper," Laurie said.

"He was sure a rotten apple."

"That's right," Laurie said, pulling Joey onto her lap. "Did you ever meet him or see him in person?"

Adam's father nodded. "Once—I saw him once, and that was enough."

"Where?" Adam asked. "When was this, Pop?"

He hesitated. His mouth twisted over to one side.

"Was it on a farm?" Adam asked.

His father nodded. "Hell of a mess," he muttered. "The place was in a shambles."

Adam glanced at the gruesome photocopies in his hands. He didn't want to upset his father too much. He hesitated, and looked over at Laurie.

She nodded soberly.

"Pop, some people died on that farm. Do you remember?"

"Yeah," his father murmured, gazing down at the floor. It seemed like he was starting to retreat into another time and place.

"Were you there when it happened? Were you there when they died?"

"I was there," he whispered.

"Pop, did you kill anyone?"

His father turned to him with a wounded look. He slowly shook his head.

"I'm going to show you a picture here," Adam said. "And maybe you can tell me exactly what happened." He ·found the least shocking image in the batch of black-and-white Xeroxed photos. The shot was taken at a slight distance with the picnic table and corpses clearly visible—and a barn in the background. "Do you remember this, Pop? Can you tell me what happened here?"

His father looked at the photo and winced. Tears came to his eyes. "They're all dead. I—I couldn't do anything." He started to weep. "I tried, but . . . I couldn't . . ."

Adam reached over and rubbed his father's shoulder.

"Pop, I'm sorry, but I need to know what happened there."

All at once, a loud buzzer went off in the hallway. It frightened Joey, who let out a startled wail. Laurie wrapped her arms around him. "What's that?" she asked—having to shout over the incessant noise.

Adam got to his feet. "It's the fire alarm," he yelled. "It goes off at least a couple of times a week here—people pulling the lever by mistake or trying to leave by one of the side doors." He helped his father to his feet and gave him his cane. "But we have to evacuate . . ."

He saw that his father was still upset and handed him a Kleenex from his pocket. He snatched up the Bartell bag and stashed the photos in it. As they filed out of the room, he grabbed his jacket off his father's bookcase. The gun was still inside it. He stuffed the jacket into the bag as well.

In the crowded hallway, the residents—many with walkers or in wheelchairs—moved at a snail's pace. Some were in their bedclothes or robes. Nurses and a couple of security guards were herding them toward the lobby and the main doors. "Calm down, everybody," the copper-haired nurse, Jodi, announced. "You people know the drill! We've all been through this before—like two days ago! Vera, button up your robe, honey. Everyone, just keep moving . . ."

Adam kept hold of his father's arm. He leaned in close to Laurie so she could hear him over the persistent alarm. "This won't take long. Are you wearing your visitor's pass? They won't let you back in without a pass."

She nodded, and shifted Joey aside long enough for Adam to see the visitor's badge on the front of her pullover. She pressed Joey's head to her chest and covered one of his ears to muffle the noise. He was still crying.

They merged with the throng into another crowded hallway.

"C'mon, folks," the husky, black, fifty-something security guard called out. He was on the other side of Adam's dad, directing the residents like a traffic cop.

Someone behind Adam slammed up against his back—almost as if he'd been pushed.

Adam glanced over his shoulder at an old man in a robe, who looked peeved. Just in back of the crusty old guy was a woman in her thirties with black hair and a long, pale face.

Adam turned forward again, and kept moving with the horde. It took him a moment to remember where he'd seen that severe-looking woman before. She'd been on the pier—at the Great Wheel yesterday.

She'd been watching him.

He swiveled around again. The woman had pushed her way forward so that she was right behind him. Adam froze.

She wore a black T-shirt and jeans. On one arm, she had some kind of leather cuff. She reached for something inside it.

Adam automatically stepped between her and his father.

Then someone put a hand on her shoulder. It was the security guard. "Miss, do you have a visitor's pass?"

She jerked away from him.

From the expression on her face, it looked as if she was about to punch the guard. Instead, she shoved aside an elderly lady and bolted through the crowd. The old woman hit the floor with a feeble cry.

"Wait!" Adam yelled. He wanted to chase her down, but his dad was leaning against him and the frail old woman was at his feet. He was trapped. "Hold it! Somebody, stop her!"

But no one did anything. They probably didn't even hear him over the alarm.

The woman seemed to vanish. Adam anxiously searched for her, but he couldn't spot her in the crowd. All he saw was a winding trail of startled, jostled people she'd left in her path. It looked like she'd headed down the next corridor—and maybe out the side door.

Adam helped the old woman to her feet. He glanced at Laurie and Joey to make sure they were okay. She gave him a bewildered look. She kept hugging Joey—and kept moving with the crowd.

The guard turned to Adam. "Do you know that woman? Was she with you?"

"No, but I think she's trouble," Adam said over the staccato alarm. "I think she might have come here to hurt my father."

"Well, it's okay, she's gone now," the guard said distractedly. Then he raised his voice again. "All right, people! Keep moving!"

Adam took his father by the arm again, and he looked at Laurie. They kept moving toward the lobby with the others. But he was still shaking over what had just happened—or had almost just happened.

The guard was wrong. It wasn't okay. And the woman may have gone.

But Adam was certain she'd be back.

Friday, 11:20 P.M.

"I'm in my dad's bathroom," Adam was saying on the other end of the line. "I don't want to wake him. So I'm fully dressed in his bathtub with the curtain closed to help muffle the sound of me talking. I'm sitting on one of those shower stools old people use. It's really quite depressing."

Laurie laughed. "I'm sorry. I shouldn't—it's not funny."

But the truth was, she needed a laugh tonight.

She was lying in bed—with Joey asleep in his little annex. She had her doors double locked downstairs and Brian's baseball bat at her bedside.

Earlier tonight, Adam had told her about the woman he'd spotted in the crowded hallway during the fire alarm. He'd been worried about her and Joey driving home alone. He'd been worried about his dad, too.

Once everyone had filed back into the building, she and Adam tried to ask his dad about Biggs Farm again, but he just got confused and disoriented. Adam walked her and Joey out to the parking lot, and waited there until after they'd driven off. At his insistence, she called him once she safely arrived home.

She baked several different types of cupcakes and

mini-pies for Gil Garrett to sample tomorrow. There was a whole batch for each different dessert sample. She decided to send a small package to Duncan, since he always liked her desserts. She'd use her old address in Ellensburg for the return address. Maybe by the time Duncan received the parcel, the police would have caught up with Ryder and his disciples. Then she could come out of hiding.

The remaining mini-pies and cupcakes were going to Don Eberhard's widow. With funerals, there was always some sort of brunch. Laurie figured the desserts would get eaten—if Mrs. Eberhard saw it in her heart to forgive her. Then again, maybe a package from her was just about the last thing Mrs. Eberhard wanted right now.

She'd been lying in bed thinking about that when Adam had called. Laurie had told him she would be up baking until midnight.

"Listen, about tomorrow," he said. "If I can't talk you out of this showdown with Gil Garrett and Cheryl, at least I can be close by—just in case you get into trouble. I went online, and checked. Medina Park is about two minutes by car from Gil Garrett's house. I can take my dad there tomorrow around two-fifteen. I'll stay there until you call and give me the all clear. In fact, not to tell you what to do, but maybe you should put my number on speed dial. If I don't hear from you by four, I'll call you."

"You don't have to do all this," she said, sitting up in the bed.

"I know, but I want to—if it'll help."

"Yes, it'll help," she replied. "That would make me feel a lot better. Thanks, Adam."

He asked her to call him in the morning, and she promised she would.

After they hung up, Laurie slid back under the covers, and then she started to cry. She had such an awful, doomed feeling about tomorrow. She was worried about Adam. A part of her felt like she didn't deserve his help and kindness.

She was also thinking about Don Eberhard, the last man who had tried to help her.

CHAPTER THIRTY-TWO

"I'm missing the Mariners," his father said—for the third time since they'd crossed the 520 Bridge.

"Pop, you're really working on my last nerve here about the Mariners game," Adam said, pulling into the parking lot for Medina Park. "You've got to let that go. We're here at the park now, and we're going to have fun, okay?"

He glanced in his rearview mirror to see if the dark blue SUV was still following him. The vehicle had been about two or three cars behind him since he'd gotten on the floating bridge over Lake Washington. For all he knew, it had been tailing him since he'd left Evergreen Manor.

He didn't mean to snap at his dad. But what with the SUV on his ass, he didn't need the old man suddenly obsessing over a missed Mariners game. Adam had asked him twice in the morning if he wanted to walk around Medina Park, and his dad had been all excited to go. He'd said he didn't care about the damn game. And now he acted like he was missing the Second Coming.

Of course, what really unnerved Adam was the idea of Laurie letting her boss drag her to Gil Garrett's house. Laurie was walking right into a trap—especially if she was right about Gil. He could very well have been the L.A. big shot who had hired local mobsters to conduct a special investigation into the Styles-Jordan murders. The investigators were dead, the people they were investigating were killed, and almost everyone with any kind of inside knowledge of what happened was now dead.

Adam had just met Laurie, and he liked her a hell of a lot. He'd already lost two people very close to him this week. He didn't want to lose her.

"Okay, Pop, let's get out and soak up the scenery," he said, parking the car. With his jacket folded up and tucked under his arm, he climbed out of his Mini Cooper. He went around to the passenger side and opened his father's door. Helping him out of the car, he handed him his cane. Adam thought about it for a moment, and then stashed his jacket—with the gun in it— under the passenger seat. Pressing the device on the key, he locked the car doors.

With his father by his side, he looked at the picnic grounds, and the people walking their dogs along the winding trails. He heard kids laughing. In the distance he could see what looked like a lagoon—and trees everywhere. Adam glanced over his shoulder toward the parking lot.

He didn't see it. He let out a sigh of relief.

He figured maybe he was wrong about the dark blue SUV.

The woman at the wheel of the SUV had pulled over just outside the entrance to Medina Park. Her cohort in the passenger seat had been preoccupied with something on his mobile device ever since they'd left Evergreen Manor. The woman didn't ask him what was so fascinating. She didn't care. She'd been busy keeping a discreet distance behind Dean Holbrook, Sr., and his son.

In the SUV's backseat, among other things, she had a thermos and Adam Holbrook's laptop computer— both stolen last night from the basement apartment of his dead brother's home. It was almost criminal how lax police security became on a crime scene after just a few days. Adam Holbrook's thermos was full of Country Time Lemonade—and enough cyanide to kill an entire family.

In this case, it just had to kill a father and son.

On Adam Holbrook's laptop, she'd composed a letter that would be sent to everyone on his mailing list:

To All My Friends,

You now know that it is true. I killed my brother, Dean, and his wife. I am Trent Hooper Incarnate. Like Trent, I am an unappreciated artistic genius. I have chosen to die as Trent did, and I'm taking my father with me. This world is not worth living in.

Adam

The e-mail was in his WAITING TO BE SENT file.

The woman had already chosen a remote woodland spot where Adam and Dean Holbrook, Sr., would be found.

The e-mail would go out in about two hours, while the Holbrooks were still alive. The friends on his mailing list—and there were many—would be concerned, of course. But there wasn't a thing they could do.

After all, finding the bodies could take days.

"Just a reminder," Cheryl said, at the wheel of the food truck. "Don't tell him my last name or mention the Grill Girl. I want him to taste the food first. Let's sell him on that before he puts it together that I'm the one who's been pestering him and his wife for a catering gig lo these many months."

Laurie squirmed in the passenger seat. In the back were trays full of tapas, mini-sandwiches, quiches, hors d'oeuvres, and Laurie's desserts. Yet all that beautiful food seemed like part of some pretense. Cheryl had another agenda. But Laurie still couldn't figure out what it was. Did Cheryl honestly think that after feeding Gil a few canapés, he'd sit down with her and tell her about his part in the Styles-Jordan murders and what followed?

Laurie hadn't said much during the twenty-minute drive that had taken them across Lake Washington from bohemian Capitol Hill to this pristine millionaire haven in Medina. But Cheryl chattered practically nonstop—mostly about the food, what to say to Gil, and what not to say. Cheryl had gotten rather dressed up for the occasion, too: a white tuxedo blouse and black slacks. Laurie wore a nice black top with beige slacks.

Gil's block was gated, with a security guard in a little chalet-style post and a crossing gate.

Cheryl pulled up to the gate, and lowered her window.

Now that they were here, Laurie felt her stomach tighten.

"I'm Cheryl and this is Laurie," she announced to the thin, thirtysomething guard. "Mr. Garrett is expecting us. We're the caterers."

He checked something on his iPad, and nodded. "It's the third house down on the right. I'll let them know you're on your way."

"We have some food trays we'd like to take directly into the kitchen," Cheryl told the man. "Could you let him know that we'll meet him in back?"

"Yes, ma'am," said the guard. He ducked into his guardhouse and raised the gate.

Laurie gazed at the clean, tree-lined road ahead. She took a deep breath. "How much do you think Gil really knows about Trent Hooper and the murders?" she heard herself ask.

"What?" Cheryl turned to squint at her.

"That's why we're here, isn't it? That's what this is about."

Cheryl shifted her focus back to the road. "This is about an important, prestigious catering job I've been wanting for nearly a year now. So please, don't blow it for me by saying stupid things like that—especially in front of Gil. Good God, Laurie, please don't do this to me now."

Laurie just shook her head. Then she turned and glanced out her window. Between the trees and the big, modern mansions, she caught a glimpse of the Lake Washington waterfront.

At the third driveway on the right, a tall double gate was open. Near one of the gateposts was a security camera.

"I'm sorry," Cheryl said, turning down the driveway. "You shouldn't kid around like that. I'm a little nervous right now."

"I wasn't kidding," Laurie said.

At the end of the long driveway, Gil Garrett and Shawna Farrell's home looked every bit as impressive as it had on the TV special with Dolly Ingersoll. The elegant Mediterranean-style mansion was surrounded by beautiful trees and potted blooming plants. The engraved double doors in front looked like something from an old Spanish church. Laurie counted five chimneys. The connecting garage looked like it housed four cars. A BMW and a Range Rover were parked in the turnaround.

Cheryl seemed to know exactly where she was going, because she turned off the driveway to a parking area by a guest house or staff member's residence, which was also Mediterranean-style, but about an eighth of the size of Gil's home. There was another turnaround, with room for several cars to park—and a walkway to a back entrance of the estate.

Laurie wondered how Cheryl knew about this. Had she studied a diagram of Gil's mansion?

"Let's put on our aprons, and bring in some of the smaller trays first," Cheryl said, parking in the turnaround. "It makes a better impression if we come to the door with food."

Laurie stepped out of the truck, then donned her maroon apron and grabbed a tray of mini-quiches. As they started toward the back entrance, she glimpsed— beyond a fence and some symmetrically pruned hedges— the stunning pool she'd seen on that television special. The back entrance was surrounded by several strategically placed potted plants, many in full bloom. The colors were gorgeous. Everything looked so clean, so perfect.

Cheryl had a tray of tapas in one hand and a fat, clunky purse hanging from her shoulder. She knocked on the tall glass panel in the door.

A short, heavyset Latino girl appeared on the other side of the glass. With a smile on her pretty face, she opened the door as if she were expecting them. Laurie guessed she was about eighteen years old. She wore a white polo shirt, khaki shorts, and sneakers. Her long, thick black hair was in a ponytail. "Laurie?" she said.

"Yes, hello," Laurie nodded, brandishing the tray of food.

"Come in, come in," she said in a thick accent. "Mr. Garrett will be right here . . ."

She guided them into a kitchen with beautiful wood cabinets that matched the polished floor. It had stainless steel appliances, marbleized-granite countertops, and in the eating area, a cobblestone fireplace. There was an island with a sink. Four barstools were lined up on one side of the island. Above it was a rack that held copper pots and pans, all polished and gleaming.

Cheryl set her tray down on the island's counter.

"Hi, I'm Cheryl," she said to the girl, talking a bit loudly and simplistically—the way some people did when addressing a foreigner. "Is there anyone else home, besides you and Mr. Garrett? Anyone else on the grounds?"

The girl shook her head. "No one else is here. Mr. Garrett is coming. Please, make yourself comfortable . . ." She started toward the front of the house.

Laurie put her tray on the island countertop. She'd never been in a kitchen this big before.

"Well, that's good," Cheryl murmured to her. "We won't have a lot of staff people here bothering us. Ye gods, can you believe this place?" She moved to the oven, turned a dial, and then opened the door to make sure the oven had started heating. "Let's start by getting the tapas warmed up . . ."

Laurie heard the Latino girl in the front of the house. "Mr. Garrett?" she called. "Laurie and her friend are here with the food for you!"

"Wonderful!" he replied, a distant voice from another room. "Be right there!"

Cheryl pulled a bottle of red wine from her big purse, and then fished out a corkscrew. Her hands shook a bit as she set them on the island counter. She picked up the tapas tray and carried it to the oven. Obviously, the oven wasn't preheated yet, but she slid the tray inside it anyway.

Laurie wondered if Cheryl was on the level after all. Was this really nothing more than a food audition for Gil Garrett? Could it be there was no ulterior motive?

She heard dogs yapping, and Gil's gravelly voice again, much closer this time. He seemed to be talking to the girl. "Sweetheart, you know how much I can't stand these little shit-machines," he said. "Would you keep them away from me, for chrissakes?"

The girl muttered an apology, and the dogs' yelping got louder. Two Pomeranians scampered into the kitchen, their paws clicking on the hardwood floor. Showing their teeth, they growled at Laurie and Cheryl. Laurie remembered there were three dogs in the CNN interview. She wondered what had happened to the third.

From the snipping dogs she looked up to lock eyes with the man who had been her elusive, glamorous godfather.

His eyes were half-hidden behind big, tinted glasses. He wore a shiny, powder blue sweat suit, and held a cigar in one hand. Laurie noticed two gaudy, jeweled rings on the fingers of that hand. His thinning hair was dyed black, and despite a dark tan, he had a waxy pallor that made him look sickly. "Well, my God, if you're not the spitting image of your beautiful grandmother!" he declared. "Look at you, darling. Aren't you lovely?" He took Laurie's hand, and kissed it.

Laurie smiled, and felt herself blushing. "It's really nice to meet you at long last, Mr. Garrett."

"What's with this Mr. Garrett nonsense?" he said, still holding on to her hand. "It's Gil—or Uncle Gil, if you must. Your grandmother was my very first love, Emily Hatch, the most gorgeous girl in Boulder, Colorado. How's your dear mother? I haven't seen her in at least twenty-five years."

Laurie realized he must not have read the note with her package of Christmas cookies. She winced a little. "Ah, my mother passed away about two years ago."

"Oh, I'm sorry to hear that, darling," he said.

Laurie nodded toward Cheryl at her side. "Gil, this is Cheryl, who owns the catering company."

"Hi, it's a pleasure to meet you, Mr. Garrett," she said, talking loudly over the barking dogs.

At last, he let go of Laurie's hand, then took Cheryl's hand and kissed it. "Please, call me Gil," he replied. "My God, I have two beautiful women working for me. I feel like Hef." Then he turned toward the front of the house. "Anita!" he yelled. "Anita, come here and do something about these mutts, will you, sweetheart?"

Cheryl fished the keys out of her big bag and handed them to Laurie. "Could you get the tray with the mini-sandwiches on it?" she whispered. "And there's dipping sauce in the fridge."

As Laurie headed to the door, she heard Cheryl going into her professional pitch: "Now I have some delicious tapas heating up for you. And this wine I've brought goes wonderfully with most everything you'll be sampling . . ."

Laurie stepped outside and headed toward the food truck. It seemed as if this food audition was indeed just what Cheryl had said it would be. She checked her watch, and figured Adam was now in the nearby park with his dad. It looked like he'd come all the way here for nothing.

Even with all his money and his past accomplishments, Gil Garrett struck her as sort of pathetic—and so archaic in his attempts to charm them. Did he actually think they'd be flattered when he said he felt like Hugh Hefner, having them work for him? Laurie had set him up on a pedestal most of her life. It was kind of disappointing to meet him now. Not only did he look a bit sickly, he also seemed slightly drunk. Then again, maybe that was just his manner.

When she stepped back into the kitchen with the mini-sandwiches and dipping sauces, Laurie got a strong whiff of Gil's cigar. The housekeeper was corralling the yapping Pomeranians into the eating area. She must have gotten out some plates and glasses for Cheryl, because the wine was poured and the tapas were plated. Gil, seated at the counter, was eating a tapa—and making yummy sounds. "I definitely want these for the party," he said. "Anita, get over here and try these . . ."

By the time he had his third helping, he'd drained his wineglass. The young housekeeper seemed to approve of the tapas as well. She had two. The dogs begged and whined at their feet. Cheryl poured Gil another glass, then started serving up the variety of mini-sandwiches with the different dipping sauces. "That's a bacon-wrapped teriyaki chicken with Swiss, and the dipping sauce is a pineapple chutney," Cheryl was saying.

Gil said the party for Shawna would be informal with tables set up in the backyard and by the pool. There would be about a hundred guests. "It's going to be a surprise," he said, his speech a bit slurred. "Anita here is sworn to secrecy. As for me, it's easy to keep secrets from my darling wife, since I rarely see her anymore—except in public. It's an arrangement that suits us both."

Laurie was a bit surprised he'd admit that to them. She figured he was indeed pretty drunk. Hunched over the counter with his smelly cigar in an ashtray, he stuffed a mini-sandwich into his mouth. The housekeeper quickly polished off three sandwiches, and announced that she liked the smoked pork tenderloin the best.

Laurie quietly stood by the counter, letting Cheryl run the show. Cheryl asked Gil if he had any particular theme in mind for Shawna's surprise birthday party. But he didn't seem to hear her. "Anita, give these damn mutts a Milk Bone, something to make them stop whining and begging, I can't stand it."

Laurie noticed the girl weaving slightly as she crossed the room and took some dog biscuits from a lower cabinet. Unlike Gil, she hadn't had a drop of wine.

The Pomeranians yelped and jumped at her legs as she held up a couple of dog treats. "Mr. Garrett, is it okay if I go to my room for a while?" she asked. "I'm suddenly really tired."

He nodded over his wineglass. "You go ahead, sweetheart. Have yourself a little nap."

Laurie glanced at the half-eaten sandwich on his plate. Then she looked at Cheryl, who was totally focused on Gil, watching his every move.

Laurie had a horrible feeling that all her suspicions about this food audition were coming true. "Cheryl?" she whispered. "Cheryl, what . . ."

The young housekeeper almost stumbled as she headed toward a hallway off the kitchen. She braced herself against a counter and then made her way to the corridor.

"Are you okay there?" Gil asked.

"I have to lie down," the girl answered in a quiet voice.

With a spatula, Cheryl set another mini-sandwich on Gil's plate.

Rubbing his forehead, Gil stared at the small hors d'oeuvre and then squinted at Cheryl. "What—what the hell did you put in these?"

She said nothing. She just stared at him.

"Goddamn it!" he cried. With one broad sweep of his arm, he knocked the plates, the glass, and the ashtray off the counter. They fell to the floor with a clatter, the glass shattering.

The Pomeranians yelped and growled as they fought each other for the fallen scraps of food.

Gil climbed off the stool, but he was teetering. He clung to the edge of the counter. "What have you done? What have you given me, you bitch?"

"Oh, God, Cheryl, no," Laurie whispered.

Cheryl was still focused on Gil, her eyes cold and remorseless. She didn't seem a bit nervous anymore. "I'm holding you accountable," she whispered to him.

She took a step back—just as Gil Garrett collapsed in front of her on the hardwood floor.

CHAPTER THIRTY-THREE

Five blocks from Gil Garrett's estate, Adam sat with his father on a bench in Medina Park. They'd gone for a short walk along one of the many trails—at one point, crossing a wooden bridge over part of a lagoon. But they didn't venture too far from the parking lot. Adam didn't want to put too much strain on his father's leg. And he wanted to be close to the car—in case Laurie called and needed him.

In the distance, he heard children laughing and shouting. But the park wasn't quite as crowded as it had been a half hour ago. Some dark clouds began to drift over the blue sky. Adam could almost smell a storm coming.

"Remember my friend Laurie from yesterday, Pop?" he asked, stretching his arm across the bench. "Remember when we were asking you about Trent Hooper? He and his followers all ended up dead on that farm. I read about it. They all drank poison—except for Trent and another guy. It looked like those two had shot themselves . . ."

His father started shaking his head.

"Pop, you—yesterday you indicated you were there that day. Did I understand you right? Can you remember any of it?"

He cleared his throat. "I need to go to the bathroom."

With a sigh, Adam got to his feet.

"I'm fine on my own," his father muttered. He stood up with a little help from his cane. But then he looked a bit lost.

Adam nodded toward the squat little building about a hundred feet away. "It's over there, Pop."

His father started off in that direction, but then he turned and frowned at him. "You've got it wrong," he said. "The papers reported it wrong. One of the women was shot, too."

Adam started toward him. "What?"

His father shook his head. "I'll be fine on my own in there," he said, turning away. "Stay put. I don't want you hovering by the restroom while I'm in there. I'm coming right back."

Dumbfounded, Adam watched him shuffle behind a trellis outside the restroom entrance. Then Adam reluctantly sank back down on the bench. His dad had sounded like he knew exactly what he was talking about. So that practically confirmed it: he was there at Biggs Farm for that group suicide. He wondered if he'd get any more information out of his dad while they were here at the park.

Biting his lip, Adam glanced over his shoulder toward the parking lot. There were fewer cars now than earlier. He didn't see a dark blue SUV among them. When he turned around again, he saw someone walking up the trail with their back to him—someone thin, all in black, with shaggy black hair.

Gaping at the lone figure, Adam started to stand up.

Just then, a woman threw a Frisbee at the person in black, who spun around to catch it. That was when Adam saw the goatee and realized it was a man with a very slight build.

He plopped back down on the bench. He heard some screaming in the distance, but it sounded like kids playing. He glanced toward the little building again. He kept waiting for his father to emerge from the other side of that trellis.

He decided he'd count to twenty, then go in there and check on him.

Adam felt a couple of drops of rain. He figured they might have to wait in the car until Laurie gave them the all clear. She and Cheryl were probably about thirty-five minutes into their meeting with Gil Garrett by now.

His cell phone rang, giving him a start.

He grabbed it out of his pocket and switched it on. "Hello, Laurie?"

There was a pause, and then a woman's voice came on. "Your father's asking for you."

The phone to his ear, Adam sat there for a moment. Then the words sank in, and he bolted off the bench and ran toward the little building. "Who is this?" he gasped into the phone. "Who's there?"

He heard a click on the other end.

He ducked into the men's room, which smelled foul. The overhead light flickered. There was only one urinal and one stall—with its door open. The spool of toilet paper was half-unraveled, leaving a trail on the filthy floor. The restroom was empty.

Adam was about to rush outside, but something caught his eye. On the wall above the sink was a stainless-steel square that served as an unbreakable mirror. It was scratched, and had some old, faded graffiti scribbled on it. But the message printed in a red laundry marker looked new:

DO WHAT WE TELL YOU

"Oh, Jesus, Cheryl," she whispered, backing away until she bumped into the refrigerator door.

Cheryl stepped on Gil's lit cigar, which had rolled onto the floor. The dogs were barking and yelping around her legs. "Help me stand him up," she hissed. "C'mon, goddamn it, Laurie, hurry! We don't have much time. We need to drag him outside, and load him into the truck. I can't do it by myself. He's heavy . . ."

"Help you?" She shook her head. "This—this can't be happening . . ." She couldn't move—or even get a breath. She'd figured Cheryl might try something here. But she hadn't expected anything this insane.

Cheryl reached for her bag on the counter, and pulled out a gun. "You can tell the police I made you help me. Tell them I forced you . . ."

Laurie shook her head. She didn't think Cheryl would ever shoot her. But then, she was still trying to fathom what Cheryl had just done. Right now, Laurie had no idea what she was capable of.

With the gun in her hand, Cheryl stood over Gil Garrett's body. "I've waited years for this moment. And you're not going to screw it up. You're going to help me . . ."

Laurie swallowed hard. "This is crazy. I won't help you. And I know you wouldn't shoot me . . ."

"You're right, it's the last thing I'd do," Cheryl whispered. "I'm sorry for this, Laurie. I'm sorry to get you involved . . ."

"Then why are you doing this?" she asked in a shrill voice.

"Because he killed them all," Cheryl said. "He orchestrated the whole thing—forty-four years ago. He was the mastermind. He arranged to have Elaina and Dirk murdered. Then he had Trent Hooper and all the others killed . . ."

She glared at Laurie, and then aimed the gun toward Gil's head. "And you're going to help me get a confession out of him—or the son of a bitch dies right here."

Outside the restroom, Adam frantically looked around the park for any sign of his father. But he didn't see him anywhere. He kept thinking they couldn't have gotten too far. Adam swiveled around and barged into the women's room. "Excuse me!" he yelled. His voice echoed slightly in the dim, empty little room.

His cell phone rang. He clicked it on. "Yes?" he answered, out of breath.

"You shouldn't be in the women's lavatory, Adam. You'll get arrested."

He hurried outside, around the trellis, and over to the edge of the parking lot. "Who is this? What do you want?" He gazed at the cars parked in the lot, but all of them looked empty.

He turned around and saw a blond woman on the winding trail, walking her corgi and talking on the phone. Then he spotted a man on a bench across the way. He was on his cell phone, too. Everywhere he looked, everyone seemed to be on their goddamn phone.

"Stay on the line with me, Adam," she said. "Just do as I say, and you'll see your father soon enough. Now, I want you to go to your car. Then I'm going to give you some easy instructions . . ."

With the phone to his ear, Adam headed toward his Mini Cooper in the lot. He heard a beep, an incoming call. He glanced at the caller ID on his keypad. It was Laurie. "Did you hear that?" he asked. "I have another call. It's important. I have to take it—"

"It's more important than your father's life?" she asked.

"Please, I—"

"Take it if you want," she said. "But I won't be here when you get back on the line. And you won't ever see your father again."

"Goddamn it," he whispered. Tears stung his eyes. It seemed too soon for Laurie to be calling with the all clear. She was probably in trouble.

And he had to ignore it.

He climbed into the Mini Cooper, and started the car. "All right, where do you want me to go?" he asked.

He glanced down at the passenger floor, and saw the sleeve of his jacket sticking out from beneath the seat.

"First, put your cell phone on speaker and set it someplace—like in your cup holder," she said. "It's against the law in Washington State to be using a hand-held mobile device while driving. The last thing you want right now is for a policeman to stop you—bad for you, and extremely bad for your father."

Adam did what he was told, and set the phone in the cup holder. "Can you hear me?" he asked.

"Loud and clear," she said. "Exit the lot, and head east on Twelfth."

Raindrops splashed on the windshield, and Adam switched on his wipers. He pulled out of the lot and turned down Twelfth. "How's my father?" he asked nervously. "Is he okay?"

"He's a little confused right now. He's been asking for you, Adam."

He squinted in his rearview mirror. "What do you want from me?"

"We'll discuss it later, when we reach our destination."

The dark blue SUV was right behind him once again, but they weren't too subtle about it this time. There was just a car length between them.

Checking the mirror again, Adam tried to make out who was at the wheel. From the driver's height and bulk, it looked like a man. Adam could barely see who was in the backseat, but it looked as if the guy was driving two people.

A car horn blared, and all at once, he saw the inter-section—and the red traffic light. He slammed on the brake. The car tires screeched, and he came to a stop. The Mini Cooper was on top of the crosswalk lines.

"You need to watch your driving, Adam," the woman said. "Remember what I told you? The last thing you want is for a policeman to stop you."

He tried to catch his breath. Clutching the wheel, he glanced down at his jacket on the floor. It had slid out from under the passenger seat when he'd stopped short. He checked the rearview mirror once more. Then he tried to reach for the jacket without being too obvious about it. He took his right hand off the wheel and stretched his arm as far as he could. His fingers grazed the rumpled jacket.

"Adam," she said calmly. "If you're looking for your gun, we have it."

"Jesus, no," he whispered to himself. He slumped lower in the seat.

"The light's green," she said. "Get going."

Adam did what he was told. He continued down Twelfth. They had his father back there—and they had him. He'd stay on this road until told otherwise.

And all the while, he'd hope to hear that beep again, the incoming call.

At least then he'd know Laurie was still alive.

"How long do you think before the police will start looking for this food truck?" Laurie asked. With a white-knuckled grip on the steering wheel, she navigated the stop-and-go traffic on the 520 Bridge toward Seattle. She had the wipers on at low speed.

"I figure we have about an hour, maybe even three if

no one comes to Gil's house and wakes up that girl."
Cheryl was in the passenger seat, holding the gun in
her lap.

Laurie's stomach was in knots. She wasn't used to
driving a vehicle this big. And they had an unwilling,
unconscious passenger in the truck section.

With Cheryl hissing orders at her, Laurie had helped
clean up the kitchen to erase all signs of a struggle. The
Pomeranians kept yapping and snapping at them—
until Cheryl tossed a couple of dog treats in the front
hallway. They'd scurried after the snacks, and then she
shut the kitchen door after them. After that, the two
dogs scratched at the closed door and yelped nonstop.

With Gil sandwiched between them, his near-
lifeless arms wrapped around each of their shoulders,
they managed to drag him out to the food truck and
hoist him into the back. Cheryl made Laurie put duct
tape over his mouth, then tie his hands behind him.
Cheryl checked her work, too—to make sure nothing
was loose.

Laurie kept looking around for security cameras,
hoping someone would see them and call the police.

As she climbed behind the wheel, Laurie furtively
reached inside her pants pocket and took out her cell
phone. She speed-dialed Adam. She figured she wouldn't
have to say anything. If he got the call, he'd know she
was in trouble and come to her rescue. He'd make it at
least as far as the gate crossing. She couldn't imagine
Cheryl really hurting anyone—except Gil and possibly
herself. Between Adam and the guard, they could put a
stop to all this.

But Adam didn't pick up.

Was it too much to hope that he'd see the missed call, and drive over here? He might beat them to the gate. He just needed some time—and so did she.

Once inside the food truck, Laurie kept stalling—dropping the keys, pretending she didn't know where anything was on the dash and steering wheel. But Cheryl obviously saw through her strategy. "Get us out of here," she growled. And Laurie obeyed.

When they finally reached the gate crossing, there was no sign of Adam. The guard opened the gate, and waved them through.

Laurie didn't know how Gil Garrett was supposed to have orchestrated the Styles-Jordan murders—or why. But something else concerned her as they neared the Seattle side of the floating bridge. "Just where are we going anyway?" she asked.

"I thought you'd figured that out by now," Cheryl said. "We're going to the house on Gayler Court, back to the scene of the crime. I want a confession. And what I can't scare out of him, the ghosts there will. You were right when you picked up on the fact that I've been inside that house before, Laurie . . ."

She took her eyes off the road for a second to look at her.

Cheryl nodded. "I was there that night."

CHAPTER THIRTY-FOUR

"The code is nine-three-zero-seven-six," Cheryl said.

Leaning out the driver's window, Laurie punched in the numbers on the keypad—on a post by the entryway. Until now, they hadn't needed to use the keypad to get past the gates. There had always been other people around—including the security guard parked on the street. But today they were alone here. The tents had been taken down and even the big trucks full of movie equipment were gone. The house was dark.

It was strange to see the place so deserted—after it had been the center of so much activity and attention the past week. The film crew would be back to set things up once again early Monday morning. But both Cheryl and Laurie knew neither one of them would be there to see it—not after today.

The front gate to the Gayler Court mansion yawned open.

"It looks almost exactly the way it did that night forty-four years go," Cheryl said. "There was just an intercom where that keypad is, but we didn't use it. JT climbed up over the fence." She nodded toward a spot in the fence near the left gate post.

Cheryl remembered watching JT from the backseat of the old, beat-up white Vista Cruiser. The seat faced the rear window, and whenever she rode in the car with other members of Trent's family, she felt isolated. Most of the time, she liked it that way.

She was twelve years old.

She wasn't supposed to be out with them that night, but she'd overheard Trent confiding in JT that they were going to "have a little fun with some movie stars." That was as much as she heard about Trent's plans before they noticed her and shooed her away. Apparently, meeting these movie stars was a big secret. She wasn't quite sure why. Trent was always bragging about the people he knew from his acting days in Hollywood— producers, directors, and actors. It was part of his charm, though she never found Trent all that appealing. Then again, she didn't care for most of the men who swept her mother off her feet.

That included her father, whom she never met.

Her mother had gotten pregnant at fourteen. Brandi Mundy refused to reveal the identity of the boy responsible, and she didn't want to give her baby up for adoption. According to Brandi's father, this act of defiance pretty much killed her mother. Apparently renal failure had nothing to do with it. One day when his granddaughter, Natalie Anne, was three months old, Mr.

Mundy drove her and Brandi to the Greyhound bus station. He gave Brandi seven hundred dollars in cash and told her that he never wanted to see her or her baby again. Then he drove off, leaving them there with four suitcases.

After her father, the other men in Brandi's life weren't much of an improvement.

She even married one of them for five months, and kept his last name, Milhaud. But no one could really pin her down. She was a drifter, who liked to hitchhike from one place to another. She often told her daughter that she was terrific "ride bait." After all, who wouldn't stop to give a lift to a young mother and her child? Natalie remembered living with a bunch of people in an artist's loft in San Francisco; then there was a ranch outside Tucson; and a farm commune in Eastern Washington. She even had a brief stint as a ward of the state in a children's shelter while her mother was in jail for shoplifting at a Sinclair station in Portland.

Somewhere along the line, Brandi got pregnant again. The baby boy was born in a free clinic in Eugene. Eleven-year-old Natalie got to name him, and she called him Buddy. From then on, he was like her own son.

By the time Natalie's mother met Trent Hooper and the three of them moved in with his tribe at Biggs farm, it seemed like just another temporary living place—and a pretty crummy one at that. But by July of 1970, they'd lived there for seven months. Natalie had her chores—mostly cooking for the group and looking after the younger children, especially Buddy, who was

ten months old. The adults seemed to have all the fun
with their parties, drugs, skinny-dipping, and campfire
singing sessions.

When Buddy got sick, Natalie wanted to take him to
a free clinic. There were a bunch of them nearby in
Seattle. Her mother kept saying it was just a cold. But
the baby was burning up with a fever and Natalie was
convinced it was something far more serious. Trent
didn't believe in modern medicine, and proclaimed the
baby would be fine if they all kept giving him "love energy."

Buddy died on July second. Natalie was heart-
broken—and so angry at her mother and Trent for letting it happen. It was utterly unnecessary, too.

The "Viking funeral" Trent orchestrated on the night
of July third was unnecessary as well. Her mother must
have been stoned out of her mind to agree to it. They
wrapped Buddy's body in a blanket and set it in an old
tin wash tub. JT had bought some fireworks for the
Fourth of July. Even though he and Trent weren't at all
patriotic and had burned their draft cards, they still
liked a good fireworks show. They stashed several sky-
rockets and sparklers in the tin washtub with Buddy, lit
them, and set the tub adrift in the farm's swimming
pond.

The pyrotechnics began to ignite, sending bursts of
color into the night sky and creating a deafening racket.
Trent and the others cheered and danced. JT and a couple of the women got naked. Trent kept going on about
how they were giving Buddy a true "Viking send-off."
But Natalie thought it was barbaric. A fire started in
the small washtub, which apparently was the point. But

she could smell the burning flesh. Glowing ash from the burning blanket floated in the air. The tub rocked crazily on the little lake—and water splashed inside it. Within a minute, the fire was out and the light show ended.

After everyone had passed out or gone to bed, Natalie waded into the pond and swam out to retrieve what was left of her baby brother's body. Shivering and cold, she wrapped the charred thing in another blanket, and loaded him in an old burlap bag. At dawn the next morning, she took a shovel, carried Buddy to some woods just outside the farm, and buried him. She used her black elastic headband to fashion a cross out of two big sticks, and marked his grave.

For the next few days, she picked wildflowers and set them on his grave. Without Buddy, there wasn't much for her to do at the farm anymore—especially in the evenings.

So the prospect of meeting a movie star seemed too good to resist.

Five nights after Buddy's botched Viking funeral, Natalie accompanied Trent and three others to the movie star's house in Seattle—only they didn't know about it. She'd snuck into the back of the Vista Cruiser minutes before they were ready to leave. No one noticed.

Her mom was driving, and Trent sat in the front passenger seat. JT occupied the back with Moonbeam, whose real name was Susan. Natalie didn't like her much, but she had a tiny crush on JT, because he looked like a grubby version of Bobby Sherman.

She stayed curled up on the floor, practically under

the seat in the very back. She heard Trent tell the others that they were going to "scare the crap" out of these people, because the couple had ripped off his producer friend, Gil Garrett, in some business deal. "If we do this right," he said, "Gil is going to put me in the movies—and none of this walk-on shit either. I'm going to be a star . . ."

Trent could be very manipulative and he enjoyed deluding people. Yet at the same time, he was pretty self-delusional, and could be easily manipulated by someone smarter than him. How much of what Trent told the others that night was a lie and how much was self-delusional no one would ever know.

About a half hour into the car ride, a cough gave Natalie away. She couldn't help it. She felt like she was choking. Moonbeam heard her. "Oh, shit, Brandi, your kid is in the back! She's going to ruin everything . . ."

Natalie's mother pulled over. She was all apologetic—especially to Trent. Would they have to turn back?

"It's too late," Trent replied. "We're almost there. You're staying in the car, wild child." Then he turned to her mother. "This couple has a baby. She can look after the kid if it wakes up while we're there . . ."

Natalie did what she was told and stayed in the back of the Vista Cruiser. Left alone in the station wagon, she suddenly wished she hadn't come. She wished it were a month ago, and she was back at Biggs farm, looking after Buddy.

After JT had jumped the fence, he opened the gate from the inside, and let in the others. They all wore dark clothes. Her mother usually favored airy, peasant dresses, but tonight she wore a black pullover and charcoal slacks. Her long curly hair was pulled back in a tight ponytail.

Natalie also noticed that Trent carried an old duffle bag. At the start of the driveway, inside the gate, he stopped and pulled a gun out of that bag. He held the satchel out for the others to pick something inside it. Natalie's mother shook her head. JT took out a hunting knife. Moonbeam chose a smaller knife.

Then they crept toward the big, dark house at the end of the driveway.

Cheryl remembered sitting in the back of the Vista Cruiser for what seemed like hours. It may have only been fifteen minutes. There was no way of knowing how long. The dashboard clock never worked, and she didn't own a watch.

But she remembered she'd never felt so alone and scared in all her life.

Now here she was in that same spot, forty-four years later, and her heart was racing. But she felt determined. She had the gun this time.

Laurie steered the food truck down the driveway toward the darkened estate. They weren't even halfway there, when all of the sudden, they heard a loud thump. The truck seemed to quaver.

Panicked, Laurie stepped on the brake. "Did I hit something?" she gasped.

Another thud reverberated from the truck.

"He's awake," Cheryl said. She took a deep breath. "This will make it easier on us. He'll be a bit groggy from the drug for the next hour, but he'll be able to communicate—and walk. We won't have to carry or drag him around." She nodded toward the house. "Go on toward the back. We'll take him in through the kitchen . . ."

Biting her lip, Laurie followed orders.

They heard another thump in the back.

"Listen to him," Cheryl said. "He must feel the ghosts already . . ."

Gil Garrett looked pathetic in his expensive blue sweats and the white loafers. One of the lenses to his tinted glasses had popped out. His wispy, receding hair was mussed. His face got more red and sweaty as he tried to yell past the duct tape over his mouth. It came out as muted, pitiful whining.

Laurie led him through the kitchen door. He staggered a bit, but at least he was on his feet. Cheryl trailed behind them—with the gun and her satchel.

In vain, Gil yanked and tugged at the rope around his wrists—still tightly tied behind him.

Laurie tried to think of an excuse to break away for a moment so she could call the police. Maybe she could dial 911 on the sly—and hope they traced the location of the caller. But Cheryl was on her guard, watching her every move.

She couldn't stop wondering about Adam. What had happened to him? That attempt to call him had been nearly an hour ago, and he still hadn't phoned back.

Cheryl locked the kitchen door behind them. "Do you know where we are, Gil?"

Laurie paused by the counter, where they'd set up the cookies yesterday. Gil just groaned and shook his head.

With the rain outside and the lights off, it was gloomy in the large house.

"Keep going," Cheryl hissed. "Take him into the living room. I want him to see it."

Laurie led him by the arm through the front hallway, where that UW student had hung himself from the balcony above them. Cheryl was right about the ghosts. Without the movie crew here, Laurie could feel something strange and otherworldly about the place. Its history was somehow more perceptible in the grayish light. Plastic sheets covered the furniture. A few cables had been left behind—along with some boxes and trash bags. But all the other movie equipment was gone.

"Do you know where you are now, Gil?" Cheryl asked.

He shook his head again. His moaning behind the tape sounded like muted protests. He wrenched free from Laurie's grasp.

"You're in the room where your onetime girlfriend, Elaina Styles, was murdered—along with her husband and their baby's nanny."

He was suddenly still. As if in shock, he stared at the room.

"You never had to set foot in here, did you, Gil?" Cheryl went on. "But they were *your* murders, weren't they? You hired a failed actor and a group of doped-up hippies to do your killing for you. Why, Gil? Why did you want her dead? Was it because Elaina stopped loving you and married someone else? Was it because she didn't want to make movies for you anymore?"

Laurie saw he was trembling. He had tears in his eyes.

"How much money, time, and effort did you pour into making her a star—only so she could turn her back on you?"

He kept shaking his head, and let out a muffled, anguished rasp. Then he started to cough, but it was stifled by the tape over his mouth. It sounded as if he were being strangled. He bent forward. His face turned crimson.

"Oh, God, Cheryl," Laurie whispered. "I think he's choking. Let me take off the tape . . ."

With the gun trained on him, she nodded. "Go ahead."

Laurie reached over and gently tugged at the duct tape on his mouth, but to no avail. She could feel the heat radiating from his face. She finally yanked the tape from his mouth, and it made a horrible ripping sound.

Gil let out a sharp cry, and then he doubled over and started coughing again.

Hovering beside him, Laurie slapped him on the back until the hacking began to subside.

"You can scream all you want, but it won't do you any good," Cheryl said. "I know that for a fact. They were here in this room, screaming for their lives that night, but no one ever came. I was right outside the house, and I barely heard them."

"God, please," he said in a raspy voice. "I—I need some water, please . . ."

Wincing, Laurie turned to Cheryl. "There are glasses in the kitchen cupboard."

Cheryl nodded.

Laurie realized this was her chance to call the police. She started for the kitchen, but Cheryl put her arm out—blocking her way. "Wait," she said. "Give me your cell phone."

Laurie reluctantly forfeited her cell. Cheryl tossed aside the phone as if it were a cigarette butt—and it landed on the shag-carpeted floor by the sofa. "If you aren't back in thirty seconds, I'm putting a bullet in his head."

"For God's sake," Gil croaked. He was looking at her. "Why is she doing this?"

Dumbfounded, Laurie gazed back at him.

"Go on, get him his water!" Cheryl hissed.

Retreating to the kitchen, Laurie found the plastic cups she'd seen in the cupboard earlier in the week. She felt so defeated about the phone. But one thing that gave her a little hope was that Gil seemed to realize she was here against her will. He'd seen she wasn't an accomplice in any of this. If they both survived, he might testify as to her innocence.

She kept thinking about Joey. If she was implicated in this, they could take him away from her. For the last hour, she'd been reassuring herself that he was in good hands with Tammy and Hank. If they were at all involved in Cheryl's insane scheme, Cheryl would have said something by now—using Joey as leverage to ensure Laurie's full cooperation.

Her hands were shaking as she filled the plastic cup with tap water. She brought it into the living room.

Gil was still clearing his throat. She put the cup to his lips, and he drank greedily. Then he nodded and she pulled the plastic cup away.

"Thank you," he gasped. "Are you—are you really my godchild?"

"Yes—"

"She had no idea I was going to do this," Cheryl cut in. "The only reason you're alive right now is because she agreed to help me get you here. I would have shot you in your kitchen an hour ago if she hadn't cooperated. You owe her your life, Gil."

He gazed at Laurie through those tinted spectacles with the missing lens. "Thank you," he whispered. He cleared his throat again. "You know, your friend here is crazy. Why would I have killed Elaina? I was in love with her."

"But she dumped you," Cheryl interjected.

"Yes, we broke up, but it was amicable, goddamn it!" he said in his gravelly voice. "I still wanted to make another movie with her. We were discussing it. I even wanted her for *Lifetime of Chance,* the role my wife got the Oscar for. I offered it to Elaina first, only she was pregnant. Elaina and I were still friends. When she was killed, it fucking broke my heart . . ."

He started coughing again.

Laurie stood beside him with the plastic cup of water. She turned to Cheryl. "Isn't it possible you're wrong?"

"No," Cheryl barked, pointing the gun in their direction. "He's lying. Trent said it in the car on the way here. He said Gil had promised to get him in the movies if he just did him this one favor."

"I don't know what you're talking about," Gil retorted. He was weaving slightly. His glasses sat crooked on his face. "I never even met the son of a bitch. It's utterly ridiculous. I found out later that we were at the same party once—along with about two hundred other people. I was there with my wife. It was almost a year before the murders. That's as close as I ever got to the sorry bastard."

He went into another coughing fit, and started to teeter. For a moment, Laurie thought he might collapse. "I need to sit down, for chrissake," he muttered. "I'm not well. I've got cancer. Take a little pity . . ."

Cheryl nodded at her. "Help him upstairs."

Flustered, Laurie looked up at the darkness beyond the top of the curving stairway.

"There's a chair in the second room off the hallway," Cheryl said. "That's where I want him. It was the baby's room."

Yesterday, during a lull in filming, Cheryl had snuck up the back stairs and peeked into what was once the nursery. Except for a few large boxes and a hard-backed chair, the room was unfurnished. It still had the light blue checkered wallpaper—slightly faded and dingy looking. But the white curtains were gone. Of course, so were the crib, bassinette, diaper pail, and the framed nursery rhyme cartoons on the wall. The baby's room was just a shell of what it had been. But Cheryl could still feel Baby Patrick in there—forty-four years later.

She wasn't sure if they would be filming in that room. Dirk and Elaina's bedroom and the living room were where most of the important scenes took place. Yet whenever Cheryl thought of this house and the murders, she remembered that bedroom—and the way it smelled of baby powder.

Dirk and Elaina must have left some windows open that warm July night, because Natalie heard the music start up. It was loud enough that even in the Vista Cruiser, parked outside the front gate, she could tell it was Dirk Jordan singing his new hit single, "Elaina."

At least the music helped pass the time while she waited alone in the car. But then it turned quiet again, and she got scared once more. Finally, she climbed out of the car and padded to the gate. JT had found a fat stick and wedged it in a spot by the post so the gate wouldn't shut all the way. The gate hinges squeaked as Natalie let herself in. She carefully placed the stick back in its place, and started down the long driveway. She saw lights on in the front of the house—but the thin white curtains were closed. She couldn't discern what was going on inside. All she could see were shadows moving about.

Earlier, she'd watched her mother, Trent, JT, and Moonbeam head down the driveway toward the back of the house. She followed the same path, hoping they'd left a door open. A dim light coming from one of the side windows made it easier for her to see her way around. Natalie noticed a screen leaning against the house. The window above it was open. Someone must have gotten a boost up, because the window was pretty high—too high for Natalie to reach. Not far from there was a door—with a crack of light along the edge. She gave it a gentle push, and it creaked open.

She found herself in a small hallway—with a powder room at her right. She moved on into the kitchen. It was very tidy—except for a box of Ritz crackers left out on the counter. She heard people talking in another room—and farther away, a baby crying.

Natalie crept toward the front of the house. She could hear someone sobbing, someone besides the baby. Moving toward the voices, she passed through the large foyer and spotted all of them in the living room. A chair and a tall potted plant had been tipped over. Trent, JT, and Moonbeam stood over three people, who were hog-tied on the shag carpet. The man was shirt-less, and wore blue pajama bottoms. Natalie could see he was handsome—even though his mouth was bleed-ing. A brown-haired girl in yellow pajamas was the one crying. She looked about twenty years old. Crouched down toward the floor, Natalie's mother was propping a Union Jack throw pillow beneath Elaina Styles's head. Natalie recognized the movie star—so beautiful with her long red hair and the lacy lavender nightgown.

"Oh, shit," Moonbeam said, gaping at her. "Brandi, your little brat is here . . ."

Her mother straightened up. "For God's sake, you were supposed to stay in the car!"

"Hey, it's cool," Trent said, brandishing the gun. He flicked back his dirty, tangled blond hair. "Go upstairs and see if you can't shut that baby up."

Natalie hesitated.

"Go on," Trent said.

"Please!" Elaina said, her eyes pleading with Nata-lie's. "Promise me, you won't let anyone hurt my little boy."

Natalie stared back at her, mesmerized. "I promise," she whispered. Then she hurried upstairs.

She followed the sound of his crying and found the baby in the second room off the upstairs hallway. It was strange to see how a pampered baby lived—in a clean bed, in Snoopy pajamas, with a big picture of Humpty Dumpty on the wall. He had brown hair and blue eyes—with a small birthmark over the right one. He was just about Buddy's age. It broke her heart to be this close to a baby again.

She could feel his diaper was damp. He stopped crying as soon as she picked him up. At that moment, Natalie knew she would keep her promise to Elaina Styles.

Hunting around the nursery, she found what she needed to change him. While cleaning him up, she kept thinking about how scared those people must be downstairs. Just last year, some hippies had killed a movie star and her friends down in Los Angeles. Those poor people in the living room had to be thinking about that right now.

"Natty?"

With the baby in her arms, Natalie turned toward the nursery door.

Her mother looked anxious. "Trent wants you to take the baby and go wait in the car—now."

Natalie quickly finished pinning on the clean diaper.

"Take the backstairs and go out the kitchen door. C'mon, hurry up . . ."

The music started up again with lush bells ringing and Dirk crooning about how insane he was for Elaina.

Natalie grabbed the Snoopy pajamas and wrapped the baby in his blanket. She hurried along the corridor until she found the back stairs. She glanced over her shoulder at her mother at the other end of the hallway.

Then she raced down the stairs. In the kitchen, she flung open the refrigerator and found a baby bottle. She grabbed it, and closed the refrigerator door with her hip. Clutching the baby in her arms, she hurried out the back door.

As she headed up the driveway, she could still hear the music—and screaming.

It sounded like Elaina.

Natalie waited in the car with the baby. Like Buddy, he was old enough that he could hold things. So he only needed a little help drinking from his bottle. She wasn't sure how long they waited before she caught a glimpse of her mother staggering up the driveway. She climbed behind the wheel, and faced forward. She was crying.

"Where's everybody else?" Natalie asked, rocking the baby in her lap.

"They'll be out soon," her mother replied, her voice hoarse. She didn't turn around. "Trent says we're going to keep the baby for a while."

Natalie couldn't believe Elaina would so easily give up her baby like that. "What are they doing to them?" she asked.

"They're just scaring them—like Trent said. That's all. Now, just—just be quiet and look after the baby, okay? I don't feel like talking for a while . . ."

Natalie didn't believe they were merely "scaring" those people in there.

Eventually, the others wandered down the driveway. Trent was carrying his duffle bag. He tossed it on the floor of the passenger seat, and Natalie heard the knives clanking. "Wash off what's in there when we get back to the farm," he grunted at her mother. The car shifted as he jumped in the front passenger seat. "We'll give you our clothes to burn, too. Got that, Brandi? Make yourself useful."

JT and Moonbeam lagged behind. He gave her a boost and she fixed something to a pointed bar at the top of the gate. It was Elaina's lacy lavender nightgown. There was blood on it.

Cheryl remembered knowing right then that her mother had lied to her.

She had the same certainty about Gil's lies. He'd manipulated Trent into committing those horrible murders—and then he'd arranged for the carnage that would follow a week later at Biggs Farm. She would get him to confess to it—or he would die in this house like so many others before him.

With the gun aimed at Gil Garrett's back, she followed him and Laurie up the stairs.

CHAPTER THIRTY-FIVE

Saturday, July 12, 4:29 P.M.
North Bend, Washington

"Well, I don't understand where we're going."
His father's voice was muffled and distant.
It came over Adam's phone, which was still on speaker
mode, and wedged in the console's cup holder.

"Don't you recognize the landscape, Dean?" the
woman asked him. None of his father's friends ever
called him that. He was Dino to them. "We're not too
far from Biggs Farm, where those hippies died a long,
long time ago. I hear your memory's failing you, but
you certainly remember that, don't you, old man?"

"I—I'm sorry," his father stammered. "I thought
my wife was coming here to pick me up and take me
home . . ."

Adam's heart broke as he listened to his father, so
helpless and confused.

For the last hour, Adam had been following the
woman's instructions, which had taken him off I-90
onto the rural roads. The delay-wipers kept sweeping

away the dull, steady drizzle from his windshield. Adam wasn't sure if Biggs Farm was really their destination— or if the place even still existed. He'd just passed the Twin Peaks Café in North Bend. They were headed toward Snoqualmie Pass and the national forest.

He couldn't help thinking that he and his father would be killed somewhere in those woods. He imagined the two of them kneeling over an open grave— and the execution-style shooting. At least there was a chance his father wouldn't understand what was happening.

For a while, Adam had tried flashing his brights at oncoming cars, hoping they'd figure out that he was in trouble. But it had been pointless, and the woman in the SUV had caught on anyway.

Outside of North Bend, they passed fewer and fewer cars. The surrounding woods were getting thicker. He braked for a stop sign at an empty intersection. Across the street was a small timber mill that looked as if it had been shut down for years.

Adam glanced at his gas gauge—half full. Maybe he could get some help at a gas station—if there was even one between here and Snoqualmie Pass. "Listen," he said, moving through the intersection. "If you plan on making us go much farther, I'll need to stop for gas. I'm almost empty."

"Well, that may just pose a problem for you—"

A loud, brief wail from a police siren cut the woman off.

In the rearview mirror, Adam saw the squad car peel around from the cross street with its strobes flashing. It came up right behind the dark blue SUV.

"Goddamn it," the woman hissed. "Okay, friend, pull over up ahead. I don't want to hear a fucking peep out of you . . ."

Adam veered over to the shoulder of the road—by the deserted timber mill. The car tilted slightly on a slope that led to a small ditch off the shoulder. He could see the SUV had pulled over, too, just a few car lengths behind him.

It seemed to take forever for the cop to get out of his patrol car, parked in back of the SUV. The siren was off, but the strobe was still flashing.

"I know what you're thinking, Adam," she said over the phone. "Here's your big opportunity to get some help from the police. Well, it's just a flunky traffic cop, and he can't help you worth a damn. In fact, his life is in your hands. He's as good as dead if you try anything. So just sit still there and let this good old boy write us a ticket . . ."

Adam watched the policeman amble up to the SUV driver's window. He couldn't quite see the cop's face. But he had a lean build, and from his gait he seemed pretty young. Adam remembered what Aunt Doris had told him about Dean and Joyce's killer—that it had to be a professional. The woman was right. A young, rural traffic cop was probably no match for the two killers in the SUV—then again, neither was he.

Adam could catch only snippets of the policeman's conversation with the driver. He said something about them running the stop sign at the intersection.

Adam kept thinking this was his last chance before they took him and his father into the woods to kill them. He could see the cop carried a sidearm. Who else could help them between here and the woods? All he had to do was clear his throat, and the cop would hear him. He could shout a warning, then shift the car into reverse and slam into the SUV. The Mini Cooper probably wouldn't do any damage to the other vehicle, but it might throw off the driver and the woman in back for a moment or two.

His hand hovered by the gear shift. Then he heard his father's voice: "Officer, I don't know these people—or where they're taking me. This one here, she has a gun . . ."

In the rearview mirror, he could see the cop looking into the back.

"Oh, Dad, be still," the woman said. "I just told you for the third time that we're going to Leavenworth. Officer, I'm sorry, but my father has Alzheimer's . . ."

Adam could see the driver, reaching for something under the front seat. The cop didn't seem to notice. He was looking at the two people in the back. It sounded like he was asking one of them to step out of the vehicle.

Adam could just make out the gun in the driver's hand. "Oh, Jesus," he whispered.

The driver pointed the gun at the cop's head.

"Watch out!" Adam screamed.

A shot rang out. Horror-struck, he saw the explosion of blood. The lean policeman reeled back from the driver's window and then flopped down on the pavement.

"Oh, my God, what did you do? What did you do?" his father cried.

"Shut up, old man!" bellowed the driver.

Stunned, Adam watched the driver climb out of the

front seat. He was muscular—with hair so close-cropped it looked painted on. Tattoos covered both his arms. He grabbed hold of the cop's lifeless arms and dragged him across the road. Then he tossed the corpse in the ditch as if it were a sack of garbage.

Over the speaker phone, Adam heard his father crying softly. He sounded so confused and scared. The woman kept barking at him to be still.

The driver walked back to the SUV and got behind the wheel. The door slammed.

"All right, Adam," the woman said calmly. "Let's get going. And while you're driving, take a moment to think about what just happened—and what your gun just did."

He felt sick to his stomach. His hands shook as he shifted out of park. Then he started back onto the rural road.

In his rearview mirror, he saw the SUV pull behind him—and farther back, the empty squad car parked on the shoulder with its flasher still going.

"Listen, ladies, aside from the fact that I'm pretty goddamned uncomfortable at the moment, all that's happened so far is I've had an unexpected afternoon nap and my glasses got broken. The damage is minimal. If you stop this now, I won't press any charges. I wouldn't want to do that to my goddaughter . . ."

Laurie was tying Gil Garrett's ankles to the hard-backed chair's legs. His wrists were still bound behind him on the other side of the chair back. With the gun in her hand, Cheryl stood over them, watching her every move. Laurie knew she'd double check her work. So there was no point in making the ropes loose.

The baby's room was dark and had that musty smell Laurie remembered from when she'd initially set foot in the house on that first day of shooting here.

"And you, Cheryl—if that's really your name—I sympathize, sweetheart. I really do. If you were really here on that night, you couldn't have been any older than ten. That's a helluva thing to live with most of your life. If you wrap this up right now before it gets any more serious, I want you to get some professional counseling. I'll even pay for it, sweetheart . . ."

"Aren't you generous?" Cheryl muttered. "Will you still want us to cater your wife's birthday party, too?"

"I'm trying to be a nice guy here!" he retorted. "For Christ's sake, I've already told you, I had nothing to do with Elaina's murder—or anything else that happened afterward. I was sick with grief—and shock. What more do you want from me?"

"The truth," Cheryl said. "And so far, I haven't heard it."

Through his broken glasses, Gil's eyes pleaded with Laurie. "Talk to her. I feel sorry for your friend. But there's a limit. I'm not a well man. I can't take this . . ."

Laurie finished tying his ankles to the chair legs. She glanced up at him. "Do you really have cancer?"

"The worst, pancreatic, like Swayze had," he grumbled. "The doctors give me six months—maybe eight if I give up the cigars." His voice dropped to a whisper. "Now, c'mon, darling, my arms are killing me in this chair. I'm counting on you. Talk to your friend, Cheryl, here. Make her understand . . ."

Laurie straightened up, and backed away from him. She turned to Cheryl. "Please, can't we stop this now?" she asked under her breath. "He's right. No one has gotten hurt yet. Listen to him. He's trying to give us a break . . ."

Cheryl brushed past her, and then crouched in front of Gil to tug at the ropes around his ankles. Then she walked behind him and tested the rope around his wrists. She sauntered around the chair until she was almost face-to-face with him. "Your goddaughter has a lot of—"

All at once, Gil slammed his head into hers.

Laurie heard a crack.

With a sharp cry, Cheryl lurched to one side and fell to the floor. The gun flew out of her hand.

"Christ, that hurts!" Gil roared. His glasses had flown off his head. He frantically nodded at Laurie. "Get the gun! Get the goddamn gun!"

Paralyzed, she gazed down at Cheryl on the floor.

She was moaning. Blood oozed from her left eyebrow, and she looked dazed. She sat up and blindly groped around for the gun on the floor—still out of her reach.

"What the fuck is wrong with you, you stupid bitch?" Gil yelled. "This is your chance! Grab the gun!"

Laurie gaped at him, and then she looked at Cheryl. She hesitated. Suddenly, she didn't know who she should help.

Cheryl found the gun, grabbed it by the muzzle, and

scrambled to her feet. She started toward Gil and raised the weapon over her head.

"No!" Laurie lunged toward her, and grabbed her arm before she could hit Gil with the butt of the gun. "God, no, please!" she cried. "Don't make it any worse . . ."

Gasping for a breath, Cheryl stepped back and jerked her arm away from Laurie's grip. Blood was dripping down into her eye, and she kept blinking.

"Stupid bitch," Gil muttered again and again. He had a bright red mark on his forehead from hitting Cheryl. He slumped over in the chair. If not tied to it, he would have fallen to the floor.

"You're bleeding." Laurie gently took Cheryl's arm. "Come on, let's take care of that. He—he's not going anywhere."

She picked up Cheryl's bag and led her out to the hallway. Laurie could almost feel the ghosts up here. Just down the shadowy corridor were Elaina and Dirk's bedroom and the room where Gloria Northrop had slept.

Laurie found a bathroom one door down, and flicked on the light. Only three bulbs worked among the eight above the long mirror. The fixtures were white and the walls were a pale green marble. Someone on the crew must have used this room as a combination lavatory and janitor's closet. A slew of cleaning products and a couple of rolls of paper towels sat on the sink counter.

Laurie lowered the toilet-seat lid and sat Cheryl down. Cheryl was obviously still a bit stunned. She no longer had the gun pointed at her. Laurie figured she probably could have snatched it away from her without much resistance. But she didn't try. She'd already killed someone once in a struggle; she didn't want to risk it happening again—not with Cheryl. She ran a paper towel under the faucet and then carefully dabbed it on the cut above Cheryl's left eye.

"Listen to me," she said. "You need to call this off, Cheryl. There's still a chance he won't press any charges . . ."

"Yeah, he's a real sweetie pie." Cheryl winced as Laurie cleaned the cut and applied a little pressure to it. "Look at this cut. And did I hear wrong or did your dear godfather just call you a stupid bitch a couple of minutes ago?"

"How do you expect this to work out?" Laurie asked. "What if you're wrong about him? What if Trent was lying about Gil? Or maybe somebody lied to Trent. I'm sorry, but I think Gil's telling us the truth."

"Well, he isn't," Cheryl said, pointing the gun at her again. "I confirmed it with someone else. The order to kill Elaina and Dirk came from one of Gil's people. Now, we probably have less than an hour before the police figure out we've come here. I'm getting a confession out of that bastard before then—even if I have to kill him. I have a small recorder in that bag. I'll get the whole thing on tape—or digital or whatever you call it. I'll have it for the police. And don't worry, Laurie. I'll make sure they know you weren't a willing accomplice in any of this."

"And you think they'll believe you?" Laurie retorted, stepping back from her. "We'll both be arrested. Your grand scheme, it's going to backfire, Cheryl. Even if Gil says that he orchestrated *everything,* the police will still say his confession was coerced. We'll end up in jail, and they'll take Joey away from me. They'll put my son in foster care. I can't let that happen. Cheryl, you're not a mother. You don't know what it's like to lose a child. You have no idea how devastating that would be . . ."

Holding a wadded up piece of paper towel to her eyebrow, Cheryl stared back at her. "Don't I?" she said.

Baby Patrick became her child that night.

She'd rescued him from that house of death. She felt obligated to honor Elaina Styles's last wish, and make sure no harm came to that baby boy. Natalie resolved never to let him out of her sight. She called him Buddy.

In the farmhouse's living room was a portable black-and-white TV with a bent hanger for an antenna. Between the TV news reports and what she heard over her transistor radio, Natalie learned that the police were getting closer and closer to finding the killers in what was becoming known as the Styles-Jordan murders. JT, Moonbeam—and her mother, especially—were worried. But Trent assured them that the news reports were bullshit. Gil Garrett's people would make sure they'd never be arrested.

One week after the murders, Natalie accompanied her mother into town on a grocery run. She took Buddy along. Her mother had been a wreck ever since the night of the murders. Natalie had wanted to run away from Biggs Farm, but her mom was certain Trent would hunt them down. After all, they were witnesses. So her mother's solution to this crisis was staying stoned or drunk most of the time. But that afternoon, she was lucid enough to drive to the store—and do all the shopping.

Natalie remained in the very backseat of the Vista Cruiser with Buddy. She didn't want to take any chances going out in public with the baby. Besides the murders, all they talked about on TV was the search for Baby Patrick. He was pretty easy to spot with the birthmark over his eye. So Natalie didn't want to take a chance bringing him into the store—even though it would have been fun to sit him in the baby seat and push him in the cart.

Her mother was clearheaded enough to remember everything on the grocery list. When they returned to the farm, she saw—before Natalie did—that something was seriously wrong.

About halfway down the long, gravel driveway, she stopped the Vista Cruiser.

A black Cadillac was parked in front of the farmhouse. Everyone sat at the picnic tables by the garden—including the two children, Fawn and Thunder, and a young teen hitchhiker JT and one of the women had picked up the day before. Ernestine, who owned the farm, was there, too. For Trent to have an impromptu rap session out there was nothing unusual—especially on a warm sunny afternoon like this. Sometimes, the adults would sit at the picnic tables and take acid. In fact, some of them already looked pretty out of it—at least from what Natalie could discern at that distance. Everyone helped themselves from a big cooler of lemonade she'd made earlier. There was nothing unusual about that either.

But three men stood beside Trent as he addressed the group, and they definitely didn't belong there. They wore nice slacks with sport shirts. One had a handlebar mustache and wore a suit jacket over his sport shirt. A fourth man, younger than the others, wore a white shirt and tie. He stood over by the Cadillac.

Watching them from the backseat of the car, Natalie wondered if they were plainclothes policemen. Or maybe they were "Gil Garrett's people," the ones Trent had mentioned a few times.

"Hide. Get down on the floor," Natalie's mother told her. "Keep the baby quiet."

Natalie wrapped her arms around Buddy and crouched down on the floor—in the very same spot she'd hidden on the way to the movie star's house that night a week ago.

"Hey, you in the car!" one of the men called. Natalie could hear him through the open window. "Come join us!"

Natalie raised her head just enough so she could peek out the side window. She saw the mustached man in the suit jacket waving at her mother. He motioned for her to come toward the picnic area.

"Stay down," her mother whispered, switching off the engine. "Don't let them see you."

Natalie heard the car door open—and then a paper bag rustling as her mother retrieved a sack of groceries. The car door slammed shut.

"Hold on! What do you have there?" the man yelled.

"Just food," her mother replied.

Natalie could see her mom headed toward the picnic area, where the two children were slumped over the table. The closer she got to the group, the more her mom slowed down—until she came to a stop.

The children's mothers picked them up and laid them on the ground. Their little bodies looked lifeless. Both women curled up on the grass beside their children, as if they were getting ready to nap with them. At one end of the picnic table, Ernestine tipped over her glass of lemonade and fell off the bench. Moonbeam was arguing with Trent about something—until JT interceded and slapped her across the face. He yanked her over to the table, grabbed the pitcher of lemonade, and forced her to drink from it.

All the while, the three strangers stood and watched. The one by the car had turned his back to the picnic area. He kept looking down at the ground and rubbing his forehead.

Natalie couldn't figure out what was going on. But her mother must have. She suddenly dropped the bag of groceries. She swiveled around and started to run toward the Vista Cruiser.

"Dino, grab her!" shouted one of the men.

The younger one by the Cadillac turned. He was the closest to her mom, but he froze.

"Where the hell do you think you're going, honey?" yelled the mustached man. He pulled a gun from inside his suit jacket and shot her—twice.

Horrified, Natalie watched her mother hit the ground, a plume of dust enveloping her.

The gunfire scared the baby, and he started to cry. Natalie held him tighter, and ducked down from the window. She couldn't stop trembling. Tears streamed down her face.

She could hear the other women screaming. Their shrieks must have drowned out the sound of the baby.

When Natalie peered outside again, the scene near the picnic tables was utter chaos.

Another woman had collapsed, leaving Moonbeam and the teenage hitchhiker huddled together close to the ground, crying and rocking each other. The others were all dead.

Natalie realized that now. The lemonade must have been poisoned.

Trent and JT were arguing with the trio of strangers. "This isn't how it was supposed to go down, Freddie!" Trent shouted at one of them. "Gil's guy promised me . . ."

JT started pushing another one of the men—like he was trying to start a fight. In response, the mustached man stepped up to JT, raised the gun just inches from his ear, and fired. JT flopped down on the ground.

Trent started screaming and cursing—until the man turned the gun on him. He shot Trent in the forehead.

His head snapped back, and then he keeled over on top of his dead friend.

All at once, it was so quiet.

There was just Moonbeam, sitting in the dirt, crying softly and waiting to die. She was the last one. The teenage hitchhiker, who had joined them yesterday, was now lying beside her, lifeless.

Buddy was whimpering. Natalie held him close to muffle the sound.

All the while, the younger man in the white shirt and tie kept backing away from the picnic area. He got closer to the Vista Cruiser with every step.

"Dino, check the car!" one of the trio called.

With her arms around the baby, Natalie ducked down in the backseat—until she was curled up on her side. She was certain she and Buddy would be killed if the man saw them.

Buddy started to cry again. "Please," Natalie said under her breath. "Buddy, please be quiet . . ."

Past the baby's whimper she heard footsteps approaching.

"See anything?" one of the men called.

"Just some groceries!" the younger one called back. He cleared his throat.

Buddy wouldn't be still. The younger man they called Dino certainly must have heard him. Natalie raised her head just far enough to see over the backseat. The man poked his head in the open window. He was staring right at her. Natalie saw tears in his eyes. "You've got to keep the baby quiet," he said in a hushed voice. "For God's sake, they'll hear it. Please, keep the baby quiet . . ."

Nodding, Natalie drew Buddy as close as she could to muffle the cries. She was terrified she might smother him.

"I thought I saw someone in the backseat!" one of the men yelled.

"I checked!" the young man called. Natalie could hear him walking away. "There's nobody! Just some grocery bags . . ."

"I count twelve," announced one of the other men. "That's how many we're supposed to have here—twelve."

Natalie realized if it weren't for the hitchhiker JT

had picked up, the trio of men would have kept hunting for the twelfth person until they found her and Buddy.

The one they called Dino had saved her life.

"Dino is Adam's father, Dean Holbrook, Sr.," Laurie said, staring down at Cheryl. "That's why you wanted a catering gig at Evergreen Manor, isn't it? You needed to get in there and talk to Mr. Holbrook. Good God, why go to such lengths? Why didn't you just go visit him?"

"I tried that—several times." Cheryl got up and went to the mirror. She winced at the cut above her eye. "The security in that place is like Fort Knox. All visitors have to be cleared through the residents' next of kin. I tried phoning Dean Holbrook, Jr., but he wouldn't take my calls. When you saw us at Volunteer Park, it was our first and only meeting. I asked to talk to his father—and even told him what it was about. But he flatly refused." She turned away from the mirror and faced Laurie. "So imagine my shock when I found out a few days later that he and his wife were murdered—and the way they were murdered."

"I don't have to imagine," Laurie replied. "I saw it on your face when I mentioned the name Holbrook."

"So, you tracked down the other son, Adam?" Cheryl asked.

Laurie nodded. She figured he'd be relieved to know that his father hadn't killed anyone at Biggs Farm. She couldn't help wondering where he was right now.

"Well, you beat me to the punch," Cheryl sighed. "I was going to try Adam next, but I was worried the same thing would happen to him that happened to his brother and sister-in-law."

"Cheryl, if you'll only let me get my phone," she said. "I'd really like to call and tell him I'm okay. Plus I'm worried about him . . ."

Cheryl was shaking her head. "You can't call anybody. I'm sorry. If the police see you made a phone call while all this is going on, they'll never believe you weren't an accomplice in this. I don't want to get you into any more trouble than I already have. You can call him when this is over." She turned toward the bathroom door.

With a sigh, Laurie followed her out to the hallway. Cheryl reached into her bag and took out a tiny recorder. She switched it on, and then stepped into the nursery.

Slumped over in the chair, Gil looked exhausted and miserable. He looked up and frowned at them.

"So, did you hear any of that?" Cheryl asked. She set the recorder on top of one of the boxes.

"Bits and pieces," he grumbled. "So a bunch of hoodlums threw my name around at Biggs Farm. It doesn't mean shit. And what's 'Gil's people' supposed to mean? I've had thousands of people in my employ. Do you even know the names of these gangsters who supposedly worked for me?"

Standing in front of him, Cheryl folded her arms and nodded. "I stayed in the back of the Vista Cruiser for at least an hour while your errand boys made the picnic area outside the farmhouse look like a mass suicide . . ."

"Not *my* errand boys," he interrupted.

"They talked a lot—mostly about how gullible Trent was, about how he'd agreed to pin the murders on JT and the women. Apparently, he felt the rest of us would just have to be sacrificed for the greater good of his film career. He thought he'd be starring in your next picture . . ."

Gil nodded emphatically, and the chair wobbled beneath him. "That's just my point, goddamn it. They were lying to him! I'd never even heard of the son of a bitch until I read in the newspapers that he was dead." He winced. "Jesus, my head is splitting and I can't see a damn thing. Are what's left of my glasses anywhere on the floor there?"

Laurie picked them up. She glanced at Cheryl, who nodded. Then she carefully put them on Gil's red, sweaty face.

"Thank you, sweetheart." He gazed at her for a moment. "Jesus, you really do look like Emily. I'm sorry about earlier when I called you a stupid bitch. It was a moment of anger and frustration."

"It's okay," Laurie murmured.

"But to your friend here, I won't apologize." He sneered at Cheryl. "I hope your head hurts *at least* as much as mine, which is saying a helluva lot, sweetheart. I feel like I have a brain hemorrhage here. Those head butts in the movies aren't at all like the real thing. That goddamn Bruce Willis makes it look so easy."

"Earlier, you asked if I knew the names of these gangsters," Cheryl said. "I heard them talking about how they had to go through the house and Trent's room to remove all evidence that he had a connection to you."

"Not me," he interjected.

"The one who saved me, Dino, he called the others by their last name. It seemed to be out of respect—Mr. Rothschild, Mr. Lawless, and Mr. Rooth. They also addressed each other by their surnames. I've had over forty years to figure out who they were. Dino is Dean Holbrook, Sr., currently suffering from dementia in a rest home here in Seattle. His older son was murdered last week because he knew too much—and maybe because someone saw him talking with me." Her voice quivered as she said that. "Larry Rooth was the one who did all the shooting, and he was gunned down himself in 2002. Arthur 'Art' Lawless died of an apparent heart attack last year, and Freddie Rothschild was murdered just a few months ago—after I spoke with him in his home in Phoenix . . ."

"Never heard of any of them," Gil muttered.

"That day at the farm, they kept mentioning a man who worked for you, someone named Arnie."

Behind the broken glasses, Gil's eyes narrowed at her. He didn't say anything.

"I asked Freddie Rothschild who Arnie was," Cheryl explained. "He said the man's name was Arnold Shearer and he worked for you for nearly two decades. That's all I could get from him. I guess Freddie figured he was safe telling me that much, because Arnold died in 1989. I couldn't find anything beyond that online, and nothing linking him to you. But I'm pretty sure Freddie must have told me the truth, because someone put a knife through his eye after that."

Gil let out a long sigh. "Well, sweetheart, you finally got to a name I know. Arnie Shearer worked for me from the late sixties through the eighties. But you won't see his name in the credits of any of my films . . ."

"I know," Cheryl said. "I looked and looked."

"Arnie handled the occasional union problem for me and he took care of other matters."

"What kind of other matters?"

"Like muzzling reporters who dug up certain dirt—you know, this leading lady has a heroin problem or that leading man has a thing for underage girls. Arnie could make those problems disappear. A little intimidation goes a long way. He was a connected guy, if you get my drift. But I never—ever—had him kill anybody for me. And to my knowledge, no one else in my employ ever used him—or even knew him. I didn't make it a habit to hang out with him. But once in a blue moon my wife and I saw him socially so he wouldn't feel insulted that I was just using him for business. So, how's that for candid and honest? Now, I don't know what kind of line this Freddie character was feeding you about Arnie, but it's just not true."

Laurie cleared her throat. "I have it on good authority that someone powerful down in Los Angeles hired three mob-connected men to investigate the Styles-Jordan murders. You were living in L.A. at the time. And that totally backs up Cheryl's story. Who else could have been behind it?"

"Well, it wasn't me, sweetheart," Gil said. "I was in no shape to do anything after Elaina was killed—except drink until I was numb. I loved that woman. She and your grandmother were the two great loves of my life."

Laurie thought it was strange that he didn't mention

his wife of forty-something years. Then again, he'd hinted earlier at his house that things with him and Shawna weren't all they appeared to be.

She heard something outside. It sounded like a car coming up the driveway.

Gil must have heard it, too, because he suddenly sat up and started yelling: "HELP ME! HELP ME!"

Cheryl lunged at him, tipping over the chair—with him in it. It crashed to the floor, and he cried out in pain. One of his shoes flew off.

Once again, Cheryl's gun fell to the floor. And again, in a panic, Laurie didn't know what to do for a moment. She stood over the two of them, unable to move.

Gil kept screaming for help. Cheryl put her hand over his mouth, but it wasn't doing any good. He kept turning his head away and yelling out again. Gil's ankles were still tied to the chair legs. Cheryl reached for his shoeless foot and pulled off the sock. She wadded it up and shoved it in his mouth. Resisting, he kept jerking his head from one side to another. But Cheryl was relentless.

Laurie realized this was her chance to put an end to this now. She went for the gun.

But Cheryl pounced on it. "Don't!" she said, turning around and pointing the gun at her.

Laurie froze. She heard car doors slamming. She wondered if it was the police. Could they see the food truck parked near the back of the house?

Gil tried to shout out past the gag in his mouth, but all that came out were strained, muffled moans. Cheryl glared at him. "Don't make me knock you out," she said, catching her breath. She raised the gun. "Don't make me hit you over the head with this. I might end up killing you. Just lie there and shut up."

"Cheryl, I think he's in pain," Laurie whispered. "At least put the gun away. If the police see you have that, they might—"

Cheryl shushed her. Gil was suddenly quiet.

Downstairs, there was a faint clicking sound of a key in the front door. Laurie heard the door open. ". . . I don't care if he's one of the producers," someone said. "If he leaves his stupid phone behind, he should go back and get it himself—instead of sending us."

"News flash, that's why they call us 'gofers.' "

Laurie recognized the voices downstairs. They were two guys on the film crew.

The front hall light went on—and it illuminated part of the second floor corridor.

"This is totally screwing up my Saturday. Let's hurry up and find the damn thing. This place gives me the major heebie-jeebies . . ."

A phone rang, playing the *Star Wars* theme.

It gave Laurie a start. Then she realized they were calling the producer's cell number to locate the phone from its ring.

She glanced over at Cheryl, perfectly still as she crouched over Gil on the floor. Laurie thought about screaming for help—just to put an end to it. But she was almost certain Cheryl would shoot Gil rather than surrender without his confession

" 'Star Wars?' This dude's a big-time producer and that's his ring tone?" The voices became fainter as they walked to another part of the house.

"There's the damn thing. I see it . . ."

Gil coughed past the gag. The chair's back legs creaked under his weight.

"Did you hear that?" one of the men asked.

"Well, the place is supposed to be haunted," the other answered. His voice was clearer now. "Hey, I'll bet you twenty bucks you're too chickenshit to go up those stairs and stand in the master bedroom for a full minute."

There was silence.

Laurie glanced over at Cheryl, who had the gun by Gil's ear.

"Twenty bucks?"

"Yeah, and you can't turn on any lights either."

Silence again. Then Laurie heard footsteps on the curved stairway. She caught a glimpse of Cheryl—and the intense look on her face. The hand holding the gun trembled.

The upstairs hallway floorboards creaked. A shadow started to sweep across the corridor wall. But then it stopped. "This is bullshit!" the man announced.

The shadow on the wall disappeared, and Laurie listened to the footsteps retreating down the staircase. The man in the foyer was laughing.

Gil began to stir. He tried to scream out past the gag.

The light went out downstairs. Laurie heard the front door slam, and then the lock clicked.

She reached over and gently pushed Cheryl's hand away so the gun was no longer aimed at Gil's head. She pulled the sock out of his mouth.

He started to cough. "Water," he muttered.

Bending over, she tried to hoist the chair back up, but he was too heavy. "Cheryl, help me," she said.

Cheryl wearily got to her feet. Between the two of them, they set the chair—and Gil in it—upright. His glasses had been knocked askew again. Laurie straightened them on his face. Then she left Cheryl alone with him. In the bathroom, she found some Dixie cups on the counter. She filled one with cold water, and then brought it in to Gil.

Cheryl was sitting on the floor, with her back to the wall. She stared at Gil, and kept the gun pointed in his general direction. It was a strange sight. They were like two exhausted fighters between rounds.

Laurie brought the cup to Gil's lips and he gulped down the water. He pulled away at last. "My mouth still tastes like foot," he said in his gravelly voice. "Thank you, sweetheart. You know, if I had any feeling left in my arms, I'd say the right one is sprained. My head's throbbing, too. I've just about had enough. I've answered all your questions—and honestly, too. Hell, I even told you about the dirty work Arnie Shearer did for me." He cleared his throat. He seemed to study Cheryl's face. "So, okay, now it's my turn to ask you something, dolly. Is all this true about you rescuing Elaina's baby?"

Cheryl nodded tiredly.

"What happened to him? I'd like to know."

"He died," Cheryl answered quietly.

"On the farm or later or what?" he asked.

Laurie sat down on one of the boxes. She remembered the "missing" poster with Charlene and her three-and-a-half-year-old "brother," Buddy.

Cheryl looked so utterly defeated. The man from whom she'd wanted a confession had turned the tables on her. Now she was answering his questions, and she seemed resigned to it.

"I remained in the backseat of that car for at least two hours," she said. "I waited until I was sure they were gone. Then I took Buddy into the house. On the way, we had to walk past all those dead bodies—including my mother's. I remember trying not to think about anything but the money."

"What money?" Laurie asked.

"Trent kept some cash hidden under a floorboard in his closet. I found it one night when everyone else was out getting high and skinny dipping. Trent had saved up about fifteen hundred dollars—from panhandling and stealing. I used it to hitchhike to Eugene. My mom had a younger brother who lived there. By the time I reached Uncle Dorian's a couple of days later, it was in the newspapers about Trent and Biggs Farm. Mom was listed among the dead. I'd managed to convince Uncle Dorian that Buddy was my brother and we'd run away before July seventh. He didn't tell the police, bless his heart. I took a new first name and went back to Mom's maiden name before she married that Milhaud loser. We lived with Uncle Dorian for almost three years."

A wistful smile came to her face. "We were a regular family. We even had a dog—a sweet, three-legged corgi named Abby. It was the closest thing to a regular home I've ever known. I was actually going to school and making friends. But I was afraid of getting too close to anyone, because I didn't want them to know who I really was—and who Buddy really was." Cheryl sighed. "But then it all went to hell."

"Why?" Laurie asked. "What happened?"

"Dorian got a girlfriend, Ivy. I used to call her Poison Ivy. She hated my guts from the get-go, and vice versa. The funny thing is, I know Dorian was gay. I guess Ivy was his last futile attempt at heterosexuality. Anyway, Ivy moved in with us, and I think she started to figure out the truth about Buddy and me. Anyway, I didn't trust her, so after a couple of months, I ran away.

"I knew the police would be looking for us, so I dyed my hair—and Buddy's. We hitchhiked to Spokane. I didn't have two dimes to rub together, so I dropped Buddy off in the lobby of a children's shelter. I managed to find work as a waitress in this greasy spoon called The Ham and Egger. It was close to the shelter, and I was able to keep tabs on Buddy. During my breaks, I'd sneak in visits with him on the playground. I thought all this was just going to be temporary until I got a place for the two of us. See, I was sleeping on a cot in a little annex off the break room in the restaurant. Anyway, I went to visit Buddy at the shelter one winter day, and he wasn't there on the playground. I found out they'd put him in a foster home—a couple from Pullman. I lost track of him after that. Then I got into the drugs . . ."

Laurie thought about the letters Maureen had collected from adoption agencies.

"Anyway," Cheryl continued, "last year, once the Grill Girl was in the black and bringing in some money, I started making inquiries. I found out this couple from Spokane had become Buddy's foster parents when he was nine. I tracked them down—only to discover they were both dead. I got ahold of their neighbor and asked about the child—who of course, by then was a grown man. Or so I figured. She said she didn't know anything about a foster son. But then she got back to me a few days later, and told me—the boy died a long time ago. He drowned a week before his twelfth birthday in a boating accident with some friends."

"Shit," Gil murmured. He seemed genuinely disappointed and sad.

"When I heard that, it was all I could do to keep from going back to the drugs," Cheryl admitted. "But instead, I decided to gather as much inside information as I could on the Styles-Jordan murders and the *suicides* at Biggs Farm."

"I thought you were there," Gil said with irony. "I thought you already knew—better than anyone else. At least, that's what you've been saying."

"I wanted confirmation about who orchestrated all of it." Glaring at him, Cheryl got to her feet. "You see, Gil, it's become my mission to make you accountable for what you did, you son of a bitch."

Gil just shook his head at her. Even though he was sweaty, beaten, and bruised because of her, there was still pity in his eyes as he gazed at Cheryl.

At that moment, Laurie realized they'd never get a confession out of him. She was almost positive Gil had been telling them the truth all this time.

And she was terrified that Cheryl would kill him before she realized that, too.

CHAPTER THIRTY-SIX

"**P**op, are you okay?" Adam asked. "Can you hear me?"

"He's doing fine," said the woman over the phone. "He's just not very talkative right now."

"I want him to tell me that," Adam replied. Hunched close to the steering wheel, he navigated the treacherous back roads winding through the forest near Snoqualmie Pass. The dull, constant rain made the pavement slick. Low guardrails were all that stood between Adam's Mini Cooper and a deadly plunge off the mountainside. His ears had already popped from the altitude change. At some curves, he'd gape out his window at the tops of evergreen trees. The dark blue SUV followed close behind. He hadn't seen another car in at least five minutes.

At different points, the road leveled off and he spotted gravel side roads that led into the forest. He wondered when she would tell him to turn onto one of those trails. Adam was still convinced they were going to kill him and his father some place in these woods.

"Pop, I'm in the car in front of you, do you understand?" he said.

"Who is that?" his father asked feebly.

"It's Adam, Pop," he said, glancing in the rearview mirror. "Are you okay?"

"Who's the fellow they shot? Do you know him?"

"Never mind about him, Dean," the woman said. "That was at least twenty miles back. Wave to your son. He's right in front of us. You and he will have a chance to stretch your legs pretty soon. You'll have some refreshments, too. Are you thirsty? I made you a Trent Hooper cocktail. It's lemonade and another secret ingredient. You're going to love it . . ."

Adam realized what they were planning. The murders of Dean and Joyce imitated the way Trent Hooper had killed forty-four years ago. Now he and his father would die in the same manner Trent and his followers had killed themselves.

They'd pin the policeman's murder on him, too. All they had to do was toss Stafford's Glock 19 in the Mini Cooper. The police would match it with the gun used to slay that poor traffic cop.

They had it all worked out. Suddenly, Adam couldn't breathe.

"Adam, that's you up there?" his father asked.

"Yeah, Pop," he managed to answer.

"Go faster," his father said.

The woman laughed. "Well, you're a regular hot-rodder, aren't you, old man?"

Adam anxiously glanced around the front seat for

something he could use to defend himself with. It was about the fifth time he'd done this since leaving Medina, and still he didn't see a damn thing. He had a tire iron in the back, but he had no way of getting at it. He looked up just in time to see the road curving in front of him. He jerked the wheel to one side and felt the Mini Cooper tilt slightly. The tires screeched.

"Watch it up there," the woman said.

"Go faster!" his father repeated.

His stomach in knots, Adam stole another glance in the rearview mirror. His poor dad was obviously somewhere else in his mind right now.

"Go faster!"

"All right," the woman grumbled. "That's enough, shut up."

His father started singing: "Pack up all my care and woe . . ."

It took Adam a moment to recognize the tune. It was "Bye Bye Blackbird."

His dad warbled that same song whenever he was "faking" during one of Dean's uncomfortable visits at Evergreen Manor. Was he actually lucid right now— and pretending to be out of it?

"No one here can love and understand me . . ."

"Okay, that's enough, old man," the woman growled. "Can it."

His dad kept on humming the tune. "Adam, go faster!" he said, and then he went back to his humming.

Adam realized his father knew exactly what he was saying. He was giving him instructions. He'd seen the driver shoot the cop. And forty-four years ago, he'd seen that group suicide at Biggs Farm. He knew what the woman meant by a Trent Hooper cocktail. He was cognizant.

Taking a curve in the road, Adam pressed harder on the accelerator. He felt the tires skid a bit. Rain pelted his windshield. His speedometer jumped up to fifty-five in the forty zone. All the while, he could hear his father singing—even louder now.

"Hey, up there, slow down," the woman warned. "And you, old man, shut up!"

"Faster!"

The road straightened, and Adam picked up speed. He glanced in the mirror, and the SUV lagged farther and farther behind. Approaching another bend in the road, he could see the treetops again past the low guardrail. White-knuckled, he steered along the curve. The Mini Cooper veered too far left and scraped against the guardrail for a second. Adam winced at the grating noise. It felt as if the car might flip over at any minute. But he didn't let up.

"What the hell do you think you're doing up there?" the woman growled. "If you want to see your father again, you better slow down . . ."

"Go faster!"

"Shut the fuck up!"

The road straightened out once more, and the terrain changed. The perilous drop on the other side of the guardrail was now a wooded gully. The guardrail ended. Adam pushed down on the gas until the pedal almost met the floor. The engine roared, and he watched the speedometer jump to eighty.

In the oncoming lane was a Jeep, the first car he'd seen in a while. Adam passed it in a flash, and he heard a whoosh. The driver leaned on his horn.

Adam glimpsed the SUV way behind him. It too almost swerved into the Jeep. The horn blared again.

Over the phone, he heard the woman barking instructions to the driver.

All of a sudden, she screamed. A loud shot rang out.

Adam quickly took his foot off the gas.

In the mirror he saw the SUV tilt and spin out of control. All he could think was that his father was in that vehicle.

The SUV hurtled toward the shoulder. There was no guardrail to stop it.

Adam slammed on the brakes. The tires squealed.

In horror, he watched the SUV fly off the side of the road. It landed with a crash in the gully and slammed into the trunk of a tall evergreen. The impact triggered the vehicle's horn. The sound was deafening in the small gorge.

Adam pulled over to the shoulder. He staggered out of the Mini Cooper and gazed down at the wreckage. The front of the SUV was bashed in. The glass that remained in the shattered windshield was splattered with blood. Through the large jagged hole in the frame, he caught a glimpse of the driver—lifeless, trapped behind a deflating airbag. Blood streamed down his face from that strange, sheared hairline that looked painted on.

Had he been shot? Adam thought he'd heard a gun go off.

He didn't see any sign of movement down there, no sign of his father either.

Adam's eyes started to tear up. He told himself there was still a chance his dad was okay. He'd been in the back—and most of the damage was in the front section of the SUV.

He hurried back to his own car, reached inside, and grabbed the cell phone. He heard static. "Pop? Pop, are you there?" he asked.

No response.

He clicked off, and pressed 911. He anxiously counted two ring tones.

"Nine-one-one emergency," the male operator announced.

"Yes, there's been a bad car accident on Rural Route Seventeen—between North Bend and Snoqualmie." He tried to get his breath. At the same time, he had to yell over the incessant blaring from the SUV's horn. "It's near Milepost Twelve—at least, that's the last one I noticed. Three people are hurt. I think one of them is dead. There's an elderly man in the backseat. The other two, they—they killed a cop just outside North Bend . . ."

The emergency operator told him to hold on the line, and kept asking him to repeat the information over and over again. "One of these people—a woman, black hair, thirtyish, and kind of severe looking—she could still be alive," he told the man. "She's dangerous. These two abducted my father. Could you send the police here—and an ambulance? I think my dad may be hurt . . ."

Though the operator expected him to stay on the phone, Adam couldn't take any more. He needed to see if his father was down there.

He clicked off the line. Popping the hatchback of his

Mini Cooper, he took out the tire iron. He figured he might need it to pry open the door on the SUV. He could also use it to defend himself. He started back down toward the gully.

He'd only been away for a couple of minutes. But when he looked down at the SUV again, he noticed one of the back doors was now open. He hurried down the slope, weaving around bushes and over rocks until he reached the wreckage. The car horn was earsplitting.

This close, he could see the driver was dead. A gaping hole was just above his right ear. He'd been shot. Adam realized his dad must have grabbed the gun from the woman—or at least, struggled for it with her while they'd sped to catch up with him. Somehow, somewhere along the line, the driver had caught a bullet in the head.

Adam glanced over his shoulder to make sure the woman wasn't anywhere behind him. He knew she couldn't be far. She could be seriously hurt, too.

The same could be said for his dad—if he wasn't dead already.

"Pop?" he yelled over the blaring horn. He started crying. He hurried around to the open back door. "God, please. Pop . . . are you in there?"

All at once, the horn stopped wailing.

The sudden quiet was such a relief. Adam heard moaning.

He glanced in the back, and saw his father slumped across the seat amid bits of shattered glass. "Oh, Jesus," he murmured, climbing into the vehicle.

He could see his dad was breathing. The old man

had one hand over his face. Blood oozed between his fingers. In the other hand, he clutched a gun. It wasn't Stafford's Glock 19. It must have belonged to the woman.

"Pop, are you okay? Can you hear me?"

His father nodded feebly.

Adam brushed the bits of glass off of his father's clothes and helped him sit up. "Can you move everything?"

He nodded again. "My nose, I think it might be broken. And my arm hurts. That woman—the strange-looking one—she got out. I think—I think she's still around here." His dad let go of the gun, and brought his hand up to Adam's face. "Are you okay?"

"Yeah," he said. "Just sit tight and—"

He trailed off when he heard the sound of a car motor starting. It echoed in the small canyon. Adam climbed back outside the car. He listened to the tires screeching, and realized it was his Mini Cooper peeling down the road. The woman must have hot-wired it.

Adam told himself it didn't matter. His dad was okay. They were both alive.

He started wondering and worrying about Laurie again.

He took his cell out of his pocket to call her. He'd need to call the police again, too, and let them know about his stolen Mini Cooper. He tried Laurie first. NO SERVICE AVAILABLE popped up in the window above his keypad. Down in the gully, he wasn't able to get a signal.

He poked his head in the car again. "Pop, think you

can make it up this hill with me? We need to get back up on the road. I had a better signal up there, and I need to call the police again . . ."

His father nodded. Then he turned to stare at the driver slumped in the front seat. "Is he dead?" he asked, wincing.

Adam nodded.

"I shot him," he murmured. "I've never killed anyone before."

Adam thought about the deep, dark family secret, and those deaths at Biggs Farm. He might not ever know what had happened back then.

But he realized his father was telling him the truth.

"I've never killed anybody," he repeated while Adam helped him out of the backseat.

"I know, Pop," he whispered. "I know."

"So what started you killing again? Was it when you heard about the screenplay?"

Shifting restlessly in the hard-backed chair, Gil Garrett gave her a weary look. Slowly, he shook his head. "Sweetheart, I haven't a clue what you're talking about."

"I'm talking about *7/7/70*," Cheryl explained. She stood in front of him with the gun poised.

Laurie stayed off to the side, near a stack of boxes. She felt a constant chill, and wondered if she'd found the cold spot in the allegedly haunted room. She also wondered when all this would end. Both Gil and Cheryl looked utterly tired and on edge—as if they were reaching their breaking point. She couldn't predict Cheryl's next move. She seemed so volatile. She had the gun aimed at Gil's head, and her hand was unsteady. Whether accidental or intentional, Laurie was almost certain the gun would go off at any moment.

"The murders you arranged were history, decades old," Cheryl went on, her voice slightly hoarse. "You didn't have to worry. You'd thought you'd covered all your tracks. But then earlier this year, a screenwriter announced he was working on a film version—with all sorts of new information. He was a threat to you—so you had him killed. That script was a threat, too. What did this writer have on you? It must have driven you crazy that the script was so closely guarded . . ."

"I may be semiretired, sweetheart," he growled. "But I still have enough clout in this business that if I want to look at a film script—*any* film script—I just have to pick up a phone. I didn't have any interest in that project. I could tell from the get-go those claims that he'd uncovered all this 'new information' were just so much hype. I remember discussing that with my wife. I told her it was utter bullshit, a way of jacking up the price of the screenplay. In fact, Shawna wanted me to option the script, but I . . ." He trailed off—as if another thought had just popped into his head.

"But what?" Cheryl asked.

"But as I said, I—I wasn't interested," he replied, still a bit distracted. "I thought a movie about that tragedy was in bad taste."

"Well, someone else didn't feel that way," Cheryl argued. "In fact, they got very nervous about the project. They had the screenwriter killed, and they did what they could to mess up the film production. After murdering Freddie Rothschild, they went after me. They blew up my food truck, but by mistake, they killed my friend—my coworker. Anyone with any kind of inside information about the murders was a target. They were tying up loose ends. They killed Dean and Joyce Holbrook, and they threw Dolly Ingersoll down those stairs—"

"Oh, for chrissake, listen to yourself!" he bellowed. "You just said *someone else*. And *They . . . they . . . they . . .* You know it's not me. You're admitting as much. This *they* you're talking about is someone who used my name to have Elaina killed. And if Arnie Shearer was truly involved in this, then they used my connections, too . . ."

Laurie noticed him trailing off again—as if lost in thought.

"My God . . ." he whispered to himself.

"What is it?" Cheryl asked, taking a step toward him.

He shook his head. "Nothing," he whispered.

But Laurie could see that he had tears in his eyes. She imagined he must have had the same look on his face when the doctor had told him about his cancer. He turned toward her. "Can I have some more water, sweetheart?"

She glanced at Cheryl, who nodded, but never took her eyes off Gil. The way they stared at each other, it was as if they'd suddenly reached an unspoken understanding. It was something between the two of them that Laurie didn't feel a part of.

She retreated to the bathroom, where she refilled the Dixie cup at the sink. Laurie started back to the baby's room, but then she stopped dead.

She heard her cell phone ringing downstairs.

Very few people had the number—the Cassellas, the Ellensburg Police, and Adam. A part of her wanted to take a chance, defy Cheryl, and run down there to answer it. And while she was at it, she could call the Seattle Police, and put an end to this.

Laurie glanced at her wristwatch. It was just after five-thirty. They'd abducted Gil two and a half hours ago. She stood in that hallway full of ghosts, uncertain what to do. The phone stopped ringing.

She heard Gil and Cheryl quietly conversing. She glanced at the Dixie cup of water in her hand. Had Gil sent her out so he and Cheryl could talk in private?

She heard something else—in the distance. It was a police siren.

Laurie figured Gil's housekeeper must have awoken by now. It couldn't have taken the police very long to connect Cheryl Wheeler and the Grill Girl II to this locale. She wondered if that phone call was from them.

She hurried back to the baby's room to find Cheryl hovering over Gil.

". . . but you can't do anything about it," Gil was saying.

"Can't I?" she asked—as if accepting a challenge. She turned away from him and grabbed her big purse from the floor. She slipped the gun inside it, then fished out a pocketknife and handed it to Laurie. "If you can't get him untied, use this to cut the ropes," she said.

The police siren seemed to be getting louder—and closer.

Bewildered, Laurie gazed at her. "Then it's over?"

Nodding, Cheryl threw the satchel over her shoulder. She touched Laurie's cheek. "I'm really sorry I put you through all this, honey. Please forgive me." She turned to Gil. "You, too, Gil."

"Let me handle it," Gil said to her, talking loudly over the siren's wail. "Do you hear me?"

But Cheryl ignored him and hurried out of the room. She headed for the back stairs.

Moments later, Laurie heard the kitchen door unlocking. Cheryl was slipping out the back—as she had that night forty-four years ago.

"Come on, darling, untie your Uncle Gil," he said in his gravelly voice.

Laurie set down the cup of water, crouched behind the chair, and started to untie Gil's wrists. She struggled with the tight, sweat-covered knot.

The police siren seemed right outside the gate, but then it abruptly stopped.

Laurie glanced toward the hallway. The red flashers from outside reflected on the wall. She wondered if Cheryl had been able to get past the police.

"Listen, sweetheart," Gil said. "You want to help your friend? Let me do all the talking with the police. And just back up everything I say. Do what your godfather says. Okay, gorgeous?"

"I don't understand any of this," she said, still tugging at the knot. "What just went on? What did you tell her?"

"Never mind, Laurie," he said. "You don't need to know. No one needs to know."

CHAPTER THIRTY-SEVEN

Monday, July 14, 6:50 P.M.
Seattle

For the moment, the North Bend and Snoqualmie Police Departments and the Seattle Police had no idea the separate cases they were working on were actually connected. It just seemed like a coincidence that these two strange abductions had started in Medina at generally the same time on Saturday. The less serious case—but the one the news services really latched on to—was the bizarre abduction of film producer Gil Garrett by a caterer who seemed to have suffered a nervous breakdown. Gil announced he wasn't pressing charges, and he wanted to help the woman get counseling once the police found her.

Deemed slightly less newsworthy was the still unexplained story behind Dean Holbrook, Sr.'s abduction, which resulted in the deaths of a North Bend traffic cop and the man who had killed him.

Still, Adam and the folks at Evergreen Manor found themselves besieged with press people once again. He spent most of Saturday night and Sunday subjected to a series of grilling sessions by detectives from Seattle, Medina, North Bend, and Snoqualmie.

Adam didn't want his father directly implicated in the notorious Styles-Jordan murders. It really wasn't necessary. He told police that his father had been abducted while the two of them had been enjoying the afternoon in Medina Park. He claimed he had no idea why it had happened, but stressed his belief that it had to do with the copycat murders of his brother and sister-in-law. This theory seemed even more viable when the police discovered in the wrecked SUV a thermos full of cyanide-laced lemonade and Adam's laptop computer—with a bogus "suicide" note among the unsent e-mails.

The police also found that the driver of the SUV had several aliases, some underworld affiliations, and a long rap sheet. His fingerprints—as well as Adam's—were on the Glock 19 used to shoot Todd Armbruster, the thirty-year-old police officer from North Bend.

Adam's abandoned car was recovered Sunday morning in a sketchy part of Federal Way. There was no sign of the woman who stole it. Police were still searching for the dark-haired, narrow-faced suspect.

After what had happened to Dean Holbrook, Sr., the Seattle Police put an officer on guard detail at Evergreen Manor. Adam had a feeling the cop was there more to watch him and his dad than to protect them.

"I feel a bit like I'm under house arrest," he told Laurie on the phone. He'd broken away from his dad for a few minutes, and now sat on a rowing machine in the rest home's physical therapy room. He had the place to himself. A large window looked out at the lobby, where the desk nurse and security guard were on duty.

Aside from leaving each other messages last night, this was the first chance they'd had to talk since their respective ordeals on Saturday. For the last day and a half, Laurie had also been busy answering questions from the police. She and Adam had agreed that for a while, they best not be seen together. Otherwise, the authorities might indeed figure out a link between the two abductions in Medina Saturday. He and Laurie didn't want them reopening the investigation into the Styles-Jordan murders, not just yet. Just two weeks ago, neither one of them had known much about the forty-four-year-old slayings—and now they each had a personal stake in what had happened back then. Suddenly they were the ones who needed to keep a lid on the case. Adam didn't want his sick father harassed. But he wasn't quite sure why Laurie felt the need for secrecy.

"Gil Garrett asked me not to say anything," she explained over the phone. "He made it clear if I agreed to keep quiet, he wouldn't press charges against Cheryl—and he'd swear that I was forced to go along with her. Anyway, I sort of feel like I made a deal with the devil . . ."

The story on the news had Cheryl abducting Gil and taking him to the Gayler Court house, because she knew it would be empty. It had nothing to do with the Styles-Jordan murders. Supposedly, she was upset at Gil Garrett, because after serving him up a spread of her best food, he'd told her he wasn't interested in hiring her to cater an important event at his house. "I guess I was a bit tactless about it," Gil had told re-porters. "I didn't realize she was under so much pressure."

The flimsy reason given for his abduction seemed entirely credible considering the frequency of work-place, school, and mall shootings over things equally trivial.

"There's a part of me that really hates perpetuating the lie that Cheryl was nothing more than a crazy, un-hinged cook," Laurie told him, "especially after every-thing she's been through. But Gil and Cheryl seemed to reach some kind of understanding at the end. He kept telling her, 'Let me handle it.' Handle what, I don't know. Anyway, so far it seems to be working. Everyone is buying the cover story. Of the three of us, no one got seriously hurt. Joey and I are together, thank God. Cheryl isn't facing any serious charges. I'm just out of a job right now—and in the public eye, something I very much didn't want to be. On the plus side, the po-lice are watching the apartment complex in case Cheryl returns—and they have a description of Ryder McBride and his two women."

"Still, aren't you scared?" he asked.

"A little," she admitted. "But I don't think he's going to try anything so soon after I was on the news—with reporters and police hanging around here."

"I wish I could be there to keep you company," Adam said.

"Me, too," she replied. "But right now, you're under house arrest and I have a gag order. But I do have to tell you something, Adam. It's about your dad and that group suicide at Biggs Farm. Cheryl was there, and she confirmed your dad was there, too. From the way she told it, your father really couldn't do anything to stop what was happening. But he saved her life—and the life of Elaina and Dirk's baby . . ."

As Adam listened to her account of Cheryl's experience, he wondered how his brother could have been so unforgiving toward their dad. Did Dean know that their old man had at least saved a couple of lives that day? Maybe their dad had never told Dean about that. Maybe all Dean knew was that their father had worked for mobsters—and he was involved in the murder-suicides at Biggs Farm.

Adam and Laurie talked for twenty more minutes—until Joey started getting cranky. Adam told her to call him later if she got scared. "Can I call you if I *don't* get scared, too?" she asked.

He told her he'd like that.

After he clicked off the phone, Adam walked down the dimly lit corridors to his father's room. He found his dad asleep on his Barcalounger with the remote in his hand. A *Cheers* rerun was on TV. He snored a bit louder with the bandage across the bridge of his broken nose. He had two black eyes, and his sprained left arm was in a sling. There was also a food stain down the front of his shirt.

Adam gently kissed him on the forehead.

Then he quietly pulled a chair up beside the Barcalounger, sat down next to his father, and watched TV.

Laurie had just finished talking with Adam when the text alert sounded on her mobile device. She had

Joey in his playpen nearby. Now that she was off the
phone, he'd stopped fussing and crying, which was
typical. She checked the message. The sender number
was blocked, and she immediately thought of the
blocked calls to the town house apartments back when
Tad had been harassing her.

Warily, she opened the text—with a picture of the
Space Needle. The message said: U did d rght tng. Stik 2 yor
story. 4giv me. Natalie.

Laurie still didn't have a clue what was discussed
between Gil and Cheryl. And she had no idea how
Maureen Forester fit into all of this. There was a lot she
still didn't know. But she was pretty sure of one thing,
because of the Space Needle photo that came with the
text.

Cheryl was still in Seattle.

For the first time since running away from her
uncle's home at fifteen, Cheryl dyed her hair. *Dark
Chestnut* was the color listed on the L'Oreal box, and it
looked slightly ridiculous on her. She was too old to
pull it off. But it really didn't matter. Very few people
saw her anyway—and those who did might have noticed that makeup didn't quite conceal a bruise over her
eye. She hid out at a Best Western on Aurora Avenue,
and lived on Starbucks and deliveries from Pagliacci
Pizza and China First. She watched the news, went online, and made it her mission to keep tabs on the activities of Mr. and Mrs. Gil Garrett.

If she'd learned anything from the events on late

Saturday afternoon, it was that all this time, she'd been wrong about Gil. She'd seen it on his face the moment he'd figured out who had ordered the murder of his great love, Elaina Styles. Early on, he'd told her and Laurie, *"It's easy to keep secrets from my darling wife, since I rarely see her anymore—except in public. It's an arrangement that suits us both."*

Apparently, it was just as easy for Shawna Farrell to keep secrets from her husband.

Cheryl had realized Shawna had masterminded Elaina's murder at about the same time Gil had. It was when he'd said Shawna wanted to buy the *7/7/70* script. Why would she be interested in that project? There certainly wasn't a major role in it for her. She hadn't made a movie in years.

No one could have had a better motive for doing away with the beautiful Elaina. Gil had never stopped loving her. He'd even first offered Elaina the film role that eventually went to Shawna and won her the Oscar. And it was a film part most actresses would *kill for.*

Obviously, it had to grate on Shawna's nerves to know her husband preferred this other woman to her—both personally and professionally. None of Gil's associates were familiar with his underworld connection, Arnie Shearer. But his wife knew him.

Gil and Shawna had been at the same party as Trent Hooper a year before the slayings. He swore he'd never met Trent. But perhaps Shawna had. Maybe she'd made up her mind that night about who would do her killing for her.

Cheryl remembered Trent and the henchmen at

Biggs Farm referring to "Gil's people." Certainly, Mrs. Gil Garrett was one of Gil's people.

"You just figured it out, didn't you?" Cheryl had whispered to him while Laurie had gone to get him some water. "Well, that makes two of us. It was your wife who had Elaina killed, wasn't it?"

"Maybe," he'd replied. "But you can't do anything about it."

"Can't I?" Cheryl had said.

According to an article Cheryl had read online this morning, Gil was on his way to Los Angeles to present a film award tonight. He wasn't going to be home.

One advantage to having been inside Gil and Shawna's kitchen was that it had given her the opportunity to copy down some of their staff contact numbers from a list by the phone. Two hours ago, Cheryl had put on a nice dress and taken one of her rare trips out of her room at the Best Western. She'd gone to Chandler's Crab House on Lake Union. There, she asked the hostess if she could use her phone to call the other people in her party. The woman obliged. Cheryl phoned the young housekeeper at Gil's Medina mansion. "I'm calling about Ms. Farrell's reservations today here at Chandler's Crab House," she said.

"There must be some mistake," the girl said in her thick accent. "Ms. Farrell—I mean, Mrs. Garrett—is staying at the Bainbridge Island house tonight."

Now Cheryl knew where to find Shawna Farrell that evening.

On the hotel's white-and-green-palm-tree-pattern bedspread, Cheryl had laid out everything she needed for her visit to Gil's wife tonight: the gun, a knife, some rope, duct tape, her satchel, the tape recorder, a black pullover, and black slacks.

The next ferry to Bainbridge Island was at 7:20.

And Cheryl would be on it.

Monday, 7:38 P.M.
Seattle

The cop in the unmarked sedan parked outside the front gate of La Hacienda was a good-looking man in his early thirties with blue eyes, receding blond hair, and a square jaw. He was in plainclothes: a plaid button-down short-sleeve shirt and jeans. He had the car window open and was listening to John Mellencamp's "Pink Houses" on his iPad when Laurie approached him.

He smiled at her and turned down the music before she reached his window. She carried a large baggie with two of her homemade cupcakes. She also had the portable baby monitor in her hand. She'd put Joey to bed—without too much fuss on his part—about ten minutes ago. "Hi, I'm Laurie Trotter," she said.

He nodded. "Yes, I know."

"Well, I brought you these," she said, handing him the bag of cupcakes. "And I just wanted to make certain you know about Ryder McBride . . ."

He assured her he'd been briefed on McBride and his two female companions. He also thanked her for the cupcakes. His name was Kurt, and his shift ended at two in the morning. He gave her his cell number to call if she had any concerns. Laurie told him to buzz her if he was hungry, thirsty, or needed to use her bathroom.

"Well, thanks to you, this detail just got a helluva lot more pleasant," he said.

Once back inside her apartment, Laurie checked on Joey, who was fast asleep. Then she decided to examine Maureen's files—for the umpteenth time. She sat on the floor and looked over the articles about the often-forgotten victim in the Styles-Jordan murders, Gloria Northrop—and her boyfriend, Earl Johnson. Laurie was still bothered by a thought she'd had the other night. Studying the pictures of Gloria and Earl in the articles, Laurie could have sworn she'd seen other photos of them somewhere else. And it wasn't online. She remembered turning pages. Had she seen their pictures in a magazine?

Then she remembered. She wasn't turning the pages—Vincent was. *"That's Maureen with the brown hair, and that's her brother. I don't know who the other girl is . . ."*

The faded color snapshots in Maureen's photo album had shown two teenage girls, a young man slightly older than them, and a baby. They looked like they were playing in a park. *"I don't know whose baby that is,"* Vincent had said.

Was Maureen the sister of Earl Johnson? Laurie remembered seeing the old income tax records in the file cabinet at E-Z Safe Storage.

Her name on the forms read *Maureen Johnson Forester.*

"Well, hi, Laurie. Where's Joey?"

Vincent had answered the door in a Mariners T-shirt

and sweatpants. Laurie could hear the TV in the background.

"Joey's asleep," she said. She took her baby monitor out of her purse and showed him. "I'm listening to him on this—only the sound isn't so good, on account of how far away I am. So I won't stay long, I promise. I'm really sorry to barge in on you like this, Vincent. But could I see that photo album again?"

"Sure, come on in." He led her into his living room, picked up the remote, and put his movie on pause. "I'm watching *Batman Begins* again!" he announced. "I own the DVD."

Laurie watched him grab the photo albums from the lower shelf of his coffee table and set them on the sofa. From her purse, she fished out one of the articles about Gloria Northrop and Earl Johnson from Maureen's files. It was the article with the clearest photo of them both. "I'm looking for those pictures you showed me the other day—of Maureen in the park with her brother, a girlfriend, and a baby," Laurie told him.

"Oh, yeah, I know where those are," Vincent said, bent over the albums on the sofa. He paged toward the beginning of one of the big books. "Are these the ones?"

Laurie gazed at the shots of the two girls in the park—with their bellbottom jeans and long hair. She looked at the young man with the dark hair and the goofy smile, who was in one of the snapshots with the girls. It was Earl Johnson—with his girlfriend, Gloria Northrop, and his sister, Maureen.

But Laurie realized she was wrong about the locale. They weren't in a park. In the far edge of one shot, she could see the side of a house. It was the house on Gayler Court.

They were on the front lawn, playing with the baby.

The other day, Vincent had said he didn't know whose baby it was.

But Laurie knew.

She remembered Tammy Cassella mentioning that Maureen had found out something about Cheryl that made them *almost like family.* Obviously, she'd helped her friend Gloria babysit Baby Patrick. And from that "missing" flier in her files, it was obvious Maureen had discovered that Cheryl—aka Charlene—had looked after Baby Patrick as well. Cheryl had mentioned Patrick's birthmark—and it was also listed as part of "Buddy's" description on the "missing" flier. Was that the discovery Maureen had made?

Laurie turned to Vincent. "You're from Spokane, aren't you?"

"Yes, but after Mr. and Mrs. Taggart became my foster parents, we lived in Pullman for a while. Then we moved to Spokane."

"Taggart? I thought your last name was Humphries."

"Maureen talked me into changing it to Humphries about six or seven months ago. Actually, my full name is Thomas Vincent Taggart. But no one ever calls me Thomas . . ."

Laurie squinted at him. "Did Maureen say why she wanted you to change your name?"

He nodded. "It was on account of some woman who was looking for me. Maureen said she might be trouble. I think she could have been after the money my foster parents left me. There are bad people like that, I guess. Anyway, about seven months ago, this snoopy woman called my parents' neighbor, Mrs. Blankenship, who was Maureen's friend, too. She asked Mrs. Blankenship about my folks and me. So Mrs. Blankenship called up Maureen . . ."

Staring at him, Laurie thought, *And Maureen had her tell the snoopy woman that you'd drowned in a boating accident a week before your twelfth birthday.*

He shrugged. "After that, Maureen wanted me to change my name. And boy, that took a lot of work, too. It was a real hassle. Maureen handled most of it. Funny thing is, less than a week before she died, Maureen said I would be going back to my old name again soon. She said . . ."

He trailed off. "I think I hear the baby," he said.

Laurie heard him, too—over the monitor. He was crying. "Oh, Lord," she gasped. "I need to run. Thank you, Vincent!" She hurried to the door, with Vincent trailing after her.

He called out good-bye to her as she ran to her own door.

She'd never left Joey alone for this long. What was she thinking? Her hands were shaking as she unlocked the door. Once inside, she raced upstairs to his room. Her heart was beating wildly.

By the time she reached his crib, Joey had started to settle down. He kicked a little and murmured some sleepy baby talk. Laurie readjusted his blanket, then crept out of his room and padded down the stairs.

She gazed at all the papers on the floor—from Maureen's files. Obviously, Maureen had started the file

after her brother's girlfriend was killed in the murders
of July 7, 1970. And she'd started the file on Cheryl
Wheeler after Cheryl had phoned Mrs. Blankenship.
She needed to protect the identity of the sheltered man
who was in her care. So, she'd had Mrs. Blankenship
lie about the child dying. Maureen made it a point to
get to know Cheryl. She did "homework" on her. She
kept her close. And then she finally discovered that
Vincent had been in this woman's care at one time, too.

She remembered what Vincent had said just before
they'd heard Joey crying: *"Funny thing is, not long before she died, Maureen said I would be going back to
my old name soon."*

Apparently, Maureen was killed in the food truck
explosion before she ever got a chance to tell Cheryl
that they were "almost like family."

Laurie realized she needed just one more thing from
Vincent to confirm that all of it was true. She would
only be a minute this time. She wouldn't even have to
step inside.

But she wanted to bring him something for his trou-
bles. She hurried into the kitchen and grabbed the
Tupperware container with the last of her cupcakes in
it. She was so rushed and so busy thinking about Vincent and Buddy and Baby Patrick that she didn't notice
something unusual in the kitchen.

She hurried out the door, leaving it ajar, because she
knew she'd be right back.

Laurie hadn't seen what was on Maureen's dinette
table. Someone had emptied out her salt shaker, and
left a little white mound beside it.

CHAPTER THIRTY-EIGHT

Monday, 8:19 P.M.
Bainbridge Island, Washington

Cheryl had the taxi drop her off three blocks away from Gil and Shawna's Bainbridge Island retreat. Lugging her bag, she stayed in the shadows along the roadside and then skulked into the turnoff—marked PRIVATE—for Sand Path Court. The beachfront houses were huge—and spaced far apart. Through the trees, she glimpsed the water. She finally reached the beautiful beachfront "cabin," which she'd seen in a *House & Garden* layout a few years ago. The sprawling house had dark brown shingles with white shutters and trim. She spotted a Mercedes in the driveway, and there were lights on inside the house. The front gate was open.

Creeping up to the front windows, Cheryl didn't see any activity—just gorgeous "rustic" furniture that looked like it belonged in a Ralph Lauren ad. She figured if a servant was there, she'd just have to deal with the extra person the best she could. At this point, she didn't care if she ended up in jail. She was going to extract a confession from this woman. She'd waited forty-four years for someone to be accountable for those murders.

At the risk of setting off an alarm on the grounds, Cheryl crept around the house and peeked into a few more windows. One of the kitchen windows was open—obviously to take advantage of the cool breeze off the water. As she pried off the screen and climbed inside, Cheryl couldn't help remembering the open kitchen window in the house on Gayler Court on that summer night in 1970.

Once she climbed over the sill, Cheryl glanced around the big kitchen—with its stainless steel appliances, tile backsplash, and granite countertops. The under-the-counter lights were on, creating a warm glow. The light fixture above the breakfast table was Chihuly glass. A bottle of Merlot and a half-full wineglass were on the counter; otherwise, the place was spotless.

Her stomach was in knots as she set her bag on the table. She took out her recorder and the gun.

Just then, she heard a noise outside, and froze. In another room, somewhere in the front of the house, one of Shawna's Pomeranians let out several yelps.

Cheryl peered out at the front hallway, where Shawna was heading to the front door. She was dressed in a sexy black nightgown and robe set. Her blond hair was tied up off her neck with a black ribbon. "Shame on you, Jeremy, making me wait!" she announced, flinging the door open.

Obviously, she was expecting someone. That must have been why she'd left the front gate open.

But no one was there. Visibly disappointed, Shawna

stepped back inside. "Hush, you," she snapped at the dog.

With a shaky hand, Cheryl clicked a button on her recorder, and set it on the table. She had the volume cranked up, and Dirk Jordan's song, "Elaina," blasted through the entire house. Within moments, Cheryl got the response she'd wanted.

Her lacy nightgown and robe flowing, Shawna rushed into the kitchen. The small dog followed her, yapping incessantly.

Seeing her, Shawna's eyes widened, and she stopped cold. "Who are you?" she gasped, a hand over her heart.

With the gun pointing at her, Cheryl pulled out one of the chairs from the breakfast table. "Have a seat, Shawna," she said over the blaring music. "You might be in for a long night."

Shawna gave her an icy, defiant stare. She scooped up the lapdog, and sat in the chair.

"Would you turn off that racket?" she said loudly.

Cheryl switched off the recorder. The sudden quiet was jarring.

"I've always hated that song," Shawna muttered. She looked Cheryl up and down. "I know who you are," she said. "You're the crazy bitch who abducted my husband on Saturday."

"Why do you hate that song, Shawna?" Cheryl asked pointedly. "Because it reminds you of the woman you had murdered?"

Shawna shook her head at her. "You're insane. You won't get away with this. I'm not the soft touch my husband is. There won't be a repeat of the incident with

Gil on Saturday. It's not going to happen. I'm expecting a friend at any minute."

"That just means both of you will die," Cheryl said—almost believing it herself.

For a second, Shawna gave herself away, and she looked a bit frightened and vulnerable.

"You should understand about collateral damage, Shawna," Cheryl said in her best ironic tone. "You didn't seem to mind that Dirk Jordan and Patrick's nanny were murdered—just as long as your killers did away with Elaina. Gil told me how Elaina was the love of his life."

She laughed, and stroked the dog. "Why the hell would he tell you that?"

"Because it's true," Cheryl said. "And because I'm not just some caterer who had a nervous breakdown. I'm a survivor, Shawna. My mother was one of Trent Hooper's women. I was there that night they killed Elaina, Dirk, and that poor girl. And I was there when your hired gunmen 'cleaned up' Biggs Farm. I saw the whole thing."

"Well, no wonder you're crazy," Shawna hissed, "You had a mother who hung out with that scummy bunch."

"I was twelve years old when I saw them gun her down," Cheryl said. She clicked the recorder mode of the little machine. "That group may have been 'scummy,' but they're the ones Arnie Shearer hired to kill Elaina for you."

Shawna stared at her. Suddenly, she didn't seem so coolly defiant anymore. "Did Gil tell you that?" she asked.

"I'll ask the questions," Cheryl said, pulling out another chair and sitting down across from her. She kept the gun trained on Gil's wife. She realized she'd stopped trembling. "It must have been such a blow to your ego to know that he preferred Elaina to you. You were this big star—back in the day when there weren't many good roles for women. And you were married to the biggest producer in the business. But he still loved Elaina. He originally picked her over you for that movie role—the one you got the Academy Award for. You were Gil's second choice. How that must have burned you . . ."

"She was an empty-headed no-talent little bitch!" Shawna screamed. "She was just a *body,* nothing else."

"So you had her murdered . . ."

"Yes, goddamn it, I had her murdered. I told the man who arranged it to make it look like another Manson thing. And I got away with it, too. No one would have been the wiser if they hadn't decided to make that stupid movie—and if you hadn't started tracking down Arnie's hit men. Is that what you wanted to hear? Are you satisfied?"

"What about all the others who were killed—besides Elaina?" Cheryl asked. "All those other lives snuffed out, all that collateral damage, was it really necessary? Did your murder scheme have to be so elaborate?"

"It worked, didn't it?" Shawna replied coolly. "Up until now, it was the perfect murder."

Cheryl switched off the recorder. She was surprised that Shawna had admitted so much—and with very little prodding, too.

The floorboards squeaked.

Across the room, in the glass door of the stainless

steel oven, Cheryl saw a reflection. Someone stood behind her. "Put the gun down on the table," she heard a woman whisper.

Cheryl slowly turned to see a woman standing in the entryway to the dining room. She was thin with black hair. She perfectly fit the description in the newspaper of the woman who had abducted Adam Holbrook's father on Saturday.

And she had a revolver pointed at Cheryl. "Put the gun down," she repeated.

Cheryl obeyed. She started to tremble again.

"You're back," Vincent said, standing in the doorway. "How's Joey?"

"Fine," Laurie said. She handed him the Tupperware container of cupcakes. "These are for you."

"Well, gosh, thank you." He eyed the cupcakes, and then smiled at her. "Did you want to come in again?"

"Oh, no, thanks. I just want to ask you for one quick favor." Laurie hesitated. "Could you—could you take off your glasses?"

"I can't see without them," he said.

"Just for a minute, please." Laurie pleaded.

Shrugging, Vincent obliged her and removed his glasses.

Laurie gazed at him. "You have a birthmark," she heard herself say.

"Yeah, it used to be bigger, but my face grew around it. Can I put my glasses back on now?"

"Yes, of course," she whispered. "Thank you, Vincent."

He put the glasses on again. "Is that all?"

She nodded. "For now, yes. But I—"

"Mommy . . ."

The distant voice came through her baby monitor. It was a man's voice, teasing and singsong. *"Mommy . . ."*

"Oh, my God," Laurie whispered. "Vincent, call nine-one-one. Somebody's in my apartment. I think they're going to hurt Joey."

Dumbfounded, he stood in the doorway for a moment.

"Please!" she cried. "I'm counting on you, Vincent."

He quickly nodded and ducked back inside.

Laurie ran to her door. It was open about an inch— just as she'd left it. She hesitated, and glanced toward the front gate. She could see the unmarked police car from here. Laurie frantically waved at it. She sprinted across the courtyard, waving her arms. She wondered if he'd fallen asleep. Flinging open the gate, she raced to the driver's window.

With what little breath Laurie had, she let out a sickened cry.

The cop sat at the wheel with his head tipped back—and a crimson slash across his throat. His eyes were still open. Blood covered the front of his plaid short-sleeve shirt. On the seat beside him was the baggie with one cupcake left.

"Where's your little boy, Mommy?" Ryder asked over the baby monitor.

Staggering back from the unmarked car, Laurie turned and ran into the courtyard again. She hadn't heard Joey crying. Was Ryder or one of his girls holding a hand over Joey's mouth? Or had they put a pillow over his face?

Laurie hurried to her apartment, and threw open the door. The papers from Maureen's file fluttered and scattered on the floor.

It was quiet. Her lungs burning, Laurie frantically glanced around the living room.

She ran up the stairs to Joey's room—where she'd checked on him less than five minutes ago. But his crib was empty now.

The baby monitor fell out of her hand onto the floor.

Laurie couldn't breathe. For a moment, she couldn't move.

Then she heard the voice in another part of the house: "Will you play with me?"

It was Joey's stuffed toy, Sparky. It was coming from downstairs.

She bolted down the stairs, almost tripping. Warily, she moved into the kitchen, where she spotted Ryder's calling card on the dinette table: the emptied-out salt shaker and a white little mound on the table's surface.

Laurie noticed the back door was slightly ajar. She couldn't tell whether Ryder had come in or fled that way. All she could think about was getting Joey back—even if it meant having to kill someone. Laurie turned around to reach for the knife rack.

Ryder was there, practically on top of her. He must have been hiding in the powder room by the back door.

Before Laurie could scream, he slapped a hand over her mouth. He pinned her against the counter. "I saw you on the news Saturday night," he whispered, rub-

bing his pelvis against her. "You're always getting yourself into trouble one way or another, aren't you, Laurie?"

She managed to pull her head back—for just a second. "Where's my baby?" she cried.

Grabbing a dishtowel, he stuffed it into her mouth,
silencing her. "One of my girls has him," he said, grinning. "I'm going to raise Tad's little rug rat as my
own," he whispered in her ear. His lips grazed her earlobe. "Somebody needs to be a parent to that little orphan."

Recoiling, Laurie tried to scream out past the gag in
her mouth.

"Tad was so crazy about you," Ryder said. "And you
shit on him. All he wanted to do was love you, but you
killed him. Tad told me that he only fucked you three
times. Well, I'm going to do you tonight—right now."
He ran his tongue along the side of her face, and
squeezed her breast. "I heard on the news you've been
serving up grub to the people on that *7/7/70* movie. It
gave me an idea while I've been watching you these
last couple of nights. I was just up in your bedroom.
You've got a pretty blue nightgown in your closet.
You're going to wear it for me. And when I'm through
with you, I'll hang the bloody thing from the front gate
in your courtyard . . ."

Ryder started to drag her toward the stairs off the
kitchen. But with all her might, Laurie shoved him and
broke free. She yanked the dishtowel out of her mouth,
and grabbed the first thing she could from the counter.
It was just a stainless steel beater attachment to her
Mixmaster. She'd used it to make the cupcakes. One

end, where it attached to the blender head, was sharp and jagged.

Ryder snickered as she waved the pointed end at him.

All she could think about was Joey.

Enraged, she took a swipe at him. But he dodged her. Then he hauled back and punched her in the face.

Laurie went crashing back into the counter and fell to the floor. She dropped the stainless steel beater. For a moment, she couldn't see anything.

Then the beater came into view—on the floor right beside her. She could hear him chuckling as he started to pull her to her feet. Laurie swiped the beater off the floor and plunged the sharp end into his right eye.

Ryder howled in pain. With a hand over his face, he staggered back and began to thrash around. He was wailing and cursing.

His cries almost drowned out the sound of the police siren.

"Where's my baby?" Laurie screamed. "What have you done with him?" She grabbed a saucepan from the drying rack, and slammed it against the side of his head. It made a hollow thud, and Laurie felt the handle vibrate at the point of contact.

Stunned, Ryder staggered back into the counter and fell to the floor. Blood streamed from his eye, and he was moaning in pain.

She heard the sirens—much closer now.

She watched Ryder crawl around on the floor. She hurled the saucepan at him. It hit his shoulder, and then rolled along the floor with a clatter.

Laurie thought of that nice cop, sitting in the un-marked car with his throat slashed. She thought of Don Eberhard—and his widow. She thought about Tad, and how he'd been manipulated into stalking her. Laurie even remembered that poor girl who had set herself on fire for Ryder—while he'd watched from inside the restaurant.

But most of all, she was thinking of Joey.

"Where is he, you son of a bitch?" she yelled. She swiped up the empty salt shaker and flung it at him. It sailed past him.

She rushed over to the knife rack and pulled out the butcher knife.

All at once, someone grabbed her arm.

Laurie spun around and found herself face-to-face with a policeman. She gaped at him.

"The Ellensburg Police want this sorry bastard alive," he said.

She heard a rumble of footsteps coming through the front door. Behind the cop, she could see a police-woman in the kitchen doorway.

"We caught a couple of his girls in back here," the cop said. "They had the baby with them. But he's okay now . . ."

After Laurie heard that, everything was just a blur.

She just caught fragments of what was happening around her: the policewoman grabbing a dishtowel and putting it over Ryder's eye as two other cops pulled him to his feet; Ryder, still moaning in agony; the po-liceman with his arm around her, leading her into the living room; the papers from Maureen's files getting trampled on by the policemen coming through her front door; and finally a second policewoman stepped in, carrying Joey. He wriggled and screamed.

Laurie gathered him in his arms, and everything was so clear again.

She spotted Vincent in the doorway. He looked worried.

She smiled at him. "Thank you, Vincent," she said. "And Joey thanks you, too."

With her hands up in front of her in half-surrender, Cheryl stood in the kitchen between the black-haired woman and Shawna. She knew this was the professional killer Shawna had hired to cover her tracks.

"I'm expecting company any minute," Shawna told the woman. Clutching the Pomeranian to her bosom, she pulled her chair away from the breakfast table and stood up. "You better get her out of here. And I don't want her body found here on the island . . ."

"Your boyfriend isn't coming for a while," the woman replied. "His car died on the ferry, a little problem with the distributor. You'll probably be getting a phone call from him very soon. Why don't you fix yourself a drink, Shawna? You're going to need it. Make it a tall one."

The woman then turned to Cheryl. "Go."

Cheryl gaped at her. She wasn't sure she'd heard her right.

"Go," she said again. "I don't have any business with you anymore."

"The hell you don't," Shawna snapped. "She needs to be killed. You work for me—"

"No, I'm working for your husband now," the woman said. "I just have one job for him. The orders are to come here and take care of you. I'm supposed to make it look like an accident."

"What?" Shawna whispered, horrified.

"Like I said, make yourself a drink, Shawna. And don't look so sad. I'll make sure your dog finds a nice home."

"My husband said . . ." Shawna echoed numbly.

The woman turned to Cheryl once more. "Take your things and go. There's a man waiting for you by the gate. His name's Michel. He'll take you to a car, then drive you to the ferry, and all the way back to your hotel, where he'll escort you to your room. Michel will make sure you won't try to contact the police—until the proper time. You need to ignore any pangs of conscience you may have about what's going to happen here tonight. Don't forget, just a minute ago, this bitch was giving me instructions about where to dump your body."

Dumbfounded, Cheryl stared at her.

The woman turned to Shawna. "Sit down. You're not going anywhere."

Hugging her dog, Shawna meekly sank down in the chair. She kept shaking her head and murmuring to herself: "No . . . Gil wouldn't . . . he couldn't . . ."

The woman turned toward Cheryl once more. "I'll wipe down the counters and put the screen back on the window," she said. "No one will ever know you were here—unless you tell them. And I'm afraid you won't live very long if you do. Once you're back in your room at the Best Western, call the police. Apologize for Saturday, and give yourself up. Stick with the story Gil gave the press. You're getting a real break. It's the way Gil wanted it."

"Who are you?" Cheryl finally whispered.

The woman shook her head. "Me, I'm nobody," she said. "I've done a lot of horrible things for a lot of horrible people—this woman included. This job tonight, for a change, I won't have to talk myself into liking it." She frowned. "For what it's worth, I'm sorry about your friend in the food truck. It was nothing personal. It's never personal with me. Now, get out of here. By the time you turn yourself in, I'll be finishing my work here. That gives you a perfect alibi. Leave the gun. I'll get rid of it." The woman nodded toward the door. "Go."

In a daze, Cheryl grabbed her bag and threw the recorder into it. Then she headed out of the kitchen.

"You can't do this to me," she heard Shawna say. "You—you're going to get yours, I swear . . ."

"I know I will—one day," the woman replied. "We all have to pay for our sins. Tonight's your night, Shawna . . ."

Cheryl opened the front door and saw in the distance a thin, shadowy figure waiting by the gate—her escort.

She glanced over her shoulder at Shawna. She was still seated in the chair, clutching her dog. Both Shawna and the animal were trembling. She looked utterly terrified. "How much is Gil paying you?" she cried. "I'll double it. Please, you can't. You were working for me! You just can't . . ."

Cheryl closed the door—and shut out the sound of Shawna's shrill voice.

As she walked up the driveway of the Garretts' beautiful beach home, Cheryl remembered fleeing the Gayler Court house that night forty-four years ago.

She felt sorry for Shawna right now.

Still, she couldn't help thinking that Elaina had handled her death scene so much better.

EPILOGUE

Sitting in the passenger seat of the black BMW, Cheryl looked out beyond a row of parked cars at Puget Sound. The water was dark and choppy. They were on the parking deck of the ferry to Seattle, and Cheryl was amazed she'd made it this far.

She'd been certain her driver would unceremoniously kill her and dump her body before they ever reached the ferry terminal. He was a young, handsome Frenchman with soulful eyes, a five-o'clock shadow, and a high, tousled, black pompadour. He was also a professional killer—or at least, he worked with one.

"What's going to happen to Shawna?" she asked, breaking nearly twenty minutes of silence between them.

"You should not concern yourself," he muttered in his thick accent, resting his hand on the wheel. "You will see soon enough on tomorrow's news."

"And if I tried to 'concern myself,' what then?" Cheryl pressed.

"I have my instructions," he replied, staring straight ahead.

Cheryl knew she wouldn't breathe easy until she was back at the Best Western, and alone in her room. She had to hand it to Gil. He'd seen to everything. He'd even provided her with this 'escort' to keep her in line. In many ways it helped ease her conscience for doing nothing while Shawna was murdered. He'd made it so she had no choice. The last thing he'd told her was that he would handle it.

An hour later, Michel walked her down the hotel corridor to her room. He insisted on coming inside. He stood just inside the door while she made the call to the police. "My name's Cheryl Wheeler," she told the 911 operator. She sat down on the bed. "I believe the police want to question me about something I did on Saturday. I'm the one who abducted Gil Garrett and held him hostage for a couple of hours . . ."

While she gave them her room number at the Best Western, she noticed Michel making a call on his cell phone. But he didn't say anything. It seemed like he just let it ring once or twice, and then he clicked off. She realized it must have been a signal to his partner on Bainbridge Island that his work here was complete.

He didn't say anything to Cheryl either. He just quietly slipped out the door.

Cheryl had a feeling the woman on Bainbridge Island had completed her work, too.

The 911 operator wanted to know if she was alone—or if she was armed. Cheryl told her she was alone, and that she'd gotten rid of the gun she'd used on

Gil. "It wasn't loaded anyway," she lied. "I threw it off the University Bridge—into the lake."

She'd already read Gil's and Laurie's fictional accounts of Saturday afternoon's abduction. She'd seen them on TV, too. Cheryl knew what she was supposed to tell the police and the psychiatrists.

It was Gil Garrett's show, probably his last production.

All she had to do was say her lines.

Wednesday, July 16

The photo the *Huffington Post* used online for the number one trending news story of the day showed a young Shawna Farrell on Oscar night. With her big blond hair, impossibly long eyelashes, and her blue-green paisley-patterned gown with the plunging neckline, she was the epitome of glamour—circa 1970. She was laughing and clutching her Academy Award. The headline read:

OSCAR-WINNER SHAWNA FARRELL DEAD
Freak Accident in Beach Home Claims Life
Of 70-Year-Old Actress and Fashion Entrepreneur

The article reported that Ms. Farrell had slipped and fallen in the shower while spending the night alone at her beach house on Bainbridge Island in Washington State. She had hit her head and bled to death. Her film producer husband, Gil Garrett, was in Los Angeles at the time. But when his calls to the beach house late Monday and Tuesday went unanswered, he sent the housekeeper from their Medina, Washington, home to investigate, and she discovered the body. Ms. Farrell had been dead approximately eighteen hours. Her blood showed a high alcohol level.

That morning, the *Seattle Times* reported a story on page two that didn't make much of an impact outside the Pacific Northwest. It was about the arrest Monday night of Richard "Ryder" McBride, and two women companions in connection with the murder of an Ellensburg police detective, Donald Eberhard. A number of other serious charges were pending—including assault, child abduction, and breaking and entering. For three hours, doctors at Harborview Medical Center struggled to save his right eye, but they failed. Ryder was held overnight at Harborview, where he was recovering from other injuries sustained just moments before his arrest.

Another patient at Harborview at the same time was Cheryl Wheeler, held two nights for observation and psychiatric evaluation. Gil Garrett took time out from his grieving to see that his lawyers got her released early Wednesday evening.

Thursday, July 17, 5:40 P.M.
Seattle

Laurie answered the door to find Cheryl on the other side, carrying a big cardboard box. It held a covered casserole dish, a Tupperware container, and a loaf of French bread wrapped in foil. She looked a little sad and frail with her hair chopped off and the bruise over her eye. "I made you an apology dinner—lasagna, garlic bread, and salad," she said meekly. "But I wouldn't blame you one bit if you slammed the door in my face."

Laurie worked up a smile and opened the door wider. "Come on in," she said.

Joey was in his playpen, quietly talking to himself and the television. He gazed at their guest for a few moments before turning back toward the TV and *Sesame Street*.

Laurie had seen Cheryl's light go on across the courtyard at around nine o'clock last night. She'd been wondering how long it would take her to come over or call.

What Cheryl had done to her was unforgivable. Yet Laurie couldn't help looking at the extenuating circumstances. In a way, Cheryl really did have a kind of nervous breakdown. And Laurie had seen the file Maureen had collected on her. She knew what Natalie-Charlene-Cheryl had been through.

She figured it was about time that Cheryl saw the file, too.

After they put the food in the refrigerator, Laurie offered Cheryl a glass of water and sat her down on the sofa. She made a quick phone call, then got out the blue folders and set them on the coffee table. "I have something to show you here," she announced, sitting down next to her. "But before I do, I need to ask you a question. It was Shawna who had Elaina and Dirk killed, wasn't it?"

Cheryl just nodded.

"Did you—have anything to do with her *accidental* death the other night?" she asked.